# Streams of Mercy

# Streams of Mercy

## First in a Series of Jenna's Creek Novels

### Teresa D. Slack

Tsaba House
Reedley, California

Cover design by Bookwrights Design
Graphic Design by Pete Masterson, Aeonix Publishing Group
Senior Editor, Jodie Nazaroff
Cover Photo by Andrea Schwagerl

Scripture quotations herein are from the King James Bible.

First Edition: 2004

**Library of Congress Cataloging-in-Publication Data**

Slack, Teresa D., 1964-
    Streams of mercy  /  Teresa D. Slack. - -  1st ed.
        p.  cm.  - -  (The Jenna's Creek novels)
    ISBN 0-9725486-5-3   (trade softcover)
1.  City and town life- -Fiction.    2.  Ohio- -Fiction.    I.  Title.
    PS3619.L33S77  2004
    813´ .6- -dc22
                                                            2004010715

Published by
Tsaba House
2252 12th Street, Reedley, California 93654
Visit our website at: www.TsabaHouse.com

Printed in the United States of America

To my husband Ralph,
My best friend and number one fan.

# Acknowledgments

A special thanks to the following people, without whom this book would never have been written:

Tom Horst, former Highland County Sheriff, for his wealth of information concerning crime scenes and police procedure.

The members of my online writers' group, CWFI, for all their prayers, answers to questions, and encouragement along the way.

My sister, Gail Jackson, and friend, Tammy Braniff, for listening to ideas, giving opinions (even the ones not asked for), and participating in impromptu polls of "What if."

John and Pat Maggard, my pastor and his wife, for the use of their beautiful property to take author pictures, and most of all, for their prayers for the success of this book.

My Mom, Dad, Sisters, extended family, and many friends for their support, encouragement, and infinite patience surrounding the completion of this project.

Special thanks goes to my dear husband, Ralph, and son, Randy: Randy, thank you for acting as a mediator when the computer program and I had our little disagreements. Ralph, thank you for mechanical, technical, and historical assistance pertinent to the 1970's and for making this dream of mine possible with your limitless support, love, and encouragement.

*For he shall have judgment without mercy, that hath shewed no mercy; and mercy rejoiceth against judgment.*
—*James 2:13*

# Chapter One

*June, 1973*

Hushed voices drifting up through the black metal heating grate on the floor of her room awoke Jamie Steele from a restless night's sleep. She threw back the tangled sheet and pushed a strand of nondescript, brown hair away from her forehead. She rolled over onto her side and propped herself up on one elbow to better make out what was being said in the kitchen directly below her. Her empty stomach growled in protest. She tried to remember the last time she'd eaten, and vaguely recalled part of a ham salad sandwich she forced down yesterday afternoon at the persistent requests of her Aunt Marty. She wanted to blame her poor night's sleep on her empty belly and the stifling heat, so unusual for this early in June, but knew immediately neither had anything to do with it.

From her position on the bed, she couldn't decipher a word of what was being said in the kitchen. She eased herself out of bed so the squeeky springs wouldn't give her away, and moved to the grate in the middle of the floor. The grate was an ideal tool for eavesdropping; she could see through it into the room below if she got down on her belly. At one time, it provided a means of discovering whatever the adults were involved in that they deemed inappropriate for her tender ears. It was how she discovered Aunt Marty and Uncle Justin would never become parents. Before that day she always thought having babies was what married people did, the same as going to work and paying taxes, until she heard Aunt Marty crying as Uncle Justin quietly explained to Grandma Cory what the doctor had said.

Lying on her belly on the floor, hovering over the grate, was where she listened to Grandma Cory argue on the telephone with the Veteran's Hospital doctors when they suggested she put Grandpa Harlan in a nursing home where he could be properly cared for. That notion went over like a lead balloon. Nobody told Cory Steele she couldn't do something properly.

It was where she listened to her repentant father explain to Grandma why yet another boss had "let him go," and then borrow money from her in the next breath. He always promised to stay out of the bars and the pool halls this time, but Jamie and Grandma Cory both knew that's where he'd be come sundown.

If not for the metal grate, Jamie would never know anything that went on in her own house.

"I only pray Jamie and Cassie don't hear anything about this; today of all days," Grandma Cory was saying from the kitchen below.

Jamie was instantly all ears. She dropped to the floor and peered through the grate. She easily pushed aside the fleeting pang of guilt for eavesdropping. Grandma Cory would throw a fit if she knew she was listening; but this concerned her and her younger sister, Cassie. She had every right to know what all the whispering was about. She was seventeen-years-old for crying out loud; almost a legal adult. Regardless of her indignation, she held her breath and remained perfectly still so the floorboards beneath her wouldn't creak.

Seated next to Grandma Cory at the kitchen table was her sister, Great-aunt Emmy Lou, and a neighbor, Grandma Cory's closest friend, Fran Mendenhall. The two women must have come by early this morning to help with the chores, like they had done for the past two days, and now they were having breakfast.

"That was so long ago, honey," Jamie heard Aunt Emmy Lou say.

"They never did find a body," Fran added.

"And they never will," Aunt Emmy Lou stated. "She's probably livin' it up in California or somewhere, not concerned in the least about all the trouble she's stirred up."

"I doubt that. She would've turned up after all these years if she was still alive."

Jamie frowned and leaned further over the opening, her nose pressed against the cool metal.

"If she's not alive somewhere, then what became of 'er?" Fran wanted to know. "There's no proof she's dead. There's no proof she's alive. How can anyone think James did anything to 'er?"

Jamie gasped and clasped her hand over her mouth, hoping they hadn't heard. Who was this person they were talking about, and what did she have to do with her dad? More importantly, why would Grandma Cory be discussing such a thing today?

The resignation sounded loud and clear in Grandma Cory's voice when she spoke again. "I don't know. I was beginning to think everyone had forgotten, I should've known no one in this town ever forgets anything."

"Nothing like this anyway," Fran agreed.

"Well, to be fair, if James would'a left that girl alone, they never would'a thought he did anything to 'er." Aunt Emmy Lou took a sip from her coffee cup and cocked one eyebrow. "Just like the Good Book says, 'You reap what you sow'."

"They were only dating, Emmy," Grandma Cory said, jumping to her son's defense as usual. "Are you saying he shouldn't have been allowed to date whoever he wanted?"

"Don't go puttin' words in my mouth, Cory. I wasn't sayin' that at all. But since you brought it up, she was a little out of his league, don't you think?"

"Why? Just because she came from one of the richest families in Jenna's Creek, she didn't have any business with someone like James? I can't believe you said that."

"There you go again, puttin' words in my mouth."

"Well then, what were you saying?"

Fran jumped in. "Ladies, let's not say somethin' we'll regret later. All that matters are those poor girls upstairs. First they lose their mama, and now their daddy. We have to think about them. They shouldn't have to see their aunt and grandma goin' at it like two ol' alley cats."

The reality of the day came rushing back to Jamie in an instant. A sick knot replaced the hunger in her stomach. The steadily rising temperature in her tiny, airless bedroom was all but forgotten. Her father, James Steele, was dead. A victim by choice of hard-drinking and fast-living, he inadvertently took his own life behind the wheel of his car three nights ago. After closing time at his favorite roadside bar, he lost control of the care while taking a curve too fast on a country road. He spent the night in a ditch, his life slowly slipping away, before a deputy sheriff found his car.

Today his body would be laid to rest next to her mother's at Bishop Hill Cemetery on Bishop Hill Road. There used to be a church there, just like at every other crossroads in Auburn County. Over time the community was absorbed into the farmland around it as it became easier and easier to travel into town for shopping and church attending. The only proof that a church—much less a community—ever existed at the junction of Bishop Hill and Dusty Ridge was the cemetery itself. A wire fence surrounding the property protected the dearly departed from the intrusion of Clyde Thatcher's cows. Suspended between the two metal posts, on either side of the gravel road leading into the cemetery, was a sign that read; Bishop Hill Community Church, Est. 1889.

The first time Jamie ever heard of Bishop Hill Road, Bishop Hill Cemetery or even the long-since abandoned Bishop Hill Community Church was five years ago when her mother, Nancy, died of cancer. When Jamie awoke on the morning of that funeral she immediately noticed the knot in the pit of her stomach. She had a sick, emty feeling inside. She had never felt so alone. So helpless. What in the world would she do without her mother? Who would take care of things when Dad came home drunk and wanted to fight, or he lost another job, or when he disappeared for a week or two without a word of explanation as to his whereabouts? She was the oldest. It was her responsibility to take care of Cassie like she promised her mother she would. But she was only twelve at the time, what could she do? She didn't know anything about taking care of things the way Mom did. She laid in bed that morning at Grandma Cory's house where she and Cassie had spent the night and cried, the dreadful knot in her stomach rendering her unable to get out of the bed.

It turned out she'd been scared for nothing. She and Cassie never went back to their own house in town after Nancy's funeral. Without consulting the motherless girls, the decision was made that they'd be better off living with Grandma Cory and Grandpa Harlan. That day their mother's parents, Grandma and Grandpa Sharborough, cleaned all their stuff out of the house in town and brought it to the farm. This way the girls could keep going to the same school, attending their own church, and continue to see their father on a regular basis. At least that's how the adults explained the situation.

Jamie had only visited the Bishop Hill cemetery a handful of times since her mother died—reluctant to see the granite marker that was the only tangible indication Nancy Steele ever existed. Her grandmother, on the other hand, was a staunch believer in honoring the dead. Grandma Cory visited several cemeteries throughout the year where her "people" were buried, to insure the township trustees were doing what her tax dollars paid for. Of course their idea of maintenance never measured up to hers, so she made the trip armed with her garden rake and pruning shears to correct the mistakes the trustees had invariably made. Jamie and Cassie were permitted to stay home during those excursions. But every Memorial Day they were expected to go along to decorate the graves of their lost loved ones, whether they wanted to or not. It was a morbid practice in Jamie's opinion, with no earthly logic behind it. Hadn't Grandma Cory herself taught them the fleshly body was simply a vessel of the spirit-man who would go on to either eternal glory or eternal punishment after passing on?

Grandma Cory scoffed every time Jamie reminded her of that. "Well, that's fine for you, Jamie Steele," she'd say. "When you're gone, I'll make sure no one comes out to clean around you. We'll just sit back and watch the brambles take over."

Her threats didn't bother Jamie. The odds were in her favor of which one of them would go first.

Fran's voice finally broke the silence in the kitchen below. "Cory, have you thought anymore about sendin' the girls to the Sharboroughs' this summer?"

"Yes, I have. I think it'd be a good idea for them to spend time with their mom's folks for a while. At least till people stop talking."

No way, Jamie told herself. She loved her mother's parents and enjoyed spending time with them, but resented being carted off to their house in the city so Grandma Cory could make sure she wouldn't find out whatever was going on around here. She wasn't a child anymore. She had every right to know what everyone in Jenna's Creek was already talking about.

Through the metal grate, she saw Fran nodding her head. "I think that's the best thing, just till things get back to normal."

"Normal?" Aunt Emmy Lou grumbled. "There's nothin' normal about this. You were wrong to keep it from them for so long in the first place."

"Maybe so, but it was my decision."

Before Jamie could puzzle too long about the decision in question, Aunt Emmy Lou's next words made the hair stand up on her arms.

"When they hear he was arrested for murder, they should hear it from you."

Jamie's heart plummeted. Murder! Her dad arrested for murder?

"Who says they ever have to hear it? And besides, he was questioned, not arrested."

"No, he was arrested," Aunt Emmy Lou insisted. "Wrongfully so, but arrested nonetheless."

Fran seemed to agree with Aunt Emmy on this point. "Cory, you can't keep tellin' yourself they'll never hear the stories about James and that poor girl. It's no small wonder they haven't heard anything before now. Nobody in this town can keep anything quiet. I remember when Vesta Purdy's husband went to fight in Korea and she started runnin' around with that Johannson boy. What was his name? Victor? No, that's not right…"

Grandma Cory interrupted Fran before she could get so far into her story she forgot the point she was trying to make. "The girls haven't heard anything because I've been careful. They've had enough troubles to grow up with, without listening to a bunch of unfounded rumors."

"His arrest wasn't an unfounded rumor!" Aunt Emmy Lou exclaimed, forgetting all about Vesta Purdy and her alleged boyfriend, whose name no one remembered after all this time. "It really happened. You should've told 'em about it years ago."

"And I'm telling you, right or wrong, it was my decision to make," Grandma Cory hissed. "Now, kindly keep your voice down before you wake Harlan. He's been a trial in himself the last few days and I want to keep him asleep as long as possible."

Last night, well-meaning relatives and neighbors had paraded through the house until late, like they always did before a burying. Grandpa Harlan was agitated by all the commotion and Grandma Cory assigned Jamie the task of keeping him out from underfoot. He insisted the house was overrun with strangers—he couldn't remember who half of them were anymore—and they were bent on stealing his belongings, especially his beloved record collection. Once he got a notion in his head, there was no getting it out. He fussed and fretted, counting the records over and over again. Cassie contributed to the melee by sneaking his favorite Hank Williams album out of the pile and pointing out its absence. By the time Jamie persuaded him to go to bed a migraine headache added further to his vexation.

A trickle of perspiration ran down Jamie's arm, pasting her bare skin to the linoleum. She shifted her position to find a cool spot on the floor and get a better view of the kitchen. The sagging floorboards creaked in protest under her weight. The women at the kitchen table snapped their heads upward simultaneously in the direction of the sound. Jamie jerked her head away from the grate. Gingerly, she rose to her feet.

"Jamie, is that you?" Grandma Cory called.

She hesitated a moment before answering. She imagined the nervous glances exchanged beneath her as they silently asked one another if they had been overheard. "Yeah, Grandma, it's me," she called back, hoping her trembling voice wouldn't betray her.

"Are you coming down to get some breakfast?"

Food was the farthest thing from her mind now. "I'll be down in a little while."

She stood quietly and listened, but they didn't resume speaking. The right thing to do would be go downstairs right now and apologize for eavesdropping, but she didn't. It would only get her into trouble. Besides, she had every right to know what happened in her dad's past, especially if he had actually been arrested for murder like they said. She knew precious little about him as it was.

After the girls' mother died, James made it clear he would not be able to care for his two young daughters; not that he had ever been much of a care-giver by any stretch of the imagination. The girls moved into the farmhouse with Grandma Cory and Grandpa Harlan where their father and uncles had grown up, and James rented a small apartment perfectly suited for a single man recently relieved of his parental responsibilities.

What he did in that apartment, Jamie could only guess. On the rare occasions Grandma Cory took the girls there to visit, the sink was always full of dirty dishes, his bed unmade, and clothes—clean or otherwise— strewn everywhere. She sometimes envied the carefree lifestyle he seemed to enjoy with no one telling him what to do or when to do it. He laughed a lot and talked really loud while showing them around, but somehow he always seemed just a little bit…pitiful. He had plenty of friends to drink with and have a good time. There were always pretty women to give him attention—even before Nancy died. But when the party was over, his friends went home to their families. James had no one. Even days like Christmas or Father's Day, he spent by himself. Jamie wished she could have told him he didn't have to be alone. He had her and Cassie and Grandma. But she knew even then, he wouldn't listen. He was a grown man. He made his choice, a choice that didn't involve his daughters and mother.

Grandpa Harlan began to stir in his room. Grandma Cory would be up soon to get him.

Cassie would wake up before long too. She would rummage through her closet for her only black dress and black shoes, which she would not find since they had been in Jamie's closet for nearly a year. She would come looking for them, grumbling because she could never find things where she left them. She wouldn't buy Jamie's explanation that it was she who put them in the closet in the first place because hers was too crowded with all her other stuff. She would insist Jamie borrowed them without asking, even though Jamie's feet were two sizes bigger than her.

Jamie opened her closet door and sank on her knees to the floor. She would find Cassie's shoes along with her own before she was asked. Her dad's funeral was in three hours and she didn't feel like arguing over who borrowed whose shoes.

At last night's visitation, Jamie had wandered around the funeral home greeting out-of-town relatives and basically avoiding the casket at the front of the room. She spent the three days leading up to this morning, distancing herself from what was going on around her. Yes, James was dead as a result of his reckless lifestyle, but that didn't mean her life had to change. It wasn't like she would miss his weekly visits and those father-daughter chats that had never happened in her entire seventeen years of living. She wouldn't grieve over the camping trips and vacations that would never take place. Now when he missed important events like her induction ceremony into the National Honor Society last year, at least he'd have a good excuse for not showing up.

Looking down at him now, lying in the casket that had been moved to the church for the funeral this morning, the only emotion she could muster was hate. Hate for herself for an inability to experience the loss. Hate for him for making her grief impossible.

All at once she was twelve-years-old again, peering into another casket; she needed him then—wanted him by her side—but he wasn't there. After the years of abuse Nancy suffered at his hands, he struck out at her one last time by refusing to come to her funeral. Jamie had been left to comfort eight-year-old Cassie. She was forced to grow up and be strong for her little sister that day, taking the responsibility off her dad's shoulders where it rightfully belonged; and she had. Now she was strong and she wouldn't show any weakness in front of him by grieving. He didn't deserve her grief.

Grandpa Harlan put a warm hand on Jamie's shoulder and turned her away from the casket. His gentle eyes searched hers for the cause of her distress. Jamie unclenched her jaw and gave him a reassuring smile. The tension in her head from grinding her teeth together, which she hadn't realized she was doing, lessened instantly. Her grandpa's anguish vanished at the sight of her smile.

Jamie took his hand. He didn't understand that his eldest son was being buried today. He didn't have to face a lot of unsettling things about James now that old age had stolen his mind. She almost envied him. "I'm okay, Grandpa. Let's go sit down." She led him to the front pew where Grandma Cory was sitting with Uncle Justin, her only remaining son, and his wife, Marty. As Jamie and Grandpa Harlan approached, their conversation ceased and all eyes turned to her.

*Don't waste your time feeling sorry for me. I'm fine,* she wanted to shout at them. She ground her teeth together in frustration. The tension in her head returned.

Aunt Marty pulled her down on the pew beside her and drew her close. Jamie kept her back straight, refusing to lean against her even though it might feel nice to let down her guard for a moment. No, she wouldn't be weak. Not like them. Not like Dad, who gave in to the bottle. Not like Grandpa Harlan, who gave in to old age. Not like Mom, who gave in to James' abuse. Not like Grandma Cory, who let life run roughshod over her. Not even like Aunt Marty, who found a reason for loving everyone. She would be strong. She didn't need any of them.

The pastor tactfully kept his words about James Steele's character to a minimum. He didn't even know the deceased man on a personal level. Raised in this very church, James hadn't darkened the doors since getting married here eighteen years ago, long before the current pastor's time.

Everyone seated in the church cooling themselves with cardboard fans stapled to thin, wooden handles—one side printed with a picture of a tow-headed child kneeling in prayer, the other, ironically bearing the name of the local mortuary who not only provided the fans, but also the arrangements for the deceased—knew everything there was to know about James' character.

These people knew what became of men like him when they came face to face with their Creator. The compassionate souls cried tears of remorse behind their cardboard fans. The self-righteous among them felt he got what was coming to him. The last group, of which Jamie was a part, tried not to think about it at all.

With Cassie on one side of her and Aunt Marty on the other, Jamie endured the funeral service with her eyes focused unseeingly on a spot on the wall above the organist's head. She didn't hear the pastor's words or the quiet weeping of several elderly aunts. All she heard was the conversation in the kitchen playing over and over again in her head. She wondered who the girl was and what had happened to her. Whatever it was, everyone in Jenna's Creek thought James was somehow involved; enough to arrest him for murder. Jamie shuddered in the small, stuffy church. Impossible. James Steele couldn't hurt anyone. Or could he? She knew first-hand what he was capable of. The slaps, the black eyes, the crashes in the night that startled her from sleep, and later, the sounds of her mother crying in the next room.

She realized even more just how little she knew of her own father. People in town who didn't even come to the funeral knew him better than she did. His drinking buddies at the local taverns could sit on their bar stools tonight and comfort one another with memories and humorous stories about the notorious, skirt-chasing James Steele—while she had nothing from which to draw comfort. Nothing but bitterness, regrets ... and now doubt.

# Chapter Two

The temperature inside the small farmhouse had risen to nearly 100 degrees. Mourners spilled out of every exit, hoping to find the slightest stirring in the air. The front porch overflowed with men lounging against posts and door frames, smoking cigarettes and making small talk about the lack of rain, how many feet was the proper distance between fence post holes, and speculating on the likelihood of Don Shula leading his Miami Dolphins to another undefeated season like last year's. The conversation was about anything other than the funeral and the man recently laid in the ground.

Women piled plates high with food from the over-laden table and sideboards, then searched the house for children and husbands. As they poured iced tea into glasses and smeared mayonnaise on bread for sandwiches, they swapped potato salad recipes over their shoulders and discussed one husband's high blood sugar and another's recent job promotion. Rather than leaning on posts, smoking and talking deliberately and casually like the men, the women bustled purposefully about. They didn't want to dwell on the real reason they were gathered here today either. The worst nightmare a mother could face had befallen one of their own. For the second time in her life, Cory Steele had buried a son.

Only the children remained untouched by the somber occasion. The heat did nothing to slow their frantic racing through the house and around the yard. They played hide-and-seek in the barn, searched the pond for frogs, and chased each other up and down the stairs, their thundering feet grating on the nerves of every adult present. Time after time they were scolded by frazzled parents, but once they were out of sight and out of danger of a swat across an unprotected back-side, they dashed off again in search of more mischief.

Jamie observed the proceedings from a distance. At the cemetery she had been helpless to escape the clumsy embraces and awkward words of condolences offered to her. Now that she was home, she steered clear of everyone. When someone approached with the unwelcome intention of comforting or consoling her, she lost herself in the crowd.

Her mother's parents, Roy and Maggie Sharborough arrived from the city just before the funeral. Jamie managed to avoid them too, leaving them to comfort Cassie, who relished the attention. Cassie would be thrilled when she heard the grandparents had conspired to get her and Jamie away from the farm for awhile. She loved staying in the city with the Sharboroughs. So much more went on, and there wasn't a cow to be milked in a thirty mile radius. Jamie, on the other hand, had no intention of accepting their invitation. She was determined to find out what the rest of Jenna's Creek already knew about her father and the missing girl, whoever she was.

She filled a glass with lemonade and went outside to sit under the sugar maple beside the house. She could still hear the voices of the men on the porch, but she was safely out of sight. She wouldn't have to worry about anyone spotting her and coming out to see if she needed anything. Above her head, the maple tree's leaves hung limply in the still air as if they were in as much need of a cool breeze as she was. She sipped the lemonade and leaned against the smooth bark, tipping her head back to gaze through the leaves at the cloudless sky beyond.

She remained motionless a long time, her mind pleasantly blank... drifting... thinking of nothing more than the still air and the occasional bird that flitted overhead. Slowly she became aware of voices nearby.

"Poor Cory. Such a sad thing." The words from a woman Jamie did not bother to turn and identify, caused a weary sigh to escape her lips. Similar sentiments had been uttered so many times by so many different people in the past few days they served only to annoy her.

She started to rise from her spot under the maple tree to put more distance between herself and any further sympathetic intrusions when another woman's words caused her to freeze in her semi-crouched position.

"I guess now we'll never know what happened between James and Sally Blake."

Sally Blake? Was she the missing girl Grandma Cory, Aunt Emmy Lou, and Fran Mendenhall had been discussing in the kitchen? She slid silently back down to the ground and pressed her back against the tree. She strained her ears for the next words, spoken softly by yet another woman, this one distinctly younger than the other two. She immediately recognized the voice as belonging to Debbie Turner from church, recently married and already rumored to be expecting a baby.

"Has there ever been any doubt about what happened?" Debbie asked the older women.

"Since her body was never found, there'll always be a doubt," answered the first.

"Not to me, there isn't," the second woman said. "We all knew James Steele. He was as guilty a man as I ever saw."

"Oh, Esther, how would you know what a guilty man looks like?" The first woman asked with a laugh.

"I know plenty, thank you very much. My Earl, for one. Every Saturday night when he comes home from Monty's, I know he's guilty of something." She laughed at her own joke and the other two joined in. Earl wasn't the only husband in town who frequented Monty's Tavern out on Route 8, arguably the rowdiest honky tonk in the county.

Jamie wished they'd forget about Earl and get back to Sally Blake, even though she almost dreaded hearing what they might say.

"I agree with you, Esther," Debbie said, her voice serious now that the laughter had ceased. "I believe we all know what happened between those two. But without James here to admit it, we'll never know the whole story, especially what everybody wants to know most. What he did with her body."

"I imagine he buried it somewhere or just got rid of it," Esther said.

"How gruesome!" the first woman cried. "Talking about Sally Blake like she was an 'it', instead of a real person; and today of all days."

"You're right," Esther agreed solemnly. "I didn't mean to sound disrespectful. We're just all a little curious about what happened."

"No one is trying to be gruesome," Debbie explained. "All any of us want to do is put this matter to rest, once and for all. But short of knowing what he did with her body, her poor parents will never be able to get past it. They'll always be wondering what really happened that night."

"I just can't imagine what the Blakes have gone through all these years," Esther said. "What a cruel and horrible thing to happen to a family. If he just would have left some kind of a clue that would lead the authorities to her body. Even if he was too much of a coward to implicate himself, he could have at least done the decent thing."

"You really don't expect the likes of James Steele to do the decent thing, do you?" Debbie asked caustically.

"Debbie, I really don't want to be having this conversation," the first woman reiterated. "As far as I'm concerned, with James Steele gone, the matter is put to rest."

Jamie held her breath and clutched the lemonade in her hand until she imagined the glass shattering and a thousand tiny slivers piercing her flesh. She wanted to stand up and defend her dad. How dare they call him a coward on the day of his funeral! Who did they think they were, making such horrible accusations?

But how far off were their comments? They certainly knew more about the situation than she did. She couldn't very well defend him when deep down in her heart was a nagging suspicion that everything they said might be true.

She continued to hold her breath, praying they would not discover her, and waited as they drifted down the garden path, their conversation turning to Grandma Cory's uncanny ability to grow hybrid roses, now standing at full glory under the hot June sun. Little did they know a gentle mist every night from the garden hose and Cassie's unbridled chatter, as if the roses could hear and understand what she was saying, was all that coaxed them into bloom. Relieved the women had moved on, and stiff from sitting still for so long, Jamie got to her feet. She caught sight of Aunt Marty perched on the back porch railing; who waved cheerfully, and started in her direction. She groaned inwardly. The last thing she wanted was companionship or advice, both of which Aunt Marty was sure to offer.

"Let's go for a walk," Aunt Marty suggested as soon as she reached Jamie's side. Helpless to refuse, the two walked across the yard toward the gate that led to the meadow. Rather than take the time to unlatch the heavy, metal gate and pull it open, they climbed to the top and dropped deftly to the ground on the other side. Sometimes it was easy to forget Aunt Marty's age. Jamie was pretty sure she had turned forty-two on her last birthday, yet she still got around like a much younger woman.

They headed north through the meadow, following a rise in the land that led to the Mendenhalls' property. They walked in silence, the tall grass rustling against their legs.

When enough distance separated them from the house, Aunt Marty spoke. "Honey, how are you holding up? Is there anything you'd like to talk about?"

Jamie shrugged, her eyes fixed on the ground in front of her. This meadow was home to Grandma Cory's milk cows. She thrust her hands into the pockets of her shorts and concentrated on placing each foot carefully in front of her to avoid a mess to clean off her shoe later.

They approached the remains of an old, abandoned plow and sat down on the axle. Jamie bent over and plucked a stem of grass from a clump on the ground at her feet and stuck it between her teeth. Aunt Marty followed suit. She cupped her hands around the blade of grass she put in her mouth and blew hard, emitting a high-pitched, short-lived chirp.

"That was bad," Jamie said, laughing.

"I guess I'm out of practice."

They picked more blades of grass and tried again. Before long they were elbowing one another and laughing at their weak attempts that didn't resemble whistles at all. Jamie tossed the chewed blades of grass to the ground and sighed. She would be happy to sit here the rest of the day, and listen to the cows lowing in the distance and the blackbirds calling to each other from the trees bordering the meadow. But thoughts of the missing girl and what the women had said kept pushing its way to the front of her mind. What made everyone think her dad had done anything to the girl in the first place? Aunt Emmy Lou said something about James being out of his league when he dated her because her family was rich. Was that enough to make people suspect him of hurting her? And where was she now, if no one knew what became of her body after all these years, what made them think she was even dead?

If all of Jenna's Creek knew about James' involvement with Sally Blake, Aunt Marty probably did too. This could be the only opportunity she'd have to talk to her alone.

Before she could lose her nerve, she blurted out, "Aunt Marty, who's Sally Blake?"

Aunt Marty's eyes widened and the color drained from her face beneath her summer tan. For a moment, only the blackbirds calling across the quiet meadow responded to Jamie's question. Finally, Aunt Marty spoke, "Uh, Sally Blake, where'd you hear that name?"

Jamie thought it best not to mention the conversation she overheard in the kitchen. "While I was sitting under the maple tree in the yard, I heard some women talking about her and Dad, like they thought he did something to her. Do you know what it's all about?"

"I think you'd be better off talking to your Uncle Justin about this."

"No, I don't want to upset him or Grandma. I just want to know what she had to do with Dad."

Aunt Marty absently picked a thistle loose from her shoe string and flicked it away between her finger and thumb. She retied her shoe and stared out across the fields. Jamie knew she was stalling—deciding how much she should tell her. She waited; rushing her wouldn't do any good. After a few minutes, she started talking.

"In a small town no one forgets the past. It always comes back to slap you in the face. That's how it was with your Dad. He made a lot of mistakes in his life, did a lot of foolish things that some folks haven't forgotten. But he's gone now. He can't change anything. Wouldn't it be better to let the past stay buried? What good could possibly come from rehashing what's over and done with?"

"The only problem with that line of thinking is that it's not in the past. Everyone knows but me. It's not fair to ask me to forget something I don't know anything about. I should be allowed to hear everything and decide for myself whether to leave it buried or not."

Aunt Marty smiled at her. "I sure can't argue with you there. But honestly, there's not much I can tell you. It all happened before Justin and I got married. You'd find out a lot more talking to him or your grandma about it. Besides, it's family business. It really doesn't concern me."

"Aunt Marty, you've been in this family for almost twenty years. And you know they won't tell me anything. Just tell me what you've heard. Please."

Aunt Marty hesitated again, clearly worried about talking out of turn. "All I know is Sally Blake dated your dad back before he went in to the Navy."

"What happened to her?"

"No one knows for sure. She disappeared and the police believed there was foul play involved."

"They thought Dad killed her, didn't they?"

The look of shock that passed over Aunt Marty's soft features told more than words ever could. "Your dad was their main suspect for a long time," she admitted. "They investigated him, but eventually had to leave him alone. I guess over time they closed the case for lack of evidence."

"Lack of evidence?"

"Sally's body. It was never found. Back then, there was no way to try someone for murder without a body. Even now, it's pretty near impossible. That's why they dropped the charges."

"So you mean he was charged with murder?"

"Now like I said, Jamie, I don't know all the details. I know he was arrested and held for a short time, but I think the local authorities really didn't have the right to do that. It's illegal to hold someone without formally charging them, and without the body … well, they had to release him."

"They didn't stop believing Dad did something to her though, did they? They just couldn't find her body so they were forced to end the investigation."

"Something like that, I doubt it was ever closed. Murder—or um —those kinds of cases are never closed until the killer—until whoever did it is brought to justice." Aunt Marty looked away from Jamie. She concentrated on digging another thistle from her shoe string. "They just couldn't hold James without some sort of physical evidence. The only evidence they had against him was circumstantial."

"What's that?"

"Well, since they dated briefly and their … um … relationship was tumultuous, the police automatically suspected him first. That's the way those things always go. He was also the last one to be seen with her the night she disappeared and the two of them were seen fighting that night in front of a lot of people."

"What do you mean by 'tumultuous'? Did he hit her?" Jamie envisioned her father's large hand drawn back and her mother cowering beneath him. She shuddered and pushed the image away.

Aunt Marty glanced away, perhaps thinking the same thing. "Uh, I'm not sure." She chewed on her lower lip for a minute, and then added quietly. "He probably did."

Jamie felt as if she had been punched in the stomach. She could see why the police would suspect James. If he hit the girl on previous occasions and they had been seen fighting that night ... with great effort, she brought an end to her train of thought. But she still had so many questions. Questions that needed answers.

"Didn't anyone ever think she may have just taken off? People do that sometimes."

"There was always that possibility hanging over the prosecution's head. But everyone figured her family would hear from her eventually if she went off somewhere. Of course, it's been so long now.... They never heard anything. It doesn't seem likely."

Jamie remained quiet for a long time. She looked out across the meadow at the cows grazing in the distance. It would be milking time soon and they would begin the slow trek to the barn. Even with her father's death, the funeral and burial preparations, and the house full of relatives, no time was taken off from farm chores. The cows still needed to be milked, the eggs gathered, the garden tended. As far as she knew, Grandma and Grandpa Steele had never taken a vacation or spent as much as one night away from the farm.

"So even though it couldn't be proven, everyone thought Dad killed that girl?" she asked finally.

"Yes." Aunt Marty's answer was soft and without hesitation.

"Do they still think so?"

"Jenna's Creek's a small town. I imagine they do."

"What about Grandma and Uncle Justin? Do they think he did it?"

"I don't know, Jamie. I believe they've spent their lives trying to forget the whole thing."

Marty slapped her hands against her thighs and rose to her feet. "It's time we got back. Everyone'll be wondering where we took off to."

Reluctantly, Jamie followed suit. As they approached the house, she could see the driveway had begun to empty of vehicles. Good. Nothing would suit her better than to not have to see or hear another person for the rest of the day.

❀

The house had an eerie, empty feeling after three days of activity. Cory Steele sat in the rocking chair next to the window and looked out, her eyes focused on nothing in particular. She was bone-tired, mentally and physically. If she could sit and rock like this for a week, she'd be content. Of course, that wasn't going to happen. She considered herself lucky if she was able to rock in the evenings, undisturbed, for fifteen minutes while she listened to the girls in the kitchen cleaning up the supper dishes.

She watched the fireflies outside the window, their tails winking in the fading light, and a sad smile crossed her lips. Her memory transported her back to a simpler time when she and Harlan would sit on the porch swing and watch three dusty, barefoot boys scurrying around the yard, their hands cupped in front of them, as they tried to capture enough of the elusive creatures to put in a mason jar to use as a lamp in their bedroom.

The smile on her lips faded. Two of those boys playing in the yard were gone now. Gone by their own hand, their own carelessness, and inability to listen to reason when she tried to talk sense into their fool heads.

She would never forget the unseasonably mild, late-March day she sent Justin to the creek to call Jesse, her youngest, only eight-years-old at the time, to supper. She remembered every detail. She stood at the kitchen stove dropping bits of dough into boiling chicken broth for dumplings. A pesky housefly buzzed around her head. She batted at it with her elbow every time it tried to land on her or in the flour. As soon as she finished the dumplings, she'd get the swatter and put an end to the fly's infernal buzzing. While she worked, she watched for the two boys out the window. Then she saw Justin. He was hurrying up the hill, from the direction of the creek—alone; her first hint something was wrong. As he got closer, she could see he was soaked to the skin and hysterical. She dropped the wad of dough on the sideboard and ran outside, leaving the chicken to boil over onto her stove and clean kitchen floor.

Justin had spotted Jesse's homemade raft floating upside-down in the rain-swollen creek. The next instant he saw Jesse's body in the water, partly obscured from view by the raft, and tangled in the branches of an up-rooted tree. The water was only chest-deep, but moving fast and Jesse's clothes had snagged on the branches, trapping his head beneath the surface of the water. The more he struggled, the more entangled he became. Justin tore off Jesse's shirt to free his body and dragged him to the creek bank. He collapsed next to his brother, horrified at the sight of Jesse's swollen body, bruised and mangled from struggling against the tree. The realization that there was nothing he could do for Jesse—except go home and tell his mother what he found—made him retch violently on the ground.

When he relayed the news to Cory, her unearthly screams were heard by neighbors a mile down the road.

Cory Steele's life had never been an easy one. She had suffered devastating losses before; but nothing prepared her for losing Jesse. He was her pride and joy, her sanity in an otherwise topsy-turvy world. He challenged her, argued with her, fought imaginary villains for her, and sought her opinion before he made a move. She was the stability he needed and he was her reason for going on.

Suddenly he was gone. She was humbled by whatever force controlled such matters—her formidable strength draining away day by day.

The worst part about missing Jesse was the emptiness of the house. Harlan, James, and Justin were still there, but she was completely alone. She was being destroyed from the inside out and none of them seemed to notice—much less care. The fury she felt toward them was unreasonable she knew, yet she gave into it all the same. She was mad at Harlan for not hurting the way she hurt. She wanted to vent, rage, throw things, slam doors; but he wouldn't allow it. He closed his mouth, set his jaw in a hard line, and went about his work, refusing to talk about their loss. She was mad at Justin—the one whose grief most likely mirrored her own—for crawling inside his self-made cocoon, and pretending the hurt didn't matter. She was mad at James for being too wrapped up in his self, to spend more time with his little brother while he was alive.

Most of all, God forgive her, she was mad at Jesse. How many times had she told him not to go to the creek alone to play when the water was high on the bank? Oh, she knew he did it anyway, but she warned him again and again of the dangers. Didn't he care about her at all? Didn't he know how much she worried? Because he wouldn't listen to her or his own common sense, he was gone forever—and she was alone.

She still rose every morning before the sun burned the dew off the flowers by the front porch. Breakfast was prepared, dishes done, floors swept, laundry washed and hung out to dry. She did her chores around the little farm and muddled through her days in a foggy haze of disbelief. The days of summer lengthened and then shortened again as the season burned itself out. The corn tasseled out, the apples reddened on the trees, and the pumpkins, growing haphazardly around the garden, turned from green to gold. Nothing in her life changed—except everything. Her heart was crushed, her spirit broken, but she continued on, dreading each sunrise over the hills, knowing it was another day like the one before, another twenty-four hours to endure.

Now it was happening all over again with James.

She reminisced this past Wednesday morning. It was early and she was still in her bathrobe when she heard tires crunch in the gravel outside. She plugged in the percolator for coffee and turned toward the open kitchen door. Through the screen she saw Henry, the old hound dog, look up, give a sleepy, indignant bay of warning, and lower his head back to his paws. A deputy, who looked barely old enough to shave, climbed out of the car. She knew right away it was something about James. Her first thought was that he had been arrested for drunk and disorderly conduct or some such offense. It wouldn't have been the first time.

After listening to the nervous deputy's report, she slumped into a kitchen chair and wondered how she would tell Jamie and Cassie, who were sleeping peacefully upstairs. Unlike after Jesse's death, this time her concerns were more for the daughters James left behind than for her own grief. God would give her the strength to carry on, He always had, but the girls, she didn't know about them.

She no longer blamed Jesse for his death. She wouldn't blame James either. They hadn't meant to die and leave her alone. It was just the way life worked out sometimes. With the wisdom her years had brought, she accepted that; but what about the girls? Would they understand or would they see James' death as yet another of his slights against them? He'd never been much of a father. She supposed that was her fault; the result of some mistake she'd made in raising him. Blame the mother! That's what everybody did these days.

As Cory's awareness of the present slowly returned, she asked herself the question, "What would happen if Jamie and Cassie found out about his distant past; a past involving Sally Blake?" They'd demand answers. They'd want to know why she'd kept it from them all this time. That was something she couldn't even explain to Emmy Lou. She'd buried James already. She didn't have it in her to allow him to be prosecuted again for a crime he didn't commit. He wasn't guilty—she knew that better than anyone. She hadn't been fooled by Sally Blake. And she wouldn't allow anyone—even James' daughters—to steal what remained of his dignity.

# Chapter Three

The Janelle Wyatt Public Library was named for a direct descendant of the founding fathers of Jenna's Creek. Miss Wyatt was tall and angular and rather intimidating, and it surprised no one that she never married. When she decided to spear-head the campaign to bring a library to Auburn County in 1914, most of the funding came from her own pocket. Her inadequate paycheck from the school board for teaching high school English did little to deter her.

She was the privileged eldest daughter of the county's coroner—a position Milton Wyatt held along with a successful full-time medical practice. With the illustrious name of Wyatt after her name, a sixth sense for investments, and an uncanny knack for being in the right place at the right time, Janelle was able to acquire a prime piece of real estate on the corner adjacent to the courthouse. She promptly donated it to the county for use as the site of the future public library. Some said she used the library to immortalize herself in the town's history. Others believed she only wished to do something good with her money since she had no heirs and believed all her nieces and nephews were spoiled ne'er-do-wells.

She was teaching the children of her first students by this time and her thin, bird-like features—earning her the nickname "Ostrich"—were more of a cause for ridicule in the classroom than the intimidation they once commanded. No one knew the real Janelle Wyatt; the Janelle who taught herself to read when she was barely a toddler while sitting on her father's lap as he read the evening news. The Janelle who lamented for the vast majority of Auburn County youth who would never appreciate the benefits of higher learning as she had. She implemented the founding of the library for no other reason than to bring the joy and love of reading to the children of the county, who may not have known it otherwise.

No one was around to ponder Janelle Wyatt's motives these days. She was long gone and seldom remembered. The only reminder of the rich, old spinster who taught high school English as if it were the highest calling given to man, was a plaque on the library wall highly visible from the front entrance. At the top was the library's name, dedication date, 1925—it took several years to convince county officials to open their tax coffers to support a library—and an etched lithograph of its founder. Either the designers or Janelle herself believed a lithograph would prove a more becoming likeness through the years than an actual photograph.

Jamie Steele was one of the many Auburn County residents who never gave the founding of the library a second thought, even though she frequented it more often than nearly anyone. It was one of her favorite places. She liked the fact that most of the library staff knew her by name and would let her check out as many books as she wanted even if she forgot her library card at home—which of course, she never did. She liked it that Mrs. Gardner, the head librarian, knew the types of books she preferred and would often set aside a new release she thought Jamie would enjoy. She was proud of the fact that she was on her tenth library card, each previous one filled up with the numerical identifications of the many books she took home and absorbed like a sponge. She had no way of knowing what the record was for the most cards used up by someone her age—cards filled up and not just lost or thrown away like Cassie and other careless kids would do. She figured she was close to the record, if she hadn't surpassed it already. She kept this small achievement to herself, aware of the ridicule it would incite by the kids at school who already thought she was a nerd and a bookworm; Cassie, more than anyone.

Like today, she usually made the trip to the library from the farm on foot. The walk into town was relatively short, especially since Jenna's Creek seemed to encroach more and more upon the surrounding countryside every year, much to Grandma Cory's dismay. She often commented she would wake up one morning and see a new Five and Dime outside her kitchen window. Jamie and Cassie, on the other hand, were thrilled at the town's expansion and looked forward to the day her fears would be realized.

Today Jamie walked alone. Often times Cassie joined her she would usually to go to the drugstore, malt shop or a friend's house, and then meet up with Jamie later. Cassie didn't have anything against the library. She'd browse the shelves in the Juvenile Department for a Nancy Drew mystery she hadn't read or something similar to wile away the long summer hours on the farm. Her penchant for reading was mild; but it kept her busy while waiting for a more interesting activity to present itself.

Just as Jamie predicted, Cassie had jumped at the chance to spend some time away from the farm when Grandma Maggie and Grandpa Roy invited them to their house in the city. The farm was too quiet and uneventful for her during the summer months, and any opportunity to get away she considered a godsend. She shook her head in disbelief when Jamie said she wasn't going. She didn't ask why or try to figure out Jamie's motives for staying behind on the farm where she would have a ton of chores to do and no one but Grandpa Harlan to talk to. She'd given up trying to figure out what made Jamie tick years ago. Grandpa Roy called Jamie one of a kind. The kids at school called her weird. Cassie's own opinion fell somewhere in between.

Jamie pulled open the heavy library door and stepped inside. At the circulation desk a young librarian quietly stamped dates on the inside flaps of a pile of books. The few patrons who had beat her here this morning were scattered throughout the small air-conditioned building, browsing through thick volumes in the reference section, jotting notes, or reading newspapers. No one noticed her arrival. She liked this world of anonymity. No one cared about what brought her here. No one asked nosy questions. If inquiries were to be made, it would be she who did the asking.

She found the microfiche machine in a tiny, earthy-smelling room at the back of the building and figured out how to use it. Newspapers from all over the area, dating back to the opening of the library, were available at the touch of a button. James Steele was born in 1928. Jamie figured 1943 was far enough to go back. That would have made him fifteen. Certainly he couldn't have gotten himself into serious trouble before then. She scanned every front page of every newspaper available. Most were dedicated to the war. She found herself repeatedly slowing down to read articles that caught her attention. Besides photos and headlines from the Associated Press that caused her to catch her breath at their intensity, the local stories were also slanted to rally support for the boys overseas. She doubted too much rallying was necessary back then. There were no anti-war protests in 1943, no demonstrations or sit-ins. Everyone wanted to see the Allies squash Marxism, Communism, and Socialism in one fell swoop, as well as put an end to Hitler's reign of terror once and for all.

By 1947 her tired eyes could barely read the clock on the wall that told her it was lunch-time. What if there was no story on Sally Blake? Maybe everything she had heard on the day of funeral was innuendo and exaggerations, and had gone unreported by the local papers. She felt woozy from the tiny words flying past her eyes, and had to look twice to make sure she saw what she thought she was seeing.

*AUBURN COUNTY GIRL MISSING*

The paper was dated November, 1947.

Jamie pressed her palms against her tired eyes. She took a deep breath and looked again. The article was there all right, on the front page in the lower right-hand column. She studied the tiny picture of the young woman and tried to imagine her dad interested in her. Details were difficult to make out in the grainy, black and white photograph, but she could see Sally Blake was very pretty with large, almond-shaped eyes and luxurious, dark hair. Squinting to make out the tiny print, she began to read.

> *Sally Anne Blake, daughter of Mr. & Mrs. Theodore Blake of Jenna's Creek, was reported missing Sunday morning by her parents. Reportedly she spent the evening with friends and failed to return home Saturday evening. Miss Blake is a 1946 graduate of South Auburn High School in Jenna's Creek. Police have no reason to suspect foul play in her disappearance at this time. Anyone with information concerning the whereabouts of Miss Blake is encouraged to notify the Auburn County Sheriff's Dept.*

That was it. Ten lines of typeset dedicated to locating a missing girl.

Jamie was disappointed. She had hoped to find out more. She had no more information than before except the names of Sally Blake's parents. Surely the Gazette had followed the case. There must be more in later issues of the paper. She checked the clock on the wall again. Nearly 1:00. Grandma Cory would be expecting her home. She had chores to do. But she couldn't stop now. She told herself she would go to the end of 1947 and if there was no more mention of the case, she would stop for the day.

November 28, 1947: *REWARD OFFERED*

> *A Five Thousand Dollar reward has been offered by Jenna's Creek businessman, Mr. Theodore Blake, and his wife, Donna, for any information leading to the safe return of their nineteen-year-old daughter, Sally. Sally has been missing since the 18th of this month when she did not return home from an evening with friends. Auburn County Sheriff's Dept. officials have exhausted all leads and are no closer to resolving the case. The friends with which Miss Blake spent the evening of the 18th have been questioned extensively. Officials claim to have suspects in the case but are not releasing information at this time. Mrs. Blake has issued tearful pleas to all area news agencies for help in the safe and swift return of her daughter.*

Suspects? Only one according to everything Jamie had heard so far.

She clicked off the machine and gathered her tablets and pens together. She would have to come back tomorrow when she had more time to look. But even if she found all the details the newspapers reported on, could she find out what really happened to Sally Blake when the authorities could not? Her discoveries could clear her father's name or condemn him forever. She didn't know if she was up to the responsibility.

Sally was no longer a faceless apparition Jamie had heard about somewhere. She was a real girl with a bright smile and a future. She had parents who cried over her disappearance and even offered a sizable reward to anyone who could help bring her home. James Steele had known her, dated her. Aunt Marty said he was the last person to see her before she disappeared. Who else was among the friends spoken of in the paper? If only she could find someone who had been there that night. Surely they could answer her questions. What about the sheriff at the time? Was he still alive? Were there any detectives investigating the case? Did Jenna's Creek even have detectives? Where could she find old police records? Probably at the court house. Which office? There was so much to figure out.

Jamie started down Myles Avenue toward home. Within ten feet of the library steps, the back of her blouse was plastered against her wet skin. The heat shimmering up from the sidewalk in visible waves was made all the more difficult to bear after her morning in the air-conditioned library. She puffed out her lower lip to blow a wisp of damp hair away from her face. She wished she had time to stop at the diner for a soda, but she had spent too much time at the library. Already Grandma Cory was going to be madder than a wet hen by the time she got home.

Myles Avenue was lined with stately old houses that had been transformed into offices. There were lawyers, eye doctors, dentists, and even a funeral parlor. Mature shade trees had been planted near the business entrances and provided lush, green canopies for the renovated parking areas in the back, unfortunately nothing was close enough to the sidewalk to block the sun from beating down on the passersby. Jamie hurried along, unmindful of the bustling activity of another workday going on around her, anxious to get to the corner and onto tree-lined Munroe Street where she could enjoy a brief respite from the sun's rays. Her notebooks in her left hand and her arms swinging loosely at her side, she picked up her pace. Her sneaker-clad toe snagged in the broken sidewalk she'd walked over a thousand times, and she pitched forward onto the uneven concrete. Her notebooks and pens scattered as she thrust her hands forward in an attempt to catch herself. She came down hard on her hands and knees.

She jumped up quickly, praying no one had noticed her tumble. She gritted her teeth against the searing pain shooting from her knees and the palms of her hands, and casually knelt down to retrieve her books and pens. She swiped at the dust and gravel imbedded in her skin and resumed walking, as if falling on her face in front of half the town was nothing to get shook up about.

As her moment of embarrassment passed, she became increasingly aware of the pain. She blinked back tears as an image of her mother popped into her mind. Any time she experienced pain, whether physical or emotional, she thought of Nancy. Her compassionate eyes that could soothe a wound from across a crowded room. Her whispered words of comfort and the gentle touch of her hand stroking Jamie's hair.

Why couldn't she be here now to take care of this pain? Jamie questioned angrily. Why did she have to go through everything alone? Nancy would've understood her inability to grieve for her dad the way a good daughter should. She would've understood why she had to find out what happened to Sally Blake.

*"You're not alone, Jamie. I'm here with you. I've always been here."*

"You're here," Jamie thought as shame filled her heart. She realized she had not called upon God since first hearing of the accident last Wednesday morning. She hadn't prayed, she hadn't opened her Bible. She'd been taught her whole life to turn to Him, the author and finisher of her faith, in time of need. Since Wednesday, she had been too angry, too bitter, too lonely, and missing her mother too much to do so.

At the corner Jamie turned left off of Myles Avenue onto Munroe Street. In the shade of the centuries-old elms that lined the street, the burning pain from the fall on the sidewalk began to recede, but not the anguish in her heart.

The day Nancy died Grandma Maggie had rushed into the waiting room of the hospital and grabbed Jamie and Cassie by the hand. Cassie started crying again. It was all she'd done for the past week. She didn't want to go back to Mommy's room. Grandpa Roy scooped her up in his arms and carried her down the hall, hurrying to keep pace with Grandma and Jamie. The girls weren't supposed to be in the intensive care unit. They were too little. Grandma Maggie had argued with a nurse about it the day before. She obviously won the argument because here they were, hurrying down the hall, not sure why. The nurses watched from the nurses' station, their faces solemn. Jamie didn't want to go into Mom's room either, but she offered no resistance as Grandma Maggie pulled her along.

Nancy's bed was cranked up to a sitting position. She looked so weak and tired, but as always, a smile illuminated her face when she saw them. She held her arms out toward Jamie. "There's my girl. Come give Mommy a hug." She squeezed Jamie tight. Jamie breathed in the strong disinfectant on the bedclothes as her tears splashed onto Nancy's nightgown. Grandpa Roy brought Cassie in and deposited her on Nancy's bed.

"Mommy, I'm scared." Cassie lunged into her mother's arms, pushing Jamie aside in the process. Jamie wished she could be scared too but she was nearly twelve, too big to act like Cassie.

"I'm scared too, baby," Nancy admitted, her smile never wavering.

Grandma and Grandpa slipped from the room unnoticed. "Mommy, are you still sick?"

"Yes, baby. I am."

"Are you gonna die?"

"I'm afraid so, sweetheart."

Cassie's luminous green eyes sparkled with tears. Even back then, her tiny porcelain features displayed a promise of rare beauty that would surpass even that of her mother. "No, Mommy. I don't want you to," she cried. "I want you to come home with us."

Nancy's tears mingled with Cassie's as they held onto each other and rocked back and forth. Jamie sat on the edge of the bed feeling out of place. She wanted to cry and cling to her mother too, but everyone expected her to be strong. They said if she cried, it would break her mother's heart. As if she could read her mind, Nancy held her hand out and took hold of Jamie's. She shifted Cassie to one side and pulled Jamie against the other. The three of them leaned back against the crisp sheets. She stroked their hair while they listened to her fragile heartbeat.

Cassie spoke what was on all their minds, "Mommy, what are we going to do without you?"

"You'll keep living at home with Daddy." Nancy tried to sound cheerful, but even Cassie picked up on the uneasiness in her voice. "Grandma Cory will help him take care of you."

"Are you going to miss us Mommy, when you get to heaven?"

"Oh, Cassie, of course I'm going to miss you. I'm going to miss you both." She attempted to pull them closer but her arms didn't have the strength. She began to cough quietly. The coughs built steadily in severity. The girls pulled away, aware of her pain. She took a tissue from the night stand and held it to her mouth. When the coughing subsided, she pulled the tissue away and folded it quickly into a small square, but not before Jamie spotted the blood-stained phlegm.

Grandma Maggie and Grandpa Roy hurried back into the room. They started to take the girls off the bed but Nancy stopped them with a raised hand. "No, no, they're fine," she gasped. "I have to tell them...I have to..."

Grandma Maggie helped her take a sip of water from a cup on the night stand. She swallowed gratefully and smiled at each of them in turn, first her parents and then her daughters. "Do you girls remember what Jesus told his disciples in the book of John when he was preparing to be crucified?" At her daughters' blank expressions, she continued. "He told them, 'Behold, I go to prepare a place for you. In my father's house are many mansions. If it were not so, I would have told you...'" She took their hands and smiled through pools of tears forming in the corners of her eyes. "That passage has always brought me comfort girls, even before this happened. But now it means even more to me."

Both girls screwed up their faces, ready to burst into tears, but she shushed them. "No, don't cry. Be happy for me. I'm going to dine with my Savior. Jesus promised me a place and I am looking forward to seeing His face. Yes, my heart is breaking to be leaving the both of you. But I know you'll be all right. You'll be joining me there when it's your time to go. So, please, don't cry. Rejoice. We'll all be reunited in a place that doesn't know cancer or sickness or parting. What a glorious day it will be when our Savior calls us home to be with Him."

Eight-year-old Cassie found no comfort in her mother's words. She began to wail and buried her face in Nancy's neck. Jamie's own tears cut loose like a tidal wave. She clung to her mother with the same desperation as Cassie, not willing to let her go.

"Please don't cry. It's all right." Nancy held onto them, her words nearly lost in the sound of her own crying.

Finally Grandma and Grandpa pulled them off. "Girls, stop, you're mommy's tired."

"Let me kiss them good-bye," Nancy said, after catching her breath. Roy held Cassie over her for a final kiss. When Jamie's turn came, she was glad she was big enough she didn't have to be held in position.

She pushed Nancy's once lustrous, auburn hair out of the way and whispered into her ear. "I love you, Mom. I'll take care of Cassie for you; just like I promised."

"I know you will. You've always been such a big help to me, Jamie. My big girl. I know you'll make me proud." She smiled into Jamie's eyes and laid her hand upon her cheek. "Find your strength in the Lord, sweetheart. He'll always be there for you whenever you call on His name."

Jamie swallowed her tears and forced a tiny smile she didn't feel like smiling. "I know, Mom. I will."

"Come on, girls. It's time to go."

Jamie didn't want the moment to end. She knew it would be the last time she'd see her mother alive. Their eyes remained locked as she backed out of the room holding onto Grandpa Roy's hand.

Five years ago and it still hurt as if it happened yesterday. Would it ever get any easier? She was seventeen now, a young woman. Would there ever come a time when the giant void in her heart wasn't so debilitating? Probably not, even though her mother was no longer here to lean on, she still had a Father in heaven who cared for her. It had always been Nancy's greatest desire that her daughters serve the Lord with all their hearts. If she was here, she would tell Jamie God wanted to soothe her hurts if she would just allow Him to. He was waiting for her to turn the doubts and bitterness in her heart for her dad over to Him. He was waiting for her to offer forgiveness to a man who never asked for it....

She hurried along Munroe Street, the tears and blood from her injury drying on her hot skin.

# Chapter Four

When Grandma Cory saw Jamie's skinned knees and hands she forgot about being irritated with her for taking so long at the library. She headed to the kitchen for ice and cold compresses, indicating with a wave of her hand that Jamie was to follow. Jamie would rather take care of the matter herself—there would be less pain involved—but it was out of her hands now. She dropped into the kitchen chair offered her and braced herself for Grandma Cory's ministrations. She chewed anxiously on her bottom lip as she recalled the last time Grandma Cory had to dig a thorn out of her foot. The pain from the thorn, the resulting infection, and the tetanus shot at the doctor's office was nothing compared to Grandma Cory—her tongue sticking out of the corner of her mouth in concentration—tearing at the flesh on Jamie's heel with a sewing needle and a pair of tweezers. Florence Nightinggale, she wasn't.

She took a pan from under the sink and filled it with warm water from the tap. She lowered herself to her knees in front of Jamie and began to swab at her skinned knees, scrubbing away the grit and dirt accumulated there. Jamie clenched her teeth and endured.

"I guess you'll remember to pick up those big feet of yours the next time you're out walking around," Grandma Cory scolded after rinsing the wounds in Bactine and wrapping them securely with gauze.

"Yes, ma'am."

Grandma Cory sopped up the water that had splashed out of the pan onto the linoleum. "There's a plate of leftovers in the refrigerator for you. After you eat, there's laundry that needs to be hung out on the line. I had no idea you'd be gone so long when you left this morning," she added scathingly, her irritation at Jamie's late return from the library once again apparent.

Jamie ate quickly, anxious to get out of the kitchen. She found the laundry basket of wet clothes sitting beside the old wringer washer and headed out the back door. It wasn't the joy of performing mundane farm chores she sought, but rather the release from the house and her grandmother's critical eye.

On another hot summer day many years before, two men in suits came to the little house in Jenna's Creek where Jamie and Cassie lived with their parents. Five-year-old Jamie was playing in the back yard. Sheets hung on the clothesline just like today, fresh air and lemon-scented laundry detergent enveloping her in a crisp, fragrant cloud. Jamie was a princess and the sheets formed the walls of her castle. An evil knight had fallen in love with the beautiful Princess Jamie and was searching for her to make her his queen. As the sheets swayed in the warm breeze, she darted in and out among them to escape the evil knight's capture.

A car pulled into the driveway. Princess Jamie jumped behind the clothesline post and peered around it. Maybe it was her prince coming to save her; or it could be the evil knight in disguise. A short man and a skinny man stepped out of the car and approached the garage where Daddy was working on his old pickup truck. It embarrassed Jamie that Daddy had a beer in his hand. She didn't know why. He almost always had a beer in his hand. Daddy talked to the men and laughed, but she could tell from the sound of his voice he wasn't really happy. Then he reached into his pocket and gave something to the short man. They smiled and thanked Daddy and walked away. Daddy watched them go with a scary smile on his face; the smile that meant he was really mad and about to start hollering. The short man got into Mommy's car and started the engine. The skinny man got into the other car and both of them drove away.

Mommy ran out the back door of the house and yelled at Daddy. "James! What's going on? Where are they taking my car?"

He took a swig of beer and stared at her with the same scary smile on his face. She grabbed his arm and made him spill some of his beer on his shirt. "Where are they going with my car?" she repeated.

He shrugged his shoulders. "It's not your car anymore. It's been repossessed."

"What?"

Jamie tried to make herself invisible behind the clothesline post. She wished Mommy wouldn't get mad and yell at Daddy like that. It always meant trouble.

"James, what are you talking about? That's my car." Mommy's voice just kept getting louder and louder. Jamie put her hands over her ears. "I worked and made the payments for it every month. How could it be repossessed?"

"No, honey, you gave me the money to make the payments. And well, I guess I missed a few." He smiled helplessly as if it was really funny once you stopped and thought about it.

Mommy didn't think it was funny. She started to cry. "What do you mean you missed a few? It was my car. I worked to pay for it. How could you miss the payments?"

"Baby, it's your own fault. You know I can't be trusted with money."

Mommy's face got really red. She threw herself at Daddy and pounded his chest with her fists, crying and yelling things Jamie couldn't understand. Daddy dropped the bottle of beer and it shattered all over the driveway.

The sound of glass hitting pavement startled all of them. Jamie cringed behind the clothesline post and held her hands tighter over her ears, but she couldn't take her eyes off the scene in the driveway. Trouble was coming. Mommy stopped hitting Daddy. They both looked down at the broken beer bottle. When Daddy looked up, he wasn't smiling his scary smile anymore. He grabbed Mommy by the shoulders and shook her. "Who do you think you are, woman?" he growled in the terrible voice that always made Jamie and Baby Cassie cry. "I'll do whatever I want around here."

Mommy didn't say anything; she just kept crying. He gave her a hard push and she fell to the pavement in the puddle of beer. Daddy knelt beside her and took a handful of her auburn hair in his hand. He mumbled something in her ear. Jamie wrapped her arms around the clothesline post and cried silently as she'd taught herself to do. Whenever she or Cassie cried out loud, it only made Daddy madder at Mommy, especially if he was holding a beer.

Still holding Mommy's hair, Daddy cursed at her and told her not to tell him what to do. He gave her head a hard shake and she cried out in pain. Baby Cassie started to cry inside the house. Daddy said a bad word Mommy didn't like for him to say and pushed her away. Then he straightened up. "Clean this mess up and go take care of your kid," he snarled.

He stepped inside the open garage door and got another beer out of the little fridge he kept there for that purpose. Slowly Mommy stood up too. Jamie uncurled herself from the clothesline post and ran to her mother, throwing her arms around her legs. "Mommy, Mommy."

"I'm okay, honey. Don't cry." She dragged a bucket out of the garage and knelt down to pick up the broken glass. Jamie squatted down beside her and carefully picked up the larger shards with her chubby fingers. She kept her back to Daddy, not wanting to see his face. She had forgotten the evil knight of her imagination. Sometimes reality was scarier than anything her childish mind could conceive.

Jamie didn't get another chance to go back to the library until Friday. Her mind was a whirlwind all week, wondering what else she might find in the newspapers concerning Sally's case. The crime had never been solved because of the lack of a body. Could that mean there was no body; that Sally Blake was not dead? On the morning of the funeral, Aunt Emmy Lou mentioned Sally living in California not the least bit concerned about the trouble she had caused here. What if it was true? Had she became mad enough at James to run off, knowing everyone would blame him for her disappearance? Maybe after the fight in front of all those witnesses, she decided to punish him by sending him to prison for her murder. Surely she would have followed the investigation and when she saw he wasn't being charged, she would've returned. Wouldn't she? How could she stay away from her family for so long?

Unless…

What if there was a terrible skeleton in the Blake family closet? What if she had to get away from her parents' home for her own safety? Maybe it didn't involve James at all. If the Blakes were involved, they would do everything in their power to convince the authorities James was responsible for Sally's disappearance. Maybe there was a demented cousin or uncle living in the basement who had done something to Sally. She had fled for her own safety after being threatened by this person.

Jamie's mind pumped out as many different scenarios as there were hours in the day, each one more ludicrous and far-fetched than the last.

She had tried to concentrate on other things. She opened her Bible for the first time since her dad's death and started to read from the book of Matthew. She took long walks in the woods. She hoed the garden and tried to teach Grandma Cory's hound dog, Henry to roll over. She wrote letters to Cassie, but only mailed one of them. Anything to keep her mind occupied. It was no use. She continued to dwell on Sally Blake and the possibility she was still alive somewhere. Wouldn't that just show those busybodies in town who had blamed James for the crime all these years?

Jamie went straight to the back room where the microfiche was kept as soon as she got to the library Friday afternoon. She was relieved to find the room empty again so there would be no interruptions. Quickly she advanced to November 1947. Her eyes began scanning the screen in search of anything pertaining to the case. November ended after a few pages and she dove into December. Each edition went by with no mention of the case. At first she looked at only the front pages, but then she went back through, carefully reading any headline inside the paper. 1947 came to a close. With a sigh of disappointment she moved the lighted screen onto the next edition.

*TORRENTIAL RAINS DELAY EASTER PARADE*

Her eyes flew to the date in the upper right-hand corner of the paper: *April 2, 1949.*

What happened to 1948 and the first three months of 1949? She rushed through a year's worth of papers, checking the dates but there was no 1948. Her heart sank. She scrolled back through the editions until she came to the original Sally Blake article. She found another newspaper and looked only at the dates. Just like the Gazette, there were no editions dated between the end of 1947 and April, 1949. She hurried from the room to find a librarian.

"Excuse me," she asked at the circulation desk in a whisper she wasn't sure could be heard over the pounding in her chest.

The young librarian, whose name Jamie didn't know, looked up from her stack of books and smiled. "Yes?"

"Do you know anything about the microfiche? I was looking through old editions of the Gazette and 1948 is missing. I looked at the Portsmouth Times and it's missing those dates too."

The librarian's smile stayed in place. "Let me see what I can do," she offered sweetly.

Jamie followed her into the back room, sure she had over-looked something. The librarian was a professional. She would solve the problem and Jamie could get back to her research.

"Hmm, let me see," the young woman mused to herself. "Oh, I see what the problem is. 1948 and part of '49 are missing."

"I know that," Jamie said. "But where are they?"

The librarian looked puzzled. "I don't know."

Jamie wanted to shake the young woman until her teeth rattled in her head, but she refrained. "Is there anyone here who does?"

"Wait here a moment and I'll see." She disappeared into the main part of the library.

Jamie sat down and studied her notes, trying to stay calm. She tapped her pencil on the table top until the young librarian returned with Mrs. Gardner, the head librarian.

Jamie stood up quickly and Mrs. Gardner smiled. "What seems to be the problem, Jamie? Are you having trouble using the microfiche? Sometimes it can be a little tricky."

"Not trouble, really," Jamie explained. "It's missing about fifteen months I was hoping to find. I thought maybe I was just looking in the wrong place."

"That could be it. Which years are you looking for?"

"1948 and '49."

Mrs. Gardner looked down at Sally Blake's smiling face illuminated on the screen and pursed her lips in thought. "I do believe 1948 was the year part of the library was damaged in a flood. Terrible rains that year and extraordinarily heavy snowfalls too. Not like this year. The library operated temporarily out of the high school building. It was well over a year before everything got moved back here. I wasn't here then, but it was very chaotic and I would assume some things got misplaced." She smiled proudly at Jamie. "You're the first one to notice anything missing. That's not bad on our part. Twenty-four years before someone found a mistake."

Jamie wasn't proud. She was devastated. Somewhere in those missing fifteen months was the information she was looking for.

# Chapter Five

Her trips to the library had turned up next to nothing. Jamie knew what people were talking about when they mentioned her dad's involvement with Sally Blake, but she was no closer to finding out what really happened the night Sally disappeared than she was two weeks ago. The mystery consumed her every waking hour. She couldn't let go of it. There had to be a way she could find out more.

Saturday morning after her chores, she started across the field that divided the Steele farm from the Mendenhall's. Fran Mendenhall and Cory had been friends since the Steeles purchased the property next to theirs before World War II. Cory was there for her friend when she got word in 1944 that her husband, Ellis, was missing in action in Europe. It took six months for the Army to send word to Fran that he had been found and was recuperating from extensive injuries sustained in Italy. Fran was already aware of this since Ellis was sitting in a rocking chair by the window when she opened the mail, having returned home by bus nine weeks earlier.

Jamie climbed over the wire fence separating the two properties, using a post for balance. She scrambled up a steep rise and stopped to catch her breath at the top. The Mendenhall farm was laid out below her, an almost exact replica of her own. It had a large barn, pig pen, hen house, vegetable garden, all surrounded by their own neat fences; and of course the standard white, two-story farmhouse with the dormer windows on the second floor and the identical narrow porches at the front and back doors. Whoever designed farmhouses fifty years ago, truly believed in form following function. What the dwellings lacked in style and uniqueness, they made up for in large, drafty windows and doors that wouldn't stay open without the aid of a doorstop.

The downward slope propelled her along until she reached the gate that kept the cows out of the Mendenhall's yard. She would find a tactful way to find out how much Fran knew about her dad and Sally Blake. She couldn't come right out and ask though, or Mrs. Mendenhall would report back to Grandma Cory.

Fran stepped onto the back porch. "Hullo, Jamie. What brings you out in this heat?"

"I was just out for a walk and thought I'd stop in to say hi."

"Well, here, have a seat." Fran motioned with her hand and lowered her significant girth onto an old folding chair that looked inadequate to support the weight. "It's good to see you, dear."

Mrs. Mendenhall was always happy to receive a visitor. Ellis had long since gone on to be with the Lord, so her days alone on the farm were long and uneventful. The land lay fallow except for the vegetable garden, which was taken over by weeds every summer. Besides a milk cow and a few pigs and chickens, most of the livestock had been sent to market years ago. She was simply biding her time between the church and her friends until she was called home to join Ellis, at which time her sons would step in and do whatever they chose with the family farm. Knowing those two ingrates the way she did, it would probably be auctioned off before her body was even cold.

She expressed to Jamie the regrets and concerns shared by the community for the Steele family. Jamie only halfway paid attention to the condolences, trying instead to come up with a tactful and almost sneaky way to ask about her dad and Sally.

"Myrtle Hadley sure was upset the flower shop didn't put a card on the flowers she and Ike sent. All that money, she said, and they couldn't even keep straight who sent what. She just carried on about it somethin' awful. I tried to tell her Cory wasn't worried if there was a card or not. She knew who cared enough to send flowers."

Jamie nodded in agreement, even though her mind wasn't on flowers. There were so many at the funeral, she didn't know what became of them all. Grandma Cory and Uncle Justin brought some home, but most of them were probably out at the cemetery decomposing on the grave.

"Mrs. Mendenhall," she broke in. "I was wondering if you remember…"

"But that Myrtle," Fran continued unabated. "When she gets riled about somethin', why there's no settlin' her down. When her father-in-law, Mr. Hadley passed away, my, my, you should'a seen the to-do she and Ike put on. You'd'a thought the old man was the king of France. Why, she wouldn't be upstaged by anyone. Of course, she never had any money growin' up, don't you know? Her poor old daddy barely hung on by the skin of his teeth. So as soon as she married Ike Hadley, well, she just went plumb crazy—she sure did!"

Jamie broke into her litany a second time. "You knew my dad when he was young, didn't you?"

Fran chuckled and folded her hands across her ample belly. "Of course, honey. Why I've known your whole family as far back as I can remember. I guess I've known plumb near everybody in these parts. Mr. Mendenhall and I moved here when we first married. Things were a lot different back then, I tell you what. So quiet around here. No noise at all on a summer night. Not like it is now with all the racket from that highway…"

Jamie listened politely until the old woman paused long enough to take a breath and then leaped in. "I always heard Dad had a lot of girlfriends back when he was a young man."

"Oh, my, you're right about that, Jamie." She chuckled again and stared out across the empty pasture. "Your daddy was a real ladies' man."

"Did you know of any girls he was particularly serious about? I mean, before he joined the Navy."

"I don't know about 'serious'," Fran said thoughtfully. "I think he liked them all. Of course, as soon as he met your mama, he forgot all the rest."

Jamie knew that wasn't true and suspected Fran did too. "So did you ever meet any of the girls he brought home, other than my mom?" she persisted. "I always heard young people did that back then, brought dates home to meet the family, even if they were only going steady."

"No, I didn't meet any of them. Cory would tell me ever' once in awhile that he was seeing this or that girl, but it never amounted to anything. And as far as I knew, he didn't take any of them too seriously. He was too busy just havin' fun. I think your grandma was a little annoyed that he played the field so much. Now, your Uncle Justin, he was the serious one. He never brought a girl home till Martha Alice," Fran said in reference to Aunt Marty. "There was no other girl in the world for him. Not ever."

Jamie had to try just one more time to steer the conversation in the direction she wanted it to go. "You can't remember any of the girls he dated. Not one of them stands out in your memory for any reason?"

"Oh Jamie, like I said, there were just too many of 'em. And my memory doesn't hold onto things the way it used to."

Jamie couldn't just up and blurt out Sally Blake's name, no matter how much she wanted to. Whatever information Fran Mendenhall had about the young woman, she would never get it out of her. "Grandma Cory'll be waiting for me," she explained, disappointed. "I need to get to my chores."

"You'd better be goin' then. Thanks for comin' to see me. Don't be a stranger. You come back soon as you get a chance. You hear me now?"

Jamie gave a final wave over her shoulder as she headed up the hill toward home. She hadn't got what she came for, but Mrs. Mendenhall had enjoyed the visit. She'd have to get over here more often to see her. She'd be old and lonely herself someday.

The delicious aroma of a roast simmering in the crock pot greeted Jamie upon reentering the Steele yard. She wondered what special occasion merited Grandma Cory's famous pot roast. Rather than question it, she rushed into the house, her mouth watering and stomach rumbling.

"Lands, girl, there you are." Cory's coarse voice sounded as she entered the kitchen. "I was wondering where you took off to. I haven't been able to keep up with you all week."

"I went for a walk."

"Well, I need your help," she retorted gruffly. "Your Uncle Justin called while you were out and invited himself and Marty over for supper. Seems he's anxious to see you tonight. So now I have all this extra work to do, like there wasn't enough already."

"What do you need me to do?" Jamie asked.

"I need you inside catching up on some housework if it's not too much of a bother. Everything's gone to rot and ruin around here the past two weeks. This place's a disaster. Keep your grandpa with you. I'm trying to get supper on and he's always under my feet. I don't know what your uncle Justin's thinking half the time. Inviting himself over without giving a'body a moment's notice."

Her grumbling was just thinking out loud now so Jamie tuned her out. She complained if Justin and Marty didn't come for dinner at least once a week, accusing them of being too busy for her, and then when they did come, she complained about the extra work.

Jamie gathered the cleaning supplies from under the sink and attacked the living room with an indignant fervor—which, of course, was a far cry from falling to rot and ruin. She gave Grandpa Harlan a dusting cloth and an aerosol can of furniture polish. It was an easy enough job. He couldn't mess it up and it kept him in sight. He told her about the chickens getting into the vegetable garden and pecking the tops off the carrots while she was at Mrs. Mendenhall's. They laughed heartily as he described in vivid detail Cory's horrified reaction when she saw the clucking hens relishing her prized carrots. That explained, at least in part, her foul mood.

Promptly at six Uncle Justin and Aunt Marty arrived for dinner. Jamie could tell Uncle Justin had something up his sleeve, but he kept it to himself until well into the pot roast and red potatoes.

"All right, Justin," Grandma Cory growled. "You look as puffed up as a Christmas goose. What's the big news you've got for us?"

"Mother, I don't know what you're talking about." He smiled innocently at her and gave Jamie a wink.

Grandma Cory had no patience for riddles. "Just spill it, Justin, before you bust your buttons."

Justin sighed, his spirit deflated by her lack of playfulness. But before he could say anything, Aunt Marty turned to Jamie. "Your uncle was talking to Noel Wyatt this morning at the drugstore about you."

Jamie turned to Uncle Justin. "Me? What about?"

His smile was back. "I told him what a good worker you are. How you're tough and dependable."

"Oh, for heaven's sake, Justin. You make her sound like a used car," Grandma Cory scolded. "What are you getting at?"

Uncle Justin kept his eyes on Jamie. "I told him he'd be mighty lucky to have a girl like you."

"A girl like me for what?"

Again Aunt Marty jumped in. "For a job; a job at the drugstore."

Jamie's eyes widened in surprise. "Me? Work at the drugstore? You mean it, Uncle Justin?"

"Noel said to bring you in Monday morning and he'd talk to you about it. How does that sound?"

"It sounds great. Thank you!"

"Well, it doesn't sound so great to me," Grandma Cory stated. "What am I supposed to do around this farm all summer without Jamie? She's got more than enough work to do here without going into town to find a job. In case you haven't noticed, Cassie's not here and Jamie's doing both their chores."

Jamie dropped her eyes to her plate. Marty raised her eyebrows at Justin. He cleared his throat nervously.

"Now, Mom. You know Jamie's growing up. You knew she wouldn't be here forever."

"Don't you talk down to me, Justin. I am perfectly aware Jamie's growing up. I am also aware I'm not getting any younger myself. Eventually I may have to hire someone to come in and help run the farm after Jamie and Cassie are gone. But I was hoping for a few more years before I had to worry about where the money'd come from for that."

"Mom, we didn't mean to upset you." Aunt Marty was often the voice of reason when Grandma and Uncle Justin disagreed. "We just thought this would be a great opportunity for Jamie. We all know she's planning to go to college after she graduates. Not only will this give her a way to save some money, but it'll teach her responsibility and independence."

"She has responsibility here."

"We know that, Mom," Uncle Justin said. "But you have to let Jamie do this. I was working by the time I was her age, and so was James."

Grandma Cory let her fork drop to the table with an angry clatter. "Well, Justin, you've got some nerve telling me what I have to do in my own home. It seems like the decision's been made for me with no thought whatsoever of how it'll affect me." She gave each of them an angry stare before fixing her eyes on Jamie.

"I suppose it's settled, young lady. You'll be going to town Monday morning with your high and mighty uncle to get a job. But let me tell you something." She glared at Justin and Marty. "Let me tell you all something. She'll still be responsible for as many chores as she's doing right now. And if they suffer, Justin Steele, I'll hold you to blame. The job at the drugstore will end. Is that clear?" Her hard eyes studied each of them in turn.

Jamie had a hard time meeting her grandmother's icy gaze. As excited as she was about getting a job in town, she didn't want her obvious delight to be too apparent to Cory, who had the ability to freeze a grizzly bear in its tracks with that stare.

# Chapter Six

Uncle Justin drove Jamie to town in his new Ford. She commented politely on the plush interior and shiny blue paint job. For as long as she could remember, Uncle Justin drove shiny, blue Fords. It was the one extravagance he allowed himself, or at least it was the only one Jamie could see.

She realized that except for his penchant for blue Fords, she didn't know much else about her dad's brother. She searched her mind for an occasion when he had opened up in her presence and talked at length about himself or anything he felt passionately about. Aunt Marty was the one who usually did most of the talking. Nancy used to say Uncle Justin was always quiet, even as a young man. Everybody had something they liked to talk about—usually themselves. She'd just see how easy it was to get him going.

Just as she suspected, Uncle Justin was eager to talk when she asked him about his new car. She noted his obvious pleasure at being asked. Cars. She'd file that tidbit away for another time. All the way into town he explained why he preferred Fords over the other cars on the market. He explained trade-in allowances and depreciation, none of which interested her, but she listened politely nonetheless. She had been the one to open this can of worms. He told her how he got the added options on the car he wanted without paying extra, dickered the sticker price down to what he was willing to pay, and remained in control of negotiations until the sale was final. He referred to it as 'invaluable advice' on how a shrewd consumer handled slick car salesmen.

When he slid the new car into the narrow parking space in front of Wyatt's Pharmacy, he was still talking. "Just let 'em think you're doing them a favor by being there," he said of car salesmen as he shut off the ignition. "Tell 'em you're going to buy a car from someone and if they don't do right by you, you'll find someone who will."

"Okay, Uncle Justin." She smiled, proud of herself for coming up with a subject he could talk about all day on her very first try.

Wyatt's Pharmacy occupied one of the largest buildings on the block. There were two entrances, the primary one opening out onto the corner of Main and High Streets, the other about a hundred feet farther down High Street. The only building rivaling its size and prestige was the Citizens Bank across the street. The drugstore was as much a part of Jenna's Creek as the bell on the courthouse lawn. Its picture was always featured in the town's Chamber of Commerce catalog. It bought more 4-h pigs and goats from county youngsters than even the banks and the grocery stores. It sponsored the Fourth of July fireworks display every summer and donated the timber, hot dogs, and marshmallows for the yearly bonfire and march through the streets of Jenna's Creek every October when South Auburn High School's very own Cyclones met their arch rivals, the Blanton Bull-dogs, for the most anticipated grid-iron battle of the year.

When Jamie was six, she was lifted out of the crowd by the store's owner, Noel Wyatt, and set onto the makeshift stage at the football field in front of the bonfire to choose the name of a raffle winner out of a huge drum. After the winner came forward to collect his prize, Noel knelt down and whispered into Jamie's ear the words to yell into a huge megaphone he held in front of her. With a smile of encouragement, he instructed her to shout louder than she'd ever shouted before. She still remembered the power behind her tiny voice as it rang out across the crowded football field, "Go, Big Green!" The die-hard fans of South Auburn erupted. Jamie was handed back down to her mother as the vibration from the stage threatened to throw her into the thundering crowd.

The bell over their heads jangled to announce their arrival as Uncle Justin pushed open the door and stepped aside to allow Jamie entrance. As usual the store was bustling with business. Besides the pharmacy that generated much of the store's business, it carried a large assortment of products, ranging from household supplies and novelties to hardware.

The heady aroma of roasted nuts that greeted each customer upon entering the store immediately transported Jamie back to early childhood. Her favorite memory was gazing up at the attractive rows of assorted candies in their glass canisters standing like sentry beside the cash registers to tempt departing patrons. On the rare occasions James brought her and Cassie along to run errands, there was always a need to stop at the drugstore. Before leaving, he would lean one elbow on the counter and smile disarmingly at the salesgirl while the girls were allowed to choose any candy they wanted. The salesgirl would dip a large silver scoop into the canister and bring out a generous portion, weigh it on the big scale, and hand the brightly colored bag to the girls, all the while blushing and giggling at something James said to her under his breath. The prettier the girl behind the counter, the more candy Jamie and Cassie got out of the store with.

To the left of the cash registers was the pharmacy counter and beyond it, the jewelry counter. When Jamie and Cassie came to the store with Nancy, they would stop and admire the cheap costume jewelry available for customers like them. The little girls would try on different pieces and laugh at themselves in the mirrors above the counters. Sometimes Nancy would let them buy a bauble that caught their eye, but usually she didn't have the money to spare. It didn't matter. They liked pretending, laughing and watching their mother get into the silliness as much as they were.

The drugstore was filled with similar memories for any Jenna's Creek child, especially the lunch counter that occupied the center of the store. When visiting the store on Saturdays with their parents, many local children were permitted to sit on the high metal stools with the red vinyl seats and order a soft drink or maybe even a milk shake, while waiting for their prescriptions to be filled. It was an occasion anticipated by all elementary-school children and bragged about on Monday mornings to the unfortunate ones who missed the trip themselves.

Justin and Jamie followed the hardwood floor's uneven boards—aged to a dark walnut brown—to the back of the store, where a short flight of stairs led up to a tiny crow's nest office. Justin knocked on the door and opened it at the sound of Noel Wyatt's deep voice.

"Justin." He rose from the chair behind his desk and pumped Justin's hand in a hearty handshake. "How are you? I was so glad to hear from you the other day. I haven't seen you or Marty in a long time. How is she?"

"She's fine. We're both fine." Justin returned the handshake with equal vigor.

"Is this the niece you were telling me about?" He looked past Justin to where Jamie stood in the doorway. "Jamie, right?" He squeezed her hand, temporarily shutting off the supply of blood to her fingertips.

He only gave her time to nod in response before motioning to two tattered office chairs with a wave of his hand. "Both of you have a seat." He returned to his own chair on the other side of the desk.

He clasped his hands together and leaned forward with his elbows resting on the desk. "So, your uncle tells me you're looking for a summer job?"

"Yes, sir."

"Did he ever tell you I gave him his first job?" Once again he didn't wait for a reply.

"Best employee I ever had. The best. I still tell people that. 'The best kid I ever hired was Justin Steele' I say. Never late for work. Never complained about the schedule. Never shirked his duties. That was your Uncle Justin. Summer of 1947."

1947. The year Sally Blake disappeared, Jamie noted.

"Remember that, Justin? How old were you then? Seventeen? Eighteen?"

"Sixteen."

Noel leaned back in his chair and propped one foot on the desk. "Good lands, man! Where have the years gone? I thought I was old back then. Now look at us. A quarter of a century gone and it seems like nothing's changed."

"When you put it that way, you make us sound ancient." Uncle Justin snorted amiably.

While the two men reminisced about the old days of working in the drugstore, Jamie heard little of what they were saying. As she watched Mr. Wyatt talk, fidget in his chair, and drum his fingertips on the desk—an apparent fireball of energy—she found herself considering the mystery that had puzzled half the county for over thirty years. Why Noel Wyatt wasn't married.

He was a good catch by anyone's standards. The gray in his hair and laugh lines around his mouth only heightened his appeal to the ladies. He still cut a fine figure; no unsightly bulge hanging over his belt or second chin that marred the appearance of most men his age. His easy-going, down-to-earth manner endeared him immediately to everyone he met. The fact that he was the last surviving male to bear the illustrious name of Wyatt and one of the wealthiest men in this part of the state didn't impair his popular standing either.

Jenna's Creek had been named for his far distant great-grandmother, Jenna Wyatt who, along with her husband Matthew, settled the area in the late 1700's. The Wyatts made their homestead on the banks of a tributary of the Scioto River. Since Mrs. Wyatt made most of the trips to the water's edge to meet her family's needs, the creek became known as Jenna's Creek. When other homesteaders moved into the area, they also used the name of the creek as reference to their location. Everyone knew where Jenna's Creek was. When the time came to establish a town, no other names were considered.

Noel was sent to college while most of his contemporaries went straight to work. In Louisville, Kentucky he attended pre-med and graduated near the top of his class. He also met Myra Curtsinger, the daughter of a wealthy businessman from Lexington. Noel, who until then only had a mind for his studies, found himself hanging on every soft-spoken, lilting word that proceeded out of Myra's mouth. She was beautiful, cultured, and sent to school with the sole purpose of finding and procuring the proper husband. She found Noel's homespun honesty and innocence rare and endearing. At Christmas, he went home to meet her family. Her parents approved immediately. Mr. Curtsinger found a soul-mate—a self-made man with brains to go along with the advantages life had given him. Mrs. Curtsinger fell in love with his manners, consideration of women—taught to him by his mother and older sisters—and the fact he could provide amply for her spoiled daughter.

Noel's widowed mother wasn't as impressed with Myra. She was used to sending young girls down the pike who found themselves in love with her son. She wanted only his happiness, but endeavored to spare him any undue heartache. She didn't want his naivete to be a vehicle by which an enterprising young thing with fluttering eyelashes and a demuring smile could take advantage of him. One day he would be a man of considerable wealth if he used any of the sense God had given him, and she was only too aware of what some girls would do to get on that gravy train, even if Noel wasn't.

"Noel, dear," she began gently after he returned home the following weekend without Myra. "She seems to be a lovely girl…"

"But…"

She smiled and jumped right in. "But… Myra appears to be a bit high-strung. She wasn't brought up like the girls around here. I don't know what the two of you will have to talk about."

"Is that all you're worried about, Mother?" He laughed good-naturedly and she felt a tug in her heart. She was too late. He was already in love and wasn't going to listen to a word she said.

She patted his arm. "You know I love you, Son. More than anything. But I don't think Myra will be happy here. She's used to the city and cotillions and country clubs. The women here will drive her out of her mind. Have either of you considered what a change this will be for her?"

Now Noel was doing the arm-patting. "We've talked about this. She's looking forward to a change. Her mother has been pushing her all her life into being what she despises. She wants to get away from all that. We want to buy a nice house on Bryton Avenue and raise a house full of kids."

"Somehow I can't see that girl changing diapers."

"Mother, please. Relax. I'm going to give Myra everything she wants. I'm going to make her as happy as Dad made you. You admitted it was a different world for you when you became a Wyatt, but you and Dad came out all right."

*I was a local girl,* she wanted to shout at him. *I wasn't a debutante. I knew what this town was like.* The words remained in her heart. Countless times over the next two years they were on her lips again, but she never spoke them. She knew nothing she could say would reach him on the lofty plane where he now dwelt.

Within weeks of the honeymoon, Myra began to loathe Jenna's Creek and everything associated with it, including her doting husband. He was a pharmacist, which told her he couldn't become a real doctor. He didn't belong to the country club, which told her he didn't appreciate his station in life. He extended credit to customers he knew wouldn't be able to settle with him, which made him a fool with his money—money that now belonged partly to her.

Noel tried for two long years to make her happy. It was possible that even Myra wanted to make things work since she hung around so long. Or perhaps she wanted to ensure she had a legal leg to stand on when she left. For a time he thought he loved her and later wondered if love had ever been possible. She was spoiled and contrary, traits he refused to see while they were courting. He secretly wished a baby would solve their marital woes, but was wise enough to know one would only amplify them.

When she told him she was going home to her mother, he asked how soon she'd be out of his house. Resourceful Myra had put some thought into her departure. She wasn't about to leave Jenna's Creek empty-handed. Noel paid dearly for the two years of wedded bliss they shared on Bryton Avenue. At least he did keep the house and a modicum of dignity. No one in town liked that Curtsinger girl anyway.

The bad marriage of his youth ruined Noel Wyatt, the people of Jenna's Creek reasoned among themselves. He lost too much money and pride with the whole affair. He didn't want to be hurt by a woman again. The right girl would come along someday and he would forget about Myra and the heartache she caused. If only the right girl could be one of their daughters...

Years passed. Noel grew older. He made improvements on the house on Bryton Avenue. He expanded the drugstore. He developed a stock portfolio to support himself in his old age. He joined the country club and learned to play golf because all his friends did. He bought a house for his mother in Florida and drove her there every New Year's Day to spare her the cold Ohio winters. He never remarried. He seldom dated. Only Noel knew the truth; and it had nothing to do with Myra Curtsinger.

"Jamie, I'll start you out like I did your uncle," Noel said, snapping Jamie out of her reverie.

"Okay," she said guiltily, forcing herself back to the present. She hoped she hadn't missed any other pertinent parts of the conversation.

What would her new boss think of her if he knew what thoughts had been occupying her mind for the past fifteen minutes?

"You'll be our new stock boy, or rather, stock girl." He smiled and she smiled back. "I'll start you out with a few days a week to see how you do and if everything works out, I'll increase your hours. You don't have anything against working Saturdays, do you?"

"No, sir."

"That's good. You'd be amazed how many young people want their Saturdays free. But Saturday is a workday like any other when you are working with the public."

Justin smiled. "Kids don't have the same work ethic we were raised with, Noel. But you won't have to worry about that with Jamie. She's not afraid of hard work. She's a good one, this girl."

Jamie blushed at the praise. She hadn't realized Uncle Justin paid much attention to her, especially her work habits.

"I hope you came prepared to work today," Noel said.

"Oh, that would be great," she replied quickly, surprised the interview—if she could call it that—was over and she had the job.

"Wonderful." He slapped the desk and stood up. Jamie and Justin rose with him. "That's what I like. Enthusiasm. Let's go downstairs and I'll show you around."

# Chapter Seven

How late is she going to be?" Justin asked his old boss on the way down the narrow staircase. "I'll be coming back to pick her up."

"That's all right," Jamie spoke up. "I can walk home."

"No, it won't be a problem. I don't want you to have to walk home on your first day. If memory serves me correctly," he added with a smile, "Noel will work you so hard, you won't have the strength to walk home."

"I guess I'll keep her until closing," Noel said after consulting his watch. "She'll be happy to leave by then."

They walked to the pharmacy counter where a woman around Uncle Justin's age, dressed in a white smock, was filling a prescription for a young mother with a crying toddler balanced on her hip. The child's nose was running and his cheeks were flushed. The mother looked like she wanted to cry too.

"What's the problem, Mikey?" Noel asked the little boy. He reached out and took him from his mother and looked into his face. "Aren't you feeling well?"

Relieved of her burden, the boy's mother put one hand on the small of her back and wiped her brow with the other. "He's been running a fever for a few days now. Doc says he has another ear infection. I thought he'd've outgrown them by now like the other kids did."

"I wouldn't worry, Bess. They all develop at their own pace.

He'll get along just fine. Won't you, Mike?" He held the boy a few moments longer talking to him while his mother completed her transaction with the woman behind the counter.

"Thanks again, Noel," she said, pronouncing it 'Nole' like everyone else in Auburn County. "I hope we won't have to come back in for a long time."

Noel patted the child on the head one last time before handing him back to his mother. Then he turned his attention on Jamie. "Jamie, this is my assistant, Noreen Trimble." The woman had been working behind the pharmacy counter as far back as Jamie could remember, but they'd never been introduced. "This place wouldn't run without Noreen. When I'm not here, you take orders from her. Noreen, this is Jamie Steele, Justin's niece. She's our new stock girl."

"Don't let him fool you," Noreen said, shaking Jamie's hand. "I don't give orders. And I couldn't if I wanted to, seeing as he's always here. It's nice to meet you, Jamie."

Jamie smiled in greeting to Noreen and began to relax. Working here would be fun. Her eyes roamed around the store as if for the first time, noticing all the work necessary to keep the doors open to the public. She hoped she was up to it. After pleasantries were exchanged between Justin and Noreen, he made his exit, reminding Jamie again he would be coming for her when the store closed.

Noel showed Jamie the time clock outside his office door. After he demonstrated how to use it, he led her to the rear of the store and through a door marked 'Employees Only'. Jamie felt like a grown-up as she passed over the threshold. For the first time in her life, she was someone's employee, a paid one anyway. Not like at home on the farm where she worked like a dog just because she'd been born to it.

A lanky, young man with sandy blond hair, probably around twenty by Jamie's estimation, stood in front of a stack of boxes that reached nearly to the ceiling, checking off items on an invoice attached to a clipboard in his hand. Noel spoke to him. "Jason, this is our new stock girl, Jamie. Jamie, this is Jason Collier. Pay attention to everything he tells you. He'll be training you."

Jason glanced up from his clipboard and gave Jamie a distracted half-smile in greeting.

"Keep an eye on her, Jason."

"Sure thing, Boss." His eyes had already returned to the invoice, checking figures against the number of boxes in front of him.

"I'll be in the pharmacy with Noreen if you need anything," Noel said to Jamie on his way out the door.

Jamie shuffled nervously from one foot to the other as Jason continued the inventory, seemingly unaware of her presence. While she waited, she examined the stockroom, committing its rows and alphabetized shelves to memory. At first glance, everything looked as if it had been thrown into the room with no sense of order. The stockroom was nearly half the size of the entire store. Along the back wall was a concrete pad and double doors she presumed led to a loading dock in the alley. In the corner were two smaller doors marked "Employee Restrooms." She was glad she had spotted them and wouldn't have to ask Jason where they were later.

After ten uncomfortable minutes with nothing to do but look around, Jason made the last mark on the invoice with a flourish. "Well," he said more to himself than to Jamie, "that's that." He set the clipboard on a beat-up desk in a corner of the room hidden among a sea of boxes stacked on either side of it.

"First of all, these boxes have to be sorted and put where they belong." He nodded toward the stack of boxes in the center of the floor. "The shelves and boxes are clearly marked for the proper department so you shouldn't have any trouble."

His emphasis on the word clearly indicated he thought only an imbecile could foul up the job. "Here, use this." He placed a utility knife in her hand. She stared blankly at the orange object, unsure of its purpose.

He sighed at her hesitation. "Like this." He put his warm, callused hand over hers and forced her thumb against the button on the side of the knife to extend the blade. "Careful. It's easy to get in a hurry and cut your hand off. Take your time."

Jamie stiffened at his words. Either the heat from his hand covering hers or the warning of possible dismemberment unnerved her. "After these are put away, we'll go out on the floor and inventory shelves to see what needs to be put out. Mondays, Tuesdays, and Fridays are our biggest days for deliveries, so we've gotta get moving."

She shook off the image of her severed limb on the concrete floor and tackled the stack of boxes. Most of the morning was spent searching for the correct place on the shelves for the items in the three boxes she opened. Jason didn't look up or offer to help when she struggled with a particularly awkward load or tried to locate a shelf. She worried what he must be thinking of her. She hoped he wouldn't run to Noel at the end of his shift and tell him what an incompetent dope she was. While she valiantly tried to pull her share of the weight, it was obvious he could've easily handled the job without her. The stack of boxes quickly diminished in his capable hands without so much as a word to her. He effortlessly set each heavy box on the floor, slit it open and deftly emptied its contents onto the proper shelves.

Finally the stack of boxes was gone. The empties were broken down and taken to the dumpster out back. At four o'clock. Jason announced it was time for their supper break. Jamie realized she had not thought to bring food with her and had no money to buy anything. But the prospect of getting off her feet made her glad for the break even if she couldn't afford to eat. After washing up, Jason led her out of the stockroom and to the soda counter.

"We eat behind the counter in this corner where we're out of the way of customers," he explained with a vague wave of his hand. He greeted the heavy-set woman behind the counter. "Barb, have you met the new girl? Um…"

"Jamie," Jamie filled in. She didn't care if he liked her or not, but was it too much to ask that he remember her name?

"Hi, Jamie," the woman said with a grin that lit up her soft features. "I'm Barb Beckman. What'll you have?"

Jamie darkened with embarrassment. "Oh, I think I'll just sit here and rest. Um… I didn't bring any money with me."

"Jason." Barb glared at him accusingly. "Didn't you tell her?" He shrugged absently and eyed a menu. "Employees eat free," she told Jamie softly. "A sandwich, fries or salad, and a drink. Whatever you like."

"Oh, thanks."

"Don't thank me, honey. Noel takes care of his help. You need a menu?"

"Yes, please," she said gratefully. Now that she was sitting within smelling range of the food, her olfactory senses set her stomach to rumbling. She hoped no one would hear.

Barb snatched the menu out of Jason's hands. "You don't need that," she said in response to his annoyed look. "Been the same things on this menu forever. Besides, you eat the same thing every day anyhow."

At that time in the afternoon, the soda fountain was almost deserted. As she ate, Barb leaned against the counter and gave Jamie the rundown on working at the drugstore. She painted a rosy picture that helped set Jamie's mind at ease. As long as Jason gave her a chance to prove herself before he gave Noel a bad report, she'd be okay. Jason said nothing during the short break, instead hastily devouring the sandwich in his hands. Half of Jamie's sandwich was still on her plate when he sucked the last of his soda noisily through the straw to indicate he was ready to get back to work. He stared pointedly at her plate and sighed impatiently. Jamie took a huge bite of her sandwich and started to climb off the stool.

"Let the girl finish her food, for pity's sake," Barb admonished.

"Yeah, let the girl finish her food."

Jamie looked up in surprise at her new defender. She recognized him instantly from school.

The boy extended his hand with a broad smile. "Hi, I'm Tate Craig."

"I know," Jamie said, shaking his hand. "I go to school with you at South Auburn."

The wide, straight smile remained in place. No recognition registered on his perfectly chiseled features.

"I'm Jamie Steele," she said hoping to jog his memory.

Still no response. Obviously she had left no impression on him during the years they attended elementary, junior high, and high school together. They passed in the hallways nearly every day. He sat behind her in algebra class and asked her more than once for the formula for a linear equation. There would be just over a hundred graduating seniors in her class when school resumed in the fall. How could he not remember her?

Why should he? she reasoned. Tate Craig was popular and gorgeous. Every girl in school dreamed of being noticed by him. He played football and dated cheerleaders. He wouldn't have time for a nobody like her.

"It's nice to meet you, Jamie," he said.

"You too," she said, realizing with a sinking heart how totally invisible she was at that school.

"So, Noel's finally hired some more help?" Tate smiled and eyed her appreciatively.

Jamie blushed under his stare. "Yes. My uncle used to work here and he helped me get the job."

*What a dumb thing to say*, Jamie, she berated herself. But she couldn't think of anything else with those huge, hazel eyes fixed on her.

"Well, I'm glad of that."

Jason had been shuffling from foot to foot during the exchange. "We've got work to do," he said finally, turning toward the stockroom. Jamie made a mental note to eat faster the next time.

"Bye, Jamie," Tate said in a throaty voice that sent shivers down her spine. "I'll see you around."

She smiled sheepishly and followed Jason to the stockroom. As he rushed from one end of the stockroom to the other, pointing out this and indicating that, Jamie tried to push Tate Craig's captivating smile out of her mind and focus on Jason's rapid-fire instructions. He kept her moving the rest of the day with little time to absorb all the data he was shoving into her head. Her muscles didn't complain as much as they did after a day working with Grandma Cory, but this work seemed harder nonetheless. There was so much to remember!

Jamie looked up in alarm when the store's overhead lights went out at eight o'clock. Then she realized her first work day was over. She heaved a sigh of relief—she had survived.

Noel appeared from behind the pharmacy counter. "How'd she do?" he asked Jason.

"Not bad," Jason mumbled.

Jamie sighed inwardly at the lack of conviction in his voice. At least he hadn't suggested that Noel fire her immediately and hire someone who knew their ear from their elbow!

"Can you work tomorrow?" Noel asked her.

"Sure."

"Good. Be here around noon. I'll make you out a schedule for the rest of the week." He turned and went back to the pharmacy counter where Noreen was going over receipts.

After clocking out in front of Noel's office door, Jamie looked down and saw she was still wearing her smock. The stockroom was dark and empty. Jason had obviously gone home for the night and wouldn't be able to find any more work for her to do. She hit the switch beside the door and a naked bulb suspended from the ceiling near her head cast an eerie pallor over the room. Now that the day's activities were over, the stockroom was all shadows and creepy dark corners. She thought about hitting the other switch on the wall to turn on the newer florescent lighting, but that would make her look like a big chicken to anyone entering the room. She glanced anxiously at the steel door leading into the alley and wondered if Jason had secured it before he left. She should check it just to be sure, but suddenly her legs lacked the strength to make it all the way across the room. What if she was too late? What if a crazed, escaped convict had already found the unlocked door in the alley and was waiting for her behind a stack of laundry detergent? When she got close enough, he would leap out from his hiding place, wallop her on the head with a stove pipe, and...

Jamie fumbled through the shadows and found the peg next to the locker that had been assigned to her. She shrugged out of her smock and hung it carelessly on the peg. She removed her purse from the locker and reminded herself to buy a combination lock like the one on her locker at school. With one last nervous glance over her shoulder toward the loading bay, she hurried to the stockroom door and gave it a yank. Tate Craig had been holding onto the knob on the other side and was consequently flung into the room.

"Whoa! What's the hurry, Jamie?" A teasing grin spread over his face.

Jamie's face flushed an embarrassed pink. "Oh, Tate. I'm so sorry. Are you all right?"

"Sure, I'm fine. I love it when a pretty girl practically pulls me into her arms."

"I... I didn't mean to... I'm really sorry..."

"No, really, Jamie. It's cool." He stepped aside and held the door open for her. "You working tomorrow?"

"Yes."

"Same shift as today?"

"Yes."

"Cool. I'll see you then."

Tate's twinkling hazel eyes made Jamie's already weak knees nearly buckle under her. "Uh, okay. Bye, Tate." She clutched her purse in front of her and hurried to the front of the store, chastising herself the whole way for not thinking of something clever to say when she had the chance.

A middle-aged woman was counting money at the front register. She looked up, irritated, as Jamie approached. "Hi," Jamie said, forcing a smile. "I need to leave. Could you unlock the door for me?"

The woman rolled her eyes heavenward. She stuffed the pile of one-dollar bills she had been counting back into the drawer and selected a key from the ring attached to her belt loop to unlock the front door. "Thank you," Jamie said politely as she stepped out onto the sidewalk, but the door was already closing in her face.

"How was your first day?" Uncle Justin asked from behind her, climbing out of his new Ford.

"I really liked it," Jamie exclaimed, relieved to be talking with Uncle Justin instead of people who made her feel so incompetent. "It was hard, but fun too. Mr. Wyatt wants me to come back tomorrow at the same time."

"Sounds like it went well."

"Oh, it did. But I don't know about Jason, the one who's training me. I don't think he likes me." She didn't mention the nasty look she'd just received from the woman behind the counter.

"I wouldn't worry about it. He doesn't sign your paychecks."

"I'm glad of that."

During the ride home, Uncle Justin was full of questions and stories from his own early days at the drugstore. Jamie answered each one enthusiastically, excited about her first day and thankful she'd made it out of the stockroom alive. But the best thing about the day she kept to herself. She didn't know if she would even share it with Cassie when she saw her again. It was too wonderful. Tate Craig had said she was pretty.

# Chapter Eight

Jamie's cheeks glowed with anticipation as she pulled a comb through her sleep-tousled hair. After tossing and turning in her bed last night, and going over her first day at work in her head a hundred times, she had finally drifted off and slept like a baby. As soon as she awoke, all her doubts from the night before about her ability to keep up with Jason in the stockroom rushed to the forefront of her mind. But she wouldn't think on them right now.

Instead she concentrated on finding a blouse that brought out the flecks of green in her brown eyes. There wasn't a lot she could do about making herself look better. While Cassie inherited their mom's delicate beauty, she had inherited Dad's wide shoulders and long legs, square jaw, and straight, brown hair. James Steele had been a handsome man. Nearly every woman in town would steal a peek whenever he walked past, partly for his dangerous reputation, but mostly for his rugged good looks. On him, it worked. On Jamie, it made her feel plain and un-feminine; especially next to Cassie.

She knew she was silly for worrying about what she wore to work. Anything she chose would be hidden under the dingy blue smock all the drugstore employees wore. But that didn't matter. Tate had asked her when she worked again. He even said, "I'll see you then." That meant she would most likely run into him like she did last night. When that happened, she wanted to look nice.

Finally satisfied with her choice, she laid the clean outfit on the bed and got into her old clothes for the morning chores. The cows waiting for her in the barn wouldn't care if her outfit brought out the flecks of green in her brown eyes or not.

Grandpa Harlan was at the back door pulling a worn pair of rubber boots on over his shoes. He didn't need the boots. It hadn't rained in weeks, but he wore them regardless of the weather. "Morning, Jamie," he called to her. "I'm going out to feed the chickens and gather the eggs." As far back as she could remember, feeding the chickens and gathering the eggs was the first thing he did every morning and every morning he told her his plans on his way out the door.

"Morning, Grandpa." She followed him onto the porch and bent down to give the near-sighted hound dog a scratch behind his ears. Henry was in his usual spot, sprawled on the back porch so he had to be stepped over every time anyone entered or exited the back door. He leaned lazily against her palm as she scratched. When she finished, he sighed, stretched, rolled onto his side, and went back to sleep.

Grandpa Harlan whistled a familiar bluegrass tune on his way to the chicken coop, swinging an empty basket in one hand and a bucket of dried corn in the other. Grandma Cory came out of the barn carrying two buckets of fresh milk. "Put Amelia and Windy in the pasture," she hollered at Jamie.

"Okay, Grandma." Jamie stepped over three barn cats lapping milk out of an old pan in the middle of the barn's straw-covered floor. "Morning, Amelia. Morning, Windy," she called out to the two milk cows. She patted Amelia's backside before opening the gate and shooing them out into the sunshine. She had claimed Amelia as her own when Grandma Cory acquired the Jersey years ago. Grandma Cory didn't put much thought into the naming of farm animals. 'Girl' or 'Brown' were suitable enough for a new heifer as far as she was concerned, but seven-year-old Jamie wouldn't hear of it. The child gave her no peace on the matter until she agreed to let her come up with a name befitting the animal's regal persona.

When the next milk cow was purchased a few months later, she wisely let Cassie pick out a name to avoid an incident. Cassie decided on a name on the spot whereas Jamie considered the matter for days. She called her Windy, after Captain Windy, the co-hostess of a popular, local kids' television program simulcast out of Cincinnati.

In those days, when they still lived in town with both their parents, Jamie and Cassie loved to spend weekends and long summer days at the farm playing with the animals. Their favorite game was Cowboys. They chased wild horses around the yard, trying to lasso them with their jump ropes. The only problem with the game was the horses were really chickens and chickens don't particularly like to be chased around and swung at with jump ropes. Grandpa Harlan reluctantly put a stop to their fun. He said laying hens couldn't lay eggs if they spent their days running from cowboys, and Grandma Cory would be very mad if the eggs stopped coming. After that when was no one around, Jamie would sometimes "accidentally" leave the gate to the chicken coop open. When the hens ventured into the yard she and Cassie were forced to round them up and chase them back into the pen, whooping and hollering the whole way, waving their improvised lassos like only real cowboys could.

With Cassie at the Sharboroughs there were double the chores for Jamie to do. She made light work of them as she hurried around the barnyard. She was anxious to show Grandma Cory she was capable of handling her job at the drugstore and could still keep up with her farm chores.

Breakfast was nearly ready when she got back into the house.

"Is it all right if I get ready for work, while I wait for breakfast?" she asked.

Grandma Cory kept her back to Jamie as she answered coldly. "Sure, go ahead. I wouldn't want you to keep them waiting."

"I can help if you want me to," she offered meekly.

"No, no." Cory flipped a piece of bacon over in the skillet with a fork. "We have everything under control. Harlan, finish setting the table."

Jamie sighed. Her efforts to get on Grandma Cory's good side seemed to be a waste of time.

She dressed quickly and put a finishing touch of blush on her cheeks and mascara on her lashes. She pursed her lips to give them a little color and admired the finished product in the mirror. Not bad, she supposed, though she would never be a beauty like Cassie. Cassie looked like their mother with thick auburn hair and huge hazel eyes. Not only did her looks warrant attention wherever she went, she also had a lively personality people were automatically drawn to. Where

Jamie was shy and self-conscious, Cassie was funny and extroverted, everyone's best friend. Jamie sighed and gave her hair a quick run-through with her fingers. *"You can't make a silk purse out of a sow's ear,"* she reminded herself. She'd have to make do with what the Good Lord gave her. She just hoped Tate wouldn't be disappointed that she wasn't beautiful.

Her grandparents were already eating breakfast by the time she got downstairs. Grandma Cory didn't look up or apologize for starting without her. Jamie took her seat at the table and scooped a portion of scrambled eggs onto her plate. She tried not to care that they hadn't waited for her. On the farm, no one started eating until everyone else was seated. Grandma Cory was just letting her know she was still upset with the job situation. But Jamie wouldn't let on that it bothered her. She would be the bigger person.

She set her empty plate in the sink and glanced at the clock over the stove. She had plenty of time to do the dishes before she left and maybe even run the sweeper in the living room. She turned on the faucet full-force and reached under the sink for the dish-washing liquid. "I can get those later." Cory's voice sounded sincere this time.

"It'll just take me a minute," Jamie told her. She'd do her share of the work without complaint. Even more than her share. She wouldn't give anyone reason to think she was lazy.

Cory cleared the table and set the rest of the dishes on the counter. "Thank you, dear." She kissed Jamie on the cheek.

What was that for? Surely Grandma wasn't apologizing for being so hard on her about the new job, or for starting breakfast without her. She didn't go around apologizing for anything. As far as Jamie knew, she was never wrong. At least not in her own mind.

Grandpa Harlan went into the living room and turned on his record player. Soon the mournful sound of a cowboy bemoaning his broken heart filled the house. Jamie hummed along in spite of herself. The record was scratched and dragged in places due to the thousands of times it had been played. The record player's needle needed replacing again. She would buy one for him tonight before she left the drugstore.

Jamie finished the dishes in a matter of minutes and rinsed out the sink. She dried her hands on an old towel and looked around the kitchen to make sure everything was in order. She gave herself a satisfied smile. A place for everything and everything in its place. How many times had she heard Grandma Cory say that?

She got the mop and bucket from the closet by the back door to give the kitchen floor a quick swipe. There once was a time in Grandma Cory's younger days that she mopped the kitchen floor every morning. Now that she moved slower and there was more and more to do it seemed every day, she couldn't keep up on things the way she liked. For the unexpected kiss on the cheek, Jamie would repay her with a shiny kitchen floor.

A short time later, Jamie stuck her head in Grandma Cory's bedroom where she knew she'd be relaxing during a lull in her work. "I'm leaving now, Grandma," she called into the cool darkness. Grandma Cory always kept her blinds pulled against the invading sun, even in the wintertime when its rays would be appreciated.

"All right, Jamie," Grandma Cory answered from her position by the window, an open Bible on her lap. "Tell your grandpa where you're going and when you'll be coming back. He worried me to death yesterday asking about you."

"Okay. See you tonight."

Cory watched Jamie back out of the bedroom and looked back down at her Bible, barely illuminated by the filtered sunlight coming in around the slats in the Venetian blinds. It didn't matter; she hadn't been reading this morning anyway. She closed the heavy book and smoothed her hand over the cracked, well-worn cover. She thought about Jamie and how much she resembled her father. Sometimes when she entered a room and Cory caught sight of her out of the corner of her eye, she'd catch her breath. Or when Jamie and Cassie were clowning around, the two of them wrestling on the floor, laughing and gasping for air, Cory could almost swear—if she was a swearing woman—it was James and Justin, kids again, playing the same games.

It was difficult for her to spend time with Jamie. The color of her hair, her brown eyes with the startling green and gold flecks, the curve of her lips, the tilted way she walked across a floor, the insolent set of her jaw when she felt she had been wronged—all reminded her of James.

With a silent groan of anguish, she rose to her feet and parted the curtains with her hand. She squinted against the harsh sunlight. She watched for a few minutes for Jamie to pass by the window on her way to town. It would be hot soon, too hot for the girl to keep making the walk into town. She had her license now. Cory thought she may give her permission to drive the old truck to work now and then, as long as she put gas in it. Of course she would; she was a responsible girl. Not the type to take advantage of a person's kindness. She was more like her mother in that respect.

The smell of pine cleaner still lingered in the air from her mopping the kitchen floor without being told. Yes, she was a good girl. Cory would have to tell her that sometime.

She sighed heavily again and let go of the curtain. Yes, Jamie reminded her of James, but fortunately, his less desirable qualities seemed to have passed over both of his daughters. Jamie had his looks and stubborn streak when she was crossed. Cassie had his sense of humor and easy-going manner. Besides that, there was very little of her oldest son left. He could have had so much to offer. His life could've been different if only he had *chosen* to be different. Was it something she did? Had she gone wrong somewhere along the way?

She choked back a sob and shook her head to clear it. She wasn't the type of woman to sit around brooding about past mistakes—or looking for ones that didn't exist. She leaned over the bed and busied herself fluffing pillows and straightening the bedspread. She missed her son. She was allowed to do that. She still missed Jesse, her baby. She even missed Harlan—the strong, virile man she fell in love with. She was so lonely; lonely and hurt. Hurt that once again, she was grieving alone. Jamie and Cassie sure weren't showing any outward signs of loss over their father. He was not the most stable, devoted father in the world, but he was the only one they knew. Why didn't they feel the grief she felt? How could they have forgotten him so quickly?

At least they didn't have the father she had, Frank Brown. The thought sent an involuntary shudder through her despite the rising temperature in the room. The image of a red-faced drunk spewing obscenities at a frightened little girl made her breakfast sit ill in her stomach. She hadn't allowed herself to think of him in years and she wouldn't do it now. He wasn't worth the time of day and she certainly wouldn't give it to him. When memories of Frank Brown flooded her mind, she pushed them aside as easily as the silly chickens that clustered around her feet when she went into the hen house. Frank Brown was long gone. Even though he was her step-father and the father of her younger brother and sister, in her mind he never existed. She was better off keeping it that way.

Her thoughts returned to Jamie and James. Other than appearance and physical mannerisms, the two had little in common. James could always make Cory laugh. Even when he brought notes home from irate teachers at school or put another scratch on the family car, he could find a way to make her smile and forget she was supposed to be mad at him.

Jamie was quiet and introverted, more like her Uncle Justin. Justin didn't get into trouble like his older brother. He never gave Cory or Harlan cause to worry about his whereabouts. He did what he was told when he was told to do it. Even in the cradle he didn't demand attention, and subsequently, he didn't get it. With two other rambunctious boys to keep Cory and Harlan busy, well-behaved Justin with his complacent personality, was often over-looked.

Perhaps she could get Justin to talk to Jamie for her. He could ask all those uncomfortable questions about how she was feeling, now that her father was gone. If she had any problems or concerns, Justin could take care of it. Maybe she was grieving more than Cory realized. Maybe James' death wasn't as easy on her or Cassie as the two girls made it look.

Oh, what was the use? In her opinion, people spent too much time these days worrying about how everyone felt about every little thing. It was better just to put the past behind you and move on. Get on with living. That's what Cory had done and things had worked out for her just fine. Jamie would have to learn to do the same thing.

Cory gave the bedspread another firm tug into place and straightened up. That was that. She had work to do. Too much work to fritter away the day worrying about something she wasn't sure she wanted to find out anyway.

❀

Jamie's second day at the drugstore went much like the one before. She stayed in the stockroom with Jason, working non-stop until he announced it was time for a break. They ate quickly without chatter. She was disappointed that she hadn't seen Tate all day. Every time the stockroom door swung open, she looked up expectantly to see if it was him. It was always another employee coming in to make use of the restrooms or find something a customer needed that was missing from the shelves out front. As soon as she realized the intrusion wasn't caused by Tate, she'd duck her head and go back to work, hoping the disappointment was not too apparent on her face. She caught Jason studying her out of the corner of his eye once, as if trying to determine what or whom she had her mind on. She avoided eye contact, sure that as soon as she looked into his face, he would recognize immediately the cause of her anxiety.

If only she could work with Tate instead of Jason, things would be much more interesting. As it was now, she seldom had time to finish a complete thought. Jason shoved boxes at her at a terrifying rate, and it was her duty to find the correct place for them on the shelf. The boxes in front of her continued to stack up as she got farther and farther behind and Jason's patience with her ineptitude grew increasingly short. She wondered if she'd ever catch on, if they'd ever have a day without deliveries made at the back of the store, and if Jason would ever smile or give her the least bit of encouragement.

She reminded herself she was here to do a job. It didn't matter if Jason liked her or not. It didn't matter if she never saw anything but the inside of the stockroom. Anything was better than spending her summer on the farm with only Grandpa Harlan's country music and the cows to keep her company.

Noel Wyatt appeared in the doorway late in the day. Wearing his usual friendly smile for Jamie's benefit, he directed his question at Jason. "How's she coming along, Chief?"

Jason shrugged noncommittally. "Fine, Boss."

Noel's smile widened, undaunted by the lack of praise. "Oh, I'm sure she is." He pulled a slip of paper from the breast pocket of his lab coat and handed it to Jamie. "Here's your schedule for the next two weeks. If there's a problem, let me know. I'm sure we can work around it."

"Thank you, Mr. Wyatt."

"Now, call me Noel," he said, pulling the corners of his mouth down into a false frown. "Everybody does." He started to leave and paused, turning back to Jason. "Take it easy on her, would you, ol' boy? We wouldn't want to lose another one."

"What does he mean by that?" Jamie asked after the door closed behind him.

"Beats me," he said again with the shrug.

"So I'm not the first trainee you've tried to chase off?" she persisted.

"I'm not trying to chase you off."

She caught the hint of a smile at the corner of his mouth. Was there a real person in there somewhere? He was almost cute when he smiled. "I bet you put a little notch on your employee name tag each time you get rid of one of us," she said.

He stopped what he was doing and looked her full in the face for the first time since they'd been introduced. For a moment she thought she had insulted him, and he was going to tell her to mind her own business and get back to work. Instead, his eyes bored into hers and he spoke in his typically flat, no-nonsense voice. "I'm too busy for such childish behavior. I believe in getting right down to business. When there's someone I really want to get rid of...well, let me put it this way; don't be alarmed if you find a few hairs missing from your comb and a little doll turns up in the restroom with brown eyes, wearing a blue smock, with a pin stuck in its back."

Jamie's eyes widened momentarily until she caught the mischievous twinkle in his eyes. Not only did he have what appeared to be a sense of humor, he had also noticed the color of her eyes. He was full of surprises.

"Ha, ha," she snorted. "Very funny."

A rare smile broke across Jason's face. "Had ya going there for a minute, didn't I?"

"No, you most certainly did not. I knew you were kidding the minute you suggested you could make a doll to match my beauty."

Jason shrugged and went back to his work.

Embarrassed that she'd spoken so boldly and disappointed the banter was over as quickly and unexpectedly as it began, Jamie checked her watch to see how much longer she would be in the stockroom. What had happened to the day? It was nearly eight o'clock and she forgot to buy a needle for Grandpa Harlan's record player during her lunch break. She remembered the cool reception she'd received from the woman at the cash register when she let her out of the store the night before. She didn't want to try to purchase something after the register was shut down for the night.

"Do you think it'd be okay if I went out front to buy something for my grandpa? I'll just be gone a minute."

Jason shrugged again, not looking up.

Taking that as a yes, she fumbled in her pocket for the money as she hurried out of the stockroom and into the main part of the store. She had no trouble locating the needle, having bought them several times before.

There was no one in line at the cash register, so she decided to take the opportunity to properly introduce herself to the woman who had unlocked the door for her the night before. *"Maybe that will sweeten up her sour disposition,"* she thought.

"Hi, I'm Jamie," she said brightly as she counted out the money into her hand. "I'm the new girl." When the woman didn't answer, she continued, "I work in the stockroom with Jason." Still nothing.

Just as she was about to give up on getting a response, the woman said, "I know who you are." She slid the cash drawer shut with a bang of her hip. She put one hand on the counter and leaned toward Jamie. "You're James Steele's girl, aren't you?"

The redness crept into Jamie's cheeks. "Um…yes, I am."

"He used to run around with my brother, Bill."

The ensuing pause seemed full of expectancy for an apology for something Jamie knew nothing about.

"Bill got into a lot of trouble back in those days," the woman continued. "Drinking and carrying on. He never could hold a job neither." Her eyes narrowed. "I guess if you run with the goats, you begin to smell like one."

Jamie bristled. She wanted to tell the woman maybe Bill should take some responsibility for his own actions and stop looking for someone else to blame them on. Instead she swallowed hard and forced a smile. "I guess that can happen to anyone." She snatched the paper bag with Grandpa Harlan's needle off the counter. "I should get back to work before Jason comes looking for me."

The woman leaned farther over the counter, her narrow chin jutting toward Jamie. "At least Bill never broke any laws. Nothing serious anyway."

Jamie had heard enough. She wasn't sure what this woman was getting at, but the insinuations were loud and clear. She had just opened her mouth to demand that she come out and say whatever on her mind, when she heard a voice behind her.

"Jamie. What are you doing out here? You off work already?"

Tate put his hand on her elbow and spun her around to face him. Off balance, it took a moment for his words to register in her brain.

"I was … um … getting this for my grandpa." She held out the paper bag toward him. "I need to get back to work."

Tate looked at his wristwatch. "Ah, there's no need for that. It's almost eight o'clock, quittin' time."

"Not yet. I've got to get back." All she wanted to do was get away from the woman behind the register and her insinuations as soon as possible. She couldn't even enjoy seeing Tate after looking forward to this moment all day. She could feel her eyes still on her as she hurried toward the back of the store.

Tate kept pace with her, anxious to talk. "Hey, I get off at the same time you do. How 'bout a ride home?"

Jamie's heart soared and her breath caught in her throat, the encounter at the register forgotten. Tate Craig, the best looking boy at South Auburn High School, asking her if she'd like a ride home! She hoped her pleasure was not as evident to him.

What would Grandma Cory think of her getting a ride home with a boy? The topic had not been addressed before since she never dreamed in a million years the situation would occur. Grandma Cory was strict, but Jamie was seventeen-years old. Surely there would be no harm in a ride home. If there was a problem, they could discuss it and work out a solution. Certainly the day would come when she would actually be asked out on a date. The sooner the rules and conditions were worked out, the better, she thought.

It took only a fraction of a second for Jamie's head to race through the possibilities with her grandmother before giving Tate her answer. "Sure. That'd be great."

Tate grinned, exposing a perfect set of white teeth, the result of years of expensive orthodontia. He gave her elbow a quick squeeze. "I'll see you out here when you're ready to go."

Jamie practically floated into the stockroom.

"I was beginning to wonder about you." Impatience edged Jason's voice.

The balloon she floated in on instantly deflated.

"Uh, sorry, I had to…" Her words drifted off as she meekly held up the paper bag, knowing no explanation would matter to him. She hurried to her locker, deposited her purchase and rushed back to work.

Thoughts of Tate's smile consoled her for the next fifteen minutes—the last, and longest of her shift.

# Chapter Nine

Tate drove a three-year-old, candy-apple red Plymouth Road Runner, the envy of every teenage boy in Auburn County. Jamie never thought she'd live to see the day when she'd be the girl in the front seat beside him careening through the streets of Jenna's Creek. He easily convinced her Grandma Cory wouldn't mind if they stopped at the Dairy Queen on the way home for a milk shake. She imagined what all the girls at school would think to see her walk in on Tate's arm, and offered no resistance.

As usual the Dairy Queen parking lot was full, but Tate still managed to find a parking space close to the front door. Jamie marveled at how fate always seemed to smile on him, even in the most inconsequential matters.

"Tate, ol' buddy," a young man called out as they climbed out of the Road Runner. "What's shakin'?"

"Nothing yet," Tate quipped with a laugh, on his way to the door.

Jamie smiled politely in the young man's direction as she ducked under Tate's arm and into the Dairy Queen. She was relieved Tate didn't stop to talk. The man was several years older than she and Tate, and from his manner of dress and long hair he didn't look like someone Grandma Cory would want her hanging around.

"So, what's your pleasure, Jamie?" Tate asked with a mock sneer as his eyes traveled quickly down her body and back again.

She reddened and lowered her eyes, embarrassed and pleased at the same time. She gave him her order and stepped back from the register while he relayed it to the girl behind the counter. Jamie didn't recognize the girl, but Tate apparently did. He leaned in and said something under his breath with a wink and a grin. The girl blushed and giggled as she totaled the order and took his money.

Tate led Jamie to an empty booth and slid into the seat opposite her. "You seem to know everybody," she said.

"Nah. Everybody knows me."

"Oh. Is that the way it works?"

He sank his straw into the thick ice cream and winked in reply.

Jamie let her eyes roam the eating area while she tried to think of something clever to say. Was this what it was like to be on a date? Was she expected to keep up her end of a witty and stimulating conversation? The silence was excruciating. She didn't want to say or do anything to make herself look stupid; to remind him of why he never noticed her at school.

It turned out Tate liked to talk, especially about himself, so once he got going, Jamie didn't have to worry about filling any gaps in the conversation. When she commented on his car and how nice it was, he was off and running. He explained drive trains, manifolds, hemi-block motors, and other things that left her totally befuddled, but she nodded and smiled in all the right places.

Finally his car topics dwindled and he directed a question at her. "How are you liking your job at the drugstore?"

"Oh, I don't mind it at all. I like keeping busy. It makes the day go quicker."

"Well, you have to watch Jason," he advised pointing at her with his straw. "He can be a real pain. I used to work in the stockroom with him and I hated it. He'll stab you in the back if you give him half a chance."

"Stab me in the back? How?" Jason's reference to the voodoo doll sprang to mind.

"He'll make you look bad with Noel. He's Mister Perfect and he likes to prove the rest of us mortals aren't."

"But how would that be stabbing me in the back?"

"Oh, you just wait." Tate gave the plastic straw another dramatic wave through the air. "Don't say I didn't warn you?"

Jamie bent over her milkshake. As long as she did her work at the drugstore she didn't see how Jason could get her in trouble with Noel. Nevertheless, she would watch her step around him.

"One thing I was wondering," she began hesitantly. "What's the deal with the woman who works the front register? I've run into her twice and she doesn't seem overly friendly."

Tate snorted in laughter and nearly spewed ice cream across the tiny table at her. "You must be talking about Paige Trotter. She's a hoot."

"A hoot? I think she hates me."

The straw was waving in the air again. "I'm sure she doesn't hate you more than she does anyone else on the planet."

Jamie opened her mouth to disagree when a voice sweeter than the milkshake she was drinking interrupted her. "Why, Jamie Steele, as I live and breathe."

A bit of strawberry from her milkshake lodged in Jamie's throat. Tracy Jenkins was South Auburn High School's resident bubbly and beautiful head cheerleader, vice-president of the student council, and voted most likely to get on Jamie's nerves more often than anyone.

"Tate," continued Tracy in her syrupy drawl, "I didn't know you knew Jamie."

Tate reached across the table and placed a possessive hand on Jamie's arm. "Oh, yeah. Jamie and me, we go way back. Ain't that right, Jamie?"

Jamie lowered her eyes to the remainder of her milkshake, but not before noting the startled and even jealous expression that flashed momentarily across Tracy's pretty face. The pressure of Tate's hand on her arm was unsettling. She had never been the focus of a boy's attention before, especially one as cute and popular as Tate. She hoped her silence would give the illusion of mystery and not tip them off to her overwhelming fear.

"Well, I guess anything's possible," Tracy said.

Tate removed his hand from Jamie's arm and patted the empty seat beside him. "Why don't you join us?"

Jamie looked up from her ice cream and gave Tracy a welcoming smile. She hoped it looked convincing. She'd rather the girl went and sat on the yellow line of the new highway.

"I can't. I'm here with my parents," she explained painfully. "But you two go ahead and enjoy your evening." She turned to go and gave Tate a lingering look over her shoulder. "Tate, I'll see you later." She smiled intimately and drifted back to her table.

Tate's eyes followed her across the room before turning his attention back to Jamie. "That Tracy. She's something."

"Yeah, she's something all right."

Tate grinned at the sarcasm in her voice. "I'm glad you started working at Wyatt's. Most of the girls there are so… well, you know."

"No, I don't know. What do you mean?"

"Harebrained. Dizzy, I guess you could say."

"Tate!" Jamie gasped. "That's not very nice."

"I'm sorry." He placed his hand back onto her arm. "You'll forgive me, won't you?"

Jamie smiled playfully and he smiled back. Her heart skipped a beat. He was so handsome. She wondered what it would feel like to be kissed by him.

He stuffed the used napkins on the table into his cup to throw away, breaking the spell. Jamie breathed a sigh of relief. She wasn't about to get her hopes up by considering such a thing with Tate Craig; girls like her weren't in his league. He dated cheerleaders like Tracy Jenkins.

Tate left the engine running when he pulled the Road Runner into the driveway on Betterman Road, but stepped out quickly and hurried around the front of the car to open Jamie's door. "Here you are, Mademoiselle, safe at home."

Jamie took his offered hand and stepped out. "Thank you, Sir."

He closed the door behind her and gave her hand a squeeze. "So, I guess I'll see you tomorrow?"

"Yes, I'll be there."

He gazed into her eyes for a brief moment. Jamie held her breath. Then he turned and walked around the car to the driver's side. "Bye, Jamie."

"Bye, Tate. Thanks for the ride, and the milkshake." She waved as he backed out of the driveway. Only after his car was out of sight did she exhale.

# Chapter Ten

As usual the Steeles were among the first worshippers to arrive at the church on a bright warm Sunday morning four weeks after Jamie started her job at the drugstore. She was relieved to have a day off. Her position became full-time by the end of her second week, and now she fully appreciated Sundays as a day of rest.

She went directly to their usual pew and took a seat while Grandma Cory and Grandpa Harlan lingered at the door, smiling and shaking hands with new arrivals. Jamie settled into the pew with her Bible on her lap and her purse on the floor, tucked under the pew in front of her. She busied herself with the familiar routine, intent on not looking to the front of the sanctuary where James' casket had stood the day of his funeral. She had successfully put that day to the back of her mind for the past four weeks, where it would remain, as far as she was concerned.

She opened her Bible and randomly thumbed through it. The Bible was another thing she hadn't seen much of in four weeks. Conviction crept into her heart. She had always been an avid Bible reader. She devoured it. She loved every sweet, comforting word. Now that she was busy with her new job, she didn't seem to have time for it. Where had her hunger gone? Her desire to draw closer to her Savior? Was it just the job at the drugstore keeping her distracted from Bible study, or her muddled feelings about her dad? Whatever the reason, she vowed to renew her commitment to serving God and reading His word.

Sensing the Holy Spirit's presence, she laid her hands reverently upon the open book and closed her eyes.

Before the words of a prayer had time to form in her heart, she felt eyes upon her. She looked up quickly, her Comforter's presence forgotten. The sanctuary was filling up and no one seemed to be paying any attention to her. Still the nagging sensation wouldn't go away. She remembered the conversation she overheard at the farm after James' funeral. The women involved were members of this very congregation. They had known all along about her dad and Sally Blake while she had not. Had they watched her sitting here before, so blissfully unaware of the whispers going on behind her back? The accusations? The suspicions?

She slammed the Bible shut with an angry thud. Why couldn't she have a father like other fathers? Practically invisible; leading a quiet, unobtrusive existence, his only purpose in life to provide for his family. Oh, no. Not James Steele. He had to have the most notorious reputation in the county with no regard as to how it would affect his family.

When the sermon began, she heard very little. The bitterness in her heart festered. While the pastor preached love and forgiveness, Jamie chewed on her lower lip and stared at the splashes of color on the hardwood floor from the sunshine flooding through the stained glass window.

The final chords of "Just as I am" were still hanging in the air when Jamie hurried out of the church. A group of teenagers stood at the bottom of stairs, laughing and jostling one another. She had grown up in this church with them. Most of them attended South Auburn High School with her, but she was not part of their group. If she joined them right now, they would look at her like she was crazy. She hesitated at the top of the stairs, dreading the moment she would have to pass between them to get to Grandma Cory's car.

She felt a hand on her shoulder. She turned to see Noel Wyatt smiling at her. He was also watching the teenagers and probably wondering why she was standing at the top of the stairs like an outcast.

"I never get much of a chance to talk to you at the store," he said.

Jamie was glad he didn't mention the teenagers. "No, you're always so busy," she said. "I guess I am too."

"Well, how's it going?" he asked, guiding her down the concrete steps with his hand still on her shoulder. "Is Jason treating you all right?"

Jamie didn't know what kind of answer he expected. Jason must have been *doing* his job well, because she was *learning* her job well. Was he treating her right? She hadn't thought about that. "I'm learning a lot," she replied.

"Good, good." He beamed down at her. "I guess you know why I put Jason in charge of training you."

"Because you don't like me?"

Noel's eyes widened, then he threw back his head and laughed. "Oh, Jamie, you're a pistol."

Jamie smiled but didn't tell him she hadn't intended to be funny.

Still smiling at what he thought was her attempt at humor, he explained. "Jason trains all my new employees. He's a hard taskmaster. I can count on him to weed out the ones who think the drugstore is a place for loafing and socializing. If you can work for Jason, you'll be able to work for anyone."

"I guess I'm all set then."

Noel chuckled again. "Yes, I guess you are." His expression grew serious with his next words. "It'll be a shame to lose him one of these days. A shame for me, that is, not for him. I admire a young man for wanting to better himself."

"What do you mean?"

"He'll be leaving me just like your uncle did. After he finishes college, he's going on to law school."

"Law school?" Jamie gasped. "I didn't even know he was going to college."

"Oh, didn't he tell you? Well, no, I guess he wouldn't. He doesn't talk much about himself. I guess that's why the two of you hit it off so well."

What gave him the idea they hit it off; the fact that they hadn't come to blows? They seldom said more than two words to each other during an entire shift. "Where is he taking classes?" she asked. She never considered the possibility he might have a life outside of the stockroom.

"At Shawnee College. He works all the hours he can to pay for it and help support his father. He gets some type of disability."

The way he said the word "disability" made her doubt Noel thought the man should be sitting at home while his son and the government supported him. She was sure her Grandpa Sharborough would feel the same way. "All us workin' men got a tough row to hoe," he often said, "but that don't mean you take charity."

Lucinda Wyatt, Noel's mother, made her way out of the church and moved through the crowd toward them. She was tiny and frail—somewhere in her eighties, Jamie assumed—yet she remained energetic and active in the church.

"Mother, you know Jamie Steele, the new girl I hired at the drugstore, don't you?" Noel asked. "Jamie, this is my mother, Lucinda Wyatt."

The elderly lady extended a tiny and withered, yet well-manicured hand to Jamie. "How are you, dear? I believe I taught your father and uncles in Sunday School many, many years ago. Of course, it's been a long time since I've taught, needless to say." She turned to Noel. "Have you invited Miss Steele to Sunday dinner, dear?"

"I was just thinking of it. Jamie, how does that sound? Would you like to join us for dinner this afternoon?"

"I don't know. I'd have to ask my grandma. I wouldn't want to be an inconvenience."

"Nonsense. You couldn't eat enough to be an inconvenience," Mrs. Wyatt quipped. "Noel dear, go ask her grandma if she would be allowed to come home with us. Invite her and Mr. Steele too. The more the merrier."

Noel disappeared into the crowd and Mrs. Wyatt turned back to Jamie. "Don't you have a sister? Katie or something? I haven't seen her in church since the … um … for quite some time. She isn't sick, is she?"

"Oh, no, she's fine. She's visiting our other grandparents, the Sharboroughs, in Portsmouth for awhile. Her name's Cassie."

"Oh, yes. Cassie." She squeezed Jamie's hand. "Such a shame about your father, dear. I always hate to hear about such things. He was a wonderful little boy when I had him in Sunday school. A mischievous character, that's for sure. He and Justin were as different as night and day. Don't you think? Justin's so serious and quiet. Now don't get me wrong. They were both very well behaved. Your Grandma Cory saw to that. But that James," she laughed softly. "How he kept me on my toes."

It was the first time Jamie had ever heard a good report on her father. She appreciated Mrs. Wyatt's generous summation, even if part of it was for her benefit.

Noel came back to where they stood in the parking lot. "Mr. and Mrs. Steele already have dinner planned at home. Your grandma says it's fine for you to come though, Jamie."

"Wonderful." Mrs. Wyatt held out her arm for Jamie to take. "Come along, dear. Rowena always prepares something delicious."

Jamie was suddenly nervous. Who was Rowena? Did Mrs. Wyatt have a cook? Or a maid? She didn't know anyone who actually had a maid. That was only on television. Maybe it wasn't too late to decline their offer. What if they served something she'd never seen before? What if she used the wrong fork to eat her salad? She didn't want to look common in front of Mrs. Wyatt, who was so proper and polite, and make her wish she hadn't invited her in the first place.

She was way out of her league, she thought as she settled into the plush back seat of Noel's Cadillac. She couldn't even talk like the Wyatts. She never felt more like a hick in her life than she did as the Cadillac headed to the west end of Jenna's Creek. Something like a fist clenched itself around her nervous insides. She didn't know if she'd feel like eating anything, no matter what Rowena prepared.

The situation was about to get worse.

The silver Caddy turned into a driveway leading to the most beautiful house in a neighborhood of houses dating back to the last century. A small economy car was parked near the walk leading to the back door.

"Oh, he got here before we did," Mrs. Wyatt lamented.

"Nothing to worry about, Mother. I'm sure Rowena's taking good care of him."

Another guest for dinner. Jamie wondered who it could be, but was so busy admiring the impressive back yard she didn't give it much thought.

The house and a dense hedge obscured any view of the back of the property from the street. The back yard was less than a half-acre in size—tiny by a country girl's standard—yet the small space was immaculately groomed, each square foot in perfect harmony with the next. Mrs. Wyatt, or someone hired by her, had coaxed nearly every kind of bush and flower indigenous to Southern Ohio into growing here, along with some that were not. Stone paths meandered from the patio, past shrub groupings and wooden benches, to rock gardens over-flowing with vibrant displays of flowers.

The french doors leading into the house swung open. "There you are," Mrs. Wyatt said to the other guest.

Jamie looked up and grimaced. Jason stood on the brick patio. He seemed as surprised to see her as she was to see him. He looked uncomfortable in a pair of crisply ironed slacks and a long-sleeved shirt accented with a dark-green paisley tie. The only thing missing from the ensemble was the sports jacket she assumed he shed somewhere inside the house.

"Hello, Jason," she said.

"Hi." He offered her his customary distracted half-smile and turned to Noel. "About time you got here. Rowena and I were thinking about eating without you." He hurried down the walk and took Mrs. Wyatt's Bible and handbag out of her arms.

"Thank you, dear. I hope you're not too hungry. We came as quickly as we could. We brought another soul to join us."

"Yes, I see that." He offered his arm and Mrs. Wyatt slipped her hand into the crook of his elbow. Smiling down at her, he guided her up the walk to the house.

Jamie almost resented how comfortable and at ease he was with Noel and his mother, as if he were one of the family. Who did he think he was anyway?

Mrs. Wyatt asked him how his family was getting along. "Not too good," he replied. "Dad was feeling poorly this morning. I ended up missing church. That's why I got here before you did."

"Oh, that's too bad." Mrs. Wyatt gazed up at him with maternal concern.

It hadn't occurred to Jamie before that Jason might be a churchgoer. After a month of working with him in the stockroom, she still didn't know anything about him. Why hadn't she asked about his family? If she had, she would've already known about the dreams of law school and his father's disability. Maybe she could have been an encouragement and offered prayer to him when his father was doing poorly.

No. None of this was her fault. Jason was unapproachable, that was all. He couldn't blame anyone but himself if more people didn't befriend him.

Passing through a cozy sun room, they entered the kitchen. Any anxieties over eating Rowena's cooking vanished as soon as the enticing aroma of roasted pork and steaming vegetables reached Jamie's nose. Her stomach rumbled noisily in reply and she quickly covered her belly with her hand, hoping no one heard. She shot a quick glance at Jason. He wasn't paying any attention to her, as usual.

A woman wearing an apron over a simple blue dress pulled a casserole dish out of the oven and set it on a trivet. Noel went to her and kissed her on the cheek. "How are you today, Rowena? I appreciate you coming in to cook dinner for us."

She swung at him with the pot holder. "Move back before you get burned," she warned sternly, but blushed at the kiss.

"Something smells wonderful, Rowena," Mrs. Wyatt said.

"Thank you, Lucinda," the woman answered. The look that passed between them resembled more of sister to sister or friend to friend than employer to employee. Rowena smiled warmly at the group, and Jamie understood why Jason felt so comfortable here. "It'll be on the table any minute if you'd like to freshen up before you eat," she told them.

Mrs. Wyatt pointed out a guest bathroom on the first floor for Jamie while Noel and Jason disappeared upstairs.

Jamie had never seen a lovelier bathroom. An antique oak vanity with white pearl handles dominated the pink and sea foam green room. A framed print on the wall bore the signature of an artist she recognized from her studies at school. In the bathroom at home, the only pieces of art were a towel rack Uncle Justin made in shop class years ago and a dime store picture of a cat sniffing a vase of daisies.

Everyone was waiting for her when she entered the dining room. Noel pulled out a chair for her at the mahogany table. As she sat down, she glanced nervously at her place setting and was relieved to see no unfamiliar utensils. She smiled graciously at her hostess. Heads bowed simultaneously in prayer and they began their meal. Just like regular people.

Jamie had never seen Jason so talkative and animated as he was with Noel. He was an entirely different person than the driven machine she worked with every day. She couldn't help but notice the quirky twist of his mouth when he smiled. If only he smiled more, a person could almost find him handsome.

After dinner Mrs. Wyatt led Jamie to the sun room, which she referred to as a solarium. She took several scrapbooks and picture albums from a bookcase and opened them on the coffee table in front of Jamie.

"You may be interested in these," she said. "I have pictures and mementos from different times in my life. Did you know I went to China several years ago?"

"No. That must have been exciting."

"Oh, it was. I love to travel. Mr. Wyatt and I both did." She stared into space, her eyes clouded with memories. "When he was alive, we used to dream of visiting all sorts of magnificent places after he retired. We honeymooned in Paris."

She flipped through the pages of an album until she found an aged photograph of a young couple standing on a bridge with the Eiffel Tower visible in the distance. "Here we are. What a magical time that was. My first trip abroad. I was so nervous. Mr. Wyatt was such a gentleman."

She pointed to another picture taken several years later of herself balancing a small child on the hood of a car. "This is Noel's sister, Genevieve. She lives on the West Coast with her family. We called her Genevieve to keep with the Wyatt tradition of naming the first daughter after Jenna Wyatt. She was always considered the matriarch of the family with Jenna's Creek named for her and all. Mr. Wyatt's mother was Janine. There were a few Jeanette's and Geneva's, a Jennifer, and I don't know how many Jenna's down through the years. I'm sure you've noticed the library's namesake. Janelle Wyatt was another oldest daughter. I guess it sounds like a silly tradition to some. But it's just something that's always been that way. We see it as a way of showing respect for the family that has gone on before."

Jamie had never thought much about family history. Everything she ever heard about the Steeles' past was more embarrassing than anything. Like Great-uncle Tobias who shot off his foot in World War I so he could come home. Or Cousin Abernathy who stole horses from Ohio farms and sold them to the Confederate Army during the Civil War. Or Great-aunt Vivian, widowed in 1924, who supported her children by questionable means while living in Baltimore. And there was of course, the alcohol. No one enjoyed beer and whiskey as much as a Steele man; and of course the bar fight that almost always ensued.

Yes, the Steeles were too busy with their other pursuits to worry about building libraries or studying medicine.

Mrs. Wyatt pointed out a family portrait of her and her husband, little Genevieve, and another baby. "Is that Noel?" she asked, pointing.

"No, that's Noel's other sister, Gwen."

"I never knew Noel had any brothers or sisters."

Mrs. Wyatt chuckled. "His sisters are quite a bit older than he is. Poor Mr. Wyatt thought he would never have a son to carry on the family name. Our girls were almost in their teens before Noel came along. We'd about given up hope. Here's what I wanted to show you." She pointed to a picture in a scrapbook after more flipping of pages. Jamie recognized a younger Mrs. Wyatt standing in front of their church building with a group of children. "Do you know anyone in this picture?" she asked.

Jamie looked closely. Her eyes scanned the rows of faces smiling up at her until she found a familiar one. "That's Uncle Justin," she cried. "And there's Dad. When was this picture taken?"

"Oh, I'd say the late '30's, more or less. Not too long before I lost Mr. Wyatt."

"Do you remember my dad well?"

"Oh, yes. Like I said earlier, he and Justin were in my Sunday school class for years. And no one could know your father and then forget him. I even remember your Uncle Jesse." She flipped through a few more pages of the scrapbook and studied pictures. "I don't think I have any pictures of him. He was such a little sweetheart. He meant so much to all of us."

She suddenly laughed and slapped the scrapbook. "Your father was always getting some friends of his to help him pull these terrible pranks. I'll never forget the best one. It was when Pastor McAfee was still with us. James, Hobie Bryant, and some other boy… who was it… the Mitchell boy I believe. Yes, Carl Mitchell! He married a Presbyterian girl so we don't see much of him these days. Those three boys sneaked into Pastor McAfee's office at the church and filled every nook and cranny with rice. Plain, white rice. Uncooked, of course. They put rice on the book shelves, the windowsills, the oil lamp, all his desk drawers, the desk caddy, even in his coat pockets. He was furious. That man never could take a joke. It wasn't a very respectable thing to do to a pastor I admit, but it was funny. Those poor boys got the worst thrashings of their lives. Your dad accepted all the blame. I thought that was an admirable thing for a kid to do. He told the other boys' folks it was all his idea, but they nearly got beat to death anyway. Pastor McAfee was still finding rice in his office six months later. You should have heard the fire and brimstone sermons inspired by that prank."

Jamie laughed. So that was where Cassie got her sense of humor.

"Did he learn his lesson after that?" she asked.

"Oh no, they still got into trouble. James could talk Hobie Bryant into anything. But that was the best one they ever pulled off. Your dad didn't get into trouble for the sake of being mean. He just wanted to be funny. He loved to laugh and make other people laugh too. He wanted to keep you guessing about what he was going to do next."

"I think that's why my mother fell in love with him," Jamie said.

"I never knew your mother very well. She was from out of town and all. By the time she came along, I wasn't getting out much. My age catching up with me, I guess. I knew her from church but she kept to herself a lot."

They sat quietly studying the pictures for a few minutes. Jamie knew why Nancy kept to herself. She suspected Mrs. Wyatt knew too. If someone ever got close to her, they might find out what was going on with her husband at home.

"Here's my ticket stub from a train trip I took while in China," Mrs. Wyatt said, changing subjects. "Look at the writing. Isn't it fascinating? I learned to write and speak a few phrases while preparing for my trip, but I've forgotten them. My mind doesn't retain things like it used to. Never take for granted the gifts God has given you, Jamie. Someday you'll wake up and find they're slipping away from you. It is a sad thing to grow old. We all do it eventually. It's nothing to be ashamed of, but it's sad nevertheless."

Her words of advice did not require a response. Jamie continued to look through the pictures and mementos that chronicled Mrs. Wyatt's life.

"What would you like to do when you get out of high school?"

"I don't know. I haven't thought about it."

"Sure you have. A girl like you is always thinking, looking ahead."

"No, really. I don't know." Jamie preferred talking about Mrs. Wyatt's exciting life and leaving hers alone. She would rather not be reminded that she'd never have interesting stories to tell when she was old.

"Are you planning on leaving Jenna's Creek?"

"Probably. I want to go to college somewhere."

"The only thing to keep you from it is you."

"What about money?" Jamie countered, a bit too gruffly. The conversation was veering in a direction she wanted to avoid. It was the precise reason she didn't like to answer questions about herself. She became defensive, as if she had to explain her motives when it was really no one else's business.

"What about it? Money—or the lack of it—has never kept successful people from reaching their potential."

Jamie bristled. What did Mrs. Wyatt know about the lack of money? She had a full and exciting life, with a bank account to match, none of which may have been possible if she had not married well. It was unlikely she would have honeymooned in Paris or rode trains in China had she married a mill worker. "Whatever I decide to do, I won't be getting any financial help from anyone. I'll have to do it all on my own." she said.

"You won't need any help," Mrs. Wyatt said matter-of-factly. "You're not the kind of person to depend on anyone else."

"Why do you keep saying things like that? I don't mean any offense, Mrs. Wyatt, but you don't know what kind of person I am. You don't know anything about me at all."

The old woman smiled kindly. "Yes, I do, dear. You're the determined sort. Once you figure out what you want to achieve in life, you won't let anything get in your way. You're strong, Jamie."

"No, I'm not," Jamie said, her voice trembling. "I'm weak. I miss my mother. You know more about my father than I do. For all I know, he could've killed a girl and took the secret of what he did with her body to his grave." Her voice rose in pitch and quaked dangerously.

"A daughter shouldn't think that about her own dad. Don't you see? I'm weak."

The tears trapped inside her since James' death escaped once she opened the flood-gate. She cried for all the times she wished him dead when she was a little girl and he hurt her mother. She cried for Cassie who was hiding her grief by running away to stay with her other grandparents. She cried for not crying earlier. She cried for the father she would never know because of his selfishness. He should have gotten to know her. He should have spent time with her and Cassie. He should have taken them for walks and picked flowers and chased butterflies and told them he loved them. He should have been there when they needed him.

An eternity passed before the tears finally subsided. Rowena slipped into the room with a box of tissues and back out again, unnoticed. Mrs. Wyatt rocked her and held her for as long as she needed to be rocked and held. She pressed several tissues into Jamie's hand and waited for her to compose herself.

"I'm sorry," she said finally. "I didn't mean to..."

"But you needed to," Mrs. Wyatt finished for her. "There's nothing wrong with any of the feelings you've been having, dear."

Jamie heaved a shuddering sigh. "Yes, there is, Mrs. Wyatt. Everything's wrong with the way I'm feeling. I shouldn't hate him. I shouldn't blame him for being dead. I shouldn't suspect him of... of... what I think he's done."

Mrs. Wyatt sighed. "Jamie, let me tell you a story. Mr. Wyatt was only fifty-two-years old when he died. I know that sounds terribly ancient to you, but believe me, it isn't. Noel was ready to start college. We had discussed trips we were going to take together. I dreamed of seeing the Great Wall of China with Mr. Wyatt, not a tour group. And then, do you know what he did?"

Jamie shook her head and blew her nose again.

"He went and had himself a heart attack. I told him he was working too hard. I tried to get him to hire a store manager to take some of the burden off himself, but he wouldn't listen. He kept working and losing sleep and gaining weight. One evening I got a telephone call from the drugstore. He collapsed while closing up. He died right there on the floor. He couldn't even wait for me to get there to say good-bye."

Her voice cracked and she pulled a tissue out of the box for herself. "I was so angry at him I could bite through nails. I thought he was the most selfish man who ever lived. Just when we were ready to start living for ourselves, he left me. So, of course, I started leaning on Noel. I expected him to be all the things his father had been. I don't know how we got through that time. I don't know how poor Noel got his education with me acting so foolish."

"But over the years I got over being angry. Mr. Wyatt was going to be who he was, with or without me nagging at him. He loved working. He loved that drugstore, just like Noel loves it now. He loved me and would've done anything for me. Except change who he was."

"But you know Mr. Wyatt loved you. He told you. He showed you every day. Dad never told me he loved me. He never showed me. I don't even know if he did or not."

"Jamie, honey, don't you think you're feeling sorry for yourself now?" Mrs. Wyatt asked gently. "Whether your dad loved you or not, is water under the bridge. I know you would feel better if you knew for sure, but it wouldn't change anything. All you need to worry about now is if you love him or not. You're still here. You can change. He can't. You can waste the rest of your life hating him and torturing yourself or you can let go of the pain and forgive him. It's up to you."

# Chapter Eleven

During a tour through Mrs. Wyatt's prized flower gardens in the back yard, a tremendous burden of guilt began to lift from Jamie's shoulders and disperse into the heavy summer air around her. She still was not completely at ease with the way she felt about her dad, but at least she no longer felt like the worst daughter in the world. If dear, thoughtful Mrs. Wyatt could be angry with her husband for having a heart attack, her reaction over James' death couldn't be that misplaced. Mrs. Wyatt said no more about the conversation in the solarium. She pointed out flowers and shrubs, sharing the biological names and information for growing and caring for them. Jamie breathed in the heady aromas with delight and allowed herself to be guided along, readily absorbing all the information given her.

As she and Mrs. Wyatt made their way down the brick path that led to the house, she mentioned she would be expected home soon.

"I can drive you," Jason offered from his deck chair. "I need to be going myself."

Before Jamie had a chance to refuse, Noel piped up, "Thanks a lot, Jason. That'd be great. There're a few things I'd like to see to around here before I head home."

Mrs. Wyatt pulled Jamie into her arms. "I hope I was some help to you today, dear. Please come back anytime you need someone to talk to. My door's always open."

Jamie was genuinely appreciative. "Thank you, Mrs. Wyatt." She embraced the small woman. "I'll be looking forward to seeing you again."

"Drive carefully now," Noel cautioned, after closing the passenger door of Jason's car behind Jamie. "I'll see you both at work tomorrow. Jamie, I'm glad you could make it to dinner. We enjoyed your company."

"Thanks for inviting me, Noel. Tell your mother I enjoyed myself."

"I will." He straightened and waved as Jason put the car in gear and backed out of the driveway.

Jamie watched the houses pass by her window, her heart lighter than it had been in weeks. A smile of relief played at the corners of her mouth. Relief from the weight of guilt that had plagued her for so many weeks. Relief in knowing her feelings toward her dad were completely natural considering the circumstances, excluding her self-pity, of course. Enough time had been wasted on that. It was time to move on.

"Are you going to keep sitting there smiling to yourself?" Jason asked suddenly. "Or are you going to tell me where you live so I won't have to drive around Jenna's Creek all afternoon trying to figure it out?"

She bristled self-consciously. "I wasn't smiling to myself." Why was it he never paid attention to her unless she was doing something that made her look silly?

"Yes, you were."

She sighed in exasperation and decided it best to ignore his comment. "I live on Betterman Road, just outside of town. Do you know where that's at?"

He nodded and turned left at the intersection.

Jamie clamped her lips together, determined to make no facial expression in case he was watching her again. She stole a quick glance at him out of the corner of her eye and saw he was the one smiling now.

"Is something funny?" she asked, perturbed though she wasn't sure why.

He shook his head and broke into a wide grin. "No. I was just thinking."

She waited a moment for him to elaborate. When he did not, she, growing more perturbed by the minute, demanded, "About what?"

Jason shrugged. "Nothing really. I was just wondering if it was Tate Craig who had you gazing dreamily out the window in that lovestruck way girls like you have."

"Girls like me. What's that supposed to mean?" she blazed. "Besides, it's none of your business if I am lovestruck over Tate Craig or anyone else! Which I'm not," she added quickly.

"Okay, okay. Take it easy. I told you, I was just thinking. Don't go getting yourself all in an uproar."

"Well, I'd appreciate it if you'd not spend your time worrying about my love life."

"It's all right, Jamie," he said, his voice low and patronizing. "I didn't mean to upset you."

"I'm not upset."

"You sound upset."

"Well, I'm not upset." She crossed her arms over her chest and watched as a car approached in the other lane and then sped past. She shouldn't say anything more. She should just sit here and keep quiet until he dropped her off at her house. But the more she thought about it, the more his remark got to her. "I don't appreciate being classified with girls who write the names of the boys they like in their notebooks and circle them with little hearts," she sneered, breaking the silence. "I'm not like that."

"Well. Aren't you the little snob?"

"What? I'm not a snob."

"Yes, you are," he insisted. "Jamie Steele would never write her boyfriend's name in a notebook and circle it with a little heart. She's above all that silly school girl stuff. And she'll never admit she could have a crush on Tate Craig, the big man on campus. That makes you," he said as he jabbed his index finger in her direction, "a snob."

"I don't have a crush on Tate." She realized too late the words came out of her mouth a little too loud and a little too defensive. "You don't know what you're talking about. I think you're just jealous of Tate and guys like him who get everyone's attention."

"Trust me. I'll never be jealous of Tate or anyone like him. I feel sorry for him. He'll never be anything more in life than he is right now."

"Now who's the snob?"

"That doesn't make me a snob," he said. "Just a realist. I can see where Tate is headed. He'll be one of those pot-bellied ex-athletes sitting in a bar here in Jenna's Creek twenty years from now, bragging about the night he scored the winning touchdown in the big game. That'll be the biggest moment of his life. I wouldn't want to be in his shoes for anything."

There was no point in defending Tate when it was obvious how jealous Jason was of him. He would never admit it, even to himself. So what if he didn't think much of Tate? She happened to like him. He was fun to be with. Not like Jason, who was beginning to give her a headache. If she wanted to be a snob, she'd be a snob. If she wanted to write Tate's name in her notebook and draw a little heart around it, she would do that too. It was nobody's business, especially Jason's.

At the edge of town, Jason turned the car onto Betterman Road.

"I'm the first house on the right around this curve," she said, not looking at him.

He turned the car into the driveway.

"Thanks for the ride," she mumbled as she climbed out of the car.

"Always a pleasure." He gave her a broad, quirky smile as he backed the car out of the driveway.

She hurried to the porch without looking back, still seething at the way he'd spoken to her. He was definitely lawyer material. Anyone who could turn every word out of her mouth around to make her look guilty of something would make an excellent attorney. He'd probably run for office someday. Fortunately, he wasn't personable enough to win. She never did particularly care for him; now she knew she couldn't stand him.

She put her hand on the doorknob and turned her head just enough to watch his car disappear around the bend in the road. From her vantage point, she couldn't see Jason watching her in his rear view mirror. Nor could she see the smile on his face.

Inside the house, she was greeted by the woeful sound of a lovesick cowboy seeking relief for his broken heart at the bottom of a whiskey bottle. Grandpa Harlan's music. How Grandma Cory despised it. Beer-drinking music, she called it. During their entire married life, she encouraged him to listen to gospel music. He would have no part of it. Gospel music belonged in church, he insisted. Why listen to it at home? The country and western music kept him content these days and out from under her feet so she eventually stopped making an issue of it.

"Where have you been, Jamie?" He shouted to be heard over the blaring music.

"I had Sunday dinner with the Wyatts, Grandpa. Remember?"

"Nobody told me about it."

"I'm sure Grandma told you after church."

"What?" He cupped his hand around his ear.

"Grandma Cory told you after church." She raised her voice and enunciated each word.

"No, she didn't," he growled through clenched teeth. "Don't you think I'd've remembered if she told me? She never tells me anything."

It was better to let a subject drop once Grandpa Harlan started to get angry, so Jamie nodded her head. "You're right. She probably forgot to tell you."

His countenance softened immediately as he shifted gears. "We had green beans for dinner, with bacon in them just the way you like. You should've been here."

"Rowena served green beans like that too. They weren't as good as Grandma's though."

"What? Who's Rowena?"

"Grandpa, why don't you turn the music down so you can hear me?"

"I can hear you just fine."

"No, you can't." She twisted the volume dial so the music and the crooner's voice faded into the background.

"I was listening to that," he snapped. He gave the volume dial an angry twist, the music instantly louder than it had been in the first place.

The floor pulsated beneath her feet. "Grandpa! It's too loud."

He turned his back to her, his mouth set in a grim line.

She reached again for the music dial. "Leave that alone," he shouted viciously, spinning around and towering over her.

Jamie shrank back. He looked just like James with his nostrils flaring and eyes wide with anger. She had never been afraid of Grandpa Harlan before.

Grandma Cory burst into the room. "What's going on in here? You're making enough noise to wake the dead. Harlan, you know I don't like hearing that racket on the Lord's Day."

When she saw her husband's threatening posture and Jamie's frightened expression, she quickly accessed the situation and stepped between them. Harlan had positioned himself as a barricade between Jamie and the record player, his fists planted on his hips. Cory reached past him, removed the needle from the spinning album, and replaced it in its cradle. The room descended into sudden silence.

Harlan opened his mouth to protest, but Cory spoke up before he was able. "The gate's open to the hen house. I think I saw a fox earlier prowling around out there. You better go and make sure everything's all right."

He immediately forgot Jamie and the music. The safety of his brood in the chicken house was all that mattered now. He hurried through the kitchen and out the back door in search of the non-existent fox, stopping just long enough to pull his rubber boots on over his shoes.

Jamie exhaled and the color slowly returned to her cheeks. "Grandma, what's wrong with him?"

"You know how he can be. He was just fine at church this morning, and then almost as soon as we got home, he flew off the handle about every little thing. It doesn't help matters that he's not seeing much of you. You're gone all week and he doesn't understand why. Now he's alone on Sundays too and he starts sulking."

Worry lines creased Jamie's forehead.

"Don't fret about him. He's none of your concern. I'll take care of him like I always have. He's due for an appointment with his doctor anyway. I'm calling the V.A. first thing in the morning. By the way, how was your visit with the Wyatts?"

"Very nice."

"I didn't recognize the car you came home in. Who was it?"

"Just Jason."

"I don't know any Jason."

"Jason Collier. From work."

"I don't think I approve of you riding around in cars with boys I've never met."

Jamie didn't remind her that she had got a ride home with Tate a few weeks ago. She must not have noticed. "But it was just Jason. I work with him every day."

"Is that supposed to make me feel better?"

"Don't worry, Grandma. If you knew Jason, you'd see there was no reason to worry. He had dinner with the Wyatts too, so he offered to drive me home."

That seemed to satisfy her. "Well, I suppose the Wyatts wouldn't have a young man in their home if he didn't have some redeeming qualities. When Justin worked at the drugstore, they invited him to dinner on a regular basis. They must think a lot of this Jason."

Jamie wondered if Grandma Cory knew they thought a lot of her too. She had also received a dinner invitation.

"Cassie called today," Grandma Cory said, changing the subject.

Jamie brightened. "She did? What did she say?"

"She's coming home this week. She's homesick, I think. At least Grandpa will have one of his granddaughters here to keep him company."

Her last comment stung. Jamie wasn't doing anything wrong by going to work everyday. She was sorry Grandpa Harlan was taking her absence so hard, but she was not intentionally hurting him. It wasn't fair of Grandma Cory to accuse her of doing so. "What day will Cassie be here?" she asked, keeping her thoughts to herself.

"Wednesday or Thursday."

"Finally." Jamie hadn't realized just how much she missed her kid sister. "I'm going to my room for awhile."

"Don't bother changing out of your church clothes. It'll be time to go back for evening service before long."

Something in the deep recesses of Harlan's mind told him a fox would not be scavenging for food in the middle of a hot July afternoon. Nevertheless, Cory said she saw one, so he kept searching. Who was he to doubt her word? Cory was always right about pretty near everything.

He remembered long ago; walking through these same woods with her by his side. They spent hours combing the woods on their farm for mushrooms in the spring, and deer tracks in the fall. In the summertime, they donned heavy pants and boots to protect against snakes startled out of hiding, while they watched the birds and any other woodland creature they may happen across. Even in winter when the forest bounty was spent, they bundled up against the cold and went on walks together. Just taking some time away from the kids and the responsibilities of the farm; enjoying one another's company as much or more than the peace and beauty around them.

That was so long ago. When he tried to recall specific details about those years, he became confused and frustrated. He knew he was Cory's husband, but he could not remember standing up in church and actually marrying her. He knew James and Justin were his sons, but he couldn't recall them ever being babies.

Occasionally a vague memory of another boy would flash across his mind. A boy with light brown hair like Jamie's and big brown eyes fringed with the longest lashes he'd ever seen. He could see the little boy, dripping wet and naked, running across the living room floor on chubby toddler legs, squealing with delight. Cory—the front of her dress soaked clean through—chased him with a towel thrown over her arms.

Her wet dress clung to her body revealing shapely legs and a narrow waist. Stray wisps of damp honey-blonde hair escaped her girlish ponytail and framed her smiling face with a golden halo. She snatched the little boy up in her arms, losing him in the fluffy towel. She nibbled at his neck with her teeth, his giggles and writhing increasing. She stopped playing with the child and smiled at Harlan over his shaggy, wet head. Harlan wanted to rush to her and take her in his arms, to lose himself in the feminine scent of her body…

Harlan frowned. An intense sadness enveloped him. The laughing, spirited woman in his mind was replaced with the tired, over-worked wife he knew today. She didn't laugh anymore. She didn't slow down from work long enough to enjoy a walk. She didn't stir feelings of passion in him anymore. Why? What had changed? He had a nagging suspicion it was his fault.

The image of the little boy also diminished until he couldn't even remember what he looked like. An empty ache in his heart remained. Where had the boy gone? Why weren't there other memories of him? Did he grow up and leave the farm like James and Justin did and Harlan just couldn't remember?

He shook his head to dispel the questions whirling inside. He lived in the present. The past confused him. The passage of time was of no relevance. Each day he did the things that made him happy with no thought of what happened the day before.

A disturbing fact was beginning to bother him. Something about Jamie. In words he was incapable of expressing, he needed her. She was his world. She meant everything to him. But somehow he was losing her too.

Nearly every day she left the house. Cory told him she was going to work. That didn't make sense. There was plenty of work to do here on the farm. When she was home, she was busy doing other things or she was tired. He didn't understand that either. She wasn't doing enough to make herself tired as far as he could see. She didn't dance to his music anymore. She didn't go for walks with him to the river—a place he was forbidden to go alone. She didn't tell him funny stories to make him laugh.

Things were changing. He had experienced the changes before. Somewhere in the past. Now with Jamie, they were happening again. And again he was being left behind.

# Chapter Twelve

J ason gave Jamie a quick smile when she entered the stockroom for work Monday afternoon. His first genuine smile directed solely at her. She turned away without acknowledging the gesture and put her things into her locker. She was still annoyed at him for his rude behavior during the ride home yesterday and she wanted him to know it. When she turned to face him, he was at the opposite end of the room taking inventory.

How dare he not even notice she was ignoring him? Well, if he could forget all about yesterday, so would she. She pasted a big smile on her face and went over to where he stood. "So, what's up for to-day?" she asked.

He opened his mouth to answer, but stopped when the door to the stockroom opened. It was Tate.

"I'm leaving early. You'll be working your shift with Tate." Jason explained as he removed his smock.

This day was getting better and better.

Jason turned to Tate. "After this delivery is shelved, the house-hold department out front needs to be stocked. She's never worked that section, so keep an eye on her."

"Aye, aye, Captain," Tate said with a mock salute.

Jason frowned and turned away. He hung his smock on a hook and left the stockroom without another word to either of them. Jamie re-membered what he had said about never wanting to be like Tate. She wondered if it was true or if she was right and he was just jealous.

When the door closed behind him, Tate spun on his heel to face Jamie, a wide grin on his face. "Now that he's out of here, let's liven this place up."

"Where's he going today?" Jamie wondered aloud. "Jason never takes time off."

"He got here early, I think," he said. "You're not missing him, are you? I guarantee you'll have more fun with me. Jason's too uptight." He went over to the desk and started rummaging through the piles of paper and debris until he came up with a radio. In the stockroom, the desk was the only thing that had not benefited from Jason's managerial skills. Tate plugged in the radio and twisted the dial to find a station that suited him. "How's that?" His eyebrows arched inquisitively, seeking her approval.

She grinned in consent. This is what she expected a job to be like. Work, but also fun and camaraderie between co-workers. Jason would definitely disapprove of the music. Her grin widened. That made her all the more for it.

"Okay, what else have we got to do in here?" He compared the invoice on Jason's clipboard with the remaining boxes. "We'll get this done in no time." He dropped the clipboard on the desk with a loud clatter and turned to the stack of boxes.

As he tore open a box, he started talking. Jamie was accustomed to working in total silence. With Tate's endless banter, she found herself often distracted. The work slowed to a snail's pace as he filled her in on all the drugstore gossip. He had an amusing anecdote for everyone who worked with them.

Jamie was an attentive audience as he gave his account of an episode when Paige, Jamie's nemesis at the cash register, cussed out a clerk at the grocery store for short-changing her on a twenty-dollar bill. She had yelled so loud and was so demeaning to the poor girl, everyone in the store came to see what was going on. The clerk was reduced to tears by the time the manager got to the front of the store. She demanded the girl be fired, claiming this wasn't the first occasion when someone there tried to pull that trick on her. When the manager refused, he became the object of her attack. Finally she left, announcing to the whole store on the way out, they'd robbed her for the last time. Unfortunately for them, she was shopping there again the following week. According to Tate, Paige had a reputation around town for being difficult with everyone from gas station attendants to traffic cops.

Jamie knew better than to listen to gossip, but she couldn't resist. After weeks of silence in the stockroom with Jason, she relished in the sound of another human voice.

The two girls who worked out front alongside Paige had started out as stock girls like Jamie before moving up, having survived Jason's stringent training program, Tate told her. "Mary graduated from South Auburn last year. She still lives at home with her parents, but I don't know how much longer that'll last. She's got this thing for older guys. Her parents don't believe in that sort of thing. I hear she's seeing some married guy over in Blanton."

Jamie gasped. Seeing a married man and her barely out of high school!

"Deidre is a senior at Blanton," Tate said. "That's where Jason went to school. I guess she has a reputation over there. I've heard some wild stories about her from some of the guys who play basketball there. You know how some girls are. They don't care what boys say about them."

Jamie looked away uncomfortably. She really didn't want to hear stories that had been passed between jocks from locker room to locker room. Even she knew there was seldom any truth involved in their accounts. "We're almost finished here," she said in an attempt to deter him from further discussion about Deidre's reputation. "You can show me how to stock Household."

"Oh, it's no big deal. Jason makes everything sound like life or death. It's not that hard. You'll find out he doesn't have a personal life, so this job is it. Work and school. That's all he has time for. He can't find a girlfriend. What girl would want anything to do with a guy like that?"

Jamie didn't respond. A pattern was beginning to emerge from Tate's stories. So far, he hadn't said one positive thing about anyone all day. She wondered what he would be telling the others about her tomorrow.

After tearing down their empty boxes, they bound them together with twine and carried them outside behind the store.

"Let's take a break before we start stocking Household," Tate said when the last bundle of boxes was discarded.

Jamie kept quiet. She'd never taken anything more than a dinner break the entire time she had worked there. It never occurred to her to expect another one. She didn't mention it to Tate though, afraid it would get him started on Jason again.

"You wait here," he said when they got back inside the building. He dusted off the desk chair with his hand and motioned for her to sit down. "I'll be right back."

Jamie sat on the edge of the rickety chair. She was sure she should be working, not lounging in the stockroom without a care in the world, even if it did feel good to be off her feet.

Tate returned a few minutes later with two ice cream sundaes and set them on the desk. He stacked two wooden crates on top of each other to make a seat for himself and sat next to her. "I remembered you like strawberry." He took one of the sundaes and began to eat. "Go ahead. They're delicious."

She smiled, flattered that he remembered she ordered a strawberry shake the night he took her to the Dairy Queen. "Are you sure it's okay to be doing this?" She put a small spoonful of ice cream from the remaining sundae into her mouth. He was right. It was delicious.

"Doing what?" he asked between bites.

"Taking a break."

"Sure. We're allowed as long as we get our work done."

"Then why are we eating in here and not at the lunch counter."

Tate smiled at her. "You worry too much. Eat your ice cream before it melts."

Jamie did as she was told. She sat back in the desk chair and guiltily enjoyed the cold, velvety treat. It gave her the energy boost she needed after working in the hot stockroom all day. She just hoped Noel wouldn't come in and catch them sitting here. Tate focused his attention on his sundae. He seemed to have no trouble relaxing.

After the ice cream was gone, they went to the household department to determine what needed stocking. The job wasn't difficult, just time consuming. They tallied and made lists. Everything they brought out had to be priced. Armed with their pricing guns, they squatted before shelves and boxes, and put a pricing sticker on each item before placing it neatly onto the shelf.

In the stockroom Tate only had Jamie to talk to. Out front, he knew everyone; customers in need of assistance, small children daydreaming about a toy their parents still hadn't agreed to buy, and of course, any attractive female in his general vicinity. All were an excuse to stop working and start talking.

Jamie couldn't decide if she enjoyed his gift of gab as much as everyone else seemed to, or if she was totally annoyed by him. He was outgoing and likable. His dry sense of humor made him fun to listen to. There was no denying he was nice to look at. But his good looks and quick wit weren't getting the household department stocked. She was forced to work harder and faster in order to get everything done. Her pride couldn't stand the thought of leaving something undone for Jason to find in the morning.

Tate was not keeping up. She tried to think of a tactful way to remind him of the work that needed to be done. He was supposed to be supervising her, not the other way around, so what could she say? As the afternoon progressed, she grew more and more irritated. It wasn't fair that she was doing most of the work. He didn't seem to care if anything ever got done. He was having too much fun socializing. The more she worked, the more he talked. It began to dawn on her he was intentionally letting her do his share of the work. There was nothing she could do about it, so she worked on in silence.

A girl in a navy-blue smock like the one Jamie wore, appeared at the end of a row and knelt down on the floor next to Tate. "Hi, Tate. Where've you been hiding all day?"

Tate's face lit up, delighted at yet another interruption. "Noel's got me training the new girl," he said in a belabored voice and wagged his head in Jamie's direction.

Jamie grimaced at his calling her the new girl. She had been here over a month and she obviously knew the job as well or better than he did.

The girl giggled and straightened up. Tate stood up beside her and propped one elbow on a shelf. Two fingers on his other hand went into the front pocket of his Levi's. Jamie recognized the signs. He was getting comfortable and ready to socialize. "Have you met Ja-mie?" he asked.

"No," she said, drawing out the word in what she must have thought sounded seductive. Jamie imagined she probably heard someone do it on television. She looked down at Jamie like she would a bug she was preparing to squish. "Hi," she said in the same slow, drawn-out, and slightly bored manner.

"Jamie, this is Deidre," Tate said.

Jamie glanced up and gave her a disinterested smile before re-turning to her work. So this was Deidre, the one with the reputation among the basketball players. Earlier when Tate described her, he gave the impression he didn't think much of her. Now it looked like they were the best of friends.

"So, Tate," Deidre said in her sultry voice, "what are your plans after work?"

"I don't have any yet. It depends on if anything exciting comes along."

She giggled again and Jamie gritted her teeth.

"Some friends of mine are getting together at The Point later to hang out. Why don't you come with us? We always have a blast."

"Sounds like fun." Tate looked down at Jamie. "Wanna come?"

Deidre's face fell, but she recovered almost instantly. Jamie consid-ered accepting the invitation just to aggravate her. However, she didn't want to go. She heard stories at school about the parties that went on at The Point, a narrow stretch of beach on Jenna's Creek at the end of a dead-end road. Besides the fact that it would be a sin against God and everything she believed in to attend such a party, Grandma Cory would kill her if she found out.

"No, thanks."

Tate persisted much to Deidre's dismay. "Come on, Jamie. It'll be great."

"I have to go straight home after work."

"Give your grandma a call and tell her you'll be a little late. She won't care just this once."

"Yes, she will."

"Okay, but you're going to miss out on a great time. Huh, De-idre?"

"Yeah ... great."

Jamie shut out their discussion of the party and viciously ripped open a box of toothpaste. She glanced at her watch. It was already after seven. Less than an hour to finish. She couldn't believe she was actually missing Jason. Not only would he help with the work, he would not let Tate get away with wasting so much time.

Eventually Deidre looked toward the front of the store and saw the long line of customers waiting at Paige's cash register. "Oh," she cried, startled, "I better get up there. I told Paige I had to take a restroom break." She giggled and sauntered away, her hips swaying for Tate's benefit.

Tate looked down at his watch. "Oh no! I've got to get my cleaning done. You're going to have to finish here by yourself."

"But, Tate, I can't," Jamie exclaimed. "There's too much for one person to do alone."

"Sorry." He hurried away.

Jamie clenched her fist and thought how satisfying it would be to give him a good smack. Because of him wasting the afternoon she had to work twice as hard to finish before the store closed at eight. There was no such thing as over-time pay if she had to stay late to finish. It wasn't Noel's fault if the work didn't get done on time. She wondered if he knew how Tate behaved when there was no one around to keep an eye on him.

It didn't do any good to grumble. She set her mind on her work. Tomorrow Jason would be back and things would return to normal. She would do what she was getting paid to do and let Tate worry about himself.

She finished stocking Household just as the outside lights were switched off. She took her supplies to the stockroom to put away. She eyed the back door, her heart rate accelerating. Jason always locked it while they were cleaning up back here. Had Tate thought of it? Probably not! She'd have to make sure. She mentally counted the steps it would take to reach the door and how many seconds she'd need to turn the dead bolt. She could have it done and over with in ten seconds. That was precisely how long it would take the crazed psychopath still hiding behind the stack of laundry detergent, to bash in her skull and throw her body in the dumpster out back. Tomorrow was trash day so she wouldn't have to lay there long before the sanitation department found her crumpled and decaying body.

She ran to the back door, her pulse racing and gave the latch a twist. The dead bolt slid into place with a loud click. Just as she thought, still unlocked. Leave it to Tate to get her killed her first night alone in the stockroom.

She went back to work and did everything just as she knew Jason would. She straightened up the disarray left by her and Tate's carefree afternoon. It had been fun, but now she was paying for it.

When she left the stockroom to clock out, the store was deserted and the overhead lights were off. Tate and Deidre were already gone, she noted irritably. If they hadn't been wasting her time she would've been done and on her way home too.

She climbed the tiny staircase to punch her time card. A light was on in Noel's office and the door stood open. He looked up from a stack of papers on his desk. "You still here? I thought I was all alone."

"I'm just getting finished up. The stocking took longer than usual," was all she said.

"It makes a difference when Jason's not here, doesn't it?"

So Noel did notice his employee's work habits even when they thought he wasn't paying attention. "I'm afraid so," she said.

"Well, don't worry about it. You're doing a fine job, Jamie."

"Thanks. Sometimes I feel like I'll never catch on."

He smiled. "No need to worry about that. It's getting dark outside. Do you have a ride home?"

"No, I was going to walk."

"I hate to see you walk in the dark. If you want to wait a minute or two until I'm finished here, I can drive you home."

"That's not necessary. I don't care to walk."

"No, no. Just go down and get a Coke or something and I'll be right down."

Jamie agreed and descended the stairs. Her feet were tired and she wasn't looking forward to the long walk home. It would be totally dark by the time she got there. She wasn't typically afraid of the dark—she knew there was a host of heavenly angels encamped about her—but she'd already spooked herself with images of deranged killers in the stockroom and no amount of reasoning would get them out of her head tonight.

She scooped crushed ice into a cup and poured herself a drink from the soda fountain. She sat on a stool at the corner of the lunch counter and leaned against the wall, propping her feet up on the trash can under the counter. She took a long drink from her Coke and closed her eyes. Her heart leaped into her throat when the eerie stillness was shattered by pounding on the front door. She sat up straight and her feet fell into the trash can.

"Noel," she called out when she caught her breath and disentangled herself from the trash can. "There's someone at the door."

"See who it is," he called back, unconcerned. "My keys are hanging in the door."

She slid off the stool and made her way through the darkened building. She imagined the crazed psychopath from the back alley bursting through the door as soon as she unlocked it. He would knock her to the floor, demand money, shoot Noel when he tried to intervene, and kill her for witnessing the crime.

Through the glass door, she saw a middle-aged woman alone on the sidewalk. Jamie unlocked the door and stepped back to let her in. As soon as the woman was safe inside the store, she locked the door behind her. It was her duty to keep the psychopath out, now that there was another potential victim. He had more than likely escaped from a home for the criminally insane and could kill three as easily as two.

"Is Noel here?" The woman was visibly upset. Her voice shook and she wrung her hands anxiously.

"Yes, he's upstairs." With a real crisis possibly unfolding, Jamie forgot about the psychopath. She led the woman to the office stairs. "Noel, there's someone here to see you."

She heard him get up from his chair and come to the door. The light from the office behind him framed him in a ghostly glow. In the semi-darkness, Jamie saw his face turn white.

"Abby?" Without waiting for an answer, he bounded down the stairs. Jamie barely got out of his way in time. He took the woman's hands and looked into her eyes. "Is everything all right?"

The woman lowered her eyes to the floor and shook her head. "No. It's Eric." When she looked up again, her eyes were filled with tears.

"Eric? What's wrong with him?" Panic was evident in Noel's voice.

The woman began to cry. Noel drew her tenderly into his arms. Sobs wracked her body as her tears came faster and faster. Noel patted her back and murmured words of comfort into her ear that Jamie couldn't hear.

Jamie turned away wishing she was anywhere but here. She moved quietly to the soda fountain and retrieved her drink. The woman's tears slowly subsided. Noel whispered something more, and she nodded and sniffed loudly.

"Tell me what's wrong with Eric," he said again as she stepped out of his embrace.

"He's sick," the woman choked. "The doctors' have finally diagnosed him with epilepsy."

"Oh, Abby, I'm so sorry. Are they sure?"

"You know he's been having problems for so long. There've been subtle signs for years. We just didn't know what we were looking for. Especially since there was no sign of it in our family history. We've had him to three different specialists. We were in Columbus all day. They ran every kind of test there is. They're sure." She began to cry again. "Oh, Noel, what are we going to do?" She collapsed into his arms.

Noel spotted Jamie over the top of the woman's head, trying to make herself invisible. He looked surprised, as if he just remembered she was still there. He awkwardly pulled away from the woman. When he spoke, his voice was flat and emotionless. "Abby, it's all right. Everything'll be fine. If he responds to treatment, it's likely he'll lead a perfectly normal life. There's no reason why he can't."

She sniffed loudly and pulled a handkerchief from her pocket. She blew her nose and dried her tears. "I'm sorry. I—I shouldn't have come. I waited until I thought you'd be alone. I was going to stop by your house but I didn't think it would look..." Her eyes lit briefly on Jamie. She sighed and patted Noel on the chest. "I knew you could make me feel better. You know so much about these kinds of things. Jack is beside himself with worry."

"Tell Jack not to worry just yet. My sister has epilepsy. You'd never know it by looking at her. As long as she takes her medication and follows the doctor's orders, she gets along fine."

"I'll go now," the woman said. "Jack'll be wondering where I'm at." She glanced at Jamie again out of the corner of her eye. Jamie hastily looked away. She poked her straw in her mouth and took a deep drink of the Coke.

Noel put his arm around the woman's shoulders and led her to the door. He kept whispering in her ear and she'd nod in understanding every once in awhile. Jamie stayed on the stool and sipped her soda. Out of the corner of her eye, she watched them at the front door. Noel gave the woman one last hug and then she was gone.

Jamie poured the remainder of her soda down the tiny sink and rinsed out her glass. Noel went past her and up the stairs to his office. He turned off the light and locked the door. His keys jingled in his hand as he came back down the stairs.

"Are you ready, Jamie?"

"Yes." She followed him to the door. Neither spoke as they stepped out onto the sidewalk and he turned to lock the door behind them.

She stayed a few paces behind him on the way to his car. She wanted to offer her sympathy, but felt awkward about witnessing the scene in the first place.

"We should've called your grandmother from the store. She's probably wondering where you are."

"Oh, I forgot all about it," Jamie groaned. "You're right. She'll be worried."

"I hope you won't get in trouble," he said.

She could tell his mind was a thousand miles away. "I'm sorry about Eric," she said.

He turned the key in the ignition. "Thanks."

"How old is he?"

"Umm... eighteen. You may know him. He graduated last year from South Auburn."

There was only one Eric who graduated last year. "Eric Blackwood?"

Noel nodded his head. "That's him."

Jamie stared out the window. Yes, she remembered Eric. Smart, a ready smile for even the uncool kids like her, dark-headed, and handsome. The star pitcher on the school's baseball team. He was voted most likely to succeed by his senior class. Hardly one you'd imagine being sick.

"I would appreciate it, Jamie, if you didn't say anything about this to anyone. For the family's sake. This is going to be terribly hard on them."

"Oh, I won't," she promised, appreciating their need for privacy. "I'll be praying for him though."

He smiled at her in the glow of the dashboard. "Thanks. He'll be needing all the prayers he can get. We all will."

The trip was quiet the rest of the way home. Jamie thought of Eric Blackwood. He had won a scholarship last year for college. She remembered an assembly where all the winners of various scholarships and awards were recognized in front of the school. What a terrible thing to happen to him!

She thought of his overwrought mother. Was she afraid he might die? Was it possible? She had lost her parents. This parent was facing the possibility of losing a child. Which would be worse? It was too terrible to even imagine.

Noel seemed to be taking the news pretty hard. It was obvious he was beside himself with worry. If Eric was family, Mrs. Wyatt would be upset too. She would give her a call in a day or two to see how she was doing.

She lowered herself to her knees beside her bed that night and prayed for Mrs. Blackwood and Eric. She prayed for Noel and Mrs. Wyatt. She prayed God would strengthen them and prepare them for the struggles ahead. She prayed they would trust in their Heavenly Father and rest in His grace. She prayed Eric would respond to the treatment Noel had mentioned—whatever it was.

She didn't pray for herself or Cassie. She didn't pray for her dad. Even after her tearful admission in Mrs. Wyatt's solarium yesterday, she still wasn't ready to forgive him. Nothing had changed to make him worthy of her forgiveness. Her guilt over her feelings for him was gone. For that she was thankful, but she wasn't ready to forgive him yet. Maybe if she found out he had nothing to with Sally Blake's disappearance she'd feel differently.

She just wasn't quite sure how to explain all of it to God.

Noel Wyatt didn't sleep well at all that night. Like Jamie, he looked to his Heavenly Father in the light of Abigail Blackwood's distressing news. And like her, he was unable to keep self out of the prayers he sent heavenward.

During the early years of the 1940's, many of Jenna's Creek's native sons were fighting for freedom on foreign soil. Not only were Noel's services required in the community, he was the last surviving male in his family. Much to the delight of Jenna's Creek and his mother, Uncle Sam told him to stay home.

The young ladies of the area rallied for the war effort and took jobs previously occupied by the missing soldiers. A bus stopped regularly in front of the drugstore and carried them to plants in Portsmouth and Ironton. Abigail Frazier was among them. Noel remembered her as a teenager coming into the drugstore with her friends to drink sodas and talk about boys. No longer the giggling teenager he remembered, she came into the store on cold mornings to wait for the bus. She and Noel found it easy to talk to one another about almost anything. A friendship quickly developed despite the ten year age difference.

For a year their relationship remained the same. Noel started opening the store a half an hour earlier just to prolong their time together. He'd fix a pot of coffee and have fresh doughnuts from the bakery awaiting her arrival. Abby sat on a stool beside him in the early morning hours, and regaled him with amusing anecdotes from her previous day at the plant. He began to dread seven-thirty when the bus would pull in and she'd hurry out the door with her coworkers to begin another day.

One afternoon she showed up at the drugstore unexpectedly. She looked excited and unnerved at the same time. She had something to tell him. Her fiance, Jack Blackwood, had been injured in Europe and was being sent home. It was the first Noel had heard of a fiance! He was certain Abby had not mentioned Jack's name in any of their conversations. His heart sank as she explained that they grew up together and always joked about someday getting married. In the letters Jack wrote to his mother and Abby simultaneously, he announced that he and Abby would marry immediately when he arrived home. As Abby related this information to Noel, she told him she didn't know how to tell her mother nor Jack's, that she wasn't in love with him, especially since they were planning the wedding even as she and Noel spoke.

"But Noel, does love really matter?" she had asked. "I really think a lot of Jack. Isn't that enough?"

Poor Noel missed his cue. He listened in horror to her words and realized he loved her more than he thought possible. Before that day, he thought she had similar feelings for him. What could he do? He couldn't steal a girl from a returning soldier. He stayed mute. In retrospect, he hated himself for not making his feelings for her known in time. He congratulated her, wished her well, and sent her on her way. The morning visits ceased. A month later Jack Blackwood returned from Italy, and Noel Wyatt's world ended.

It was thirty years later and he still loved Abby as much as he had that day in 1944. But there was nothing he could do for her. She was still another man's wife. He didn't have the right to comfort her tonight as he wanted to. He couldn't hold her in his arms and rock her to sleep, assuring her everything would work out with Eric. He couldn't dispel the myths about epilepsy to ease her fears. He couldn't even apologize for passing it on to his son.

# Chapter Thirteen

J amie stepped over the gate into the hog pen and aimed the garden hose into the trough. Under the intense July sun, the water trough dried out quickly and had to be replenished several times a day. The hogs clustered around the spray, squealing and pushing to get closer to the cool water. "Don't fight," she scolded. "There's plenty for all of you."

She turned the hose on them and gave each one a good dousing. Grandma Cory would say it was a waste of water. The hogs could lie in the dust in the shade next to the shed when they got hot. But Jamie didn't see any harm in indulging them in a little afternoon shower. She pointed the hose straight into the air over her head and let the cool water splash down over her and the eager swine. The hogs crowded against her, their wet, scratchy hides irritating the bare skin on her legs.

"Hey, guys, watch it. Easy now." They jostled against her, throwing her off balance. It was all she could do to stay on her feet. Time to stop the fun before she ended up head first in the water trough.

As she shut off the hose and climbed out of the pen, she thought she heard a car door slam. Uncle Justin had probably pulled into the driveway while she had the water running and couldn't hear. He stopped in several times a week to see how things were going on the farm. She slowly made her way to the water spigot, rolling the hose up across her arms as she went. She shut off the water and hung the hose on the hook by the spigot. She combed her fingers through her wet hair. She tossed her head back and tiny droplets of water rained down on her. The droplets dried instantly in the hot sun, leaving pale splotches on her grimy skin. She gave her head another powerful shake, tucked her hair behind her ears, and headed for the house. After every few steps, she leaned over and swiped at the smears of dirt the hogs left on her legs. Her wet hands only made things worse. It didn't matter. Her chores were done and she was ready for a cool refreshing shower.

At the corner of the house, Jamie gasped in horror. Tate's red Road Runner was parked in the driveway. What was he doing here? She forgot all about being aggravated with him for slacking off at work yesterday. All she wanted to do was get into the house undetected. If he saw her in her present state, she would die of embarrassment. She stepped over Henry and crept to the back door. Through the screen, she saw Tate and Grandma Cory sitting at the table. Tate said something and Grandma Cory laughed merrily, a rare sound in the Steele kitchen these days.

"There's Jamie now," she heard Tate say.

She thought of turning and running to the creek for a quick dip, but it was too late. "Come in here, Jamie," Grandma Cory called out. "You have a visitor."

"Hi, Tate. Hi, Grandma," she said as she stepped into the kitchen and smiled sheepishly.

Grandma Cory gasped. "Good lands, girl. It looks like you've been rootin' with the hogs."

Jamie held her tongue.

"Maybe I caught you at a bad time," Tate said, stifling a laugh.

"Not really," It was too late to worry about embarrassment. She decided to make the best of things by laughing at herself. "I got prettied up just for you."

"Well, whatever you've been doing, you sure did manage to make a mess." Grandma Cory rolled her eyes at Jamie and shook her head apologetically at Tate. "Why don't the two of you go into the living room while I get dinner started? It was nice meeting you, Tate."

"You too, Mrs. Steele."

Jamie sat awkwardly on the edge of the sofa, her cut-off shorts still damp. She tucked her tangled hair behind her ears again and swallowed her humiliation. "I'm really sorry about this, Tate. I feel ridiculous. If you want to wait here, I'd feel so much better if I could go upstairs and get cleaned up."

"No, it's my fault for dropping in unexpected. I should have called first." He looked pointedly at her filthy clothes and grinned. "Believe me. Next time I will. But there is a reason I'm here. I was thinking maybe you'd like to ride into town with me later and get something to eat. Or, you know, something like that."

"Er... I don't know." Was this a date, or was he just being friendly? Wouldn't he have asked her earlier if it was an actual date? Nobody went on dates on Tuesday nights, did they? Maybe he just wanted to share a pizza with someone, but then, he did come all the way out here to ask her. That had to mean something, he could've just called. She told herself to calm down. She didn't want to read more into his invitation than what was truly there.

Still, it was Tate. A date, or almost-date with Tate Craig. She had dreamed of this moment since the onset of puberty. She'd be out of her mind to refuse.

"If you already have plans, that's all right," he said at her hesitation.

"No, that's not it," she spoke up quickly. "I was just wondering— um—what time were you thinking of?"

"Anytime's okay with me, whenever you want."

"How about seven?"

"That's fine." He stood up to go. "I'll go home and get ready and give you a chance to get ... Are you sure seven o'clock is late enough? That's only three hours from now."

"Ha, ha. Very funny!" She walked with him as far as the front porch. As he drove away, she reminded herself he hadn't called it a date. He didn't even have specific plans or a time in mind. She mustn't over-react, they were only sharing pizza. Regardless, she floated up the stairs to her room, mentally searching her closet for an appropriate outfit to wear on her first date with Tate Craig.

She filled the bathtub and immersed herself in the steaming bubbles. She soaked with her eyelids closed, a smile playing dreamily on her lips until Grandpa Harlan knocked on the door.

"Jamie? Are you in there? Is everything all right?" he wanted to know.

She sat up and reached for a towel. "I'm fine, Grandpa. I'll be right out." She slipped into her bathrobe and hurried out of the room. "Sorry I took so long."

His answer was a blank stare. He turned and went into his room leaving her alone in the hallway. He was feeling left out, but her mood was too light to dwell on a momentary pang of regret.

Three times she went to her closet and three times she put on an outfit she thought would be the most flattering. In the end she wasn't happy with the choice she settled on, she was just out of options. She pulled her best shoes out of the closet and set them by the door. She looked down at them dismally and wished for the thousandth time in her life she had tiny, delicate feet like Cassie. No matter how pretty a pair of shoes looked when she first saw them at the store, they never looked as good when the clerk produced a pair in her size.

Her straight brown hair stubbornly resisted the modern style she tried in vain to maneuver it into. She bent over at the waist and let it fall in front of her. She brushed it a few dozen strokes upside down and then threw her head back. She pulled a strand back on each side and pinned them in place above her ears with matching clips. That was a little better, but not much. Her make-up attempt was more successful. She'd learned a lot this summer about applying make-up from paying attention to the fashionably dressed women who came into the drug-store. A pair of tiny gold earrings Aunt Marty and Uncle Justin gave her for Christmas completed the casually elegant look—she hoped.

She stood in front of the mirror attached to her closet door and surveyed the fruits of her labor. Not bad. It could be worse. Anything was a drastic improvement over this afternoon.

Having done all she could to make herself presentable, Jamie went downstairs to wait. She watched the hands on the clock as they dragged around the face. Seven o'clock came and went. Ten trips she made to the front door. Every time a car was heard in the distance, she hurried to see if it was Tate. Each time she was disappointed. Grandma Cory checked on her a few times, but didn't comment. At seven-thirty, tears threatened to spill down her cheeks and ruin her make-up.

Where was he? Should she phone? No, she wasn't going to do that. He should call her. If his plans changed, surely he would let her know.

At half past eight she angrily yanked the clips out of her hair and stomped upstairs to her room. She threw herself across the bed and buried her face in her pillow. She would kill him. She would literally tear him apart. Who did he think he was? How dare he treat her so callously! There was no excuse for not showing up or calling with an explanation. She would never forgive him. She hated him.

A quiet voice sounded in the hallway, "Jamie?"

"What?" She bit her tongue, immediately regretting her bitter tone.

"Grandma's popping corn. There's a movie coming on the television. It might be pretty good," Grandpa Harlan said hopefully.

"I can't, Grandpa. I don't feel well."

"Are you sick?"

"A little." She wasn't actually lying. She did feel sick.

He hurried into the room and sat on the edge of her bed. He put a gentle hand on her forehead and smoothed her hair back from her face. "What's the matter?"

"Nothing really, Grandpa. I just need some rest."

"Shouldn't you get out of that pretty dress then before you go to bed?"

"You're right." She gave him a weak smile. "I wouldn't want to wrinkle it."

"Okay then." He got up and left the room, his shoulders still slumped. She heard him trudge back down the stairs.

Jamie unzipped her dress and climbed out of it. As she hung it back in the closet, Grandpa Harlan's disappointed face danced before her. Earlier, she regretted that he was feeling left out of her life. So what if Tate stood her up? Did that mean she had to be exiled to her room and feel sorry for herself all night? Why punish Grandpa? At least one man wanted to spend an evening with her, even if it wasn't the one she planned on. She put on her nightgown and bathrobe, washed the make-up off her face, and went downstairs to eat popcorn and watch a movie with her family. Tate Craig wasn't worth it.

✺

The ringing of the telephone awakened Jamie the next morning. She groggily checked the time on the clock by her bed. Eight-thirty. She hadn't slept this late in ages. She had stayed up until well after midnight watching scary movies. At first she was too depressed about Tate to enjoy herself. As the night progressed, she forgot about him and let herself have fun getting scared with Grandma and Grandpa.

Grandma Cory never was one for TV but last night she made an exception. It wasn't often that she did something on Jamie's behalf. Jamie came as close to being spoiled as a Steele child could. Her opinion was sought about which movie to watch. She was given the most comfortable chair in the room—the one usually occupied by Grandma Cory. Cory even prepared her a soda with an entire tray of ice the way she liked it and brought her a bowl of popcorn from the kitchen. The extra attention was unheard of. In this house, it was every man for himself. Cory felt she worked too hard as it was to be given the extra burden of carrying food to people with two good legs.

"Jamie, are you up?" Grandma Cory called from downstairs. "The phone's for you—it's Tate."

Mixed emotions filled her head. Anger at how he treated her combined with excitement of talking to him again. Why was her heart betraying her? Didn't she remember how mad she was at him? She tried to calm the pounding in her chest as she pulled on her robe and hurried downstairs.

"Hello?" She hoped he wouldn't detect the tremor in her voice.

"Hi, Jamie? It's me, Tate."

"Oh."

"Hey listen, Jamie," he began. "I'm sorry about last night. I know me and you were supposed to get pizza or something, but something came up. You know, at the last minute."

Was this his idea of an apology? It wasn't a very good one. What about an explanation?

"Jamie? Are you still there?"

"Yes, I'm here."

"You're not mad at me, are you? I guess I should have called."

"Yes, you should've." She didn't tell him she waited for him all night. She didn't want to sound pathetic.

"I'm really sorry but, well, you know. It was last minute and all."

He still hadn't explained what it was that kept him from keeping their date—if it had been a date. Was it a family emergency, car trouble, or did someone better come along? She feared the last was true. He wasn't saying and she wasn't about to ask.

"Well, whatever, Tate."

"I hope you're not mad." The pitiful whine in his voice was beginning to get on her nerves. "I'll make it up to you, I promise. You forgive me, don't you?"

She couldn't stay mad at him, no matter what he did. After all, it was Tate. She didn't want to say she forgave him, even though she already had. She would string him along—make him suffer. It was unlikely he ever suffered through anything. He had acted irresponsibly last night, but they didn't actually have a date. Out of consideration he should have called, but she wasn't his girlfriend or anything. It was a simple misunderstanding. The next time he wouldn't stand her up, and if something did come up, he would call to let her know.

She sighed into the phone so he would hear. "I'm not mad, Tate."

"I'm so glad. I knew you wouldn't be. You're all right, Jamie. Hey, I'll talk to you later, okay?" With that he hung up.

"Uh... okay... bye," she said to the dead air on the other end. She stared at the phone in her hand for a moment before hanging up. Had he been sorry after all, or was he merely calling to appease his conscious?

Grandma Cory was wiping off the kitchen counter. Jamie knew she had been listening to her end of the conversation. She was embarrassed to have forgiven him so easily. "Something came up last night," she explained. "That's why he couldn't make it."

"Uh huh." Grandma Cory kept wiping in circular motions without looking up. Jamie could tell she thought it was a dumb excuse, and she was thinking the same thing.

# Chapter Fourteen

Jamie Steele called me the other day," Lucinda Wyatt told her son.

"Um," Noel nodded, his thoughts more on the fresh cream cheese croissant in his hand than what his mother was saying.

"She expressed her sympathy to me about Eric Blackwood's medical condition."

Noel nearly choked on the croissant. "She—she did?"

"Yes, she did. Imagine my surprise when I discovered Eric Blackwood has a medical condition. Especially since it took me a moment or two to even remember who the boy is. It seems she's under the impression we're related to him."

Silence.

"Where do you suppose she got that idea?" Lucinda was pleased at the look of trapped desperation on his face.

He made a visible effort to bring himself under control. "How am I supposed to know what goes on in that girl's head?"

"I'm just trying to figure out why she thought we were related to the Blackwoods of all people." She watched his face for a reaction. He shoved the rest of the croissant into his mouth and began to systematically lick each finger. Lucinda pressed on. "Did you say anything to her to that effect?"

"No, Mother." He wiped his mouth with a paper napkin and wadded it into a ball. "Abby Blackwood came in the store the other night to tell me about Eric, and Jamie was there."

"Why did she do that?"

"Do what?"

"Why did Abby Blackwood tell you about Eric? After the store was closed?"

He focused his eyes on a spot on the wall slightly past her right shoulder. Quietly, he answered, "I don't know."

"Noel, I want you to talk to me."

"There's nothing to say. The Blackwoods have been customers of ours for years. Abby was very upset and I guess she just wanted to vent her frustration. I don't know. It's nothing to be concerned about." He turned back to her, his face placating.

Lucinda knew there was more to it than he was telling her, but she wasn't sure if she wanted to hear the whole truth. "After Jamie got to talking, it took me a few minutes, but then I remembered where I'd heard Eric's name before. Wasn't he last year's recipient of the science scholarship award you sponsor?"

"You already know he was," Noel replied testily.

"He was also the only high school senior you considered, even though there were applicants from all over the county equally eligible."

"I considered each kid fairly."

"Not last year, you didn't," she stated. "I sit on that committee with you, Noel. You wouldn't listen to anything about any other student. I mean, I know it's your money but…"

"But what, Mother, what are you getting at?" His sharp tone surprised them both.

"What is his condition anyway?" she asked suddenly, switching topics.

"What condition?"

"His medical condition."

"Oh. Epilepsy. According to his mother, he's been undiagnosed for years."

"Did he have an injury sometime in his life?"

"No, not that they're aware of. They're stumped as to what caused it." Noel slowly realized what she was driving at. "Abby—er—his mother said there's none of it in her family history."

"It sounds like the situation with your sister, Gwen. She was about the same age as Eric is now when her's was first detected. You were so young, I doubt you remember. She had problems off and on for years before it was finally diagnosed."

Noel turned slightly in his chair to face the window, absently rolling the paper napkin into a tighter and tighter ball. "And it's just like what happened to your father's brother, Horace, and his two oldest girls." Lucinda continued, "They all had the same condition that showed up about that age." She stood up and went to the coffee pot to freshen her cup. She knew he was still listening even though he seemed to have taken a great interest in whatever was going on outside the window. "I was so thankful, it didn't claim you. I think it was easier on Gwen. At least she has a husband to support her. She doesn't have to worry about holding down a job or anything. With her medication, she can lead a perfectly normal life. It will be much harder on poor Eric. Isn't it convenient that he won your full four-year college scholarship? He won't have to work his way through school now, thanks to your generosity."

Noel rose quickly to his feet. "I've got to get to the drugstore. Noreen's probably got a hundred prescriptions that have been called in by now. Thanks for breakfast, Mother." He kissed her wrinkled cheek and hurried out the kitchen door.

Lucinda waited until she heard his car backing out of the driveway. She thought for a moment, her eyes staring blankly out the same window that had held her son's attention moments before. She moved slowly and arthritically to the living room. In the top drawer of her roll-top desk she found the newspaper article announcing Eric Blackwood as the recipient of the scholarship, Auburn County's most coveted award, initiated by Noel three years earlier for an outstanding student in science. Noel had always excelled in science. He had won many competitions and awards himself when he was young. Just like his father. Cut from the same cloth, she always said.

She folded the clipping in her hand and went to the staircase. Her other frail hand on the banister for support, she slowly climbed the stairs to Noel's old room. She didn't get upstairs much these days. Rowena kept it clean and aired out, but it still felt musty and stale. It needed children and laughter and dirty laundry. She smiled wryly and thought of the house full of children she and Mr. Wyatt dreamed of having. The only rowdy, raucous behavior this house experienced was Noel's friends tearing through the halls on their way to a neighbor-hood ball game.

She opened the door to his room with near reverence. He hadn't slept in the twin bed for forty years, but the room was still the same. She opened the closet and began to search the top shelf. Noel was a meticulous organizer so she found what she was looking for right away. She sat on the narrow bed and opened the annual to Noel's se-nior picture. So many awards and accolades. He had been involved in everything; sports, editor on the school paper, the debate team. He excelled in everything he put his hand to.

She looked at the picture of her beloved son dressed in a smart, dark suit, smiling for the camera and groaned aloud. There it was, staring up at her. It was so obvious, how could she have over-looked it before? The straight nose. The square, aristocratic chin. The wavy, almost black hair with the stubborn cow-lick on the left side. The same cow-lick that frustrated Mr. Wyatt and every Wyatt before him.

She placed the newspaper article with the photograph of Eric be-side the picture of Noel. Eric was also dressed in a dark suit and smil-ing for the camera. The two pictures were nearly identical. If not for the hairstyle changes in the past forty years, Lucinda would have a hard time telling which young man was which.

She closed her eyes to their smiling faces. "Oh, Noel, what have you done?"

Noel drove too fast to the corner and was forced to mash the brake pedal in order to come to a stop at the intersection. He was angry and knew he shouldn't be. He was angry with Jamie Steele for opening her mouth to his mother. He had asked her not to say anything about Abby's visit to spare the family the pain of public scrutiny. At least that was the reason he gave her. She hadn't really gone against his wishes. After the display she witnessed the other night, she assumed the Black-woods were related to his family. Why else would a woman unburden herself on Noel's shoulder late at night after the drugstore was closed? Jamie thought she was being considerate by checking in on his moth-er, doing the Christian thing. Noel should appreciate her concerns.

He was also angry with his mother. She had a sharp mind and didn't miss a thing. She had probably already figured out the whole story. The scholarship awarded to Eric, the epilepsy which ran rough-shod on the Wyatt's side of the family, Abby's visit the other night. Separate, they meant little, together, they painted a clear picture if someone took the time to look.

In the mid-1950's Noel Wyatt was in bad shape. He had gained thirty pounds since Abigail Frazier walked down the aisle to marry Jack Blackwood. He hadn't seen her since Jack came home from the service. She came into the drugstore only out of necessity. Noel avoided all contact with her. She belonged to another man. He knew his place.

He smoked two packs of cigarettes a day, even though he knew better. His only exercise was to amble across the street to the diner for his customary two hot dog lunch which he bolted down between errands. He worked twenty-hour days and ate his dinner standing over the sink in the beautiful, mahogany kitchen designed by the in absentia Myra Curtsinger. The chest pains that plagued him for two years were ignored and went unreported to the family doctor whom he never visited.

He was forty-two when his heart decided the chest pains weren't enough and did something drastic to get his attention. A mild heart attack sent him to the emergency room one Sunday afternoon while enjoying a sirloin steak at his mother's house. Had it happened at home, he would have ignored it and possibly died as a result. But his mother and Rowena muscled him into Lucinda's Packard and drove him to the hospital.

With his father's medical history staring him in the face, he listened to the doctor's advice. He wasn't thrilled with the diagnosis, but he wasn't ready to die at forty-two either.

The doctor prescribed one month out of the drugstore. The telephone was not to ring with problems for him to solve or customers for him to advise. No exceptions. He strongly suggested a vacation to Lucinda's winter home in Florida, but Noel refused to go that far. It was enough the meddling quack insisted he waste an entire month doing absolutely nothing. He was to rest and relax, preferably without a cigarette or a chili dog in his hand.

A nurse came in twice a week to check his progress. Noel didn't mind at first; he was too sick and weak to complain. He hated to admit he needed the rest and change of lifestyle. He had been foolish with his health. As he began to feel better, he became cantankerous. He had never sat around doing nothing in his life. He did not make a good patient. His mother bought him a new-fangled television set, which he refused to turn on. Just because his body had turned to mush, didn't mean his brain had to follow. He snapped at anyone who made the mistake of visiting him. He fussed and fretted and paced the floor. All within the first seven days.

His second Monday morning was spent laying on the couch in his bathrobe reading the Wall Street Journal. He heard someone come in the back door. A feminine voice called his name. His first thought was; that blasted nurse, she wasn't supposed to come today. He modestly straightened the bathrobe across his bare legs and sat up. What kind of man lays around the house with his legs exposed for the whole world to see on a Monday morning anyway? He was disgusted with himself.

It wasn't the nurse.

Abigail Blackwood appeared in the doorway and gazed in at him. Her eyes were moist. He barely had time for a sharp intake of breath before she burst across the room and sank to her knees in front of him. "Oh, Noel," she cried, her tears dampening his bathrobe. She threw her arms awkwardly around his neck. "I can't believe it. Oh, Noel."

He tried not to notice the smell of her freshly shampooed hair or how her slim body felt next to his.

"I just heard today," she sobbed. "They were talking about it at the beauty parlor. Linda said you almost died. It was all I could do to sit there until she finished with me. I had to come straight over."

"I didn't almost die, I'm fine," he said soothingly. He stroked her hair, reveling in the silky softness under his fingers.

"You didn't have a heart attack?" She peered up at him through her disheveled locks and sniffed loudly.

"Well, just a mild one," he said gently, brushing the hair away from her face. "That old coot, Dr. Montavon, told me I needed a vacation. I'm supposed to get some rest, lose a few pounds, and throw out the smokes."

"Are you sure that's all there is to it?" Her blue eyes were doubtful.

"I wouldn't lie to you."

Relief slowly replaced the fear on her face. She got off her knees and sat on the edge of the couch next to him. He scooted against the back cushions to make room for her.

Gently she laid her hand against his cheek. Their eyes locked. She imperceptibly leaned forward. Noel raised up off the cushions toward her. Their faces came together. It was happening so slowly, he could almost count her long, light eyelashes. An eternity later, their lips met. She sighed and sank against him. His arms went around her back and pulled her close. After a long moment, she drew back.

Tears came to her eyes again. "Why did you have to do that?" she asked breathlessly.

"I wanted to," he whispered. "I want to again."

"No." She pulled away from him and stood up. "Why couldn't you have done that ten years ago?" Her eyes filled with sudden rage. "I hate you, Noel Wyatt," she yelled at him. "I hate you. You ruined my life." She covered her face with her hands and her shoulders shook with sobs.

Noel was shocked into silence. He stared at her, his mouth hanging open. He struggled to his feet, unaccustomed to the bathrobe flapping open around his knees. He put his hands on her shoulders and tried to look at her face. She jerked away. "Leave me alone," she wailed, her voice losing its venom. Quietly, mournfully she said, "Just leave me alone."

"Abby, please, I'm sorry. Just tell me what I've done."

Her arms dropped to her sides again and her shoulders sagged. "Oh, forget it. It's too late now anyway. Nothing can be done about it."

"Done about what?" He was thoroughly confused.

She saw the confusion in his eyes and shook her head, dejected. "I'm sorry. I shouldn't have come. It's obvious you don't feel the same way I do. I really don't hate you. At least not all the time." She turned toward the door.

"No, wait a minute. Don't go." He put his hand on her shoulder and turned her around to face him. "Talk to me. Please."

"No... I just thought... I thought you still..." She shook her head at the futility of the situation.

"You thought I still what?"

She attempted a weak smile. "I think I've misinterpreted everything, Noel. From the very beginning. It's not your fault."

He was beginning to see the light. "You think you've misinterpreted that… I love you?"

Her eyes widened.

"Abby, I love you. I've always loved you."

He cringed at the reappearance of her tears. "Then why didn't you say anything? Why did you stand there like an idiot and let me marry a man I didn't love?" When he didn't respond, she asked again, louder, her voice an angry shriek, "Why?"

"I…" Beads of sweat popped out on his brow. He wiped them off with the back of his hand. The emotional and physical exertion was getting to him. "I thought… I thought you were in love with Jack Blackwood."

"Did I ever tell you that?" she demanded.

"Well… no. But you seemed so proud to be marrying a war hero. I couldn't compete with that. You said your families had always expected you to marry him. You said…" His voice trailed off as he realized his error.

"I was trying to give you a chance to tell me how you felt about me. You never did, you know? We talked about everything else. I thought my feelings for you were so obvious and I thought you… But you never said a word. You just talked and talked about things that didn't matter. I even came in that day to tell you Jack was coming home. I thought for sure you would say, 'Don't do it, Abby. I love you. Don't marry him.' But you didn't."

"But I… I… oh, Abby, that's not how I remember it at all. I thought you were telling me you didn't love me. I thought you were in love with him. I thought all along you only saw me as a friend."

"Why couldn't you have just asked me?" She said with a half-hearted chuckle. "Funny, isn't it? When I told you I was going to marry Jack, I thought you saw me as nothing more than a friend. I was so crushed. I cried every night until my wedding. And the whole time you were thinking I only cared for you as a friend. You know, if you would've called me at any time before I said 'I do', I would've stopped the ceremony. I even looked for you while I was walking down the aisle. I thought it would be so romantic if you burst into the church at the last minute and professed your love for me in front of everyone. I fantasized about you sweeping me off my feet, wedding gown and all, and carrying me away. Isn't that ridiculous? Oh well, it didn't happen that way, did it?"

Noel's head was pounding. He didn't know what to say. If only he had known. "Oh, Abby, I was such a fool. I had no idea. I'm so sorry." His words were inadequate, but he couldn't think straight.

"You know what else is funny?" she asked. "If you had told me how you felt back then, you probably wouldn't have had your heart attack or whatever it was. I would have been here and I wouldn't have let it happen. I would have made you take care of yourself."

Noel wanted to cry. He wanted to go back in time and change that dreadful day in 1944. His life suddenly seemed more hopeless than he imagined. He'd been self-destructive with his health without even realizing it. Without the woman he loved in his life, he hadn't seen any reason to take care of himself.

"If things had been different, I wouldn't be scrimping to get by on Jack's paycheck," she was saying. "I wouldn't have to worry about light bills and insurance premiums. Oh, I'm sorry. I didn't come here to complain about missing out on an easier way of life. I was truly concerned about you. I had to find out for myself that you were all right." She sank onto the couch and he sat down gratefully beside her, his legs wobbly from exhaustion.

"Jack treats me fine. I guess he even loves me. My girls are great. I wouldn't trade them for anything. But I'll never feel for Jack the way I feel for you. Every time I drive past this house, I wonder what it would've been like to live here with you. I know that makes me sound like a terrible person. But it isn't about the money or my lack of it. I just wonder what it'd be like to live in this big house; to put my feminine stamp all over it. To fill it with dark-headed kids that look just like you. To drive a car that doesn't die in the middle of an intersection and leave me stranded." She hammered her fists against her knees in frustration. "I'm a terrible person! I hate myself for thinking this way. I hate myself for not appreciating Jack and our girls. And that's why I hate you, sometimes."

Noel didn't speak. He was still beating himself up inside. He put his arm around her shoulders. She relaxed into him and sighed heavily.

"It's all right. You're not a terrible person." He gave her a small smile. "It's okay if you want to hate me. I don't mind."

She turned her face toward him and returned his smile gratefully. Once again their lips met, tentatively at first, and then more ardently. Wisdom told them to get up and walk away, but neither had the strength.

The affair lasted three months. Noel felt like a hypocrite sitting in church every Sunday. For his own benefit, he wished the whole town would find out. Everyone would know. They would hate him for awhile, call him vicious names behind his back, and then forget about it. At least then he would have Abigail all to himself. He despised himself for lying and sinning against God and man, but he didn't hate himself when he was in her arms.

For Abby's benefit, he hoped no one ever found out. She loathed their behavior—but like him—she couldn't find the strength within herself to stop. He knew for her sake, it would have to end. Nevertheless, he prayed every night for one more day in her arms.

One day she asked him to meet her in their usual place. As soon as he saw her standing there, his heart sank. This was the day. He wouldn't try to change her mind. It wouldn't be right. Nevertheless he felt as though his world was ending for a second time.

She got straight to the point. "Noel, I'm going to have a baby. Your baby."

For a moment he was elated. Then he realized it wasn't good news.

"I can't keep doing this. Not now," she said. "I'm going to be the wife Jack deserves. I've been praying for the strength to do what we both know needs to be done. I've repented and I'm going to start serving the Lord again."

He put his hand on her cheek. "This isn't another opening for me to sweep you off your feet and carry you out of here, is it?"

"If you did, I think I'd throw up." She smiled wanly. "I love you, Noel Wyatt. I always will."

His face grew serious. "I know. I love you, too. I'm sorry things couldn't be different. I'd give up everything for you and for this baby."

"Don't," she said, "or I'll start crying again. This is for the best.

I've been struggling with it since it started. I take all the blame. I'm the one who went to your house that day. I should have stayed home where I belonged. I'm torn between my love for you and my duty to Jack. Nothing will change the fact that I'm a married woman. Whether it's a good marriage or not doesn't matter. I owe Jack my fidelity. I am so sorry, Noel."

She studied her hands for a long time before looking at him again. "This baby will be raised as Jack's. No one will ever know it doesn't belong to him; not Jack, not my kids. This way, it will just be you and me who have to suffer for what we did."

He looked away, his jaw clenched. His child would be raised by another man. His only chance to carry on the Wyatt name. Abby was out of his life again. This time she was taking his child with her. With bitter resolve he decided he would never have anything to do with another woman. Abby owned him, heart and soul. Loving her had been the most wonderful thing in his life; and the worst.

Noel pulled his car into the parking space behind the drugstore. His space. He had been parking in the same space for twenty-two years. Thanks to wise decisions and a natural business savvy, the family business he inherited from his father had become more successful than the old man could've dreamed. With diet modifications and exercise, he lost the excess weight and kept it off. He was healthy and athletic. His life was full, albeit lonely at times.

The only thing he couldn't claim as his own was redemption.

Forgiveness was there, waiting for him to accept it as a free gift, but it eluded him. He held onto Abby's memory like he had held onto her. He wanted her; not redemption. He would give anything to have her for his own; to change history, to change that day in 1944 when she told him Jack was coming home to marry her. He lived that day over and over in his mind, wishing for all he was worth, he had done everything differently. If only he had opened his mouth...

On the outside he was the same. He went to church, served on the usher board; but not on the council since he didn't qualify without a wife, went to work, and to the country club where he became a member. He was widely respected throughout the community. Every mother in town wanted him for a son-in-law. Little did they know he was hopelessly lost without a Savior. On the inside he was filled with rage. He blamed God for the emptiness in his life. He felt he was a good man—an honest, caring businessman who never cheated anyone out of anything. Wasn't he entitled to the things other men took for granted? Didn't his mother deserve a grandson to keep her family name alive?

One Sunday morning during Sunday School, the Lord spoke to him. He hadn't been paying attention to the lesson. He was there for appearances only. He found himself thumbing through Deuteronomy, a favorite Old Testament book. In the ninth chapter, he read how the Lord was about to send the Israelites over the Jordan to possess the land He had promised them. In verse four, Moses warned them not to say in their hearts the Lord brought them in to possess the land because of their own righteousness. They had done nothing to earn God's grace. Noel continued to read to verse seven where Moses reminded the Israelites how they had provoked the Lord to wrath in the wilderness. From the day they departed out of Egypt until they came to this very place, they had been rebellious against the Lord.

Noel stopped reading, his spirit troubled. He went back to verse four and read the passage again. Over and over he read the verses, knowing there was something in it for him.

The longer he read, the more troubled he became. His vision blurred, and he realized he was crying. Deep in his spirit a gentle voice chastened him.

*"You haven't earned anything by your own righteousness. It is by My grace that you are blessed."*

Noel thought about the words he heard as he reread the passage. The Israelites hadn't earned God's favor by their own righteousness. His favor was given to them because of His goodness and mercy. The still, small voice dealt with him again as he sat on the wooden pew and experienced God's infinite patience and love for him; patience and love he did not deserve.

*"Be thankful, Noel Wyatt, you are not getting what you deserve. The wages of sin is death. That's what you deserve. You have sinned before the Lord. You committed adultery with another man's wife. Her sin has been blotted out; cast into the sea of forgetfulness. Yours remains."*

He couldn't wait until the end of the service when he found his knees on an altar of prayer. He cried openly in the church, surprising everyone. With the release of his tears, flowed the grief, weight, and burden of the sin that had enslaved him for so long.

That day he was forgiven of his sins. His soul was washed whiter than snow. He left the church a new man, redeemed by the blood of the Lamb. He accepted the fact that his son was growing up in another man's home—calling another man, 'Daddy'—as a consequence of the sin he committed. He lived a comfortable life in his comfortable house and wondered quietly about the son he would never know. His forgiveness was complete, but he would always have to live with the consequences of his actions.

He founded the Benjamin Wyatt Memorial Scholarship Fund, in honor of his father, three years before Eric graduated in order to make a way to send his son to college. Other than that, he was totally uninvolved with the boy's life. With each passing day he paid, within his own heart, for the sin he committed. He understood more than anyone why the Bible warned that adultery and fornication were sins against one's own body.

He would never have a family; children and grandchildren. He still got a lump in his throat when he read in Psalm 127, *"children are an heritage of the Lord"* and *"As arrows are in the hand of a mighty man; so are children of thy youth."* He accepted the parts of his life he couldn't change and improved the parts he could. With confidence, he would face his Maker some day and hear the words, "Well done, thou good and faithful servant."

# Chapter Fifteen

The summer progressed like the channel 12 weatherman predicted; with drought-like conditions through June and July. Finally on Thursday morning when Cassie was due back from the Sharboroughs, the skies split open and poured much needed rain on Jenna's Creek and the surrounding community.

Several days before the meteorologists in Columbus predicted rain would again fall on the sun-baked Ohio Valley region, Cory knew the rain was coming. Her joints that had been silent since April began to rage. They awakened her in the middle of the night, her fingers and wrists stiff and drawn. As she hurried about her chores the following day, her aching fingers lost their grip on the feed bag and most of the grain missed the trough, landing on the barn floor instead. Her wrist popped painfully as she lifted the milk buckets from under the cows tied in the stall. Her shoulders wearied from the weight of the water buckets and she had to stop halfway to the garden to set them down for a moment's rest. She searched the sky for the rain clouds, still three days away. Yet she knew they were coming.

Arthritis had plagued her since the boys were in school. Back then, the pain was easily dismissed. She was a strong woman, accustomed to hard work. Pain and discomfort were a part of life for a farmer's wife. As time passed the arthritis worsened, the pain increased, and it became harder to ignore.

No one was aware of how badly she suffered. She took a few aspirin when no one was looking and went on about her business. She never complained, never slowed in her work to nurse aches and pains. She believed that was how people got old—by acting old. It wouldn't happen to her. Old age was something she could not afford to give in to.

When the pain was particularly acute, like it was before a big rain, a worrisome thought would worm its way forward from the back of her mind. What would happen to Harlan if something happened to her? Who would take care of him? Of course Justin and Marty would offer to take him in, and perhaps give him an easier life than the one she provided, but the change might be more than he could handle. He was set in his ways. Even Cory, who understood his moods and temperaments, had a rough time dealing with him sometimes. He would eat sweet-natured Marty alive.

He became irritable at times and was still perplexed that James was gone. He seemed to have forgotten Jesse, who had not been mentioned in the house for nearly forty years, but she wondered sometimes how much he really remembered when he got a faraway look in his eyes. He was visibly dismayed when Jamie spent more time away from the house than in it. When the time came for her to leave for good, Cory knew the routine of emotions he would go through; anger, frustration, loneliness, and finally resignation.

It had been a mistake to let him become so dependent on Jamie. She could see that now. At the time, it seemed harmless. Harlan always loved Jamie more than just about anyone. She was patient and attentive with him, even when she was small and his condition was first showing itself. She had an understanding heart most adults lacked. After Nancy died and the girls came to live on the farm, Jamie took it upon herself to look after her grandpa. Cory supposed the little girl needed to be important in someone's life.

How important she had become to Harlan! When he was petulant, she was the one to get him to do what needed to be done. When he was sick, he called Jamie's name for comfort. Cory's reasons for letting Jamie take over the position as Harlan's primary care-giver were selfish ones. She was tired. She needed a break. When he was demanding Jamie's attention, it gave her a much welcomed rest. Maybe it had not been a good idea, but the damage was done now.

He would never understand what became of Cory if the Lord took her first. She could imagine him sitting by the front window, looking out, waiting for her return. Vanity had nothing to do with her assumption. She just knew how his mind worked.

She hated it when her mind started wandering in this direction. It was because of the rain. She had too much time to sit around and think about her future and about Harlan's. Tomorrow he had an appointment at the V.A. hospital. That would make her think even more; going from one waiting room to the next, consulting with doctors, arguing with nurses, and enduring Harlan's tempestuous outbursts. At least with the rain still coming down, there wouldn't be much she could get done around the farm anyway. It was as good a day as any to waste feeling sorry for herself at a hospital.

Thursday morning—while the rain continued to fall and Hank Williams belted out the immortal question, Why don't you love me like you used to do? on Harlan's record player—Cory scrubbed the kitchen from floor to ceiling. There was little to do outside in this weather, so at least today she could clean the house like it had been begging for all summer. Besides, Maggie Sharborough was coming to visit. She was no better than Cory, had never professed to be, but she had a nice big house in a nice neighborhood with everything she could want. It only came after years of struggling for her and her husband. Cory didn't begrudge them that. But she'd be lying if she didn't admit deep down in her heart it bothered her that by all appearances Nancy Sharborough had married down when she accepted James Steele's marriage proposal. Although she was positive the Sharboroughs didn't see things that way, she didn't want to give them a reason to think the Steeles weren't as proud and hard-working as they were.

By the time she finished with her cleaning, the kitchen glistened in the artificial light above her head. The rain had stopped but low, threatening clouds gave the appearance of night.

In the living room, Hank Williams continued to bemoan his love's cold, cold heart—as if the weather wasn't depressing enough. She thought about going in and shutting off the record player. There would be the devil to pay if she did. She yearned for Harlan to develop a different taste in music, but it wasn't likely. Not after all these years. Harlan would be the same until the day he died.

For the thousandth time she missed the man she married. He was strong, handsome and virile back then. He promised her the moon, and spent most of his adult life trying to deliver it. Then he just got old. The doctors said his mind was deteriorating faster than his body. "Senile Dementia" they called it. Didn't that mean demented? Insane? What a terrible way to describe the finest man God ever put on earth. Her husband was old. He had a disease. That didn't make him crazy.

The disease took some people quickly she was told. They were the lucky ones. Harlan had been suffering now for years. Of course, he wasn't suffering nearly as much as the people who loved him. If only the Lord had taken him in the beginning. She wouldn't have to worry about what would become of him now if something happened to her. She would've been left with her memories and only the girls to care for. Now she was just old and tired.

The sound of a car in the driveway brought her out of her reverie. Her spirit was as heavy as the clouds in the sky, and just as dark. She put the teakettle on to boil and went to greet her granddaughter. Seeing Cassie was sure to lighten the oppressive mood that settled over her.

The rain had started again just as Jamie left the drugstore. Grandma Cory had insisted she take the truck to work this morning, knowing it would be pouring outside by the time she got off work. Jamie wondered if she might also still be feeling sorry for her that Tate stood her up the other night. Whatever. It sure did beat walking. The truck's defroster took forever to warm up and driving was terribly slow. By the time she got from the truck to the back porch, her hair and clothes were plastered to her body. Despite her condition, she rushed into the house beaming. Now that Cassie was home, she realized how lonesome the place had been without her.

The evening found the sisters sprawled across Jamie's twin-size bed, listening to the rain beat a steady tattoo on the roof as they filled each other in on what they'd been up to.

Jamie told Cassie about her job, but kept the part about Tate and how he stood her up to herself. She wasn't ready for her kid sister to tell her what a dope she was for letting a boy run all over her. Jamie always felt like the immature little sister when it came to matters between boys and girls. At only thirteen, Cassie was the one who understood how those things worked. She would read Jamie the riot act when she found out how Tate got away with treating her so badly.

Jamie hadn't seen anything of him at the drugstore since Monday, so she hadn't gotten a chance to talk to him yet. After she heard his explanation—she was sure he had a good one—she might admit to Cassie she had a little bit of a crush on him.

When Jamie told Noel that Cassie was back home from her other grandparents, he gave her Friday and the weekend off. It was the longest stretch she'd had without working all summer.

Friday was spent on the farm catching up on chores. The barn was cleaned out. Fallen sticks and limbs from the storm were gathered from the yard and pasture and piled up to be burned later in the season, after they dried out enough. The garden was weeded and hoed and thirty-five jars of tomatoes and green beans were canned and taken to the cellar for storage.

It was nearly midnight before the girls stumbled up the stairs to bed. Once again, they met in Jamie's room after their baths to talk.

"I thought I missed being home." Cassie collapsed on the bed, her hair leaving a wet spot on Jamie's pillow.

"I thought I was on vacation." Jamie landed beside her and both girls laughed.

"There's going to be more tomatoes and beans ready at the first of the week," Cassie moaned.

"And cucumbers. Don't forget the cucumbers."

"Ugh! Doesn't she ever get tired of making pickles?" Grandma Cory's collection of jars in the basement contained nearly every pickle variety known to the free world. "How many can one family eat?"

"Obviously a lot," Jamie said. "With all this rain, we're going to be swimming in cucumbers. You should see the slaw she's already put up."

"I think I'll call Grandma Maggie and tell her I'm ready to go back."

"Oh no, you don't," Jamie warned. "You're not leaving me here alone again."

"You can come with me this time."

"No, thanks. I'm starting to enjoy myself at the drugstore." Jamie rolled over on the mattress and stared up at the ceiling. "I wonder what she has in store for us tomorrow," she mused.

"Surely we'll get the day off."

"Don't be so sure. You know how she gets this time of year. 'You've got to make hay while the sun still shines'." Her imitation of Grandma Cory was flawless.

"Don't mention hay," Cassie wailed. "Remember what that was like?"

Both sisters shuddered at the memory of those summers putting up hay. Cassie and Jamie were too little to stay at the house by themselves back then. There was no one to stay with them so they went to the fields with the adults. While their tender skin fried in the summer sun, they would ride on the tractor or sit perched at the top of the growing pile of hay bales. Nancy and Cory took turns driving the tractor while James, Grandpa Harlan, and whoever wasn't driving threw the bails of hay onto the wagon. A local youth was usually hired at slave wages to help out with the back-breaking job.

One such day, with the wagon loaded as high as it would go and the group seated precariously on top, Nancy headed the tractor for the barn. She backed the wagon up against the barn under the loft door. James and the hired boy climbed into the barn loft. Cory and Harlan climbed to the highest point on the wagon and began to hand the bales inside to be stacked in the loft. Cassie climbed down the side of the wagon to get out of the way. Neither James or Cory had patience for children underfoot. Jamie wasn't quick enough.

As Harlan lifted a bale from the stack and handed it up to James, a six-foot long, field-mouse fed, black snake fell from the bale and landed in Jamie's lap. Jamie screamed at a decibel-level that would shatter glass while the black snake recovered from its rude awakening. Grandma Cory reached down and plucked the big snake from the child's lap and tossed it over the side of the wagon.

"Oh, hush up," she snapped. "You shouldn't've been there in the first place."

Tears of shock from the snake's sudden appearance and hurt from her grandma's words, spilled down Jamie's sunburned cheeks as she stood up on wobbly legs. She could still feel the weight of the snake on her lap. She spotted her dad watching from the loft doorway, understanding in his eyes.

"Hey, Jamie. You had yourself a big'un there, didn't ya?" He winked and laughed. Jamie relaxed and laughed too.

"Maybe if we get up early and make breakfast," Cassie suggested after Jamie's retelling of the story, "we can butter Grandma up. Then when we ask to do something fun, she'll give in."

"Maybe you should ask her then," Jamie said.

"Why me?"

"Because she'll be more likely to say yes to you than me."

"What makes you think that?"

"She likes you more than she does me. Everybody knows that. And she's still in a good mood about you being home."

"You're crazy. Grandma doesn't like me more. She just likes to act cranky. It's part of her charm."

"Maybe. I just think we have a better chance if you ask. You know me and Grandma don't get along that well."

Cassie slapped the pillow to make a point. "That's because the two of you are so much alike."

"We're not alike at all," Jamie exclaimed. "Grandma never wants to talk. She's always busy working on something, and she's always in a bad mood."

Cassie laughed. "Jamie, you just described yourself."

"I did not."

"Yes, you did. You'd rather work than hang out with your friends… if you even have any. You're serious all the time. All the kids at school think you're a snob. You're just like Uncle Justin and he's just like Grandma Cory. That's why the two of you can't get along."

Jason had told her she was a snob too, but what did either of them know about anything? "I still say if you want to go somewhere tomorrow, you'll have to be the one to ask Grandma about it."

"Fine, I'll ask her. I'm not afraid of her."

Jamie crawled under the blanket and closed her eyes. "Well then, get off my bed. If we're going to do something tomorrow, I need my sleep. And get the light on your way out."

Cassie's plan worked just like she predicted. They arose at six-thirty and hurried downstairs to fix breakfast. Grandma Cory heard them from her room and came out to investigate. She didn't say anything as she walked past them and outside to milk Windy and Amelia. When she came back in, the table was set and breakfast was waiting.

The smell of sausage and biscuits lured Grandpa Harlan downstairs earlier than usual.

Cory washed her hands and seated herself at her end of the table. She asked the blessing and said, "Looks good, girls."

They smiled across the table at each other and began to eat. They didn't know if it was the food, the clean kitchen, or the long hours of work they put in the day before that prompted a quick affirmative answer from Grandma Cory when Cassie asked if they could get away from the farm for the day. She didn't ask for an explanation of their plans or even when they would be home, which was good since they hadn't worked out the details yet.

"Just give me your help until ten o'clock," she said, "to finish the morning's chores and do up these dishes. Then you can have the rest of the day to yourselves."

The girls were delighted. They jumped up and kissed her on opposite cheeks. "Thank you, Grandma. Oh, thank you," they gushed.

She dismissed them with a wave of her hand. "Good lands. Don't go gettin' all tore up about it. It's not that big of a deal."

# Chapter Sixteen

The back seat of Grandma Cory's car was loaded with bags and packages when Jamie and Cassie pulled into the gravel driveway and parked next to Uncle Justin's Ford. It had been a long, hot afternoon, the humidity was unbearable after all the rain. The car had no air conditioning and both girls looked like they'd lost ten pounds each. Regardless, their spirits were high.

Aunt Marty threw the door open and rushed out to meet them with the enthusiasm of a teenager. She locked Cassie in a fierce embrace. "Oh, honey, I'm so glad you're home."

"It's good to see you too, Aunt Marty. Come see what we bought."

Cory was right in figuring the girls would run out of money before they thought to stop somewhere for lunch. After they left the house that morning, she called Marty and Justin to tell them Cassie was home, and invited them to dinner. By the time Jamie and Cassie deposited their packages on their beds and got back downstairs, their stomachs rumbling, the table was set and loaded with enough food to rival Thanksgiving dinner.

Cassie monopolized the conversation during dinner, as was her custom, with the same stories she told Grandma, Grandpa, and Jamie the night before; along with a few new ones from their shopping excursion. No one seemed to mind. Without her animated chatter, meals were often about nothing more than the consumption of food.

She was still talking after the dinner dishes were washed, dried, and put away. Grandpa Harlan stopped listening, out of sheer exhaustion, and went into the living room to watch television. Grandma Cory suggested that Cassie take her and Aunt Marty upstairs to show them her purchases; to give the girl a new subject to talk about.

A pronounced silence hung in the kitchen after Cassie's departure. Uncle Justin and Jamie sighed in relief. Jamie dried the draining rack with a towel and put it under the sink. She pulled out a kitchen chair and sat down across from Uncle Justin.

"She had to get that from the Sharborough side of the family," he smiled wearily. "There isn't a Steele alive who can carry on like that."

"I think you're right," Jamie agreed. "The Sharboroughs love to talk."

They sat in silence for a few minutes enjoying the respite. Since going to work at the drugstore, Jamie barely had time to think about her dad and Sally Blake, let alone look for answers to her questions. Sitting across from Uncle Justin now, brought all of them flooding back to her. She dreaded turning to him for answers, but he was probably the only chance she had to find out anything new. July was nearly gone and another opportunity such as this one might not present itself. She'd have to talk fast before Grandma Cory came back downstairs.

"Uncle Justin," she began hesitantly, "did Aunt Marty tell you anything about what she and I were talking about the day of Dad's funeral?"

"Do you mean about your dad and Sally Blake?" he said without hesitation. He had obviously been waiting for this moment.

"Yes. She told me you found out about Sally and were wanting some answers."

"If you knew I wanted to talk about it, why didn't you say anything?" Jamie asked.

"I figured you would come to me when you were ready."

All this time she had been afraid to approach Uncle Justin and he'd been waiting on her. He reminded her of Jason. Why couldn't men just say what was on their minds without waiting for an invitation? Did they always have to make things so difficult?

"So, what can you tell me about them?" she asked.

"What do you want to know?"

"Everything. As much as you know. Tell me who she was, how Dad got mixed up with her, what really happened to her; and most importantly, tell me why everyone thinks he did something to her."

"You're not asking for much, are you?" He smiled teasingly, but she was too tense to appreciate it. "All right. I suppose I should start at the beginning. I warn you, it could take a while."

"Your dad loved Sally Blake for years," Justin began. "Since elementary school, Sally was the one girl he couldn't have. Maybe that's why he was so fascinated by her. He always had girlfriends. He could get any girl he wanted, and he never dated the same one for very long. I guess you could say he had kind of a bad boy reputation, but it didn't seem to matter to anybody. The more girls he dated, the worse his reputation got, and the more popular he became.

"Not me though." He smiled at the memory. "I was terrified of girls. I could never figure out how James did it. He was two grades ahead of me, but it's a small school so we saw a lot of each other. I would see him in the halls between classes or having lunch with his friends. He was at ease in any situation. He didn't get good grades but everybody liked him, even the teachers. I guess they enjoyed his clowning around too, as long as it didn't go too far. He could always sense when it was time to back off. He would even walk down the hall with the principal sometimes, the two of them going on like they were old friends.

"Don't get me wrong. He got in trouble a lot. He got in fights with boys, who the day before had been his best friends. He got his face slapped by girls he dated more times than I can remember. He had detention at least once a week and Mom was called in pretty regularly for conferences. That's the part I couldn't understand. He was loved one minute and hated the next. How did he keep it balanced? But he was cool. He had it all together. Everybody wanted to be his friend. There was only one girl who wasn't impressed with him."

"Sally Blake," Jamie interjected.

He nodded. "Right, Sally Blake." She was a world apart from every other girl at South Auburn High School. Her family had money and power in the county and they didn't raise their little girl to be a mouse. She wouldn't take anything off anybody. She knew who she was and what she wanted. Oh, she liked James like everyone else did. He was funny, handsome, and had that certain quality high school girls can't resist. But unlike everybody else, she used him instead of the other way around. I think she was aware of the hold she had on him and took advantage of it."

"What do you mean?"

Justin didn't answer right away. He leaned back in his chair and stretched his arms over his head. Jamie began to grow impatient. She wanted to repeat her question, but knew it would be pointless. After a few minutes thought, he continued.

"It's hard to explain if you didn't know Sally. I didn't really know her that well myself. I just observed her at school. She was ahead of James by a year, so that put her way ahead of me. She wouldn't have spoken to me if she'd tripped over me. Kids like me didn't get noticed by kids like Sally. That's what always puzzled me. Why did some poor kids from the wrong side of the tracks, like James, fit into the 'popular' crowd when the rest of us didn't?"

Jamie smiled to herself. She too often wondered what labeled some kids "popular" and others "invisible."

"Sally was a real mystery to me. If you didn't serve her purpose, then you weren't worth her time. You know what I mean?"

"I think so. There are girls like that at every school."

"You're right, but Sally was different. She had the whole thing down to an art. Everything she did was to further the purpose she set up for herself. Sally only made friends with kids who could benefit her in some way. She played up to certain teachers who she thought may do something for her later on. If you were smart, you could always tell where you stood with her. She didn't waste her time on you unless you had something she wanted. The only problem was, no one was smart enough to see through her. She had everyone fooled, or at least I thought she did, until the night she disappeared."

"That's what I don't understand, Uncle Justin. What happened that night? I can't find any real details. Everything I've read is so vague."

"That's because nobody knew what happened. No one knows to this day. Only Sally knew for sure; and the person who killed... I mean the person involved in her disappearance. I'm still not convinced she's dead. If it suited her to take off and never let anyone know, then that's what she'd've done."

"But surely she wouldn't leave her mom and dad without letting them know she was all right—especially after all this time?"

"Probably not. But how are we supposed to know what goes on in another person's head. As I've gotten older, I've learned there are some people who'll do just about anything, even if it doesn't make sense to anyone else. They rationalize their actions in their own minds and they think that makes it all right. Look at the mess society has gotten itself into today. 'Do your own thing', they say. 'As long as it doesn't hurt anyone else, then it's okay'."

"But it isn't okay, is it?" Jamie asked, worry creasing her brow. "The Bible hasn't changed. Don't we have to follow its absolute truths, regardless of what society is saying?"

"That's what we believe, yes. But society today is teaching there are no absolute truths. You make up your own truths as you go along to fit your circumstances at the time. If something is right in your eyes, who am I to come along and say it's wrong? You have the right to decide for yourself what's truth and what isn't."

"But that isn't right," she said adamantly. "The Bible has said the same thing for centuries. How can it suddenly change because society wants it to?"

Justin covered her hand with his. "It hasn't changed, sweetheart. Man has changed. We don't want to be told what to do; so the modern thing is to challenge the Bible and everything it represents. Society says God is dead. The principles written out in His Word are considered old-fashioned and judgmental by today's standards."

Tears of frustration and fear glistened in the corners of Jamie's eyes. "But if that's true and God is dead, then why are any of us here? What is our purpose for being on this earth? How'd we get here?"

"That's what scientists have been trying to figure out since Darwin. They've wasted years and millions of tax dollars trying to understand what has been in the Bible all along. They will never find their answers by studying rocks and the stars, because God isn't dead. All you need is faith to believe that, Jamie. Don't ever let anyone take that away from you. You'll get out in the world some day and your faith will be challenged, but stand firm in your beliefs. God has a divine purpose for each life on this planet. It may not look that way all the time, but who are we to challenge His wisdom? He's God. He knows what He's doing. He's not up in heaven looking down on us and wringing His hands and saying, 'Oh, no, they don't believe in Me anymore. What will I do? Should I send plagues of locusts down on them so they'll know I'm still here? Should I strike those nay-sayers with bolts of lightening?'."

"I would if I was Him," Jamie stated. "I'd let them know I was up there and I wasn't happy."

"But His Word has already done that. Remember the parable of Lazarus and the rich man? The rich man asked Abraham if he could send one from the dead to tell his evil brothers to repent before it was too late. But Abraham told him if they wouldn't listen to Moses and the prophets, they wouldn't listen to one risen from the dead."

"I think they'd've listened if someone came to them from the dead."

Justin smiled gently. "No, they wouldn't. Jesus was referring to himself. He rose from the dead, and most of the world still hasn't listened."

Justin was quiet for a moment while Jamie digested his words.

"You or I would never dream of leaving without letting anyone know what became of us," he said. "I couldn't hurt Marty like that. I know she loves me and she'd be out of her mind with worry. But there are people who only think of themselves. Now, I'm not saying that's what Sally Blake did. I'm just saying it's been known to happen and it could've happened in this case."

"What do you know about that night?" Jamie asked him again. "Did Dad ever tell you anything? Could he have been…" her voice trailed off. She didn't have the nerve to ask him the question that had troubled her all summer.

"Well, now," Uncle Justin said slowly, stalling, as if deciding which parts of the story to tell her and which ones to leave out. "It's been such a long time. James had dated Sally a few times. Nothing serious. I think she was stringing him along for a few laughs. Like I said, she knew he was crazy about her. But it was serious to your dad. He was in love with her. I think he'd've done anything for her."

"What if he figured out she wasn't serious about him? Could he've been mad enough to…?"

"I don't know, Jamie. This town's been speculating about it for twenty-five years. Let me tell you about what I do know."

She clamped her mouth shut, determined not to interrupt again.

"They were going to a party that night with two of Sally's friends, Tim Shelton and Noreen Trimble."

Jamie couldn't keep quiet. "Noreen Trimble!" she burst out, "Quiet, shy Noreen Trimble who works behind the pharmacy counter at the drugstore?"

Justin laughed at her reaction. "That's her. She wasn't always a pharmacist's assistant, you know. At one time, she was a sweet, old-fashioned girl interested in nothing more than talking on the telephone and giggling about boys with her friends."

"I suppose so. It's just hard to imagine."

"Noreen and Tim were quite an item back then. Everybody thought they'd get married some day. But after Sally disappeared, they just... I don't know... they fizzled out, I guess you could say. It was a shame too. Noreen wasn't the same after she broke up with Tim.

"But anyway, Sally, Tim, and Noreen were best friends. They were always together. It didn't make much sense. Them being so close, I mean. Tim's family owned a big dairy farm north of town. They had some money, I guess. but not a lot. Noreen's dad, on the other hand, was the pastor of the Nazarene church; not exactly a country club member either. I never understood their relationship at all. I don't know what they could've had in common. Noreen didn't fit the mold of Sally's other girlfriends.

"For whatever reason, they spent a lot of time together, the three of them. Tim loved Noreen, or at least, that's what it looked like, and Sally was always tagging along behind. She usually had a different fellow to make it a foursome. At this particular time, the fourth fellow was James.

"They dated for about a month, always the four of them. James wasn't happy about the arrangement. He wanted to be alone with Sally. But if she'd told him their next date was going to be on the moon, he would've gone. He was so happy to finally have her attention, he'd do whatever it took to please her.

"That night they went to a party; an engagement party a bunch of them put together for Noreen and Tim. James told me later, Sally was acting strange all night, like she was looking for a fight. Your dad was never one to back down from a fight, so I guess they got into it pretty hot and heavy more than once. It wasn't much of a big deal since they had fought before. She was a hothead just like he was. He said it was one of the things he liked about Sally. He could never predict when they were going to get into it about something. She was a challenge, he said.

"According to him, that night was the worst he'd ever seen Sally. Everyone at the party was drinking heavily and Sally started flirting with several other men there. I mean, really coming onto them. Their girlfriends didn't like it and neither did James. She was fooling around with some guy… I can't remember who, and his girlfriend got all worked up. I guess she and Sally exchanged a few heated words. Sally laughed it off, but the other girl was furious. I think they were close to coming to blows themselves before James stepped between them."

Jamie leaned forward in her chair. "Who was the other girl?"

Uncle Justin shrugged. "I don't know if I ever heard who she was. She went to the college with Sally and her friends. I don't know if she even lived in Auburn County."

Jamie tried not to get too disappointed. The girl's identity probably didn't mean anything anyway.

"After your dad got between them," Uncle Justin continued, "he told Sally to settle down and behave herself before she got into trouble. Maybe he said a little more than that because Sally slapped his face and cussed at him. Right there in front of everybody, he slapped her back. The whole room got deathly quiet. Then Sally started screaming and cussing and swinging at him. He twisted her arms behind her back to keep her from hitting him again. He was cussing and yelling just as much as she was. I guess they knocked over a lamp and a table of food and drinks. They made quite a mess before he dragged her out of the house.

"Everybody there witnessed the whole thing. They watched James physically drag her to his car, both of them fighting and screaming the whole way. Even as they were driving away, they could hear Sally screaming at him from inside the car."

Jamie sat in stunned silence. Finally she found her voice. "And no one saw her after that?"

"Right. The next morning her parents called the police and said Sally hadn't come home from her date. Her bed had not been slept in."

"What did Dad say about it? Didn't he take her home?"

"Not exactly. It wasn't until after he was arrested that he would talk to me about that night. He acted very strange after she disappeared. He didn't talk to me, Mom or anybody. I know that's what made so many people think he was guilty. You couldn't blame them. I still don't know if he told me the whole story."

"So he was actually put in jail?" Jamie was horrified.

"Yes. The Prosecutor was under pressure from the Blake family to make an arrest in the case. The investigation wasn't going well. All they had was circumstantial evidence against James, but there was a lot of it. He was arrested and held for a short time, although they really didn't have the right to hold him at all. Mom got hold of a lawyer from Portsmouth who said they had to formally charge him or release him. So they let him go.

"Jenna's Creek was in an uproar. The whole town thought he was guilty. We got death threats at the house. Mrs. Blake even called and begged Mom to make James tell her what he did with Sally. And James was no help, he acted like it was a big joke. He practically thumbed his nose at the Blake family. Underneath though, you could tell he was scared. One night after an obscene phone call, he broke down and told me his version of what happened.

"He said after he and Sally left the party, he drove around for a long time. They stopped at a carry-out and bought a cheap bottle of wine. Of course, when questioned by the police, no one from the carry-out could remember them stopping in. James said he got Sally to drinking again and that calmed her down. They went parking on some deserted country road. He said he had no idea how late it was by that time. It must have been early in the morning when he was finally ready to take her home. But she didn't want to go home. She wanted to go back to the party. She said she'd just spend the night there at the house with Noreen. He was tired by this time, and especially tired of listening to her, so he did what she wanted."

Jamie and Uncle Justin turned their heads toward the front of the house when they heard Grandma Cory and Aunt Marty coming down the stairs. Uncle Justin went to the refrigerator and poured himself a glass of tea. Jamie listened as they moved into the living room and sat down in front of the television. Uncle Justin was waiting too. When it was obvious that they were not coming into the kitchen, he continued talking, his voice slightly lowered.

"When they got back to the house—it belonged to some relatives of Noreen's, they were out of town or something—there were still lights on and they could hear music coming from the house. James was so drunk, he didn't pay any attention as to who was still there. The police asked him later and he said he didn't know. He could see lights in some of the windows through the trees and he could hear music playing. The only car he remembered seeing was Noreen's. It was parked in front of an old barn or shed or something like that a little ways from the house. He dropped Sally off at the end of the lane close to where Noreen's car was parked and drove away. He was so sick of her harping at him, he didn't go in the house with her. He wanted her out of his hair so he could go home and go to bed. So who knows? What happened from the time he let her out of the car and she made it into the house, is anybody's guess."

"Did they ever find out who was still at the party?"

"They interviewed everyone. The last ones to leave the party said James never came back. They said they never saw Sally come in again either. Noreen said she never left the house; she was there all night. She never saw Sally come back. So who were the police supposed to believe. After all, James' story was pretty flimsy."

"But what about that other girl? The one who was arguing with Sally. Did anyone think she may be mad enough to do something to Sally?"

"Not really. She was just a girl at the party who didn't want Sally hanging all over her boyfriend. Anybody would've reacted the way she did."

"But they should have looked into the possibility that she could have done something to her. I mean if no one knew her that well… her being from out of town and all, maybe she was capable of more than anyone knew about."

"The only one the authorities were interested in was James. The evidence was against him. She would have just been a long shot."

Jamie sat back in her chair sick to her stomach. She wanted to believe the unknown girl had a score to settle with Sally, but even to her, it didn't seem likely. She could see why the authorities never gave her a second glance. In a small voice, she said, "It does look like Dad's guilty. Is it possible he could've…"

Justin didn't answer right away. The silence between them lengthened. "Jamie," he said finally, "we may never know what happened to Sally. It may look like you're Dad was guilty, but remember, the police couldn't make a case against him. No matter how it looks, it's still all circumstantial."

"But what else could have happened then?"

"I know it looks bad, honey. But I know my brother. He was a lot of things. He had a reputation for being rough, but I can't accept that he was a murderer. I honestly don't think he was capable of that."

"I wish I was as confident as you, Uncle Justin. You probably knew him better than I did, but I saw what he did to Mom. I know how bad his temper was. The littlest thing could set him off. I can't help thinking he was capable of just about anything."

Justin looked mournfully at his hands. He didn't respond.

"I have to know for sure. I have to find out what happened to Sally."

"I understand why you need to know, really I do. For a long time the rest of us felt the same way you do now. Mom kept every newspaper clipping she could get her hands on in a shoe box in her room. She went over them with a fine tooth comb trying to find some discrepancy, anything that would prove James didn't do it. There was just nothing to find. You have to remember the most important fact in the case. They never found a body. The police couldn't make an arrest because of that simple fact. And we can't convict him either—even in our minds. It doesn't make it any easier to sleep at night, but that's the way it is. And maybe I don't want to know the truth. Maybe I'm afraid of it."

Jamie nodded, understanding his meaning. She wasn't sure she could live with the truth either, if it turned out her worst fears were realized.

# Chapter Seventeen

Grandpa Harlan's appointment at the Veteran's Hospital in Chillicothe was first thing Monday morning. Jamie claimed she wanted to sleep in. She was afraid Cassie would decide to stay home too, but at the last minute she said she was going with them. Just as expected, Cassie couldn't stand being cooped up on the farm even though she'd only been home less than a week. Whenever she got a chance to leave Jenna's Creek and Auburn County, she grabbed it.

Jamie waited in her room until she heard the car back out of the driveway and start down Betterman Road. She bounded out of bed and hurried downstairs to look out the front window to make sure they were gone. The driveway was empty, the front yard deserted. She had at least three hours to find what she was looking for.

Her curiosity had been piqued by Uncle Justin's words. She finally knew something about Sally Blake and the relationship she had with her father. Still, there was more to learn. She had to know what happened to her. Uncle Justin thought it was possible she was still alive. Had she been murdered like the whole town suspected? What about James? Had his story to Uncle Justin been completely honest? How much of the truth had he left out to make himself look innocent?

Anticipation spurred her along as she moved quickly to Grandma Cory's room. She flicked on the light, dispelling the gloom that shadowed the room. She glanced over her shoulder one last time, fearful that somebody in the car realized they had forgotten something and had come back to retrieve it. If Grandma Cory found her in here, snooping around… she shuddered, not wanting to think about what would become of her.

She went immediately to the closet. Her grandma was a fanatic about organization. Jamie knew that if the shoe box of newspaper clippings Uncle Justin told her about still existed, it would be stored somewhere in this closet, probably in a neat chronologically ordered stack. She knelt on the floor and began to go through boxes, starting with the stack that looked like it had been there the longest. Most of the shoe boxes were quickly dismissed, actually containing shoes. Others were full to overflowing with canceled checks from the bank dating as far back as the 1950's. *What would possess someone to save checks written to the gas company and Ohio Bell for twenty years?* she wondered. She set each box aside, making sure they would go back into the closet in the same order as they had come out. That was her grandma, a pack rat almost to the point of obsession. It was a good sign though. If she'd keep old phone bills, she'd surely hang on to the newspaper clippings as well.

It only took thirty minutes of searching before she found the one she was looking for on the floor of the closet. It had been pushed way to the back and was under a box of owners' manuals and warranties for everything from the deep freeze, purchased from Sears in 1958, to a Huffy bicycle Cassie outgrew when she was ten. Jamie's heart skipped a beat when she opened the lid and saw old newspaper clippings inside. She sat on the edge of the bed and carefully spread the clippings in a semi-circle in front of her.

Many of the clippings were of no interest. There were obituaries of long-gone relatives and neighbors, wedding announcements, recipes, and how-to articles on gardening and crocheting that Grandma Cory couldn't bring herself to throw away. She laid them aside in orderly piles, being careful to leave no evidence of her invasion. She turned over a partial article about rising interest rates and saw the, now-familiar, face of Sally Blake staring up at her.

Jamie gazed at the grainy, newspaper-quality photograph and wondered what made James Steele fall in love with her? According to everything Jamie had heard, he had his pick of most of the girls in Jenna's Creek. There had to be more to his attraction to Sally than her appearance. Was she funny? Clever? Mysterious? What made her irresistible? Why was she the one girl Uncle Justin said Dad had to have?

A disturbing thought occurred to her. What if he never got over Sally Blake? If she was the one true love of his life, did he still love her when he married Nancy? It would explain so much of his cruel behavior toward her. If he had still been in love with Sally, maybe he was unable to treat her with the love and respect a wife deserved from her husband.

"Don't make excuses for him!" she shrieked at the walls in the quiet bedroom. "He had no right to treat Mom the way he did. She deserved to be treated like a human being, whether he loved another woman or not."

She wiped angrily at the tears rolling down her cheeks. She wouldn't waste her time beating that dead horse. She had already spent too much time over the years wishing her parents were like other parents; a loving, attentive father and a smiling, contented mother. It had never been that way and it was too late now to wish it was.

She focused her attention on the scrap of paper in her hand. It was the same article she found at the library announcing Sally's disappearance. She reread it carefully, hoping to glean some sort of clue from the short, succinct sentences, wishing she could find something the authorities had missed, something to prove they were incompetent, and that James was wrongfully accused.

No such clue existed. She went on to the next article, one she had never seen before. It was dated *February 1, 1948*. The headline read; *SUSPECT RELEASED.*

The article told of the circumstantial evidence against James Steele. The Prosecutor regrettably announced that the authorities could find no physical evidence against the suspect and he was being released. By the tone of the article and the Prosecutor's comments, it was obvious to Jamie that he thought he was sending a guilty man back into the community.

She couldn't entirely blame the people of Jenna's Creek for their opinions of her father. No wonder most of them thought he was guilty after reading the slanted articles the newspaper printed. The media had done a good job of trying and convicting him before he ever went to trial. Had she been around in 1948, with a family of her own, wouldn't she have wanted to know of the possibility of a killer living in her midst? She would warn her children and start locking her doors at night. If she met James Steele on the street, she would probably cross to the other side to avoid him.

The next clipping her fingers found was dated three months later. It was from the social page, obviously submitted by Cory, announcing James' graduation from Basic Training at the Great Lakes Naval Academy.

Jamie knew he had been in the Navy for several years before he met and married her mother, but she didn't know he had been practically driven out of town by an angry mob. Was his decision to enlist an indication of guilt? She was sure the town, particularly the Prosecutor, thought so. Was he simply looking for a fresh start away from Jenna's Creek and all its questions and suspicions?

What if he was innocent? What if the Prosecutor had no leads in the investigation, but the Blake family was pressuring him to do something, anything? The commissioner and mayor were breathing down his neck. He was handed James Steele in a neat little package. All his problems were solved. If he got a conviction, all the good citizens of Jenna's Creek could sleep peacefully at night again, and of course, a successful career in the local political arena would be his for the taking. How much did it matter to him if James was guilty or not?

She looked over the February 18th article again until she found the Prosecutor's name. David Davis. *What was Mrs. Davis thinking when she gave her little boy a name like that?* Jamie shook her head to chase away her stray observation and forced herself, instead, to concentrate on what was really important. Was the man still alive? He may have been a doddering old litigator in 1948 and now long in his grave. On the other hand, he might've been a young hotshot attorney trying to make a name for himself and still living in Auburn County today. Mrs. Wyatt was sure to know all about David Davis. Jamie would give her a telephone call as soon as she restored Grandma Cory's room to its original, tidy condition. She looked through the remaining articles, but found nothing she didn't already know from talking to Uncle Justin.

As she carefully placed the box's contents back in their proper position, her fingers felt a thick packet at the bottom of the box. She withdrew several letters held together by a yellow hair ribbon. She carefully untied the ribbon. Masculine handwriting was scrawled across the pages. She unfolded the first letter and read the salutation: *"My beloved Sally,"* she gasped and scanned to the bottom of the page. *"Love, James."*

Waves of guilt caused her hands to tremble as she started to refold the letter. She had no problem at all digging through Grandma Cory's closet to find the newspaper clippings about the case. The newspaper was a matter of public record, printed for anyone interested to read. But these letters—love letters obviously—were off limits to her. The letters were meant for Sally's eyes only. She didn't have the right to be invading her privacy like this after all these years.

But how did they come to be in Grandma Cory's closet?

Her eyes stole to the top line of the letter. *"It seems like so long since I saw you last. I can't believe it was only last week."*

The lines lacked eloquence, but they professed James' feelings for Sally. Jamie knew she should read no further, but she was unable to make herself stop. She uneasily read the awkward phrases and youthful professions of love. It bothered her to think of her dad in love with a woman other than her mother. For the first time, she began to almost hate Sally Blake.

Against her better judgment, she went on to the next letter, its tone entirely different from the first.

> *Dear Sally,*
>
> *I'm sorry about the other night. I didn't mean it. You just make me so crazy sometimes. You know I love you. I love you so much. I never want to hurt you. But when you treat me so bad it isn't my fault what I do. Please forgive me. I'll do anything for you. I want to make you happy. You are all that matters to me. If I ever lost you, I don't know what I'd do. I can't live without you. I love you. I hope you believe me. Please call me. I'll be at Mike's Friday night. If I don't hear from you before then, please meet me there.*
>
> *Love always, James*

A wave of nausea washed over Jamie. She had heard James' *"forgive me's"* and *"I'm sorry's"* more times than she cared to count over the years. Only then they had been directed at her mother. Nancy was

the one with a bruised cheek or black eye. He would beg for forgiveness, though never accept the blame, and it would inevitably happen
again. According to his letter to Sally, Nancy had not been his first
victim. By the time she came along, James was obviously an old hand
at asking for forgiveness from the women he claimed to love, but ul-
timately caused pain.

The third letter was by far the most disturbing. By the time Jamie
finished reading it, her hands were shaking so badly, she could barely
make out the words.

*Dear Sally,*

*I told you the other night what I would do if I saw you
with him again. I'll kill you both. If you think I'm kidding,
just try me. I love you, Sally. Can't you see that? Even though
we fight, I know you love me too. Why are you always trying
to make a fool of me? If you know what's good for you, you'll
stop seeing him. Stop talking to our friends about my temper.
Everything I do is your fault. You make me so mad. I can't help
myself. No man likes to be made a fool of. I love you, Sally, and
I want you. If I can't have you, no one will. I'll kill you with
my bare hands if I have to. I swear I will. You're mine, Sally.
You belong to me. I promise I'll make you happy someday. I
will give you everything you want. Just don't see him anymore
or I'll make you sorry.*

*Eternally yours, James*

It was the rantings of a madman; a man capable of murder. Of
that Jamie had no doubt. No wonder Grandma Cory hid the letters
in the bottom of her closet. If they'd ever gotten into the Prosecutor's
hands, James would have been convicted. This was the physical evidence the police needed.

What man was James referring to in the letter? Who had Sally
been seeing that put him into such a rage? Was he just a friend of hers
and James' petty jealousies had caused him to jump to conclusions?
Would the man's identity put her any closer to solving the puzzle of
Sally's disappearance? Probably not.

There was only one thing for her to do. She had to try to set up a
meeting with the Prosecutor to see if he would tell her anything he

knew that had not made its way into the papers. She folded the three letters she'd read and stuffed them back into their envelopes. She retied the yellow ribbon around them, along with the remaining unopened letters, and slipped them into the pocket of her jeans. She hurriedly stuffed the other papers back in the box and shoved it to the rear of the closet. She didn't bother returning things to their previous order. If Grandma Cory found out the letters were missing and came looking for them, she would have to explain why she helped her son conceal a murder.

# Chapter Eighteen

A quick call to Mrs. Wyatt confirmed the Honorable Appellate Court Judge David Davis was very much alive and still residing in Jenna's Creek. He had moved up through the ranks of local government and occupied the Probate Court's bench for several years before he was elected to the district's Appellate Court. He had retired from public office last year when his wife was diagnosed with multiple sclerosis. Her condition was currently under control with medication, yet the judge felt his place was beside her, according to Mrs. Wyatt, who seemed to hold the man in high regard. Jamie hung up the phone, unsure of how to proceed.

What was Mr. Davis like? Would he want to talk about a case that never went to trial because he couldn't prove anything? Would he be willing to talk to her or would he think her a nuisance? While her mind whirled with questions, she looked in the phone book for a home listing for the judge. No matter what he was like or what he had to say, she had to meet David Davis and talk to him.

She took the keys to Grandma's old pick-up truck from the key hook by the back door and set off. Twice today, her curiosity had got the better of her, and twice it would probably lead to trouble.

❀

Haversham Road was a few miles out of town, left off of Potter, and another left off of Bell Hollow at the bottom of the hill. Many of the mailboxes were not marked with names or house numbers. Jamie kept losing her place while searching for 6680. The farther she drove, the more she assumed she had missed it. Then she saw a sprawling, newly built, ranch house set far back off the road. A split rail fence separated the front of the property from the road. Young trees lined the quarter-mile long driveway that ended near the side of the house. She put the truck in neutral with the motor idling and admired the sweeping view of the countryside surrounding the house as she wondered what in the world she was hoping to accomplish by coming here.

A farm tractor pulling a wagon load of hay approached. She put the truck in gear and eased over to the edge of the narrow, secondary road to make room for it to pass. The farmer operating the tractor brought it to a stop alongside the truck. He pushed the straw hat away from his face and smiled down at her.

"Need any help, young lady?"

"No thanks, I'm just out for a ride," she answered. Although her nerve was failing fast, she hated to think she came all this way for nothing. She blurted out, "Well actually, could you tell me if that's the Davis' house?"

He shaded his eyes from the sun with his hand and peered in the direction her finger pointed. "Yes, miss, that's it."

"Do you know them very well?" After the words were out of her mouth, she realized how pushy and impolite she must've sounded to him.

He cocked his head reflectively and said, "They keep pretty much to themselves."

"Well, thank you," she said, her hand reaching for the gear shift at her knee.

"What would you be wanting with the Davises?" he asked, stopping her.

"Um, I was interested in an old case the judge was involved in while he was County Prosecutor." She hoped she sounded nonchalant.

"Goodness. That was some time ago, I believe," the old man observed, scratching his bristled chin.

She decided honesty would work best. "Yes, but it involved a member of my family, and I was hoping he could answer some questions for me."

"I'll tell you what," he said, "I'm taking this load of hay to the barn. If you'd like, you can go with me and introduce yourself. Maybe the judge'll be in a talkative mood this afternoon."

Jamie was suddenly nervous. Everything was happening so fast. Was she ready to face Judge Davis? What if she offended him with her questions? The last thing he would want to do is waste time explaining the way he handled old cases. She considered leaving, but the old man was so friendly, and she did tell him she had questions.

"I don't want to be an inconvenience," she explained.

"You may as well try. It's hard to say when he'll be home again this time of day."

Jamie acquiesced. She maneuvered the truck around on the narrow road and followed the tractor at a snail's pace to the Davis' house. The farmer shut off the tractor's motor outside the new barn and climbed down. She pulled the truck alongside him and got out.

"It's a lovely place out here," she commented. "So quiet and peaceful."

"It was built just a few years ago," the farmer said. "The judge and his wife love horses and I suppose they thought they needed the space. Would you like to come in the barn and see a some of their stock?"

She hesitated. "I don't know if I should…"

"Oh, they won't mind. The judge loves showing off those horses." He swung open the door and the pungent smell of fresh hay, leather, and horseflesh assailed Jamie's nose.

Three of the six stalls in the large barn were occupied. Jamie didn't know horses—Grandma Cory said there wasn't a need for any on the farm once she could afford her first tractor—but she knew a beautiful animal when she saw one. The farmer led her to each stall to admire the magnificent creatures. He extended his hand to a tall, regal-looking mare who sniffed at it and backed away.

"They're a haughty bunch," he explained. "They're offended that you're in here."

"Maybe we should go," she said nervously.

He laughed lightly. "Don't worry. They're not going to stampede or anything."

She tried to relax, but stayed a step behind the farmer just in case.

"David? Who's your guest?"

Jamie and the farmer turned to see a woman standing in the doorway. She was wearing old jeans, torn sneakers, and a faded blouse.

Her light brown hair was pulled away from her face in a youthful po-nytail. Jamie looked from the woman to the farmer. Had she called him David?

The farmer smiled good-naturedly and extended his hand to Jamie. "I'm Judge Davis," he said, "and this is my wife, Bernice."

Bernice came forward and shook Jamie's hand. Up close, Jamie could see she was quite a bit older than she first appeared. Even with-out make-up, she was pretty and her figure would make most wom-en half her age envious. There were no indications of the debilitating disease Mrs. Wyatt had mentioned that caused Judge Davis to retire early, but then again, she had no idea what to look for.

"Pleased to meet you," she said to Mrs. Davis. "I'm Jamie Steele. Why didn't you tell me you were the judge?" She looked accusingly at the farmer.

"I didn't exactly tell you I wasn't."

"Oh, David, really," Mrs. Davis said. "What can we do for you, Jamie?"

The judge answered for her. "She's come to inquire about an old case of mine. Steele. That name rings a bell. Oh yes, how could I forget? And you're Jamie Steele. I assume that means you're James Steele's daughter?"

"Yes, sir, I am."

"How interesting," he said, wagging his head thoughtfully.

"Jamie, would you like some lemonade or a soda or something?" Mrs. Davis asked.

The judge answered for her again. "How about Miss Steele and I make an arrangement first?" He turned to Jamie. "You help me un-load the hay into the barn, and after that, I'll answer your questions over a nice glass of lemonade."

Jamie was in no position to object. Mrs. Davis disappeared into the house. The judge tossed Jamie a pair of gloves and they set to work unloading the wagon. It took longer than she expected. By the time the hay was stacked neatly at the rear of the barn, she was ready for the lemonade.

The judge led her to a newly-constructed, wooden deck that wrapped around the back of the house. Mrs. Davis brought out a tray with a pitcher of lemonade, two glasses of ice, and a plate of cookies and set them on the glass-topped patio table. She put the plate of cookies near Jamie and gave her an encouraging smile. She poured both glasses to the rim with the lemonade and went back through the sliding glass doors into the house.

Jamie took a long drink of the lemonade. She kept her tired hands wrapped around the frosty glass, its coolness relieving the stinging pain caused by the blisters currently forming on the fleshy pads of her hands.

The judge drained his glass and ate three cookies before he spoke. "I heard about your dad's death on the radio last month. I'm sorry."

*Justice finally finds James Steele. Are you really sorry, Judge Davis?* she thought.

The look on his face was sincere. She immediately regretted her cynical thoughts. The judge was a nice man. He had a nice wife. She couldn't imagine either of them rejoicing that her dad was dead.

She said nothing as she stared at the crystal pattern the sun made on the table top as it shone through the ice cubes in her glass. Once again, she questioned the good sense behind her decision to seek Judge Davis out. Reading his name in the newspaper an hour ago, she knew she had to meet him, face to face; to force him to tell her why he believed James was guilty of killing Sally Blake. After finding the love letters James had written, she was no longer sure he was wrong. Making him look like the bumbling fool she thought he surely must be now didn't seem so likely. He obviously knew a thing or two about her father that she did not. He wasn't even easy to dislike, as she had hoped.

"Miss Steele? Are you all right?" he asked.

"I shouldn't have come," she answered. "I don't know what I expected from you."

"An apology, maybe?"

She looked up in surprise.

"You want me to apologize for pursuing your dad as the prime suspect in the Blake girl's disappearance. Because of me, the public wouldn't acquit him, even if the courts did. Consequently, it ruined his life and possibly drove him to an early grave."

"I don't want an apology or revenge. All I want is the truth."

"And what truth would that be?"

She looked up from her glass of lemonade into his eyes. She noted the deep blue intensity there. He was sincere. He wanted to help her. She could trust him. She took a deep breath and blurted out, "I want to know if my dad killed that girl."

The deck was quiet. A hummingbird hovered at a red feeder hanging from the roof between two brightly colored, non-stop begonias. It drank the syrupy fluid from the feeder and buzzed away. A moment later, it flew back for another drink before buzzing to its nest high in a tree. Horses shuffled aimlessly around the corral, munching grass and swishing flies with their long, glossy tails. A car passed on the road, leaving a cloud of dust suspended in the late morning air.

Judge Davis refilled his empty glass from the pitcher. He topped off Jamie's glass and returned the pitcher to the tray. After another long drink and two more cookies, he sat back in his chair. "I've wanted to know that too, Jamie, for twenty-five years. But with your dad gone and so many years passed, I don't think we ever will."

"I have to know. There has to be evidence that was somewhere overlooked that can prove his guilt or innocence." She didn't mention the letters she found at the bottom of her grandmother's closet.

"Jamie, we left no stone unturned. We were under tremendous pressure from everywhere to close the case. There's nothing that wasn't done."

"But there has to be," she insisted. "The body was never found. No physical clues. There's no such thing as the perfect crime. There had to be something that linked the guilty party to Sally Blake."

"You're right. There should've been. If evidence ever existed, I imagine it's gone by now. It's been too long."

"How could you have proven there was even a crime?"

"That's exactly what we couldn't do. With no body or physical evidence, we had to drop the charges against your dad. The case was never closed, but it was eventually put on the back burner and forgotten."

"Where are the files on the case now?" she asked.

"I imagine in the basement at the court house."

"Could I see them?" Her eyes brightened at the prospect.

"Any files remaining on the case would be public record."

"You mean anyone has the right to look through them?"

"Yes, if someone has ten or twenty years to spare sorting through all the junk down in that basement."

"Will you help me find them? I wouldn't know where to begin."

He shrugged. "Neither would I."

"Surely you want to know what happened to Sally Blake as much as I do."

"I stepped down from my bench to be with my wife," he explained. "She was here twenty-five years ago when I was first making the Blake case. It became an all-consuming fire to me. I don't know if I can put her through that again. I don't know if her health can take it."

"I understand," Jamie said, trying to stay composed. She could tell he was only seconds away from giving in. "Would you be willing to ask her and then get back to me?"

"There's one condition you have to agree to first. No matter what the outcome, you have to accept it and get on with your life."

"I can do that."

"No, I don't think you can. You haven't been able to do it yet. The outcome might be the one you most dread." He paused. "The case could be impossible to solve."

Jamie had considered that possibility before.

"If I agree to help you," he continued, "and between the two of us, we can't discover anything new, you have to be willing to let it go and get on with your life."

"I'll try," she said meekly.

"I must admit, I'd give anything to see an end to this case."

"So, are you going to help me?"

He chuckled at her tenacity. "I guess I don't have a choice, do I?"

❧

Judge Davis watched as the old pick-up truck disappeared down the gravel road. He hadn't thought about the Sally Blake case since he retired; or at least he tried not to think about it. That, however, was an impossible task. The case had haunted him throughout his career. Even while working on the Appellate Court Circuit, it was like an albatross around his neck; the one case of his career that made him feel like he had not done his duty to the community.

In his heart of hearts, he believed James Steele was guilty. And he had been unable to prove it.

Sally Blake's disappearance should have been the easiest case in the world to solve. A pretty, bright young girl with everything going for her disappeared in the night without a trace. She wasn't a runaway, he was positive of that. She had nothing to run away from. She had no enemies, except a hot-headed boyfriend with a history of violence. They got in a fight in front of witnesses that very night. It was an open and shut case, if only they had found a body.

The judge shook his head dismally. That was the only reason they couldn't prosecute James Steele. Since that time courts in other states had been successful in prosecuting cases without the physical evidence of a body, but not in 1947. Back then they needed a body. And it was the one thing they lacked.

He should call Jamie Steele and tell her he changed his mind. He would not be able to help her with her investigation. She seemed like a good enough kid, and he didn't want to be the one to prove her old man was guilty.

Jamie knew she should have told Judge Davis about the letters in Grandma Cory's closet. He was being so helpful and honest with her. She would tell him. She didn't like being deceitful, but now wasn't the time. She thought about his warnings. Would she be able to accept whatever outcome they found, and get on with her life? What if her dad was proven guilty? He looked more guilty with each passing day. Could she bear it? Or even worse, what if they searched and searched and the truth was never discovered? Could she let go of it? She gripped the steering wheel and stared at the road in front of her.

For the first time in a long time she prayed, earnestly, searchingly. Not with her head instead of her heart, as had become her custom. Not for others' needs. This prayer was honest and heart-wrenching. She needed Him. More than ever, she needed the strength only her Heavenly Father could provide.

*I can't face not knowing the truth any longer by myself. If it's Your will that I never know what happened between Dad and Sally Blake, then I'll accept it. Or at least, I'll try. But I can't do it without Your help. I'll lean on you. Give me peace in my spirit, Lord. Peace that You are still in control and You know the truth, even if the rest of us never do.*

# Chapter Nineteen

It took Cory three days to discover that the letters were missing from her closet.

"You've been in my room!" she exclaimed, barging in on Jamie unannounced.

Jamie sat resolutely on the edge of her bed, her jaw set, and said nothing.

"Explain yourself, young lady," Grandma Cory demanded.

Jamie snatched the letters, still tied together with the yellow ribbon, from under her pillow and held them high in the air for Grandma Cory to see. "Explain these."

Cory's countenance turned ghostly white. One hand clutched at her throat and the other reached out for the bed's foot board to steady herself.

Jamie leaped to her feet, her eyes filled with sudden concern. The image of Grandma Cory having a heart attack caused her own face to go white. "Grandma, are you all right?"

Cory's knees buckled and she sank onto the bed. Jamie lowered herself beside her and put her arm around her sagging shoulders. "I'm sorry. I shouldn't have shown them to you like that. Are you okay?"

Cory smiled weakly, the color slowly returning to her cheeks. She patted Jamie's knee. "You've always been the one asking questions about stuff that I thought kids shouldn't worry about. I should've known you'd be the one to discover my secret."

"Your secret? Weren't they Dad's secret?" Jamie asked, motioning with the letters in her hand.

"No, he didn't know they still existed. I think he forgot all about them, or was hoping Sally destroyed them before she disappeared."

"How did you get them if Dad didn't know they were still around?"

"I stole them from Sally Blake."

Jamie's eyes widened. "What? How did you do that?"

"Oh, Jamie, things were such a mess back then. I didn't know what I was doing. I was very upset and confused about everything going on with that girl. I wanted to protect my son, that's all. I didn't want to see him hurt."

"Grandma Cory, what are you talking about?"

"I never wanted to talk about those times again. After James was acquitted, I wouldn't allow Sally's name to be mentioned in this house. I refused to hear anything about the case, the disappearance, anything. As far as I was concerned it was over. Oh, I know, the poor Blakes had lost their daughter; it would never be over for them, but what could I do about that. I wanted for this family to get on with living.

"You know how people are. They wouldn't let us forget. They harassed us with phone calls in the middle of the night. They vandalized the farm. They even killed all the chickens one night. It was a terrible thing. It was affecting Justin's life too. It wasn't fair to him or any of us.

"As long as the townspeople kept insisting James got away with murder, I knew things wouldn't get any better while he was around. I suggested, rather severely, he leave town. He joined the service and after some time went by, people settled down. Our lives began to go back to normal. Justin, your grandpa, and I lived here in peace for the next five years. Justin married Marty and we began to forget the awful time when Sally Blake was in our lives."

"Grandma, forgive me, but you almost act as if all this is Sally's fault."

Grandma Cory sighed heavily and slowly shook her head.

Finally she spoke. "Everyone thought Sally Blake was a sweet, old-fashioned girl. She was from a nice family. She was educated. But they didn't know her like I did. She wasn't a sweet, old-fashioned girl. She had lots of boyfriends; or maybe I should say men friends. Either her parents didn't know or they chose not to see the truth. But she was fast. At least, that's what we called it in my day. She wasn't the kind of girl a mama wants her boy to marry."

She raised her hand in apology and looked toward the ceiling. "Forgive me, Lord. I shouldn't be speaking ill of the dead." She turned to Jamie. "You found the letters. You deserve an explanation as to why I have them. I know you've been trying to find out what really happened to her."

Uncle Justin or Aunt Marty must have told her about Jamie's questions. Maybe Fran Mendenhall realized the true reason for her unexpected visit a month ago.

"I don't think any of the details are fit for a young girl's ears," Grandma Cory said, "but James was your daddy. I guess I owe it to you to tell you what I know and what I did. I'm warning you though, you may not like hearing what I have to say."

Jamie nodded, acknowledging that she understood.

Cory began her story with a heavy heart. "James was no saint. I'm not trying to imply that he was. You've heard all the stories of his conquests, I'm sure. He got into trouble all the time, and most of it was over girls. I knew what he was up to, but a mother always has hope. She wants her boy to settle down, find himself a good girl, and do the right thing. He did with your mama for awhile. Nancy was the best thing that ever happened to him. He was just too foolish and hard-headed to see it."

At the mention of her mother, Jamie gulped hard to keep herself under control, and concentrated on what Grandma Cory was saying.

"James worked off and on at different places after he graduated high school. He wasn't a steady worker like Justin. He would get mad at his boss or a foreman and quit the job. I worried about him day and night. He dated a lot of girls and did things I didn't approve of. Then I got wind that he was seeing Sally. They only dated for a month or so before ... well, you know."

"James told me he was in love with her. He said she was the woman he always wanted and now he had her. For a few days I believed him. Then he came home one night with blood on his shirt. He laughed and said he and Sally got into it and she socked him in the nose. I didn't really believe it, but I didn't know what else to do. Another time I overheard him on the telephone with her and it was obvious they were having a terrible fight. I asked Justin about it and he said they fought all the time. Not just arguments; vicious, horrible fights. He heard rumors around town that Sally was dating an older man, a married man, I guess. James probably heard about it too. Well, your dad always did have a jealous streak a mile wide.

"I tried to talk to him about it. I told him maybe they oughta break up. He laughed and said she was the woman he was going to marry. Well, I don't have to tell you that sent a shiver up my spine. I started nagging at him to get away from her and that made him more determined than ever to see her, so I backed off."

"Matters just kept getting worse. He was staying out till all hours. He was going to work late. I knew it was only a matter of time before he lost another job. He wasn't eating right. He started losing weight. I could see he was upset all the time. He was changing. He had always been so cheerful and talkative before that. When he'd come home from work, he would come in the kitchen and talk to me about his day while I was fixing supper. We'd laugh and talk and carry on. Let me tell you, those times meant a lot to me. Harlan and Justin—God love 'em—never were much company. I admit I shouldn't've spoiled James like I did, but he made time for me. I guess I felt like he enjoyed being around me more than the other two."

Jamie wondered if Grandma Cory felt the same way about her. Did she wish for more time spent with her granddaughter, but felt Jamie was always too busy?

"After he started seeing Sally," Grandma Cory continued, "he stopped talking to me altogether. He was sullen and always mad at someone or about something. He wasn't being himself at all. I just hated to see the change in him and I sort of hated Sally Blake for causing it. I know I shouldn't've felt that way but I couldn't help myself. Things were getting to the boiling point. There was nothing I wanted more than for that girl to get tired of James like she did every other man, and just drop out of our lives.

"One day Sally showed up here at the house. James was at work. Justin was upstairs getting ready to leave for his job at the drugstore and Harlan was off somewhere, so it was just me and her. I'd never seen her up close before. I remember thinking that girl was too beautiful for her own good. She had all this thick, dark hair that went halfway down her back, and her eyes, I'll never forget her eyes. They were a different shade of brown than I ever saw. It was like they could see right through you. She was agitated about something. I invited her into the house, hoping I could maybe talk some sense into her since I wasn't having any luck with James. She was like a nervous cat. Her eyes kept darting all around the room and she couldn't stop fidgeting. I could see she had problems. I just wanted her to leave my son alone.

"As soon as she got in the house, she said James was going to kill her. She was afraid for her life. I told her that was ridiculous. She said, 'I knew you'd say that.' She took some papers out of her purse. They were tied together with a yellow ribbon. She unfolded one and held it up for me to see. I recognized James' handwriting right away. Then she read from it. 'I will kill you with my bare hands. I swear I will.' My heart just about stopped. I tried to tell her James was always a blow-hard; just trying to scare her, to get her attention. She shouldn't pay it any mind. But she laughed in my face. She said she was taking the letters to the police and they would have James arrested. From the look in her eyes, I believed her. I had to stop her. I couldn't have that girl ruining my son's life.

"I talked her into going to the kitchen with me and I fixed us some coffee. She put the letters back in her purse and didn't look at them again. We talked for quite a while. She told me her version of their relationship. She said she was afraid of James most of the time. She thought she loved him, but now she wasn't sure. If only he wasn't so mean to her. The longer we talked, the more she started to settle down. I think she was glad I was there to listen to her. Maybe that's all she wanted; someone to talk to.

"All I wanted to do was protect James. I didn't doubt for a minute he'd made those threats. I knew how he could be when he get riled. I also knew he was all talk. He didn't mean it. But I didn't want her going to the police. They wouldn't understand.

"Before she left, she said she was on her way to work and she asked me to have James call her there; they had things to discuss. Then she left. She hadn't mentioned the letters again. They were still safe in her purse as far as I knew, but I couldn't take the chance that she'd give them to the police like she said she would."

"I prayed she'd go straight to the drugstore without stopping by the police station first. Later that night, I went to the store with some excuse about needing to see Justin. While I was there, I sneaked back to the stockroom, telling him I had to use the restroom. No one else was back there, so I got into Sally's locker. Back then, they didn't keep them locked half the time. The letters were still in her purse, still tied with the yellow ribbon, so I grabbed them. I tucked them in my pocket and left. I didn't know what I'd do if she found them missing and figured out it was me. I guess I figured I'd worry about that when the time came.

"I planned to burn them, I didn't want them around if Sally came looking for them, but it was late at night by the time I got home. I figured they'd be safe 'till morning. I put them in a bureau drawer and forgot all about them. Sally never did come back. I don't know if she thought she'd misplaced them or changed her mind about going to the police and just didn't need them anymore. It was only two days later that she—er—disappeared.

"It was then that I remembered I still had the letters. When James told me she hadn't gone home the night before, I immediately got them out of my drawer and hid them in the closet where I thought they'd never be found. For years they were inside the torn lining of an old coat."

Jamie interrupted, "Didn't you feel a responsibility to turn them over to the police? They were evidence."

"Evidence that would'a sent your daddy to prison," Grandma Cory snapped. Then her voice and demeanor softened. She turned imploringly to her granddaughter. "I couldn't do it, Jamie. I know it was wrong, but he was my son. I couldn't do something that I knew would help convict him. I even asked him. I came right out and said, 'James, did you do something to that girl?' He swore to me he was innocent, and I believed him.

"The afternoon after she disappeared the police came to the house and talked to him. After they left, I went up and searched his room. I found the clothes he wore that night. They were clean. I mean they weren't torn or bloody or anything. And he wasn't acting like he'd just killed someone. Not that I know how a body'd act if they just killed another person. What I mean is he was acting perfectly normal. He was worried about her, but he thought she just took off. He said she was always threatening to do that. He kind of hinted about her seeing this married man and he thought maybe they'd left town together. He was crushed. I could see it in his face. It wasn't until he was taken into the station for questioning a few days later that he started to get scared."

Jamie thought of the letter she'd read; the one in which James threatened Sally if she didn't stop seeing some other man.... "Was she really seeing a married man? If she had been—"

"Now, Jamie, I don't know if she was or not. It could've just been a rumor. You know how small towns are. All I know is that girl was into a lot more than most people knew about, and it's hard to tell what actually did happen to her."

"You don't believe he did it, do you?"

Grandma Cory didn't hesitate. "No, I don't. I know for a fact he didn't do it." She took a deep breath to pull herself together. "Like I said, the look in his eyes when he told me she may have left with another man—well, it just near broke my heart. Even with those horrible letters staring at me, I believed him when he said he was innocent. If I had thought he was guilty, I would have turned the letters over to the police. I'm a mother, but I'm also a God-fearing woman. I still believe a guilty man should pay for his crimes; but, Jamie, my son wasn't guilty."

"When the police came around to search the house, they didn't even look in my room. They searched James' room from top to bottom, along with his car, but the rest of the house just got a glance. I think they felt uncomfortable about going through our things. It was the first missing person case in Auburn County's history and I don't think they knew quite how to handle it. I kept the letters there all through the investigation. I didn't even tell James I had them. I can't explain why I didn't throw them away. Like I said, I wanted to put it all behind me. I think I convinced myself they didn't exist."

Grandma Cory sighed and put a tired hand to her forehead. "I was just thankful that girl was finally out of our lives. That way she couldn't hurt my boy anymore."

"You're not saying you're glad something happened to her?" Jamie asked, horror-stricken.

"No, I'm not saying that. I just have my doubts that anything did happen to her outside of her own control. I believe she knew all along what she was doing and I was glad when it was over."

Jamie wasn't sure she agreed with Grandma Cory's line of thinking, but she appreciated hearing her version of what happened. "Thanks for telling me all this, Grandma," she said sincerely. "I know how hard it is for you."

She gave her a thin smile. "I hope this will help put your mind at ease, child."

"I still don't know what did happen to Sally. If Dad didn't do anything to her, then what happened? Is she still out there? Who else might have had something to do with her disappearance?"

"Oh, Jamie, why can't you let it be?"

"I don't know. I just can't."

Grandma Cory shook her head slowly and stood up. "Well, there's nothing I can do to stop you. Go ahead and pursue it. But don't be surprised when you don't find anything. The police spent months and even years trying to solve the case. They never could. I don't know what makes you think you can."

She started toward the door. "Grandma," Jamie called after her. Cory stopped and turned back to look at her. "Thank you."

She nodded wearily and went out.

Jamie kept the letters in her room. After Grandma Cory was gone, she opened the envelopes one by one. Her curiosity wouldn't subside until she had read every word. There were seven envelopes in all. Each one was penned in James' handwriting. She had been unable to look at the most threatening letter since first reading it. Even now, after three days, its menacing tone made her blood run cold. How could she keep telling herself there was a chance he didn't do anything to Sally when the evidence against him was so overwhelming? Grandma Cory was convinced he was innocent, but why did she keep the letters hidden all those years? Was there more to the story than what she'd told Jamie?

Jamie laid the three letters she had already read and the four remaining unread letters out in front of her on the faded pink bedspread, and stared down at them, their lines blurring and running together before her unfocused gaze. What would she tell the judge? The presence of the letters would surely prejudice him against James, making him all the more positive he was guilty. He may see no need then to help her find out exactly what happened.

What if it had happened just like the authorities believed? James and Sally got into a big fight at the party. James took her somewhere to be alone. Like he had told Uncle Justin, they got to drinking and instead of him taking her back to the party, they started arguing again and things went too far. She said something to set him off and he slapped her; maybe too hard. Jamie knew first hand how easy it was to say the wrong thing to James at the wrong moment and send him into a fit of rage. Sally would've fought back like she always did, so he hit her again, and again. What if her head hit the car window or a rock on the ground? What if—too late—he realized she wasn't moving; wasn't breathing?

It could've been over so quickly. James would have panicked. He would know the police would immediately suspect him. So without thinking twice, he put Sally's body back in the car and drove...

Jamie rubbed her hands roughly over her face and bit back the sob rising in her throat.

The letters were so incriminating how could it have happened any other way? She would have been better off had she never overheard the conversation in the kitchen on the morning of his funeral. She wished she had never gone into Grandma Cory's closet looking for those newspaper clippings. Why didn't she let well enough alone, like everyone advised her to do? She knew more now than she ever needed to know, but still it wasn't enough. No matter how things looked, there were still too many unanswered questions. She had started this. She would have to finish it; to see it to the end.

She picked up one of the remaining unread letters. The old envelope opened easily when she slid her thumb along the underside of the flap. The love letter was much like the others. Threatening, yet oddly loving at the same time. It was short, not taking up half the page it was written on. A slip of paper fell to the floor as she unfolded it. She picked it up and turned it over in her hands. It was a bank withdrawal slip. Sally had cashed in a $1000 savings bond. Even if she only received half the money for cashing it in early, it was still an enormous amount of money for a young girl to have in 1947. The date on the withdrawal slip was November 16th. The very day she spoke to Grandma Cory. Only two days before her disappearance.

Hope rose up inside Jamie, dispelling the dread in her heart. Why had Sally Blake cashed in such a large savings bond? What was she planning to do with so much money? Had her parents known she cashed it in? It was probably a gift from them or her grandparents. A gift to be saved for college, marriage, her future. The only plausible explanation was she was planning on going somewhere. Somewhere far away and for a long period of time. Did she plan on going alone or did the married man truly exist and they were leaving together? Maybe Grandma was right; maybe Sally knew what she was doing all along.

What happened to the money? Did she have it on her when she spoke to Grandma Cory? She had the withdrawal slip with her, why not the money? What if someone she worked with saw it and decided to steal it. Would they want it bad enough to hurt her to get it?

So many questions. So many possibilities.

# Chapter Twenty

Jamie tapped gently on Grandpa Harlan's bedroom door and stuck her head inside. She had to be at the drugstore early that morning, and didn't want him thinking she left without saying good-bye. Her absence from the farm this summer had been upsetting for him so she had decided to make a conscious effort to pay more attention to him. She remembered what Grandma Cory told her about James being the only one in the family who ever talked to her, and vowed she'd spend more time with both her grandparents.

"Grandpa? I'm leaving."

"Jamie? Is that you?"

"Yes, Grandpa. I have to be at work early this morning. It's Friday."

The fact that it was Friday meant nothing to him. To her, it meant delivery trucks arriving early to unload. "When are you coming home?" He asked her the same question every day. She knew he was worried that someday she would say she wasn't coming back at all.

"Four o'clock," she answered, "if I don't have to stay late." He didn't answer. "Good bye, Grandpa." When no response came, she assumed he had gone back to sleep and quietly shut the door. She hurried down the stairs and tried not to feel guilty.

The store was quiet when Jamie arrived. The front door was unlocked, but the overhead lights were off and the closed side of the sign that hung on the door still faced the street. Noel didn't open up until eight A.M. these days. The citizens of Jenna's Creek had no need for his services as early in the day as they once had.

He stood at the pharmacy counter opening the register and getting his books in order. He glanced up as she walked in, and smiled in her direction. "Morning, Jamie."

"Morning, Noel," she said as she made sure the door had closed all the way behind her.

His head was already bent over his patient records again, so she moved on through the quiet store. She was one of the few employees that had arrived. The soda fountain didn't open until ten, so Barb hadn't come in yet. Noreen wasn't there either. She didn't come in until noon on Fridays, working the late shift, so that Noel could leave early.

Jamie clocked in like she did every morning and went straight to the stockroom. It was empty. She was puzzled briefly over Jason's absence and wondered if anything was wrong, before pushing the thought from her mind. This was the first time she had ever beat him to work. What would she say when he came in late? It would feel good to rub it in. No, she wouldn't say anything. She'd just give him one of those disapproving looks he was always directing her way. She practiced a few in the restroom mirror while buttoning her smock, just to make sure she had it right.

With a disdainful look securely in place, she turned to face the door when it finally opened ten minutes later. It wasn't Jason. It was Tate.

"Morning, Jamie," he sang out cheerfully, exposing his perfect, white teeth.

"Good morning, Tate. I haven't seen much of you lately."

"I know. I haven't seen you around either."

"If I didn't know better," she said, "I'd think you've been avoiding me."

"Now, why would I be avoiding you? Maybe you're the one avoiding me."

She sighed. Everything was a joke with him. Couldn't he see she was serious? "Isn't Jason working today?" she asked, changing the subject.

"Nope. You're stuck with me." He laughed out loud.

She groaned inwardly, remembering the last time she pulled a shift with Tate instead of Jason. She'd pay attention this time and not let the occasion repeat itself. The continuous 'beep beep' of a truck's back-up signal sounded in the alley behind the store. She would have to wait to ask him why he hadn't showed up at her house to take her out for pizza, and where he had been keeping himself since. No matter what, she didn't want to sound like it meant that much to her. She only wished it didn't. She uttered a quick prayer for patience, which she was sure she would need today. and opened the loading bay door.

The truck driver jumped out of the truck and handed her an invoice. "Morning, Jamie. You're here early."

"Yeah, well, somebody has to be here since you insist on showing up at this hour! That means it's all your fault," she added with a smile.

He raised the back door of the truck and climbed inside. Tate came over next to Jamie and deftly removed the invoice from her hand. "Let's see what we have here." He laid a hand on her shoulder while he perused the invoice. Jamie moved out from under his hand and stepped out of reach. She no longer found his familiar behavior flattering.

It took over an hour for the three of them to unload the truck. Tate had his own way of checking items off the invoice, which seemed to take forever. Jamie noted irritably that Jason could have had it done in half the time. Tate also liked to talk. She stood by helplessly as he and the driver discussed the Cincinnati Reds' chances for a pennant in the fall. Reared in a predominantly female household, she'd never had to endure such inane discussions. Who cared? Professional sports were just a legalized way for overgrown boys to get paid obscene amounts of money by exploiting a child's game. She wished the two of them would shut up so they could get on with their work.

"So, where were you the other night?" she asked Tate when the truck pulled away and they were alone in the stockroom. It didn't mean she was desperate if she demanded a simple explanation from him, she told herself. He owed her that much out of common courtesy.

Tate fumbled with a bulky box at the top of the stack. "Oh… well, it was like I said. Something came up."

Jamie was tired of hearing those words. "I have no problem with something coming up," she said sharply. "But there was no reason why you couldn't've called. Maybe I had something better to do myself, but didn't do it, out of consideration for you."

He gave her a dubious look. "Oh, really. And what else would you have had to do?"

"That doesn't matter, Tate."

"Yes, it does. If I'd've known you had other plans, I would've waited till another time. All you had to do was tell me," he said piously. "I wouldn't be getting all mad at you like you are with me right now."

He was not going to turn this around to be her fault. "The point is, Tate, you were rude, just like you are now. And I don't appreciate it. Believe me, I'm not mad. I don't care enough about you to be mad." A slight fabrication on her part. "All I asked is why you didn't call and let me know you weren't coming."

"And I told you, something came up. I would've called if I could've, but I couldn't, so I didn't."

Jamie looked away and took a deep breath, her cheeks hot. Fighting back the words she wanted to hurl at him, she forced herself to control her anger. If she lost her temper, he would know his actions hurt her feelings; that she did care enough about him to be hurt when he treated her wrongly.

She closed her eyes and turned to her Heavenly Father instead. *Lord, forgive me for losing my temper. Help me to not take everything Tate says personally. That's just the way he is and he isn't going to change to please me. I think he needs You in his life, God. Let me be a light that he may come to know You someday. Amen*

When she opened her eyes, Tate was staring at her, his eyebrows raised in a puzzled arch. She smiled and began shelving the items they had unloaded from the truck.

How easy it had been to forgive Tate. All she had to do was seek forgiveness for herself with a contrite heart and her feelings of animosity dissipated into the air around her. Was that all it would take to find the strength to forgive her father?

All summer she had looked for a way to forgive him; a way to forgive him without letting go of the bitterness and disappointment that went along with it. If she truly offered him the forgiveness Jesus described in the Lord's Prayer, that meant she would also have to forget. That was the hard part. She didn't want to forget the miserable way he had treated her, her mother and Cassie. She wasn't ready to let go of that anger yet. It was a part of her; a comfortable blanket she wrapped around herself to keep from experiencing his death like she had her mother's.

It had been easy to forgive Tate. The pain he caused was insignificant and fleeting. Nothing like what she had experienced at the hands of her dad. His mistreatment of her went much deeper than anything Tate Craig could ever do. Forgiveness for him would be much harder to find—maybe even impossible. Someday Tate would disappear from her life. She would forget all about him. Not so with her dad. He would always be with her, whether she wanted to think so or not. Every time she looked in the mirror she would think of him. Every time she remembered her mother, she would think of him. When she someday looked into the face of her own child, she would undoubtedly be reminded of James Steele.

Deep in her heart she knew if she couldn't find forgiveness for him, she would never be free. Redeemed. Worthy of the same forgiveness she wasn't willing to offer. Still, she clung resolutely to her anger. She would give him her forgiveness when he did something to deserve it; such as being innocent of any involvement in Sally Blake's disappearance.

For the first time since coming to the drugstore, Tate worked without talking. He seemed to get it that Jamie wasn't in the mood to kid around. She didn't notice the morning slipping away until he announced it was time for lunch.

She glanced down at her watch. "It's only twelve-twenty. Jason always waits till after one."

"Jason isn't here," he pointed out, "and I'm hungry now."

"It's too early. There'll still be customers at the counter."

"I wasn't planning on eating here," he said. "I thought you and I could have lunch at the diner for a change."

"Don't we have to eat here?"

"Boy, Jason sure keeps you on a short leash. You don't have to eat here every day just because he does. He only eats here because it's free and he's cheap."

Jamie bit back a retort. "I'll wait until one."

"You're probably right. The diner'll be crowded right now anyway. We'll wait till one."

She wondered if his invitation to lunch was an apology for standing her up. It was probably the closest she'd come to getting one from him. She wanted to believe he was sincerely trying to get back into her good graces; that he was truly sorry for hurting her feelings. Still his snide comments about Jason were uncalled for. Jason was simply trying to better himself. He didn't make a fortune working for Noel, yet he was putting himself through school and helping his family out more than either she or Tate were doing. He also took pride in his work. That was no reason to insult him behind his back.

"So what are your plans for the weekend, Jamie?" Tate asked, his sudden interest making her suspicious.

"The usual," she answered. "Work on the farm and work here."

"That doesn't sound like much fun. Maybe we could do something."

"You've got to be kidding, right?"

"Oh, come on, Jamie. You're not still mad at me, are you?"

"No, I'm not mad," she replied, honestly this time. "I'm just not making anymore plans with you, that's all."

"Why? You too good for me all of a sudden?"

"No, I didn't say that." She fumbled for an excuse to avoid hurting his feelings. She didn't know why she bothered, he certainly didn't concern himself with hers. "My sister just got back from my grandparents' house last week and I want to spend some time with her. Let's not talk about it right now. Let's just finish our work before one." She squatted down and busied herself stacking cartons on a low shelf.

"Come to think of it, I've never seen you date anyone," he observed thoughtfully. "Why is that, Jamie? You too good for everybody?"

She sighed, exasperated, but didn't take her eyes off the cartons she loaded onto the shelf. "Tate, I don't think I'm too good for anybody. I just never had the opportunity to date that much before, that's all. Now, could we drop it."

He didn't say anything for awhile. She hoped he had forgotten about her. The sound of his voice so close to her ear startled her. "I hope I didn't make you mad," he said softly. "I was just teasing. I really am sorry for not calling you the other night."

"I know you are. Let's just forget it even happened." She wished he'd go away. His close proximity was making her uncomfortable.

"That's all I want." He began making circular motions on her back with his hand. "I really do want you to forgive me."

She jumped to her feet, feeling trapped between him and the metal shelves. He stood up too and smiled. He seemed to sense her discomfort and was enjoying the moment. "I do forgive you, Tate." She hurriedly stepped around him and went to her locker. She unbuttoned her smock, hung it on the hook and stepped into the restroom. She washed her hands for an extra long time before stepping back into the stockroom. "I'm getting something to eat," she announced over her shoulder as she headed into the main part of the store.

Just as she seated herself on her usual stool in the corner, Tate arrived at the lunch counter. "You sure left in a hurry. You must be starving. Are you ready to go?"

"Where are you two going?" Barb wanted to know.

"Jamie and I are going to the diner for lunch."

Jamie opened a menu and studied it as if she didn't already know every item on it by heart. "No, I'm staying here."

He sat on the stool beside her. "I thought you wanted to go to the diner."

She didn't remember saying anything to give him that idea.

Mary and Deidre, Tate's biggest fans at the drugstore approached. Mary sat next to Tate and Deidre squeezed her voluptuous figure into the small space between him and Jamie. "Who's going to the diner?" Mary asked.

"Jamie and me." Tate leaned forward on his stool to see Jamie on the other side of Deidre. "Are you ready to go?"

Jamie glanced up from her menu. "No. I told you I'm eating here."

"Jamie's mad at me." He thrust out his lower lip at Deidre and Mary. "One little misunderstanding and she won't forgive me. Isn't that right, Jamie?"

She didn't answer.

"See what I mean. She's so touchy after being in that stockroom all summer with Jason."

Jamie's cheeks reddened, but she didn't look up from the menu. Deidre tossed her long hair over her shoulder and leaned toward Tate smiling, her eyes on Jamie as if hoping to make her jealous. Mary put her hand on his shoulder and squeezed her ample chest against his arm.

Jamie wished they would all go away so she could eat her lunch in peace.

"Why don't you go?" Barb urged her. "I'm sure you're tired of eating here every day."

"No, I don't mind."

"Your loss," Tate said lightly. He put one hand on Mary's shoulder and the other on Deidre's. "How about you two? Want to go to the diner with me?"

"Oh, we can't," Mary moaned. "We already had our lunch breaks."

"I wish you had asked us earlier," Deidre told him, an irritating whine in her voice.

"Shouldn't you two be getting back to work then?" Barb admonished.

They groaned and rose from the stools. "Bye, Tate," they chorused in sugar-coated voices that turned Jamie's stomach. "Good-bye Barb." Neither acknowledged Jamie's presence as they sashayed away.

"Well, seeing's how I hate to eat alone, I guess I'll stay here with you." Tate leaned against Jamie and surveyed the menu over her shoulder. "What're you having?"

Ignoring him, she gave her order to Barb.

"That sounds good. Make it two."

Jamie ate in silence while Tate kept up a constant flow of conversation with Barb. She wished he had gone to the diner with Mary and Deidre. She listened as he spun his yarns about people he knew and things he had done. She marveled at the ludicrous exaggerations he came up with. Barb surely didn't buy his long-winded tales, did she?

Was she being too critical again? Maybe his life was terribly exciting and everything he said was true. Maybe he had a psychological disorder that made him unable to distinguish fact from fiction. Maybe he was just a jerk.

Jamie smiled down at her egg salad. Yes, that was it. She should've noticed it before. Tate was a jerk.

# Chapter Twenty-one

J udge Davis wants you to call him tonight," Grandma Cory told Jamie when she arrived home that evening.

Jamie's mouth dropped open. "Really? What did he say?"

"He didn't say anything. He just asked me to have you call him when you got in."

"Did it sound like good news or bad?"

"It didn't sound like anything," she retorted. "I just took the message."

Jamie headed for the telephone. She'd change out of her good clothes to help with the chores after hearing what he had to say. Grandma Cory's disapproving voice stopped her.

"I don't know why you had to drag him into this. It's our family business."

Jamie stopped in her tracks. "It's his business too. He was the County Prosecutor."

"That's right. He *was* the County Prosecutor. He's not anymore."

"He wanted to help," Jamie tried to explain. "He's as anxious to get to the bottom of this as I am."

Grandma Cory rolled her eyes. "Oh, I'm sure he has nothing better to do with his time than go running off on a wild goose chase with you. Why don't you leave the poor man alone and let him take care of his wife like he's supposed to do?"

"It's not a wild goose chase. We're going to find out what really happened to Sally Blake."

"And then what?" Grandma Cory crossed her arms over her chest and fixed on Jamie with an icy stare. "What are you going to do once you find out? Break her mother's heart all over again?" Her voice cracked. "Or mine?"

Jamie didn't know what to say. She didn't want to hurt her, but she couldn't go on without knowing the truth. "I— I'm sorry, Grandma," she said in a small voice.

"No, you're not. You're selfish. I never should've explained those letters to you. I should've just ripped them up right in front of you and thrown them away. You probably told him all about me hiding them too, didn't you? You'd be happy to see an old woman locked up for hiding evidence from the police, wouldn't you?"

She opened her mouth to defend herself, but Grandma Cory stormed past her into the kitchen. She turned in the doorway to add, "You can make your phone call after you finish your chores. The judge's news'll wait."

While she hurried around the barnyard doing what needed to be done, Jamie agonized over the situation with Grandma Cory. It seemed she couldn't win, no matter what she did. She truly was sorry for hurting her, but she wasn't being selfish. It was more selfish of Grandma to ask her to stop looking for answers in the case, than for her to insist on finding them. James was her father. She had a right to know what happened. Now that she knew of Sally Blake's existence, she couldn't be expected to forget her and stop wondering about what became of her. Her brain just wasn't going to let that happen. Every time she thought of James, she would automatically think of Sally and wonder if he was in any way involved in her disappearance.

She did not want to see her grandma go to jail for complicity in a murder case; she hadn't even considered the possibility of that happening. Wasn't there a statute of limitations on something like that? She'd have to ask the judge to make sure no one got in trouble. But she had to know the truth. How could she live the rest of her life fostering these suspicions about James? They were eating her up inside. She wanted to forgive him for the way he treated her, Cassie, and especially her mother. She wanted to forget the past and move on like Mrs. Wyatt advised, but it was impossible without knowing the truth. She had listened to everyone's advise on the matter, meditated upon it, stewed and debated. The fact was, she could not get past the question of James' innocence or guilt.

Grandma Cory would just have to understand why she had to know the truth. Judge Davis would have to understand if she couldn't stand behind her promise to him of letting the case go if they didn't find any new answers. God would have to understand that she needed the whole story before she could offer her forgiveness.

She rested her forehead against Amelia's warm flank, her fingers working the cow's teats on their own, with no conscious thought on her part. The rhythmic szzt... szzt of the milk as it landed in the bottom of the pail reprimanded her. She knew her reasoning was displeasing to God. He offered His forgiveness unconditionally and she was required to do the same. Seventy times seven, Jesus had said, was how many times she was supposed to forgive a brother who had wronged her. *Seventy times seven. That sounds about right,* she thought bitterly. That was probably how many times James Steele had hurt his wife and daughters while he was on the earth. If she didn't forgive him in this instance, that would make them about even.

Exercising tact to spare Grandma Cory's feelings, Jamie waited until after the supper dishes were washed and put away before calling Judge Davis. She had hardly been able to eat any of her supper, from the anxiousness of waiting, but she managed. The telephone rang four times on his end before he finally picked up.

"Good evening, Judge." She hoped she didn't sound over zealous. "My grandma said you called. I'm sorry I couldn't return your call earlier, but I had chores to do."

"I understand," he said with a chuckle. "I had chores to do myself."

Her impatience got the better of her and she dispensed with the usual niceties of conversation. "She said you had some news for me?"

"Actually I do." She could tell he was smiling into the receiver. "I must say, after talking with you the other day, my curiosity got the better of me. I couldn't wait for you to get some time off work, so I went to the courthouse this morning."

She could barely keep herself from jumping up and down. "What did you find?"

He chuckled at her enthusiasm. "It didn't take as long as I thought it would. I didn't figure I'd find anything the first time out. I almost believe there was some divine intervention involved. I started working on a stack of boxes and I could tell by the dates I was on the right track. The very last box in the stack was the one I was looking for."

"What was it? What was in it?"

"Whoa now," he said. "Slow down. You'll have to come out here and see for yourself. I haven't even looked at it yet. By the time I found it, the morning was almost gone. As soon as I realized what it was, I shut the lid, loaded it ino my car, and brought it home."

"You have it at your house?"

"Yes. I thought it would work out easier, if we could go through it here. I didn't want to start investigating until you were here though. After all, it's your case."

Jamie blushed at his thoughtfulness. "Thank you, Judge. This means a lot to me."

"I know it does, Jamie. I don't know if we're going to come up with any answers," he said, reminding her not to be overly optimistic, "but we can try."

"When would be a good time for me to come over?" she asked, hoping he would say right this minute.

He paused as if checking a schedule. Jamie held her breath. "How about Monday? Are you free then?"

"Not until the evening. I have to work."

"Just stop out after work then. We'll see what we can do."

"Judge," she began slowly. "There's something else I need to tell you."

"Yes, what is it?"

"Last week, before I came out to your house, I found some letters in my dad's things. They were letters he wrote to Sally Blake." She held her breath, afraid he would yell at her for keeping them to herself. It was highly likely the existence of the letters could change the entire investigation.

The line was quiet on his end for several moments. Finally he said, "Would you bring them with you Monday? I'd like to look at them."

She took a deep breath and asked hesitantly, "Holding onto them all these years isn't going to get anyone in trouble, is it?"

"Well, I really don't see what good that would do at this late date." She imagined he knew who she was wanting to protect. Who else but a mother would risk interfering in a capital case to protect her child? "I don't think you need to worry about that," he finished.

"So you're still going to help me find out what happened to Sally?"

"Of course. Why wouldn't I?"

"You'll see when you read the letters."

Tonight was Friday. Jamie would have to wait the whole weekend to get started, but she had no choice. She thanked him again and hung up the phone. Waiting until Monday would take all the patience she had on reserve.

It was too hot to go outside. It was hot inside too, but inactivity in front of the rotating fan and sheltered from the blazing sun was better than nothing. Sunday afternoons were always the slowest part of Jamie's week. They seemed to be three days long. It was a good time for a nap—that's how Grandma and Grandpa escaped the heat—but seventeen-year-olds were incapable of sleeping in the middle of the day. She'd tried before.

Cassie was upstairs in her room with the door closed, laying crossways on the bed in her underwear, flipping idly through a back issue of Tiger Beat Magazine. Jamie wandered from the kitchen to the living room, her hands wrapped around a glass of iced tea. She sat heavily on the couch and positioned the fan so its air currents would hit her directly in the face. She pulled her hair into a knot with her fist and held it up off her neck to allow the moving air to dry the trickles of perspiration running down her neck into her blouse.

She decided she hated summer. She longed for the cool, crisp air of October. The upholstery of the sofa made her even hotter so she slid onto the hardwood floor, taking the electric fan and the newspaper that was folded on the end table with her. She spread the newspaper out in front of her, fighting the air currents from the fan to keep the pages flat on the floor. It was the local Jenna's Creek paper. It only came out twice a week, since so little went on in the community worth reporting.

She wasn't really interested in the top story concerning the preservation of the pre-civil war Bentley house, on Elm Street, as an historical landmark. It seemed there was some controversy over what to do with the old house. It had been left to the city a generation ago and now lack of funds had the town officials divided over its fate. The Ladies Historical Society, a small but vocal community organization, wanted to utilize the house for the new location of the Human Services Organization. The town leaders believed it would take too much money to convert the elegant house into a proper location for a public service building. They wanted to abandon the house and erect a new set of office buildings on the edge of town for Human Services.

The Ladies Historical Society was livid. Why do away with a part of Jenna's Creek history to put up new office buildings that they felt would rob the town of its heritage and small-town charm? The town leaders felt the Historical Society was standing in the way of progress. Jenna's Creek needed to keep up with the twentieth century, they insisted.

The only problem with the officials' leverage in the argument—although this key issue was not addressed by the newspaper—was that most of their wives made up the Ladies Historical Society. They could say whatever they wanted at town meetings. They could debate from their podiums and address answers from the crowd, but at the end of the night, they had to go home with the lovely, well-dressed members of the Historical Society.

The fate of the Bentley House was a foregone conclusion. If the Ladies Historical Society wanted to preserve it, then they would get their way. But for appearances sake, the city officials held firm to their convictions, if only for the benefit of the press.

Jamie perused the article on the front page along with the announcement of a new business opening on Main Street, and an article accompanied by a picture of the Mayor addressing the Senior Citizens Organization. Inside the paper she skipped over the obituaries and social calendar. The comics were on the last page with Dear Abby. She would read that for a laugh. Usually Dear Abby was more amusing than the comics.

As she struggled to turn the newspaper pages against the mechanical breeze of the electric fan, her eyes fell on an advertisement she had seen her entire life, but never paid any attention to before. It was for a local real estate agency. There were several pictures of houses for sale with descriptions, locations, and asking prices. An announcement for an upcoming farm auction with a long, tedious list of implements and machinery available for sale droned on and on. At the bottom of the ad was a blacked-out block with white writing to catch the reader's eye.

*Theodore E. Blake, Inc. Realtors and Appraisers since 1934*
*Brokerage/Auction Service/Appraisals*
*221 North High St., Jenna's Creek, Ohio*

Next to the company name and logo was a list of the names Jamie assumed were Mr. Blake's associates. At the top of the list was Tim Shelton, along with his telephone number.

Tim Shelton.

Jamie's heart skipped a beat.

One of the last people to see Sally Blake alive now worked for her father. What did it mean? Probably nothing. Just because Tim Shelton was an employee of Mr. Blake didn't necessarily mean anything. Jamie knew she was only trying to find someone else to blame in Sally's disappearance. She was grasping at straws.

Her eyes moved down the page to an auto dealer's ad. She could not get her mind to focus on the used cars for sale. She started to turn the page, but kept coming back to Tim Shelton's name printed at the bottom of the real estate ad. Something was wrong, she could feel it. But what?

She went to the telephone hanging on the wall in the kitchen and dialed Uncle Justin's number. He answered on the first ring. "Hello?"

"Hi, Uncle Justin, it's me, Jamie."

"Hi, honey. What's up?"

"I was wondering if you could answer a question for me?"

"Sure. What is it?"

"Do you by any chance remember what Tim Shelton did for a living before Sally Blake disappeared?"

"Tim Shelton? Why do you want to know that?"

"Um, I was just wondering," she said. "He works for Mr. Blake now, and I was wanting to know what he did before that."

"Yes, he's worked for Mr. Blake's realty company for years. I think he's been there longer than anyone."

"Was he always a real estate broker?"

"Yes, mostly. His family did operate a dairy farm and he worked there at first. It wasn't a huge operation, but enough to keep him and his old man busy."

"So Tim quit working for his own father and went to work for Sally's? Does that make sense?"

"Well, why not? I guess he didn't want to be stuck on that farm his whole life. A lot of folks aren't cut out for farming. It's a hard life. I chose another path myself."

"Do you know when he went to work for Mr. Blake?"

"It couldn't have been too long after Sally disappeared," Uncle Justin answered after a moment's thought. "Like I said, he's been there forever. I think he started working for him about the same time they arrested your dad."

"Did he know Mr. Blake before that?" she asked.

"I couldn't really tell you. He knew Sally pretty well so he probably knew her parents too."

"Doesn't it strike you as odd that Mr. Blake would hire Tim away from his own father at the same time the police were investigating his daughter's disappearance? I mean, isn't that a strange time to be hiring new employees?"

"I don't know. To tell you the truth, I never really thought about it before. Just what're you getting at, Jamie?"

"I'm just trying to understand why Mr. Blake would be making major business decisions at a time like that. How could his mind be on real estate and not on his missing daughter?"

"His hiring Tim didn't have to be a major business decision. Maybe he felt sorry for the boy and wanted to help him out. Tim has made a nice living for himself over the years. Maybe he always wanted to sell real estate and had applied for a job a year before the position opened up. It's impossible to tell what was going on."

"Yeah, I guess so."

"And whether it makes sense to us or not, businessmen are always thinking about the all-mighty dollar, no matter what's going on in their personal lives."

"You're probably right." Jamie felt deflated in the oppressive heat.

"Jamie?"

"Yeah?"

"Don't go making mountains out of molehills, okay? Tim Shelton is a nice guy. I know what you're thinking. But he didn't have anything to do with harm coming to Sally Blake."

After hanging up the phone, Jamie stretched out on the couch in front of the fan. Uncle Justin was right. Mr. Blake had a right to hire anyone he chose. Still a suspicion nagged at the back of her mind and wouldn't let her rest. Something didn't seem right with the whole situation. She wondered if it would be worth mentioning to Judge Davis. He would probably react the same way Uncle Justin had; that she was making mountains out of molehills. She was still puzzling over it when Grandma Cory came out of her bedroom and told her to help get dinner on the table before the evening service at church.

# Chapter Twenty-two

A dark brown, cardboard box with cut-out handles sat on the judge's dining room table. Mrs. Davis led Jamie into the dining room where Judge Davis was seated at the head of the table. He offered the empty chair beside him with a wave of his hand.

"Could I bring you a soda or an iced tea, Jamie?" Bernice Davis asked.

"A soda would be fine, please."

"David?"

"The same." He exchanged loving smiles with his wife. She sighed accommodatingly and left the room.

Jamie sat in a high-backed chair and pulled herself up to the table. "So this is everything about my dad's case."

"Actually it's Sally Blake's case. Your dad just makes up a lot of it." He eyed the mountain of paperwork. "Quite overwhelming, isn't it?"

She nodded. The files looked like a whole lot of nothing to her. She suddenly understood why everyone hated paperwork. "Where should we begin?"

The judge chuckled. "Wherever we want. I'm afraid nothing's in any particular order. Every file and report will have to be gone over and sorted through. Much of it won't be of any use to us, but then again, the least important detail could be exactly what we need to put it all together."

A knot of apprehension tightened in Jamie's stomach. "Okay," she said, "I'm ready. But first let me show you the letters I found."

She handed him the packet of letters tied together with the yellow ribbon. He opened the one on the top of the stack and scanned its contents. Then he looked up at her. It was impossible to tell what he was thinking. She held her breath, waiting for him to explode for not telling him about them in the first place.

"It may have been a good thing we didn't have these in 1947," he said.

"What do you mean?"

"I mean, if we'd had these in our possession twenty-five years ago, I can tell you, we would've definitely considered the case closed; that we had our man. If you and I find out your dad was innocent, we would've convicted an innocent man, simply on the basis of these letters."

Jamie sighed in relief. Even after knowing of the letters existence and having tangible proof of James' violent temper, Judge Davis wasn't willing to consider the case solved. He wanted the whole story as badly as she did.

"There's something else." She pulled the withdrawal slip from her back pocket and handed it to him. "You'll notice the transaction date is two days before Sally disappeared," she pointed out as he looked over the faded document.

He nodded thoughtfully. "Yes, this opens up a whole world of possibilities."

"I've been hearing rumors that Sally may have been involved with someone other than my dad. A married man." she added.

"You realize that falls under the category of hearsay," Judge Davis explained. "Something you heard someone say that they heard someone else say cannot be considered evidence."

"Oh, I understand that," she said quickly. "I just thought it might be interesting to keep in mind when we're considering the different possibilities."

"You're right about that. We'll leave no stone unturned this time."

The judge turned his attention back to the letters James had written to Sally while Jamie dove into the cardboard box on the table. She carefully read every file she picked up. The judge was right. Most of it didn't seem to be integral to their own investigation. Many were police reports that said the same thing over and over again, just written differently by a different officer. She finally came to a folder that caught her attention. It was full of accounts of what happened on the fateful night according to friends, family members, and guests at the party. After reading each statement, she handed it to the judge for him to read. Many of the statements were redundant or hard to understand, but it gave her an idea of the emotional roller coaster the community was on because of Sally's disappearance.

They decided to write down the pertinent information from each statement in a notebook, to find any conflicting accounts in the eye-witness reports.

Jamie was currently reading Hobie Bryant's statement. Hobie had been James' best friend for as long as Jamie could remember. Even Mrs. Wyatt said they were in cahoots in the infamous rice incident in Pastor McAfee's office at the church when they were boys. She remembered him coming around the house when they lived in town before Nancy died, to hang out in the garage and drink beer with her dad. He had not been invited to Noreen and Tim's engagement party that night; he didn't hang with Sally's crowd. Still, he was James' closest friend and knew him better than anyone. His intentions were good, but he painted a bad picture of James' relationship with Sally.

He wrote of James' love for Sally; how it had started in fourth grade, the first time he laid eyes on her. She was older than him, but it didn't stop his advances. He had always been able to win any girl's affections in short order, until Sally came along. He swore to Hobie someday she would be his. James never felt about any other girl, the way he felt about her. She was his world. If he couldn't have her, his life wouldn't be worth living. The image Hobie portrayed was that of an obsessed man who would defy reason to have the woman he loved. Jamie felt sick after reading his statement. His words alone were al-most enough to convince her James was guilty.

She read a few more statements from people she had never heard of. She read them carefully and took notes, but found nothing that seemed relevant. So far, they were all telling the same story; the story she knew all too well. James and Sally got into a heated argument at the party and then left together. Sally was never seen or heard from again.

When she came to Tim Shelton's statement, she read it with ex-treme caution. The only thing she found of interest to her was that

Tim had not worked for Mr. Blake before the disappearance. He wrote about working on his father's farm and didn't mention aspirations of doing anything else with his life. Of course, why would he? A police statement was not the place to make known one's hopes and dreams for the future. Uncle Justin was probably right. Going to work for Mr. Blake was not a crime and did nothing to implicate Tim in the disappearance. Still, she sensed something was there. Maybe she simply wanted to implicate someone—anyone—bad enough to see things that didn't exist?

# Chapter Twenty-three

A plume of diesel smoke rose in the early morning mist as the backhoe roared to life. It lumbered the short distance from the trailer on which it had been riding, to the remains of the dilapidated chimney. Mom had been on him for years to clean up this place. It was an eyesore and a potential danger to the grandkids. Although no one came back here anymore as far as he knew, he guessed she had a point.

He almost hated destroying the history surrounding this place. His great-grandparents had built the home place in the 1800's when they first bought the property. They had farmed the original hundred acres to earn enough money to pay the bank for the lien against it. When their children were grown, the oldest son—his grandfather—built the house now occupied by his parents. Great-grandma and Grandpa remained in the old house until they died. After their passing, the outdated house fell to ruin. No one else in the family wished to occupy it, but yet they couldn't bring themselves to tear it down.

When he was a boy, the only things remaining of the original house were the remnants of a stone foundation and the chimney rising into the sky. He, his brother, sisters, and various cousins spent countless summer days playing pioneers, hide-and-go-seek, or cowboys and Indians here. Now the chimney stood barely eight-feet high with more broken, home-made bricks reclaimed to the soil every year.

As he maneuvered the backhoe across the field, he thought of the people who settled the area and wished he knew more about them.

He should have paid closer attention when Grandma and Grandpa were still alive and wanted to tell the kids stories of their younger days. Back then, he just thought his grandparents were old and dull with nothing worth telling, but he'd give anything now to sit down and listen to them talk for as long as they wanted.

The bucket of the backhoe swung in a small arc and gave the chimney a gentle nudge, reducing the labors of his ancestors to a pile of bricks and dust. He scooped up a bucket of debris and headed to the waiting dump truck. He looked over his shoulder to check his progress and saw he had run over an old well, exposing a gaping hole that once provided sustenance and convenience to the home's residents.

He doubted it was very deep, but deep enough to be a hazard if one of the grandchildren tumbled into it. After depositing the shovel load of bricks into the bed of the dump truck, he climbed down from the seat and went to investigate the well.

It was dry as far down as he could see. Even if it still held water, it was a good half mile as the crow flies from the present house and barns, through the woods and down an overgrown lane; too far away from everything to be put to use. He would build a cement cover for the top before the weekend if he found the time—another mundane task to add to his list of chores, in order to maintain his parent's property. His brother had been the smart one—moving away before their parents grew too old to see to their own needs.

As his eyes became accustomed to the lack of light in the hole, he noticed something laying at the bottom. The more he looked, the more bewildered he became. What was that? Various pieces of rocks or something... No that wasn't it. Long, slender objects scattered...

Behind the seat in the truck was a flashlight. He dug it out from among the rags and tools, and got down on his belly next to the hole. The beam of light permeated the darkness of the long forgotten well. Bones, just like he thought. The shape and size indicated they could not belong to an animal. He panned the beam across the bottom of the well. A skull—definitely human—possessing a perfect, full set of teeth grinned eerily up at him. A chill in the summer morning air passed over him, causing the hair to rise up on the back of his neck. He scrambled up, nearly propelling himself into the well in his haste, and switched off the key in the backhoe's ignition. The sudden stillness echoed in his ears as he broke into a trot, taking the shortcut through the woods he and his siblings had used as children, to his parents home. His breath was coming in short gasps and a painful stitch grabbed at his side by the time he got to a telephone.

Jamie immediately recognized Judge Davis' voice on the other end of the line when she picked up the telephone.

"Jamie?" he said, excitedly. "They haven't announced it on the news yet, but I just got off the phone with Vernon Patterson, the County Sheriff. I wanted to let you know before you heard about it in town. Human remains were found this morning in an abandoned well on Will Trimble's farm."

The significance was lost on Jamie. "Will Trimble?"

"Yes. It was Will Trimble's property where they had the party the night Sally Blake disappeared. They're sending the remains to the forensics lab in Franklin County to check into the possibility that they could belong to Sally."

"You're kidding?" Jamie cried. "You mean they may have found her?"

"We won't know that for a couple of weeks, but it is a possibility."

"Oh, I can't believe it." Jamie suddenly sobered. "Is this good or bad, Judge? I mean, I was beginning to think Sally just took off. Now we know she didn't. That means Dad could have done something to her after all."

"Jamie, you're jumping to conclusions. In the first place, we don't even know if it's Sally's remains in that well. And even if it is, that doesn't mean your dad had anything to do with her being there."

"I know. I know," she murmured.

"Don't let yourself get worried just yet," he advised. "Give them a few weeks to identify the remains. It's possible they may also be able to determine the cause of death. When that's all said and done, we'll figure out how to proceed. The police may be able to answer all our questions for us."

Jamie hung up the phone, but she found no solace in the judge's words.

Everything was happening so fast. First they found the files on Sally's case and now a body had been discovered in a well where the party had taken place.

While Grandpa Harlan sat in front of the television set later that evening, Jamie asked Cassie and Grandma Cory to join her on the front porch. Neither of them had been out of the house or listened to the radio all day so she knew they hadn't heard the news yet.

"The police found the remains of a human body in an abandoned well this morning," she reported inaccurately. Unbeknownst to her, the police were not involved at all. The Sheriff's Department was handling the case.

"Oh my gosh!" Cassie exclaimed. "Who was it?"

"They don't know yet. It'll take awhile to find out."

"I wonder who it could be," Cassie mused. "How do you suppose he got in a well? Did he fall in? Was he pushed?"

"No one knows yet, Cassie," Jamie told her. "They just found the body today. They don't even know if it's a man or a woman."

"This is so exciting," Cassie went on. "A mystery in Jenna's Creek. Just think of it. It could be a convict who escaped from prison. Maybe he was wrongfully accused and trying to get home to clear his name. Maybe it's a kidnapped heiress whose family paid the ransom, but she was killed by her captors anyway. Or it could be..."

"Oh, Cassie, for heaven's sake," Grandma Cory snapped. "There's nothing wonderful or romantic about it." She turned to Jamie with fire in her eyes. "They think they know who it is already, don't they?"

"Well, uh— they're investigating certain leads," she said, hesitantly.

Grandma Cory sprang from the rocking chair she was sitting in and stormed into the house, letting the screen door slam behind her.

"Jamie," Cassie whispered, "what's wrong with Grandma? Who do the police think it is?"

Cassie had been gone most of the summer and had no idea what Jamie had found out about their father. She would fill her in later when everything was over. She didn't know if she was up to giving her all the sordid details just yet. "They think it could be Sally Blake, a girl Dad used to date," she said, telling her just enough to get her to stop asking questions. "Grandma Cory knew her pretty well."

"Oh no. Poor Grandma."

Jamie's face mirrored her sister's concerns, but for totally different reasons.

Cory sat on the edge of her bed and stared out the open window. The breeze on her face and soothing night sounds did little to calm her this evening. A helplessness, to which she was unaccustomed, washed over her.

For the first time in years, she thought of Estelle McNeilan and Frank Brown. The helplessness brought them rushing to her mind's forefront. She spent her adult life trying to repair the damage done by the two of them. For the most part, she had been successful. Not tonight. Here they were—in all their glory—to torment her again.

Cory McNeilan was born too early. Five years too early in fact. She didn't know why people stared at her and her grandmother when they walked down the street. She did not understand the indignant lift in her grandmother's chin when she heard old women whispering and pointing. And she certainly could not imagine what happened to her daddy. Everyone she knew had a daddy, a daddy who lived in the same house. But her daddy was missing. Maybe he was lost. Grandma and Mommy didn't talk about him. She didn't even know his name. It didn't stop her from praying every night, in the bed she shared with Mommy, that someday he would find his way home.

Then out of the blue it happened. Daddy came home. Or at least a reasonable facsimile. He suited Mommy and that was what mattered. Mommy said his name was Daddy. Grandma said his name was Frank. He laughed a lot and his breath had a sour smell that Cory didn't like, but she got used to it.

She got used to Frank coming in the house and swooping her into the air, her belly doing flip-flops while he laughed and Mommy laughed and Grandma watched with a strange look on her face. She got used to tiptoeing through the house in the middle of the day while Frank slept because he had a "headache." She got used to sleeping in Grandma's soft feather bed instead of with Mommy. She even preferred it. She got used to Mommy and Frank waking her up in the middle of the night, laughing and singing off-key, as they made their way to bed after a night of what they referred to as visiting friends. She even got used to raised, angry voices behind their bedroom door and the disturbing sound of an occasional slap. She was never sure of who slapped whom. But what Cory could not get used to was the

sad-angry-frightened expression Grandma wore most of the time now
that her Daddy-Frank had come home.

Grandma was Cory's world—she always had been, even before
Frank entered it. She didn't know how Mommy would be feeling from
one day to the next. Sometimes she would get mad and slap Cory over
a small matter. Other times, she would be sad and pout for days with
nary a word to her worried, little girl.

Not Grandma. Cory knew how she would be every morning when
she woke up and ran downstairs to greet her. Grandma would smile
and bend over to give her a kiss and a hug, setting her in a kitchen
chair as she prepared breakfast. She would tell Cory a story from the
Bible or have her sing a song she learned in Sunday School. Cory loved
being with Grandma. She was Grandma's "Morning Glory."

What Cory did not know until she was much older, was what Grace
McNeilan went through protecting her "Morning Glory" from the
harsh reality that was her life. Grace had expected a son-in-law before a grandchild, but Estelle always had her own way of doing things.
Grace wondered how she could be so selfish as to let something like
this happen. Estelle never apologized to God or anyone for having an
illegitimate child with a man whose identity she refused to reveal. She
told Grace she did not care what anyone thought of her. But Grace
cared. She especially cared about what it would do to a child growing
up in an unforgiving society.

Grace took it upon herself to shelter the innocent product of her
daughter's irresponsibility from as much harm as possible. She took
the adorable bundle to church as soon as she was born and ignored
the judgmental glares from the congregation. She knew God did not
hold her or the baby to blame, but He would if Grace did not do her
part in seeing that the little girl was brought up properly. She hoped
to avoid the same mistakes she felt she must have made with Estelle
that caused her turn out the way she had.

Grace was a long-standing member of the church and Cory was
an irresistible baby, so the ladies of the congregation soon warmed up
to them both. Maybe the Holy Spirit convicted them, causing them to
overlook the unfortunate circumstances surrounding Cory's birth.

After Frank moved in life for Grace became almost intolerable.
She told Estelle she and Frank would have to marry or get out of her

house. Estelle promptly informed her if they left, Cory left too. Was she prepared to throw her granddaughter out in the street? Grace backed down... for a while.

Frank worked sporadically. He drank incessantly. He and Estelle fought viciously. Grace did her best to comfort the child during the fights that grew more frequent and more volatile. Finally she could stand it no longer. She packed their belongings and set them outside the door in cardboard boxes. When Estelle got home and saw the boxes, she began to scream at her mother who was inside the house with Cory.

"Give me my daughter, Mama!" she blasted.

"Be reasonable, Estelle," Grace said from the other side of the locked screen door. "You and Frank can start fresh, just the two of you like it's supposed to be, and Cory can stay with me."

"I want my daughter. Send her out now."

"Please, Estelle. Let her stay with me. It's for the best."

"Listen to her, Estelle," Frank interjected. Grace heaved a sigh of relief, glad for once that Frank was on her side. "Let's get our stuff and get out of here."

"NO!" Estelle turned on him, her face purple with rage. "That old woman has wanted my baby from the beginning and she's not going to get her. She's mine. If she's kicking me out, I'm taking what's mine with me."

Grace and Frank both knew it was pointless to argue with Estelle when she got like this. Cory, who was no stranger to fights, sensed something traumatic was transpiring. She began to wail and clung to Grace's skirts. Grace tried to reason with Estelle one last time. "Please. I'll do anything. Let her stay with me. I promise I'll do anything you want."

"It's too late for that." Estelle grabbed the screen door and yanked on it until Grace finally reached out and unlocked it. Estelle snatched Cory by the hand and dragged her out the door.

Cory screamed, kicked, and fought for all she was worth, but her enraged mother would not be dissuaded. She was thrown into the back seat of Frank's Plymouth, where she continued to wail, her panicked, tear-stained face pressed against the glass.

Grace watched helplessly from the front porch as her determined daughter loaded her meager belongings into the trunk of the car. Frank resigned himself to the situation and bent over to retrieve a box. He didn't want to be burdened with Estelle's woods' colt, but there was nothing he could do about it now. Since he was pretty sure the little girl's real father wasn't going to materialize anytime soon, he needed to make Estelle see the benefits of letting Grace raise her. Otherwise he'd be stuck with her. When she calmed down, maybe he could talk some sense into her fool head.

Not another word was spoken to the terrified, bewildered little girl in the back seat as Frank and Estelle did what they had to do and drove away in a burst of dirt and gravel. Cory watched out the back glass until the white, frame house and her entire world were out of sight. She could not begin to comprehend how much her sheltered life was about to change.

Estelle and Frank were married the following week by the Justice of the Peace simply because no one would rent a house to them as long as they were living in sin. Grace was not invited to the ceremony. Frank was unsuccessful at convincing Estelle to send Cory back to her mother's house. It was several years before Cory saw her beloved grandmother again.

She was no longer anyone's "Morning Glory."

Frank Junior was born within a year. Cory was forced to grow up fast. She discovered her mother had little patience for teething infants and dirty diapers. She tried to become the buffer between Estelle's temper and little Frank's babyness, a daunting task for someone just entering her seventh year. By the time Emmy Lou came along, Cory had settled into her role as the family's resident baby-sitter. She knew what was expected of her to keep peace in the household. Or at least as much peace as was possible in the home of two drunken, angry parents and three neglected, hopeless off-spring.

She was fifteen when Frank left. One morning, he was just no longer there. Estelle did not explain his sudden disappearance and the children knew better than to ask. His departure was a relief and a sadness all at the same time. Now Estelle's frustrations were heaped upon Cory and the younger children. Cory knew there was nothing that would make Estelle happy, so her only hope was to lessen her misery.

She took housekeeping jobs to assist in the family's finances. She was mature, organized, and efficient, making her a much-desired commodity among the older ladies of the neighborhood. While working for a retired doctor and his wife, she met Harlan Steele, the young man who did their yard work. She knew him from around town—he was several years older than she—and they began to see a lot of each other. She felt obligated to stay with her family until Frank Jr. was older. She knew Estelle needed her, even though she was never told as much. Harlan was patient and understanding, as any young man in love would be. When Cory felt comfortable enough to leave Frank and Emmy Lou alone with Estelle, she married Harlan and they settled down to a life together on a farm which they worked for rent, and eventually bought.

Cory worked hard to become the mother she never had. She fashioned herself after the example Grace set, who had died when Cory was in her teens. She ran her home like a business, organizing everything down to slightest detail. Her three babies were fed on a schedule from which she never deviated. Even their diaper changes were scheduled into her regular household chores.

She was a successful doting mother and wife, doing everything right for the four men who depended on her. But her success came with a price. Her pursuit of perfection alienated the ones she loved most. They didn't question her love for them, but were dubious as to whether or not they could ever live up to the high standard she set for herself. Would she accept them when she realized their shortcomings? Their humanity?

Only Jesse, the youngest of her three boys, had not been threatened by her drive and determination. Cassie reminded her so much of him, with her easy laughter and infectious joy that sometimes made Cory forget life wasn't as carefree as they made it look. Jesse had been only eight when he drowned in the creek that ran behind the house. Occasionally a tight fist of fear would wrap itself around Cory's heart and a tiny voice would whisper that Cassie could be taken from her as easily and unexpectedly.

Cory continued to stare out the window. She had driven James away with her rigidity and iron strength. What she saw as personal attributes, he deeply resented. Now she seemed to be doing the same thing to Jamie. What could she do to prevent the cycle from starting all over again?

While Cory stared out her bedroom window, Jamie was in her own room staring holes through the ceiling.

Why couldn't her grandmother understand how she felt? She had thought when she approached her about the letters she had found, Grandma Cory empathized with her. Apparently not.

She wanted to be excited about the possibility that Sally Blake had been found. Solving the decades-old mystery seemed closer than ever. But since Judge Davis called to give her the news, frustration filled her heart. She found herself sympathizing with Grandma Cory. Maybe she was right. Maybe they were better off not knowing what happened to Sally? The sympathy she felt only angered her and added to her frustration.

When she thought of the remains in the well—now on their way to Franklin County—trepidation filled her heart. She didn't want to admit it—even to herself—that Grandma Cory was not the only one who dreaded what the forensics lab may discover.

# Chapter Twenty-four

The sound of glass breaking followed by gravel being slung by spinning tires woke Jamie with a start. Cassie was standing beside her bed in an instant. "Jamie? Are you awake? What was that?"

Jamie found her slippers and robe in the dark, and she and Cassie hurried out to the hallway. They clutched each other's hands in fear and crept down the stairs as one. A lamp was lit in the corner of the living room, it's dim glow casting shadows into the hallway. Grandma Cory was at the bottom of the stairs holding a broom and dustpan.

"Grandma Cory, what was it?" Cassie asked.

"Some kids, I guess," she answered. Her voice sounded old and tired.

"Here, Grandma, I'll do that," Jamie offered. She took the broom and dustpan from her grandmother's hands. Cory didn't resist.

Cassie grabbed Grandma Cory's arm. "Do you think whoever it was will be back?"

"Not likely. They've had their fun. They sat out front for a few minutes with the radio turned up. That's what woke me up. I heard a car door slam before they threw the rock."

Cassie tightened her grip on Grandma Cory's arm. Her green eyes were wide with alarm. "But what were they doing here? Why would they be throwing rocks at our house?"

Jamie straightened up with the dust pan of glass fragments. She met Grandma Cory's gaze over the top of Cassie's head. She lowered her eyes self-consciously. The motion wasn't wasted on Cassie. She looked from Jamie to Grandma Cory in something nearing a panic.

"What? What's going on?"

Grandma Cory put her hand over Cassie's and pried it loose from her arm. "It's nothing. They were just hoodlums. Don't worry about it. Just go back to bed."

Jamie could see Cassie wasn't satisfied with the answer, but even she knew when it was pointless to try to get information out of Grandma. That meant she'd be bugging Jamie about it later.

She gestured toward the window with the dustpan. "Should we cover the window with something tonight?"

"No, it'll be fine. You girls go on back to bed. I'll take care of it later."

"Are you sure, Grandma?" Cassie's voice trembled. "Maybe we should all sleep down here with you tonight."

Grandma Cory sighed heavily. Usually Cassie's endless questions got on her nerves, but tonight she didn't have the strength to get mad. She put her hand on Cassie's cheek. "No, honey. Everything's fine now. I'll see you in the morning."

Jamie dumped the broken glass into the wastebasket in the kitchen. Cassie did not take two steps away from her as they returned to Jamie's room. With no word of explanation, Cassie slid into her bed. Jamie sighed. It would be a tight fit, but there was no point in trying to convince Cassie the threat of danger was over.

"Jamie?" Cassie's voice said as soon as they situated the thin sheet over them. "Why did those kids break our window? That kind of stuff doesn't happen around here."

"Grandma said not to worry about it," Jamie said. "Just go to sleep."

"I can't go to sleep. I know there's something going on." Cassie propped herself up on her elbow and looked down at Jamie. "Why didn't Grandma go out and run them off before they had a chance to throw a rock at the window? Or at least call the police? Any other time she would've thrown a fit if somebody'd been sitting out in the driveway with their radio blasting."

Jamie didn't say anything. There was nothing to say. Cassie was right. Grandma Cory had no fear when it came to telling anyone what she thought about unacceptable behavior. Playing loud music in someone's driveway in the middle of the night certainly qualified as "unacceptable behavior".

"Come on, Jamie," Cassie hissed. "I saw that look Grandma gave you. You know what's going on, and so does she. I have a right to know too. I'm thirteen. It's bad enough that Grandma treats me like a child. I don't know why you have to."

Jamie didn't want to be the one to tell Cassie what she knew about their dad and Sally Blake. She almost wished she didn't know herself. But she remembered how resentful she was the day of her dad's funeral when she found out everyone else knew all about the situation except her. It wasn't fair to do it again to Cassie.

"Remember the remains they found in that well. They think it's the girl I told you about who dated Dad."

Cassie was watching Jamie intently. Whatever she was about to divulge, Cassie didn't want to miss a word of it.

"The last time anyone saw her was the night she got into a big fight with Dad," Jamie continued reluctantly. "She's been missing since that night. Twenty-five years ago."

"So everybody thinks Dad killed her?"

Cassie's instant and matter-of-fact response took Jamie aback. All these years the two sisters had never talked about what went on in their parents' house while their mom was still alive. Jamie remembered the hurtful comments and put-downs directed at Nancy by the man who would say he loved her in the very next breath. She remembered coming home from school to find Nancy in the kitchen sitting at the kitchen table with her head in her hands, her shoulders shaking with sobs. But she thought she was the only one who did remember.

Surely Cassie had been too young to remember. She was only eight when Nancy died. That was too young to notice all the things going on in that house—wasn't it? Nancy never brought it up, even when Jamie caught her crying. She would just take Jamie's hand, give her a reassuring smile, and pull herself together. She'd set a plate of cookies on the table for a snack and then ask Jamie about her day; the tears forgotten. At least Jamie assumed they were forgotten. But *she* never forgot. She never forgot the wounded look in her mother's eyes, or the way she'd flinch when James came up behind her suddenly and pulled her into his arms.

He loved doing that; startling her. Reminding her of the power he held over her just by the touch of his hands. It was times like that when Jamie hated him most.

But not Cassie. She never hated anyone. Why should she? She was everybody's darling. The self-confident, effervescent one who could hold a roomful of adults in the palm of her hand by the time she could walk.

Jamie nodded. "I figure that's why those kids were out in the driveway tonight. They've heard the story from their parents, who have probably been reliving it ever since they heard about the remains being found in that well. It's probably the biggest gossip going around Jenna's Creek right now."

"How could anyone think Dad would do something like that?"

Jamie opened her mouth to answer; to say something reassuring and hopeful that would put Cassie's mind to rest. Then she realized Cassie was thinking out loud more than looking for an answer. She did remember. She hadn't forgotten the look in her mother's eyes, or the subtle warning in her father's hands when he'd take hold of his young wife. Anyone who knew James Steele knew it was within his power to commit a violent crime against a woman—especially the two sisters sharing the narrow twin bed.

Jamie had just dozed off when she heard the tapping of a hammer against the door frame downstairs. She climbed out of bed again and went to investigate—alone this time. Cassie was sound asleep.

Grandma Cory had attached a piece of plywood over the broken pane in the door's glass. Her mouth was full of nails and her eyes moist.

"Grandma? I thought you said we could fix the window in the morning."

She drove in the last two nails before she turned to answer. "They killed Henry," she said brokenly.

Jamie's mouth dropped open. "What?"

"I found him in the driveway. He must have went out to see who was there and they... they clubbed him in the head with something. A tire iron, most likely."

"Oh, Grandma, no." Jamie burst into tears and threw her arms around Cory's neck. "How awful! Poor Henry."

"Hush now. You'll wake Cassie." Grandma Cory soothed her, patting her back and stroking her hair. Their tears of grief mingled together. After the tears were spent, Cory said, "I put him in the barn. If you'll get up early, you can help me bury him. We'll tell Cassie what happened later, when she's not so scared. I don't want your grandpa to know about it at all. He doesn't need to go getting upset."

Jamie squeezed into the bed next to Cassie. She turned her face into the pillow and cried herself to sleep.

A gentle nudge roused Jamie from a fitful sleep. She dressed quietly so as not to wake Cassie and then followed her grandmother downstairs. The sun had not yet broken on the horizon as Cory pulled the wheelbarrow out of the shed and headed toward the barn. Jamie followed silently, dragging the shovel behind her, dreading the job ahead. As she had gotten older, Henry's existence had begun to mean less and less to her. He became another fixture on the back porch—much like Grandma Cory's potted plants that she also overlooked—but she hated to think anyone would intentionally harm him.

Just like Grandma said the night before, Henry was laying in the empty manger in the barn. The sight of his lifeless body brought fresh tears to Jamie's eyes. A small cut on the side of his head and a trail of dried blood running from inside his parted mouth down his chin, were the only signs that he had been injured. He stared up at her through half-open eyes.

"Is there a blanket or something we could wrap him in?" she asked. She couldn't bear the thought of putting Henry in the cold ground with nothing to keep him warm.

"There should be a blanket or rug around here someplace."

Together they lifted the dog out of the manger and placed him as gently as possible into the wheelbarrow, as if afraid of disturbing his eternal slumber. He was much heavier than Jamie anticipated. She wondered how Grandma Cory got him to the barn by herself last night.

A quick search of the barn turned up the remnants of an old blanket used to cover seedlings in the garden when there was the threat of a late frost. Jamie wrapped the blanket securely around Henry's form.

Jamie opened the long, metal gate and Cory pushed the wheelbarrow into the pasture, past the gaping, curious cows, until they were out of sight of the barn. It was imperative the grave be far enough away from the house that it not be discovered until enough time had lapsed for Henry's simple existence to slip into the gray recesses of Harlan's memory. As far as Cassie was concerned, she would walk up and down Betterman Road today, calling Henry's name, wondering where he may have gone off to. She would stop along the way and ask the neighbors if they had seen him. Eventually she would tire of her search and return home, figuring he had been scared off the night before by the noise and would find his own way home in due time. After a few days she would realize he wasn't coming back. She would imagine he wandered off into the woods somewhere to die of old age. She seldom ventured beyond the pasture, and it was unlikely she would find the fresh mound of earth. After shedding a few tears she would assume he was happier on that big back porch in the sky where no one tripped over him on a regular basis.

Grandma Cory rested against the wheelbarrow as Jamie began to dig into the hard, unforgiving soil. Her hands were blistered and a trickle of perspiration traveled down her spine by the time the hole was deep enough to satisfy her that Henry would be safe from other animals that might smell his remains and try to dig him up.

Cory did not say a word until the dog's blanket-wrapped body was lowered into the hole. She took the shovel from Jamie and carefully laid a scoop of fresh dirt into the hole on top of him. "Good-bye, Henry," she said. "You've been a good friend."

Her simple sentiment surprised Jamie. She had no idea Grandma Cory perceived Henry as anything but a worthless bag of bones, always underfoot.

Cory smiled at her expression. She put an arm around Jamie's shoulders and pulled her close. "Yes, dear. Henry meant a lot to me. He always had time to listen to an old lady's complaints."

Jamie gulped back the tears in her throat. Just when she thought she understood her grandmother, she said or did something that threw off her whole perception of her. She never suspected Grandma Cory was the type of person who needed someone to listen to her complaints. Jamie always assumed she was too strong to need anything from anyone. Everyone relied on her, not the other way around. What a shame her complaints were only voiced to a dog because no one else took the time to listen.

Jamie grabbed the handles of the wheelbarrow. "Come on, Grandma. Let me give you a ride back to the barn."

Cory looked at the wheelbarrow and then at Jamie. She laughed. "Not on your life. If I sat in that thing, I'd never be able to get back out."

"Aw, come on. Let's take 'er for a spin."

Cory looked skeptical. "You won't dump me out, will you?"

"Not if I can help it."

Cory shrugged and plopped down into the wheelbarrow. She reclined back with her legs dangling over the side and held the shovel across her knees. Jamie couldn't remember the last time she saw anything so funny. She covered her mouth with her hand and tried not to laugh.

"Hey, none of that," Grandma Cory said with a wide smile. "I didn't know I was gonna to be subjected to ridicule."

"Sorry." Jamie gasped. She pulled herself together, gripped the handles and lifted. The wheelbarrow barely came off the ground. Laughter erupted out of her throat again. She was not prepared for the reality that her grandmother was not a petite woman. She took a deep breath and heaved again. This time her attempt to lift the back of the wheelbarrow off the ground proved successful.

"Keep it balanced. Keep it balanced," Grandma Cory squealed as Jamie lurched forward. "Steady. Don't dump me out."

Once Jamie got the weight of her load balanced, the going became easier. She pushed through the tall grass, up the steady grade until they were in sight of the barn. Her knees buckled under her just as she reached the top of the grade. She set the wheelbarrow down and leaned against the handles, gasping for breath, partly from suppressed laughter and partly from fatigue.

The milk cows were waiting outside the barn door. When they spotted them at the top of the hill, they ambled in their direction, the cow bells around their necks clanging in the still morning air. It was milking time and they couldn't understand the delay. "Let's go, Jamie. The girls're waiting. Don't worry. It's all downhill from here."

Jamie gripped the handles and raised them hip-high. "Okay. Here we go."

Going downhill had its advantages. Now the wheelbarrow and the force of gravity took over more of the work. The disadvantage was that Jamie could barely keep up with it. As it careened toward the approaching bovine, she struggled to keep her grip on the handles. Grandma Cory could tell by the increasing speed, her operator was no longer in control.

"Slow down," she shouted, too late for driving lessons. She realized she'd have more luck yelling at the cows instead. "Out of the way! Get out of the way, you stupid cows!" She tried to wave her arms, but the shovel bouncing up and down painfully on her knees prevented her from doing so.

Jamie tried to slow the wheelbarrow's progress, but it was all she could do to hold on. The cows were coming closer, Grandma Cory's cries were getting louder, and Jamie's sore hands were slippery with sweat. She was barely able to keep her legs under her as she stumbled after the runaway wheelbarrow. To make matters worse, a bubble of laughter began at the bottom of her throat and started working its way up.

The cows were only a few feet away when their simple minds registered that they were about to be hit. They turned and lumbered back down the grade toward the barn, the wheelbarrow right on their heels. Grandma Cory hollered, "Move it! Move it!" at the top of her voice.

Jamie chuckled, softly at first. The longer she looked at the rear ends of the fleeing cows, the harder she laughed. The ground leveled off and she slowed the wheelbarrow to a walk. She was laughing so hard that when the front wheel hit a rut in the pasture, she lost the battle of keeping the wheelbarrow upright. The wheelbarrow, shovel, and Grandma Cory hit the dew-covered ground with a thump. Jamie fell on the ground beside her in a heap, her side aching from running and laughing.

"It's... it's... not... it's not..." Grandma Cory was laughing as hard as Jamie. She tried to catch her breath to tell Jamie something. Each time they looked at each other, they fell into fresh fits of laughter.

"It's... not..."

"It's not what?" Jamie gasped.

"It's not good… to make… the cows… run… like that."

Jamie rolled onto her back and stared up at the sky, her eyes wet from laughing. "We won't be getting much milk this morning."

"Did you see their faces when they thought we were going to hit them?" Grandma Cory asked through fresh laughter as Jamie helped her to her feet.

"You should've seen yourself in that wheelbarrow," Jamie snickered. "I thought I was going to wet my pants."

"I think I did," Cory admitted. "I should have known better than to let you gimme a ride, at least downhill. Big mistake."

"It's a good thing no one saw us."

Grandma Cory agreed. "I can see the headlines tomorrow morning. Young girl and fat woman terrorize cattle with runaway wheelbarrow."

Jamie righted the wheelbarrow, set the shovel inside, and pushed it toward the barn. She turned and looked at her grandma as if seeing her for the first time. Grandma Cory's eyes sparkled and her cheeks were still flushed from her experience down the hill. Jamie couldn't recall the last time she looked so young and refreshed. Maybe Cassie was right. Maybe they had more in common than Jamie thought. If she began to see Grandma Cory as a friend rather than an adversary, maybe there was hope for a relationship between them after all.

# Chapter Twenty-five

Tate was outside Noel's office door clocking in when Jamie arrived at the drugstore. She smiled and nodded a greeting while awaiting her turn to punch in for the day. He found her timecard among the others, but held onto it.

Her mood was still light from her morning with Grandma Cory. Whatever Tate had on his mind to do or say, she would allow without comment, and then he'd be on his way. His biggest crime was just wanting to be the center of attention. Things would go smoother if she just let him get it out of his system.

"Hey, Jamie."

"Morning, Tate. How was your weekend?"

"Great!" he answered, enthusiastically. "I went to a party at the Point. A lot of kids from school were there along with some older people. You wouldn't believe all the beer we drank." He laughed and told her a story of someone at the party drinking too much and falling into the water. It wasn't long before most of the inebriated teens followed suit, many still fully clothed, others only barely so.

As the story wore on, Jamie glanced pointedly at her watch, hoping he'd get the message that it was getting late and both of them should be getting to work.

"You should have been there, Jamie. It was wild."

"I'm sure it was." She reached for the timecard he still held in his hand.

"Oh, that's right, I forgot. You don't go to parties. You go to church."

"Could I please have my card? I don't want to be late clocking in."

"Oh no, we can't let our Jamie be late," he mocked derisively. "Wouldn't that be terrible? You might lose out on employee of the month. It's usually a toss-up between you and Jason, huh? Don't worry. I bet he'll let you win." He nudged her playfully with his elbow and put her timecard in her hand.

Jamie slid the timecard into the slot without responding. She returned the timecard to its position on the board and turned to go downstairs.

"Everybody in Jenna's Creek knows they found that girl," Tate said, "Your dad's old girlfriend." Jamie froze on the stairs. "And everybody knows how she got in that well."

"They do not know whose remains they are," she said, turning around to face him. Her hand gripped the railing for dear life. Her knuckles went white. "They don't even know if it's a man or a woman."

"That ain't what I heard. I heard they found her with an ax still buried in her skull; an ax with your dad's fingerprints all over it."

Jamie's eyes flashed. She stepped forward, her nose nearly touching his. "You better watch what you're saying, Tate?"

He chuckled nervously and took a step backward, raising his hands in front of him as if to shield himself against her coming wrath. "Whoa now, don't get mad at me. I'm just telling you what I heard."

"Would you two get out of the way? Some of us have work to do." Barb spoke up from the bottom of the stairs.

Jamie stepped away from Tate, hating it that someone had overheard their conversation, but too angry to care.

Tate brushed past Jamie to give Barb a disarming smile on his way down the stairs. "Sorry, Barb." He patted her on the shoulder as he breezed past.

Barb smiled as she watched him head to the front of the store. Then she looked up at Jamie still at the top of the stairs and shook her head. Jamie hurried down the stairs avoiding eye contact. She knew what Barb was thinking. It was written all over her face. *Tate didn't mean any harm. He was just trying to be funny, and maybe she needed to learn to take a joke.*

Jamie knew how to take a joke, when something was funny. Tate was not funny. And if he didn't keep his mouth shut today, well, she didn't know what she'd do. Fortunately, Jason was already at work in the stockroom. She hoped he was staying. She doubted if she could handle working with Tate this morning. Jason glanced up and nodded at her in greeting when she walked in before going straight back to work. He didn't even notice her flushed cheeks or shaking hands. Good. She was so angry she didn't know if she'd be able to utter an intelligible word if she had to.

She had never felt such anger toward another human being as she did toward Tate Craig right now. How could he be so callous and unfeeling? How could she have had even the slightest crush on him just a few weeks ago? The bond she sensed developing between her and Grandma Cory, along with the warm glow that came with it, were forgotten. Now all she could think of was Tate's cruel words. Had he been involved in what happened to Henry last night? Did he know who was? There had been no sensible reason to hurt that old dog; no reason to get mad at her family at all. Even if James had been involved in Sally Blake's disappearance, he was long gone. Why bother her, Cassie and Grandma Cory?

Was Tate only repeating what was all over town already, like he said? She was home on the farm all day yesterday, so she didn't know what had been said after the discovery was announced on the radio. Maybe he just thought he'd let her know about the rumors before she was surprised by them out on the street.

Yeah, right. An ax imbedded in the skull! How ridiculous! Wouldn't Judge Davis have told her something so gruesome?

At least she prayed it was ridiculous.

Jason sliced off the top of a carton of hand creme and slid it across the floor for her to put away. She hefted it onto the shelf and turned to wait for the next box. She eyed Jason thoughtfully. He never showed signs of judging others or enjoying whatever pain they were experiencing. She needed a sympathetic ear. Perhaps she could talk to him.

"Have you heard anything about human remains being found in an abandoned well on Old County Road 24?"

He didn't look up from his work. "Yeah, my old man was talking about it last night."

"Who do you think it could be?"

He shrugged noncommittally. "Don't know."

She wasn't going to let him off that easily. "Have you ever heard about a girl from around here named Sally Blake? She disappeared about twenty-five years ago? They think it could be her."

"Do they?" A box of floor wax slid across the floor and landed against her foot.

"Yes. What do you think?"

"About what?"

He had to be the most frustrating man on the planet to try to talk to. "About the remains in the well belonging to the girl who disappeared; Sally Blake."

"Oh. What did you ask me again?"

The box at her feet was still untouched. Another one careened across the concrete floor and thumped against the first. Jason looked at the boxes and then at Jamie, consternation evident on his face. He straightened up and folded his arms across his chest. What was wrong with her today, why was she not keeping up, his expression demanded.

Finally, she had his full attention. "Jason, do you ever listen to me when I talk to you?"

"What kind of a question is that?"

She closed her eyes briefly and shook her head. Then she sighed, opened them again, and asked, "Could you please give me a straight answer without asking another question in response? I don't know what they teach you people over in Blanton, but around here, we pay attention when someone else is speaking to us, and we answer their questions if those questions are reasonable."

"I'll try to remember that in the future, Miss Steele."

"Good. Now will you please answer my question?"

"At the risk of sounding redundant, what question would that be?"

She put her hands on either side of her head and clutched her hair with her fists. "Aaaah! You are driving me insane. By the time this summer is over, I am going to be totally white-headed."

He grinned at the spectacle she created. "You crack me up, Jamie.

I have such a good time messing with you. You take everything so seriously."

"Me?" Her arms fell to her side. "Well, let me tell you something. You're the one who's serious all the time. I try to talk to you, but you always have your mind on work."

He glanced around the room with widened eyes. "That's because we're at work. I take my work seriously. You take life seriously."

"No, I don't," she countered. "You're the one everybody talks about. You're the one they think is an old stick in the mud."

"That's funny. That's what I've heard about you."

"It is?"

He nodded.

She slapped her forehead with the heel of her hand and moaned dramatically. "So everyone thinks I'm just like you?"

He nodded again, a smile tugging at the corners of his mouth.

"No wonder they think I'm weird," Jamie sighed.

"No, they think I'm weird because I'm just like you. You know what else they think? They think we'd make the perfect couple. They think we're meant for each other," Jason countered.

It was impossible to tell if he was kidding or not. A blush rose in her cheeks at his suggestion, although it wasn't as distasteful as she once thought it would be.

To avoid embarrassment in case he was only kidding, she put her hands on her hips and steered the conversation back to their original topic. "Jason, you still aren't answering my question."

She thought she saw disappointment flash across his face, but as quickly as it appeared, it was gone. His playful manner diminished as well. "I don't know if the missing girl is the one they found in the well or not. I guess they can find out, but I don't see what good it's going to do. They'll never figure out how she got in that well."

Jamie was a little sorry he was back to his old no-nonsense self, but she wanted to hear his opinion on the remains in the well. "What makes you say that?"

"How could they? There won't be any evidence left. The trail's gone cold by now."

"Everybody in town thinks my dad did it." She swallowed hard. "They think he killed her."

His eyes darkened. "Yeah, that's what I heard," he said slowly. "I'm sorry."

Jamie stared at the boxes at her feet. "Someone killed our dog," she blurted out, her eyes still focused on the floor.

"What?"

"We heard a car in front of the house last night. They were shouting and spinning gravel. Then someone threw a rock through the glass in the front door. My grandma went out to investigate after they left and found our dog, Henry, in the driveway. They killed him." By the time she finished, she was crying.

"Oh, Jamie, I'm sorry." He hurried over to her and put his hand on her shoulder. "Is there… can I do anything for you?"

She stiffened and pulled away. His hand dropped ineffectually to his side. "No, I'm fine," she sniffed and with great effort, regained her composure. "I didn't mean to bother you with my problems."

Jason opened his mouth, but before he could get the first word out, she turned and hurried toward the restroom. Out of the corner of her eye, she saw him shrug his shoulders and bend down to retrieve the two boxes she left on the floor. Just as she thought. He didn't care anything about hearing her problems. All he ever cared about was work.

She washed her face with cool water and inspected her face in the mirror. She had wanted to tell him everything. To unload. But she couldn't. Now she was glad she refrained. He said she took life too seriously. He would say she was over-reacting again. She would keep her thoughts to herself. None of it was his problem.

Noel Wyatt was sitting in his office with the chair turned toward the wall while Tate tormented Jamie about the remains found in the well on the Trimble place. He was preparing to intervene when he heard Barb's voice bring the altercation to an end. Poor Jamie. She would get stares and whispers all over town for a long while. Discovering her father was innocent would be the only thing that might spare her and her family months or even years of renewed suspicion. Noel remembered Sally Blake's disappearance well. She worked for him at the store, like many of Jenna's Creek's teenagers, to earn spending money while she went to school. She didn't need the job as badly as some kids—her parents had plenty, but she was a good worker if he could keep her attention focused on the work and off the boys. Her disappearance was all anyone talked about. The community convicted and sentenced James Steele within the first week. Justin had been the object of his sympathy then. He gave the boy work to do in the stockroom so he wouldn't have to see the stares or hear the vicious remarks about his brother. The public's reaction became so volatile that for a time, Justin was forced to take a leave of absence.

Things cooled down significantly after James left town to join the Navy. Justin came back to work, and slowly Jenna's Creek moved on to something else.

In his own mind, Noel also suspected James had done something to Sally. Although he never voiced his opinion to anyone, he could see no other logical explanation. The girl was high strung, that was for sure, but it was not plausible to him that she would just take off without a word to anyone. He'd heard the rumors that she'd been seeing a married man. He wouldn't put anything past her; she liked all men, but who was he to judge. He acknowledged that he didn't know all the details. There may have been more to the story than he or anyone else knew. Who else would have a motive or the capacity to kill her? No one as far as he could tell.

Now with the remains of a body being found on the same property where she was last seen alive, the mystery was back in the forefront of everyone's minds. Old-timers were telling younger folks the story, probably embellishing the facts to suit their thirst for the sensational. Like the story of the ax in the skull Tate mentioned to Jamie. It was a product of someone's imagination—probably Tate's.

Noel had not been in his office staring at the wall for nothing. He had bought the high-backed leather office chair when he realized he needed somewhere to hide from the constant needs and demands of his employees and patrons. The chair worked perfectly. By the time anyone found him, he was unwound and ready to go back to work.

Today his reason for hiding was Abigail Blackwood and their son, Eric; the son who was supposed to belong to Jack Blackwood. Abby called him last night to let him know how Eric was accepting his medication. So far, things were going well, God be praised.

His mother had figured out Eric's lineage, Noel was sure of it. She hadn't approached him about it—and knowing her—she never would.

Still, somehow she knew. If she could deduce the truth, who would be next? What if Eric ever needed a blood transfusion for surgery? When Jack Blackwood offered his blood, would the doctors realize he was not the boy's biological father? What about physical appearance? Had no one ever noticed the incredible likeness between Eric and the man who owned the town's pharmacy?

His mind went from Eric to the remains in the well, and back again. Worrying over either situation would not change the outcome. He thought of how true it was that ignorance was bliss. A month ago, the possibility of his relationship to Eric becoming public knowledge never crossed his mind. Most of Jenna's Creek had forgotten all about Sally Blake. Now the town's peaceful existence, protected by ignorance, could be rocked by either or both revelations.

# Chapter Twenty-six

Thank you for seeing me, Donna."

"It's not a problem, David." Donna Blake stepped away from the door and motioned Judge Davis into the foyer. "I always have time for an old friend. How's Bernice?"

He stepped inside the foyer and glanced around awkwardly. If he was here on a social visit, he would not be ill at ease. The conversation ahead of him was the cause of his discomfort. "She's fine. Every where I go, people are concerned about her. I don't think she realized before this, how many caring friends she had."

"She's a wonderful woman," Donna said. "Please come in and sit down. I know you didn't come here to tell me about Bernice's health, although I'm glad to hear she's doing well."

The judge sat carefully on the edge of an elegant, upholstered sofa. Donna seated herself across from him and offered him a drink.

"No, thank you."

She looked at him expectantly with raised eyebrows.

"Donna. The last thing I want to do is upset you."

Her brow furrowed and her gaze darkened as she waited for him to go on.

"I'm here to ask you something that I know you aren't going to want to talk about. I'm truly sorry to have to do this."

"Please, David. I cannot bear the suspense. Just ask me what you came here to ask. I'll help you if I can."

"It's about Sally," he said quietly.

All the blood drained from Donna Blake's face. Her garnet-tinted lips stood out against the stark whiteness. "Sally?" she breathed. "What— what about Sally?"

"Donna, I know Vernon told you and Ted the remains they found on the Trimble's property could belong to... It could be... Sally."

There was a sharp intake of air before she spoke. "Are you telling me they found out already who...?"

"No, no. It isn't anything like that," he assured her. "Before they found the remains, I was researching her case again on my own." He didn't think it was necessary to mention Jamie's name, especially since there was a Steele attached to the end of it. "I could say it has to do with my vanity," he replied with a small smile. "Her's was the only case I never saw closed."

She stood up and began to pace the floor. "David, I don't know if I am prepared to go through this again. I realize I may have to if they tell me..." She dropped wearily into her chair. "Believe me, I want to know what happened to her... or I think I do."

He leaned toward her. "Is there anything I can get you? A glass of water, perhaps."

She waved her hand at him in response. "No, no. I'm fine. Ted and I have been trying to prepare ourselves for this. Twenty-five years ago we were told to prepare for the worst. But the news never came. We waited and waited. Finally, I gave up waiting." She turned imploring eyes to him. "Is that horrible, David? A mother giving up on her daughter. I just couldn't... I couldn't spend another day running to the window every time I heard a car in the driveway." Her voice dropped to an anguished whisper. "I just couldn't do it."

"You didn't do anything wrong, Donna."

"You know, I always had it in my head she just took off. I suppose it was easier to accept that she hated me so much she wanted me out of her life, than to think she'd been murdered. I didn't want to think about her suffering. I couldn't. So I let myself suffer instead. The last time I saw her we had a big fight. She was getting ready to go to that party." She stared into space as the years retreated back to that night. "She was wearing a dress I had never seen before. I hadn't bought it for her and I know Ted never would have. Well, I thought it was much too revealing for a girl her age, and I told her so. We were both hot-headed. Ted always said neither of us knew how to lose an argument. We said too much. She left mad. I was mad. And she was still wearing that blasted dress. That was the last time I saw her."

"I convinced myself she had grown tired of little, insignificant Jenna's Creek and her meddling mother. She always said she would leave here someday anyway." Donna sat back wearily in her chair. "I pictured her living somewhere, married to a wonderful man, with a few children and a mortgage. If she was, then I knew she was happy, even if she wasn't here with me. I learned to accept it." Her face hardened. "But I could not accept that she had died at the hands of... of a jealous boyfriend."

Judge Davis waited quietly as her eyes focused on him again.

"Well, you said you had a question for me."

"Yes, I do. And again I apologize for disturbing you. What you were saying about Sally leaving town was a possibility I had been looking into myself." He seriously doubted it now, since the remains had been found, but he wasn't going to overlook any detail this time.

"I discovered something a few days ago, and it's been bothering me. I cannot make any sense out of it."

She leaned forward in anticipation.

"I found a withdrawal slip from your bank that indicated Sally had cashed in a significantly large savings bond." Again he kept Jamie's involvement to himself. "I believe it was worth a thousand dollars. Would you, by any chance, know what need she would have for that much money?"

Donna brushed an imaginary wisp of hair away from her face. "Ted and I were aware of the transaction," she said. "And yes, I do know what it was for."

When he realized no more information was forthcoming, he asked, "Could you fill me in?"

With a resolute lift of her chin, she said, "I really do not see how knowing that could help you find out what happened to Sally."

The judge had made a decent living for himself by convincing people it was in their best interest to tell him things they did not wish to divulge. He learned to read each individual to discern what would make them comfortable enough to talk. Donna Blake was nobody's fool—much like her daughter. Yet he knew under that tough exterior was a loving mother who wanted to know what became of Sally.

"You could be right," he agreed. "There could be no reason at all for me to know why she needed so much money. But twenty-five years ago, we missed something. We overlooked something that may have let us know what happened to her." He could see she was interested in the point he was trying to make.

"Now, like it or not, in a few days, we may find out…" he tried to put it delicately, "what became of her. I know if that's the case, you and Ted are going to want to know exactly what happened when she disappeared. The information you have about the money could prove to be crucial in finding that out."

Although not completely convinced, he could see she was weakening. "It was a family matter, David. I don't want all of Jenna's Creek knowing our business."

"I respect that, Donna. I truly do. Just because you tell me, doesn't mean it has to become public knowledge."

He did not know what he expected her to say, but he wasn't prepared for her announcement.

"Sally was going to have a baby."

His mouth dropped open in astonishment. He clamped it shut again in hopes of regaining his professionalism. "Oh. I had no idea."

"No one did," she said. "That was the point. The money was not for an abortion," she said quickly, "if that's what you're thinking. We wouldn't sink that low. She was going to take the money and elope, stay gone for a week or two, and when she came back… well, you know. The baby would be born—perhaps a little too early for respectable people—but we hoped the town busybodies would lose count of how many months transpired since the honeymoon."

"Sally was going to elope with James Steele?"

"Oh, goodness, no!" Donna shrieked, her cheeks crimson. "Tim Shelton. He was the father."

The judge shook his head to clear it. "What? Now, back up a minute. I'm confused. Tim Shelton? I thought Sally was seeing James Steele. Wasn't Tim engaged to Noreen Trimble?"

"Yes," she nodded her head, "that's right. Sally was seeing James Steele and Tim was engaged to Noreen, but they were in love with each other."

The situation reminded the judge of a scene from an afternoon soap opera. "Donna, how do you know all this?"

"Because they both admitted it. Tim came to the house with Sally one night to tell us she was expecting. They said they weren't proud of what they had done, and Tim was distraught over his treatment of that poor Trimble girl. But with a baby coming and all, they knew they had to set things right."

"And by setting things right, you mean Tim intended to jilt Noreen after becoming publicly engaged to her. Then he and Sally were going to disappear for a couple of weeks and come home with a lie for the whole town. Is that it?"

"Oh, David, you make it sound horrible," she said, disapprovingly. "Do you have any idea how many young people get married when a baby is already on the way, and spend the rest of their lives pretending it wasn't?"

"But what about Noreen...and James? Didn't they deserve the truth?"

"What point would that have served? It would have only added insult to injury. We all agreed this was the best way to spare them as much pain as possible."

"Oh, come on, Donna. You weren't thinking about them. You weren't even thinking about Sally and Tim. You were thinking about your reputation in the community. You didn't want to look bad to your country club friends."

The resolute set of Donna's chin was back. "Those are your country club friends too, David. You would want to avoid an uncomfortable situation yourself, if you could."

He took a deep breath and reined in his aggravation at her sanctimonious behavior. "Didn't you think James and Noreen would figure everything out when Tim and Sally disappeared together?"

"We were going to cross that bridge when we came to it."

"Why didn't Ted give them money to run away on instead of having Sally cash in a savings bond?" he wanted to know. "That wasn't very prudent, financially speaking."

"We did not want anyone to know that we were privy to their plan. We wanted to look as shocked as Tim's parents."

"So, you had it all worked out?"

"We thought we did."

"What went wrong?"

Donna sighed and shook her head. "Sally never was the most tactful thing. Ted and I assumed she told James about the baby and he did something to her in a jealous rage."

"Why didn't you tell the authorities? It would have been motive—something we didn't have. It might have been enough to make a case against him."

"If you had done your job, you could've made a case without our help," she snapped.

The judge swallowed his anger. This was not the time to lose his temper. "Had we been in possession of this juicy tidbit of information," he couldn't keep the sarcasm from his voice, "it could've changed everything."

"And it may've changed nothing. James Steele still could have gotten away with murder. I wasn't going to risk my daughter's reputation for a slim-to-none chance."

He sighed heavily. "Don't you realize this opens the way for a whole new set of motives and possible suspects?"

"What do you mean?"

"I mean, Sally and Tim were behaving in a way that can make a person a lot of enemies. Tim was engaged to Noreen Trimble. They even had their engagement party the night she disappeared. If Tim was going to run off with Sally, why did he plan a big, costly celebration with Noreen? Did you ever think he may not've been as anxious to marry Sally as he seemed? He may've had his doubts about the baby belonging to him. I know I would have."

"That's enough, David."

"What if Sally told someone else about the baby, not James?" the judge said, thinking about the alleged married man Sally had been rumored to be seeing. "What if she accused him of being the father, and he didn't appreciate her threats? Maybe this man had a lot to lose, and he couldn't afford to have Sally tell the whole town she was having his baby."

"David!" Donna shrieked. "You do realize that's my daughter you're talking about, don't you? I don't really know what you're trying to get at, but none of it's true. The baby belonged to Tim and that's all there is to it."

He reminded himself he was not interrogating a witness. Donna was a friend; he didn't want to make an enemy out of her. Softly he said, "There's a possibility that Tim had a motive."

"Tim? You've got to be joking. He's the sweetest boy we ever met. He was from a good family. He could never have done something to Sally. It wasn't in him."

"How do you know that, Donna? Whatever happened to the money from the savings bond?"

"I don't know," she admitted.

"That's a lot of money to just vanish. Tim was the only one who knew about its existence. Maybe he actually loved Noreen like the whole town thought. Maybe he wasn't interested in being someone's daddy just yet, and all that money right in front of his nose…"

"Well… no…" She was visibly rattled. "You're wrong, I know you are. Ted gave him a job. How could he have come to work for us if he had…oh, the very idea is absurd! I don't know how you could suggest such a thing."

He abandoned the attorney role and went back to being her friend. "I just wish we had all the facts back then, Donna. We may've had an easier time getting to the truth. It's what we all wanted." He patted her hand consolingly.

"As far as I'm concerned, we did get to the truth. James Steele found out Sally was seeing Tim—and maybe about the baby too—and he… well, you know what a temper he had."

"Even if that was true, we probably didn't have enough evidence against James. I mean, we don't know for sure that Sally told him about the baby, and we had no way of finding it out. Sally wasn't here to tell us and I'm sure James would've lied about it if she had."

"That's why we didn't tell you about the baby," she reasserted.

He had to know one more thing.

"Is all this the reason Ted gave Tim a job?"

"Yes. We discussed it the night they told us about the baby. Ted would set Tim up in business so he could provide a nice living for Sally. After the disappearance Ted didn't see any reason to change those plans."

So Jamie's suspicions had been accurate. There was something significant about Tim's employment coinciding with Sally's disappearance.

He stood up to leave. "I appreciate your honesty, Donna. I cannot say I understand why you handled things the way you did, but if I was in your situation, what's to say I may not have reacted the same way?"

Always the hostess, she smiled cordially and walked him to the door. "Give my love to Bernice," she said, as if they had spent the afternoon discussing more pleasant matters.

On his way down the stone path to his car, he considered keeping this newest development from Jamie. On one hand, Tim Shelton could be considered a suspect if there was more to the story than Donna Blake knew or was telling. On the other hand, the case against James was stronger than ever. Tim was most certainly the man James had referred to in his threatening letters to Sally. He had vowed to make her sorry if she continued to see him. If he had found out about the baby … if Sally had been stupid enough to tell him … well, it was hard to tell what the man was capable of.

Dr. Lou Gochberg was Auburn County's coroner. He had carried the illustrious title for the past sixteen years. Every time he was up for reelection, he was easily voted in. Most of the time his name was the only one on the ballot because no other doctor in the county wanted the hassle.

Today he wished anyone else had the job. He had just gotten off the phone with Sheriff Patterson. The remains from the well had been identified and returned to Auburn County. They were now sitting in a back room of Lou's office building. The sheriff would call Mr. and Mrs. Blake and tell them to meet him at Lou's office. When they received Vernon's call, they would immediately recognize the significance of it. Like the rest of Auburn County, they were awaiting the results from the forensics lab. They would be the first citizens to hear the news.

It would be Lou's job to officially inform them that the remains found in Will Trimble's well belonged to their daughter. Then he would explain in layman's terms, the exact findings from the forensics lab.

There was a ninety percent probability that Sally's death had resulted from a blunt trauma to the back of the head. In all probability, she was dead by the time she was placed in the well. It was all the information he had. They would want more. They would demand answers. But Lou did not have them. Their questions were beyond answering after all these years.

He would also give them Sally's personal effects found at the well site. It wasn't much. It had been bagged separately and placed in a small box about the size of a man's shoe box. Lou had examined the contents when he received them this morning. The box contained a severely, dilapidated pair of shoes, a leather belt—so shrunken and weathered that only the buckle made it easily recognizable, one gold earring, an imitation gold necklace and a ladies' watch.

Lou had seen almost everything in his medical career. This was definitely not the first time he had to tell parents their child was gone forever. As county coroner and medical examiner—one and the same in Auburn County—he had grown accustomed to seeing things that woke him up at night, drenched in a cold sweat. Still, his throat constricted tightly and tears threatened to spill onto his tie as he went over each item. His own daughter was grown now, with a daughter of her own, but he couldn't imagine the pain the Blakes would be forced to endure all over again when they saw their child's belongings in the box.

The watch had particularly stirred Lou. Even with its exposure to the elements in the well, it had obviously once been a beautiful piece of jewelry. On the back side—with the help of a magnifying glass—he could still make out an inscription: To our beloved daughter.

When the Blakes' arrived, Lou could tell by their grave expressions and red, swollen eyes that they realized why Vernon Patterson had brought them to his office. He seated them at his desk across from him and tried to make them comfortable. Vernon stood anxiously at the door and shuffled from foot to foot. It only took a few moments for Lou to give them all the information he received from Franklin County. It took considerably longer to answer their questions and wait for the crying to cease. Finally he set the box on the desk and slid it across to them.

Like so many had done before them, the Blakes opened the box in his office, extracted and examined each item, before laying it reverently on the desk and going on to the next item. Fresh tears spilled from Donna

Blake as she held the items that had once belonged to her daughter. Lou thought she could not have handled them any more gently had they been Sally herself.

The watch was the last thing to come out of the box. She put it in the palm of her left hand and examined it closely, turning it this way and that so it caught the light. When she finally looked up, the sorrow in her eyes had been replaced by confusion.

Ted looked from the watch to Lou and back again, the same puzzled expression on his face.

"It's Sally's watch," Lou explained gently, his voice respectfully low.

Mrs. Blake extended the hand holding the watch toward him. "No, it isn't. I've never seen this watch before."

It was Lou and Vernon's turn to be confused. They exchanged glances over the Blakes' heads. If the watch didn't belong to Sally, then whose was it? And how did it come to be in that well?

# Chapter Twenty-seven

A television crew from a neighboring county came to film Dr. Gochberg and Sheriff Patterson making the announcement that the forensics' lab had identified Sally Blake's remains. The Steeles and every other citizen of Auburn County watched the now-familiar story unfold on Channel 12's six-o'clock news.

A serious-looking reporter stood on the courthouse steps and explained Sally Blake's disappearance to the viewing audience. The first picture Jamie had ever seen of Sally in the newspaper at the library flashed across the screen while the reporter's voice continued off-camera. The camera went back to the courthouse, only now Dr. Gochberg and the sheriff—looking sweaty and uncomfortable staring into the camera—had taken the place of the reporter. The coroner said the remains of the body had been positively identified as the girl who had been missing from the community for over twenty-five years. He gave the probable cause of death as blunt trauma to the back of the head. When the sheriff took over for Dr. Gochberg, the scene on the screen changed to the image of the abandoned well. Vernon's voice went on to say that the remains had been found by the son of the property owner while doing clean-up work. He assured the viewing audience the case had never been officially closed and local law-enforcement would do everything in its power to put an end to the case once and for all. The reporter reappeared on the screen and spoke of the Blake family's grief with a plea to anyone who may know anything about the case to please contact the Auburn County Sheriff's Department.

No mention of James Steele or any other suspect was made, much to Grandma Cory's relief. She'd been holding her breath since first hearing the news, afraid some reporter would call the house requesting an interview. The entire segment lasted just over two minutes. The good people of Jenna's Creek went to bed that night disappointed at the story's lack of sensationalism. They realized glumly that most viewers watching the story outside their local area would forget all about it by morning.

Jamie and Judge Davis had spent the days leading up to the forensics lab report looking over all the old case files again and again. Both agreed an illicit love affair between Tim Shelton and Sally Blake could make enemies. And if there had been a third man in Sally's life—someone who may have had a lot to lose if it became public knowledge she was carrying his child—it wasn't unreasonable to think this person may have wanted her silenced for good.

For days they discussed different scenarios that could have led up to Sally's disappearance. Nothing they found coincided with their speculations. Jamie began to doubt she would ever have answers to her questions. She prayed every night for God to help her accept that possibility.

She sat at the table in the Davis' kitchen. Bernice and the judge sat at opposite ends, surrounded by files, pictures, and statements. The remaining files spread across their kitchen table had to go back to the courthouse this afternoon. Since the public wanted the case solved, the judge would have to do his investigating at the courthouse like everyone else. Whatever there was to find, they hoped to find it today.

Bernice had grumbled good-naturedly about the mess in her kitchen and losing her husband to his old profession again, but she had grown as curious about the case as Jamie and the judge. She wanted answers too.

Jamie studied the picture in her hand. She had seen it a thousand times. Why did she keep coming back to it? There was something in the picture. She was sure of it.

It was a police photograph of the house where the party had been held. Even though the police could not officially become involved in a missing persons case for twenty-four hours, as a personal favor to Mrs. Blake, they had gone to the house the next day, questioned Noreen who was the only one there, and taken a picture of the front of the property. The photograph was faded and blurred, but details were still easily discerned. A sheriff's deputy must have stood at the end of the driveway to take the picture. It showed the front and west side of the house, the garage, shed, and barn.

She continued to study the picture. Her reasoning told her there was nothing there to see, it was only a picture of Will Trimble's farmhouse. Her gut told her to keep looking. Something was there.

The day Grandma Cory came into her room angry about her being in her closet came to mind. What was it she had said?

Jamie recalled her saying, *"I remember thinking Sally was too beautiful for her own good. She was not a sweet old-fashioned girl. I couldn't have her going to the police with those letters. They wouldn't understand. That night I went to the drugstore with some excuse about needing to see Justin. I got in Sally's locker. Back then, they didn't keep them locked half the time."*

Jamie shook her head. *What was she thinking?* Something was bothering her about her grandma's words. And the picture; how did it all tie together? She was missing something. She wracked her brain trying to recall the rest of what Cory had said that day. Jamie wanted Sally Blake out of their lives.

*"She was not a sweet old-fashioned girl."* Those words stuck in Jamie's mind.

The judge leaned back in his chair and stretched his long arms above his head. "I need a break," he announced. "Anybody want ice cream?"

"Sounds great," Bernice said.

He went to the refrigerator and opened the freezer door. "Okay, we've got vanilla, maple nut, and it looks like a little bit of the cherry cordial's left. I'll take that." He pulled out the container and set it on the counter. "Bad news, Jamie. We're out of cherry cordial. What'll it be? Vanilla or maple nut?"

"Hmm… oh, vanilla's fine."

"Okay. And maple nut for you. Right, Bernice?"

"You know it," Bernice said with a smile. "And don't go skimpy on it. I'll count calories tomorrow. Isn't that right, Jamie?"

"Yes, I'll take vanilla."

"David, I don't think Jamie's paying attention to us."

"I'm afraid most people don't anymore, dear."

"Oh, I'm sorry." Jamie tore her eyes away from the photograph. "Did you say something?"

The judge scooped ice cream into the three dessert dishes he had taken from the cabinet. "Are you onto something, Jamie?"

"I don't know. I'm just trying to remember something." She held the photograph out in front of her and tried to remember everything Grandma Cory had said.

When she looked away from the picture, the Davises were staring at her. "It's something about this picture," she tried to explain, motioning with it. "I'm forgetting something and for some reason this picture reminded me of it. I just can't figure it out." She set the picture down in front of her and attacked the stack of files. She sifted recklessly through the pile, paying no mind as some of the papers slid onto the floor.

The Davises watched her inspection in silence. When she found the paper she wanted, she sat back in her chair and began to read. The judge set her dish of ice cream on the table in front of her, but it began to melt, forgotten. She read the paper carefully and then read it again. After three readings, she held it out to Bernice.

"Would you read this and then look at this picture?" she asked. "See if you come to the same conclusion I have."

Bernice did as Jamie asked. When she finished, she gave her a blank stare. "I'm afraid I must be missing it, honey."

The judge had been reading over his wife's shoulder. He was also unsure of what Jamie was getting at. She took the picture and tapped it with her index finger. "See right here?" she said. "Now read this paragraph."

Once again they did as they were told. Excitement was mounting in the bright, airy kitchen. Three bowls of ice cream now sat abandoned on the table. The Davises knew she had found something crucial. Their eyes twinkled with vivid realization as they looked from the paper to her.

"I think you may have found the smoking gun, Jamie," the judge exclaimed. "Possible proof that someone was lying," he said with a tap of the picture. "When I go to the courthouse this afternoon, I'll discuss all this with Vernon. With what we've found out lately about Sally, this could point us in the right direction."

The three ate what remained of their ice cream, lost in thought. The elation over the discovery dissipated as they contemplated what the consequences could be.

Vernon Patterson, the county sheriff, was the only man on the force who remembered the Sally Blake case first-hand. Over the past few weeks, he had been going over the particulars with the new fellows—several of whom were younger than the case itself. Today his office was packed with the same five men who had assisted him in recovering the remains at the well site, along with Blaine Michke, the current county prosecutor, Eldon Spears, his investigator, and Judge Davis. The door to the small office had been left open to provide enough space for the nine men to sit, stand or lean, and to allow air to circulate from the only window in the room. Even though the office was on the second-floor, they attempted to keep their voices down so not to be overheard from the street below.

Dr. Gochberg had just finished explaining, in detail, the lab results from Franklin County. He explained about the watch that had been found in the well with the remains, but did not belong to the victim.

Lt. Hollabahl, the only man in the room besides the doctor not originally from Auburn County, had the most questions. He had never heard of the case and couldn't understand why it remained unsolved for twenty-five years. Vernon, Dr. Gochberg, and the judge took turns fielding his barrage of questions. It was apparent he assumed these country bumpkins couldn't solve a real case when it was handed to them.

When Judge Davis finally got an opportunity to speak, he immediately mentioned the watch. "What are your theories on where it came from?" he wanted to know.

Blaine Michke jumped in. "There could be a number of reasons why it was there. Sally could have borrowed it from a friend that night to wear to the party."

"It could have been accidentally dropped into the well when it was still in use, by anyone living in the area," Eldon Spears added.

"But the most likely scenario is, it was dropped by the killer while he was disposing of the body," the Prosecutor finished.

"But doesn't the presence of the watch in the well with the remains of the body imply the killer was a woman?" asked the fair-haired deputy, who looked barely old enough to shave.

"Not necessarily," Blaine Michke was the first one in the room to recover from the suggestion that a woman could commit such a crime. "The watch could have belonged to anyone at that party. Maybe the killer had taken it from a girlfriend to have repairs made on it. Or he could have stolen it from the owner during the evening. It's even possible it belonged to someone else entirely and we don't know why the killer had it in his possession."

"So, you're saying the only physical piece of evidence we have may not be a clue at all?" Sergeant Toomey, the most seasoned veteran in the room other than the sheriff, grumbled.

"No. All I'm saying is the watch in itself doesn't implicate anyone. We need more than that."

The judge spoke up from his seat on the windowsill he shared with Sergeant Toomey. "We have found out recently there may have been a theft at the party. Maybe the thief took more than we first suspected."

"And just who is 'we'?" Lt. Hollabahl demanded sarcastically.

All eyes turned to the judge, the lieutenant's question reflected in their eyes.

"A friend and I have been doing a little investigating of our own lately," he answered vaguely. He would divulge Jamie's identity when it suited him. "And the two of us may have found a discrepancy in a statement by one of the witnesses. It could be proof that someone lied during the investigation."

"I think that goes without saying, Judge," Eldon Spears said raising an eyebrow.

"Touché," Judge Davis quipped with a smile, and the tension in the small room erupted into good-natured laughter.

After it died away, he recounted the information Jamie had pointed out earlier in the day. He added the pertinent information given to him by Donna Blake, including the thousand dollars that had never been recovered. As far as he was concerned, there was a motive and substantiated proof of a lie to investigators. The watch placed the new suspect at the scene. It was enough for them to be brought in for questioning.

The meeting broke up soon after the decision. Sheriff Patterson and Judge Davis were left alone in the room. The judge leaned back in the leather desk chair recently vacated by Dr. Gochberg, and stared at the ceiling. The sheriff sat in his chair on the opposite side of the desk. Neither man spoke for a long time.

Vernon eventually broke the silence. "This isn't good. This isn't good at all."

"I don't know how Jenna's Creek is going to handle this."

"A prominent citizen arrested for a twenty-five year old murder. This isn't good," he repeated.

"If we open this can of worms and then can't prove anything, you won't be elected dog catcher."

"Lucky for you, you're already retired."

The judge nodded in agreement. "Do you think we could be wrong?" he asked, already aware of the answer.

"Anything's possible," the sheriff conceded. "This is one time I would love to be wrong. If we hadn't been so fixed on James Steele in 1947…"

"How are you going to handle it?" the judge asked.

"Well, when I know the suspect like this, and there's no flight risk, I often call them in. They come to my office, we discuss it, and if an arrest is necessary, I do it right then."

"You're kidding?" Judge Davis asked in disbelief.

"I don't do it for everyone. Just those I know well. It spares folks the embarrassment of being picked up in a cruiser. You know, keeps the neighbors quiet."

"I can't believe you get away with that."

"You've been in the trenches too long, Judge. You've become jaded. This is Jenna's Creek where we know and trust our neighbor. We don't need to be hard-cases."

"Who am I to say you don't know what you're doing?"

"This one is special though. If I do have to go out to the house, I'd like to have you there with me when I do the questioning."

He nodded. "All right."

"I'm going to call first."

"You're going to what?"

"Hey, it's the middle of the week. I can't just pop in unannounced or expect them to drop everything to come into town. It's just common courtesy. Didn't your mother teach you anything?"

"Vernon, this is a murder investigation."

"I'm aware of that, but I know this county. You have to show respect. It's the only way to get things done in a small town. Most of these people will live here till the day they die. Even the guilty ones who serve time always return."

"You're right. I've been away too long. I learned not to trust anyone."

"That attitude won't fly around here. Benefit of the doubt, that's what people give you, and that's what they expect in return."

The judge glanced at his watch. "What time have you got?

"A quarter till six."

"Should we call now?"

"Maybe we should wait till after supper. A body's got a right to enjoy their meal without the telephone ringing."

Neither man moved toward the telephone. They were stalling and they both knew it.

"You got the number?" the judge asked.

"I'll have to look it up." Again neither one moved.

Vernon chewed his lower lip. He laced his fingers together behind his head and leaned back in his chair to stare at the ceiling. Finally, slowly, his big hand reached for the telephone book. When he found the number he wanted, he began dialing. He gave the judge one last look for moral support.

The judge heard someone pick up the phone on the other end. He listened to Vernon's side of the conversation.

"Uh, yes, hello. This is Sheriff Patterson. How are you tonight?" "Good, good." "Hope they're not keeping you too busy." A longer pause followed by good-natured laughter. "Yes, I know how that goes. Hey, listen. I've been thinking… well, Judge Davis and I… you remember the judge, don't you?" Vernon smiled at David while he listened to the other end. "Yes, he retired last year." "I agree, it must be nice, some folks got it made," more laughter and a wink in the judge's direction. "Oh, she's fine, doing real good out there in the country."

Judge Davis smiled. Everyone in the county must have Bernice's health on their minds.

"Well, anyway, like I said, the judge and I have been going over some old files in the Sally Blake case. A few troubling questions have come up. We were wondering if you could come in tonight and…" "All right, yes, that'd be fine." "Okay, sounds good. We'll see you after while."

"That went well," the judge observed after Vernon replaced the phone in its cradle.

"Yup, looks like you and I are going for a ride." Vernon said without a move to get up from his chair.

Judge Davis leaned back in his chair and toyed with his lower lip with his finger and thumb. "Well, whenever you're ready."

"Let's wait a few more minutes. I hate to disturb someone's supper." Sheriff Patterson put his hand out to the phone again. "Speaking of which, how about I call the diner and see if Herb can send one of those kids he has working for him over here with a bite for us? I'm starved."

The judge smiled and shrugged. He was hungry too.

❧

Two more cars than expected were parked in front of the little frame house on the end of Maple Street. Vernon and Judge Davis exchanged curious glances and climbed out of the car. The door opened as they started up the walk. Noel Wyatt stepped out onto the porch.

Noel extended his hand. "Sheriff. Judge. We've been expecting you."

He opened the door and stepped back for them to enter ahead of him. Vernon removed his hat. The judge cleared his throat nervously. He had never been involved with an investigation such as this. He felt like a drunken line-backer at a ladies' tea party. He didn't belong here. Neither did Vernon. There had to be a mistake. This couldn't be right.

At the first sight of the suspect's face and downcast eyes, he knew there was no mistake. He knew a guilty person when he saw one. This was not how this case was supposed to end. When Jamie approached him about researching the case with her, he had imagined bringing a vicious killer—a fugitive who had eluded capture—to justice. Now the fugitive was before him, and he saw no malice, only contrition. In the place of brutality, he saw repentance.

Instead of the thrill of justice prevailing, he felt sick. He wanted to cry. He wanted to run. This was Vernon's job. Let him earn that meager civil servant's paycheck. Never had he felt so low and despicable in all his life. He could tell by the way Vernon was turning the brim of his Smoky Bear hat around and around in his hands, he felt the same way.

A young man the judge did not recognize was sitting on the sofa next to the suspect. Both looked like tears had flowed recently. Noel motioned for them to have a seat. They obliged.

Vernon took a notepad out of his pocket and cleared his throat.

"I have some questions I have to ask," he said softly, almost as an apology.

The suspect nodded. The young man spoke up. "We've already discussed everything, Sheriff. We're ready to give you a statement, but we'd prefer to do it at your office with an attorney present."

"I've already called my attorney," Noel added. "He'll be meeting us at your office. He has to come from Portsmouth, so it may be an hour or two before he gets here."

Vernon nodded, flipped the notepad closed, and slid it into his pocket. "That sounds good."

The judge tried not to stare. He could not get over how effortlessly things were working out. He almost wished for a fight, an out-right denial. Justification would come much easier if the suspect was not sitting so piously on the sofa, hands twisting anxiously in the lap.

Vernon got to his feet. "Okay." He looked down at the suspect. "You can ride to the station with Noel if you'd be more comfortable."

The suspect nodded and stood up.

The others, including the judge, who had spent the last fifteen years of his life denying requests for dismissals of sentences to murders, rapists, and thieves—and loving every minute of it—followed suit.

"Is there anything you need to get before we leave?" Noel asked gently.

"My pocketbook," the suspect answered quietly. "It's in my room."

"I'll get it," the young man offered. The judge learned later he was the assistant pastor at the Nazarene church.

The suspect, the sheriff, the judge, and Noel Wyatt waited quietly in the living room for the young man to return. He handed the white, summer pocketbook to the suspect and stepped away. Tears glistened in the corners of his eyes. His lips twitched as he tried to offer an encouraging smile.

The sheriff came forward and offered his arm to the suspect. Noreen Trimble slipped a hand into the crook of his elbow. Vernon smiled gently and escorted his prisoner out the door toward the waiting cars in the driveway. To the seasoned judge, the scene resembled a father escorting a bride down the aisle to meet her groom instead.

# Chapter Twenty-eight

It would be another first for his long and colorless career. The end of a twenty-five-year-old case would make the state news—maybe even national. But Vernon Patterson wasn't looking forward to it. National notoriety on any other case would have pleased him immensely. But he didn't want to be remembered as the man escorting plain, unassuming Noreen Trimble into the jailhouse. It would be an embarrassment, not a triumph.

His heart ached for her. A sad ending to a sad case.

It was his first year with the sheriff's department when Sally Blake disappeared. He remembered thinking things like this weren't supposed to happen in Auburn County. Was it a foreshadowing of things to come in his career? No. In the twenty-five years that followed, nothing compared to that one sensational case. Paperwork, drunks, more paperwork, kids tearing up the streets on Saturday night, and drudgery summed up his public service career; but nothing like this.

Nothing compared to arresting Noreen Trimble, the spinster daughter of the pastor of the Nazarene church, for murder.

He escorted Noreen to Noel's silver Cadillac parked in the driveway, and shut the door gently behind her. Then he joined Judge Davis in the cruiser. He backed out onto the street, the engine idling, and waited for Noel and the young pastor to finish inside the house. Neither man spoke. What else was left for them to say?

Noreen stole one last glance at the house. Noel had gone through each room turning out lights and checking locks. Now he was locking the front door. He must think it will be a while before anyone will be home again. She would have to remember to tell him to give the keys to her sister-in-law. Someone would have to come in and water the plants. She wondered who would stop her mail and cancel her magazine subscriptions. She envisioned Blanche Harris' face down at the post office when the next piece of mail addressed to Noreen Trimble came across the counter. Her cheeks burned from the shame. What would everyone think of her?

The assistant pastor was standing beside his car toying with the keys while he waited for Noel to come outside. He would follow the sheriff's car, which would be following the Cadillac on its way to the courthouse. He wanted to be there for moral support. He caught her eye and smiled. She tried to return the gesture, but choked on the huge lump in her throat.

Her entire adult life, Noreen had tried to learn to live with the truth; or rather in spite of it. She buried herself in her work. She put others' needs before her own. She stayed active in the church; anything to pay her penance. Nothing worked. She couldn't absolve herself of the crime that haunted her. She was a guilty woman. Nothing said or not said would change that. She had committed the ultimate sin. She had taken a life. She had shed innocent blood.

She twisted the tiny diamond ring on her finger around and around like she always did when she was agitated. The diamond came from her mother's engagement ring. When she died two years ago, Noreen's dad had the jeweler reset the stone and gave it to her. She supposed he finally accepted the fact his forty-plus-year old daughter would never marry.

She was thankful that, at least, her mother wasn't alive to see her shame.

She kept her eyes on the ring and not on the world outside the Cadillac. She couldn't bear thinking she would probably never see her little house again. She had never been as proud as the day she signed the deed. She still had seven years on her mortgage. What would become of her house while she was gone? Her dad couldn't afford to make the payments and maintain his own house. He would probably sell it and put the money in a trust for her while awaiting her release, if there ever was a release. Would she be there until she died? What about the possibility of the death penalty? Who knew? She had no concept of bail or parole or plea bargains. All she knew was that she was going to Vernon Patterson's office to write and sign a confession. She would sign away her freedom. Noel contacted his attorney for her. She didn't know why. It seemed like a waste of good money. She was guilty. Attorneys were for people who were innocent, or who refused to admit they were not.

She was nervous because she didn't know what was going to happen to her. But at the same time, she felt as if a huge weight had been lifted from her shoulders. No longer would she have to lie to people she loved. No longer were there secrets to be kept, words to be watched. The hiding and the lying were finally over. Whatever was about to happen to her would have to be better than that.

When Vernon called to tell her he was coming out to ask her some questions about Sally Blake, she knew. She knew it was over. She called the assistant pastor at her church and Noel Wyatt and told them she needed them at her house immediately. She could not call her father, who was still the head pastor of the Nazarene Church, to seek his counsel. Not just yet. By the time Vernon got there with Judge Davis, Noel and the assistant pastor knew the whole story.

Noel offered no counsel—only the comfort of a friend and a listening ear. He called an attorney friend of his from Portsmouth and told him to come to Jenna's Creek before the evening was over. They would be in need of his services.

Noreen sought the assistant pastor's advice. He told her what she expected to hear. He said she only had to be concerned with answering to God. She did not need to fear man who could only destroy her mortal flesh, but she had to fear the Creator who could destroy her eternal soul. He cried when he said Christ had already died for the sins she had committed. She was forgiven as far as God was concerned. He added with pain and regret evident on his face, that she could not answer the sheriff falsely and expect to meet her Savior in the air someday.

Of course she already knew everything he said was true. She had struggled with it for years. She had wanted to confess many times. Once, years ago, she dressed in her best church dress, had her hand on the doorknob, the car keys in her hand, and had every intention of driving to the sheriff's office and turning herself in, but at the last minute, couldn't go through with it. She could not walk out the door. She was too afraid. Afraid of punishment. Afraid of what people would say. Afraid of losing her freedom.

Freedom. She scoffed at the irony of the concept. She had not been free for twenty-five years.

If time had been an ally, it would have lessened the memory of that night; but it had not. She remembered every detail as if it happened yesterday. She remembered the recipe for the hors d'oeuvres she served. She recalled the way she wore her hair. She remembered breaking the heel off her shoe while coming down the stairs and being forced to change out of the new blue dress she was so anxious to show off to her girlfriends. She had to settle for the black sheath dress they had seen several times before. Tim couldn't understand why she had to change her dress and accessories because of one shoe. His ignorance of women and fashion made her laugh and forget her frustration over the shoe. How could men be so thick? Actually it was endearing. She had so much to teach him.

She never got the opportunity.

Noreen fought back tears. This wasn't the time to think about Tim. He was gone, just like that night. Her entire life, her future, had changed in one instant.

So many factors could have made all the difference. Insignificant things that didn't seem important at the time. If she had not thrown the party when her aunt and uncle were out of town. If James and Sally hadn't gotten into a fight. If she had not worried about cleaning the house that night and gone to bed instead. If Sally hadn't come back. If Uncle Will had not placed that old-fashioned, cast iron boot scraper by the front door…

Noreen was on her knees in front of the fireplace, scrubbing at an irregular-shaped wine stain on the rug in front of the fireplace. Its shape had reminded her of Australia, an absurd thought to be having at two o'clock in the morning. Then again she was bone tired and wanted nothing more than to give in to the immense desire to fall into the soft bed upstairs that was calling her name. But she couldn't do that. If her aunt and uncle came home and saw their house in this condition, they would never forgive her. Aunt Paula would never let her forget it. Irresponsible; that's what she would say of her. They had left her here to watch the house while they attended the funeral of a distant cousin on Aunt Paula's side of the family in Somerset, Kentucky.

Noreen was not irresponsible in any sense of the word. This was the first time in her life she had let her hair down to do something reckless, like giving a party, without her aunt and uncle's permission.

She planned to clean the worst of the mess—the things that would leave a stain that would never come out—tonight and finish tomorrow. Uncle Will and Aunt Paula were not due home for two more days so they would never have to know what had happened to their beautiful home. She sat back on her heels and wiped her sweaty brow wearily. She was startled to see her best friend watching her from the open doorway. "Sally?" she gasped. "What are you doing here?"

"I came to talk to you and Tim."

"He's already gone. The party's over. I'm the only one left." She looked past her and through the door. "I didn't hear a car pull up. How did you get here?"

Sally shut the door behind her and sat on the sofa. "James dropped me off at the road." She was quiet for a few moments and then commented absently, "Some mess you've got here."

Any other time Noreen would have told her to grab a brush and start cleaning since the biggest part of the mess was due to the fight she had with James, but she could tell there was something on Sally's mind. She could almost see the gears turning in her head. All she could think of was that she was going to be stuck driving her home after she said what she came to say. "Did something happen between you and James?" she asked.

"Nooo," Sally said slowly.

Noreen straightened up and brushed off the knees of her pants. She worked the kinks out of her legs while she waited for Sally to say something. Silence. She was becoming impatient. She had too much work left to do to play any of Sally's games. "Well, Sally, is there something I can do for you?"

"Yes, there is. I came here to talk to you with Tim. But since he isn't here…"

"Sally, it's late and I'm tired. Just tell me what you want."

"I'm trying to. This isn't easy, so I'm just going to say it. Tim was supposed to be here to help me do this, but I guess he chickened out.

I'm sorry to have to be the one." She paused and wrung her hands anxiously. Noreen imagined it was for effect. "Tim and I have been seeing each other for a few months behind your back, Noreen." she blurted out.

Noreen's mouth dropped open. It took her several moments to find her voice. "What? I ... I don't believe you," she choked out.

"I didn't expect you to." Sally lowered her eyes in shame, but Noreen didn't miss the smug smile tugging at the corners of her mouth. "But it's true. I can't go on lying to you another day. I care too much for you, Nory."

"Care for me?" Noreen cried. "How can you say you care for me when you're lying about having an affair with my boyfriend?"

"I'm not lying. It's the truth."

Noreen's legs buckled under her and she sat down hard on the hearth. She put her hands over her face. "I can't believe you're telling me this. Tim and I are engaged."

"I told you Tim's a chicken. He didn't even have the guts to tell you himself. He didn't want to break your heart. But I can't let you marry him. I just can't do that. In the first place, I am in love with him. And in the second place, you can't marry a man who's been lying to you all this time."

Noreen sighed heavily and looked at her friend. It took every ounce of resolve within her to keep from slapping Sally's angelic face. "I don't believe you. This doesn't make any sense. You come in here out of the blue with this unbelievable story. You were at our party all evening; hanging all over every guy here, I might add. Why didn't you say something then? If you've been seeing Tim all this time, how could you come here with James and act like nothing was going on?"

"I was trying to spare you, Nory," Sally explained, her voice pleading. "I didn't want to embarrass you in front of everyone. Not at your engagement party."

"Well, thank you, Sally. That was very big of you," Noreen said icily. "But I'm sorry, I just don't believe it. Tim is in love with me. We're getting married. I don't believe he's been seeing you and I don't believe he's in love with you."

"I guess it doesn't matter what you believe. I'm telling the truth. I have no reason to lie about it."

Usually slow to anger, Noreen was becoming enraged at Sally's calm demeanor. "Tim has never shown any interest in you, Sally. The only reason he's even polite to you, is because you're my friend. He would never have anything to do with someone like you."

Sally's eyes narrowed. She tried to maintain her contrite demeanor, but her true nature was peering through the cracks. "Don't be so sure, Noreen. He's not the choir boy he pretends to be."

Noreen stood up and towered over Sally sitting on the sofa. "I won't listen to another word of this until Tim is here to tell me his side of the story."

"I know this isn't easy for you to hear, Nory." Once again, her tone turned tender and apologetic. "And you shouldn't have to hear it from me. Tim should have told you when it first started. You deserve better than this. You deserve better than a man who would string you along, and all the while be sleeping with your best friend."

Noreen inhaled sharply, barely maintaining her composure. Sally's words were tearing her apart, but she tried in vain not to show it. Sally continued on in her conciliatory manner, enjoying her control of the situation. "I am truly sorry that it's come to this. Please believe me. I would give anything for this not to have happened. But what can I do about it now, except tell you the truth?"

"Sally, I've heard enough. I want you out of here. It's late and I'm tired. I'm going to talk to Tim first thing in the morning and get this straightened out."

Sally spoke fast—almost desperately. Her next words cut Noreen to the quick. "Haven't you ever wondered why the two of us are friends? Everyone else wonders why I would spend my time hanging around a loser like you. Could it be all this time, I've been polite to you only because I wanted to get close to Tim?"

"Get out of this house," Noreen screamed. "I don't want to see your face." She stormed around the couch and to the door. She turned the knob, intending to open it to show Sally the way out.

Sally jumped up and grabbed a fistful of Noreen's hair with one hand and slammed the door shut with the other. "Don't you turn your back on me!" she hissed viciously in Noreen's ear. "I'm not through with you yet. You will listen to what I have to say."

In the back of her mind, Noreen began to fear for her safety, but her awakened anger would not give way to Sally's threats. She was an inch or two taller than Sally and a few pounds heavier. She spun around to face her and easily broke out of her grasp. "I've listened to all I'm going to from you. Now, I'm not going to tell you again. Get out of here."

To her utter amazement, Sally buried her face in her hands and began to sob. "Oh, Nory, I'm so sorry," she cried into her hands. "Please forgive me. I didn't mean it." The tears fell like rain. Noreen found herself almost feeling sorry for her.

"I don't want to hurt you. You're my only friend." She moved toward the sofa, still crying helplessly. Noreen followed her and sat mutely on the sofa beside her. "I have been so upset lately. With everything that's happened, I feel so lost. Dad is furious with me. Mom can't even look at me."

"Can't even look at you? Sally, what are you talking about?"

"The baby. I'm talking about the baby," she shrieked. "I'm pregnant. I'm going to have Tim's baby." The tears flowed faster and with greater intensity.

Noreen felt like she had taken a sharp blow to the stomach. "You're lying," she spat. But her voice lacked the conviction it had earlier.

"I wish I was," Sally moaned, her tears slacking off. "Oh, if only I was lying or this was all a crazy dream..."

"Maybe you are pregnant," Noreen conceded, "but I refuse to believe the baby belongs to Tim. What about James Steele? He's the one you've been spending all your time with. He would do something like get a girl pregnant. But not Tim. Not my Tim."

"Tim cares for you, Nory. That's why he's not here telling you this. He respects you, but he loves me. He couldn't help himself. We couldn't help ourselves. That's how it is when you're in love. You do things, even when you know they're wrong."

"I still don't believe you, Sally. I don't think Tim had anything to do with you getting pregnant... if you are, that is. James Steele is the father of your baby and you know it ... or maybe you don't know who the father is."

The transformation she was becoming so familiar with, came over Sally so quickly Noreen didn't see it coming. Sally cursed vehemently, calling her names that should never be spoken aloud. Noreen drew back as if slapped. "Tim is the father! Don't you get that! You are so stupid, so naïve. I hate you. I always have. You whimpering, weak..." She cursed again, drops of spittle flying from her mouth as her rage intensified.

Noreen jumped up from the sofa as if Sally was a snake poised to strike. "Please leave Sally." She struggled to keep her voice level. "I'll talk to Tim tomorrow."

Sally stood up and grabbed Noreen's shirt collar. "You're not talking to him tomorrow. He'll be with me by then. I've given him what you never could, you frigid cow. He's mine now."

Noreen felt tears of hurt and anger sting her eyes and nose. Could Sally's words be true? Did Tim think the same of her as Sally did? No. She wouldn't take Sally's word for it. She had seen her do this to people before. It was a game to her; stringing people along merely to get a reaction. Sally thought it was funny. She was trying to plant the seeds of doubt in her mind about Tim. No, she wasn't going to fall for it. She grabbed Sally's wrists and jerked free from the hold she had on her blouse. She shoved her backwards into the sofa.

Sally stumbled against the sofa, but maintained her balance. She plowed into Noreen and landed a lop-sided punch to her jaw. Noreen tried to resist without actually fighting Sally. Even though she was furious, her reasonable nature told her they could settle this in the morning when Tim was here to defend himself against Sally's ridiculous accusations and Sally was in a more stable frame of mind. Sally, on the other hand, seemed determined to solve the problem physically. Neither girl was an experienced fighter. They slapped and pushed and clawed at each other—Sally after blood and Noreen simply trying to defend herself— neither inflicting serious injury upon the other.

The struggle only served to stoke Sally's anger. She put her hands against Noreen's chest and pushed as hard as she could. Noreen back-pedaled and fell onto the stone hearth of the fireplace, her head banging soundly against the mantle.

The jarring pain that rattled Noreen's teeth in her head, ended any resolve to avoid physical conflict. She ran forward, propelling herself full tilt into Sally. Both girls fell on the sofa and flipped over the back, landing on the other side. Noreen heard a sharp, metallic thump just before her head hit the floor and the wind was knocked out of her. For a moment she was disoriented. The room was suddenly quiet. She could feel a goose egg already rising on her forehead right at the hairline where she had whacked it on the hardwood floor. She had landed on top of Sally—cheek-to-cheek—their limbs entangled. Her nose was against Sally's ear; her soft dark hair tickled Noreen's skin and she could feel the coolness of an earring resting against her cheek.

The silence, the knot on her forehead, the smell of Sally's hair; all sensations registered within a moment to Noreen's brain. The next sensation was that of sticky wetness on her nose. She thought at first she had bloodied it in the fall. Then she realized there was no pain.

She put her hands on either side of Sally's body and raised herself up. A drop of blood fell from the end of her nose onto Sally's cheek. The blood was not her own. A crimson pool was widening under Sally's head. Her exotic tiger-brown eyes were staring blankly at the ceiling. Noreen awkwardly scrambled to her feet as realization hit. During the fall, Sally's head had banged against the cast iron boot scraper near the front door.

Noreen put a hand to her mouth and stifled a scream. Even before she put trembling fingertips to Sally's throat, she knew there would be no pulse. The blank, lifeless eyes stared up at her, accusing her. The lips were parted in what resembled a mocking snarl. *"You'll pay for this, Nory,"* they seemed to be saying. *"I'll have my revenge. You'll never get Tim Shelton now."*

She stood motionless, staring down at Sally's inert body, willing her to blink, sit up, and laugh about the cruel joke she had just played on her. *"You should've seen your face, Nory,"* she would say. *"It was hysterical. I wish I had a camera. You're so simple. You'll fall for anything."*

She waited. Nothing happened. The blood continued to spread across the hardwood floor. Absurdly, she noticed it was headed for the sofa. Aunt Paula would kill her if she ruined her good sofa, it was practically brand new. She could hear her bragging about the amount of money Uncle Will had paid for it. No one else in the family could afford such an extravagance, certainly not Noreen's father. Uncle Will made good money, which Aunt Paula was always quick to point out. Even in the leanest depression years, they'd been able to maintain their comfortable lifestyle because of his wise business choices. She loved to remind Noreen's mother—in the subtlest of ways—that she would never enjoy the same comforts on a pastor's salary.

Noreen shook her head to rid it of Aunt Paula's image. Sally was lying on the floor in a pool of her own blood and she was worried about the sofa. She spurred herself into action. She dashed downstairs into the basement Uncle Will had converted into a workshop. He liked to tinker around down here, building chests, gun cabinets, and whatever else someone wanted to buy. It was possible for one item to take him half a year to build; it depended on the difficulty involved and the amount of time he was able to dedicate to the project. He was incredibly talented with his hands and his work sold on reputation alone. Noreen often wondered if he came to the basement more as an escape from Aunt Paula's mouth than a desire to build beautiful furniture.

She found the box of cleaning rags she was looking for and rushed back upstairs. Sally hadn't moved. Had she expected her to? In the back of her mind, she was still hoping it was all some sort of cruel prank on Sally's part. She couldn't be dead. She just couldn't. Everything had happened so fast. They were fighting... over what? Her mind drew a blank. Panic set in as she frantically tried to remember what had started the fight in the first place. Oh yes, Tim... and something about a baby. A sob forced its way out of Noreen's throat.

A baby! Had there been a baby? Had she taken two lives tonight?

No, it wasn't possible. It was an accident. She was angry at Sally; angry at her allegations. But she wasn't angry enough to kill her. Was she? She had to call the police. What would she tell them? It was an accident. Wasn't it? She would explain in a rational manner how Sally had berated her with a vicious and heartless attack of words. She had relentlessly pushed and pushed until Noreen was forced to retaliate. She hadn't wanted to fight back. She tried to avoid a physical confrontation. She had never raised her hand in anger to another person in her life.

Would anyone believe her? Why should they? It would be her word against the body of a slain woman on Aunt Paula's living room floor. Sally's mother would want vengeance; an eye for an eye. The Blakes always got what they wanted.

There was no one to link her to Sally. No one had seen her come back here tonight. How had she even gotten here? Oh, yes. She said James dropped her off and left. No one would have to know what had happened. Everyone knew how impulsive Sally could be. They knew about the fight at the party. They would think she was just mad and to prove her point, just left town; walked away from everything.

People did it all the time, didn't they? If they couldn't find Sally, there would be no questions, no investigation. There had to be proof of a crime first, didn't there? Without her body...

She couldn't do it. She couldn't just pretend there was no crime. She couldn't pretend Sally left town on a whim never to return. What about the Blakes? Sally's poor mother, she would be devastated. She would never stop searching for her; never stop asking questions. She wouldn't rest until she knew what happened to her daughter and the guilty party was punished—punished to the fullest extent of the law.

Punished...

She would have to be punished...

Noreen swooned, staggering on her feet. Prison, she would go to prison. The thought of it filled her with terror. She had seen movies about what happened to people in prison. Yes, she was guilty, she didn't deny that. But she didn't deserve prison; or even worse, the electric chair.

*You've shed innocent blood. Your blood will be required of you.*

Oh, God, no!

What about her own parents? They would be devastated if their daughter was sent to prison. The shame, the heartache; they didn't deserve it. They had raised her to know right from wrong; and she did. Sally was the selfish one. She was the one who used and hurt other people, not Noreen. If Sally hadn't come here tonight... If she hadn't told those awful stories ... If she hadn't tried to purposely come between her and Tim, just to hurt her... None of this would have happened.

It was Sally's fault. Noreen was an innocent pawn in her games. Sally was to blame. She brought it all on herself. She had been the one to start the fight. Noreen hadn't meant to kill her. It was an accident. She fell and hit her head. It wasn't Noreen's fault.

Noreen forced her mind back to the task at hand. She threw the rags into the congealing blood on the floor and sopped up the worst of it. In sheer panic, she put her arms under Sally's armpits and lifted with all her strength. She dragged her through the house to the back door. She lowered her body to the floor to have a free hand to open the door. Only then did she realize her car was parked next to the barn. She refused to look down at Sally's body as she stepped over it to go out the door.

Keys, where were her keys?

It seemed like an eternity of fumbling before she found the keys in her pocketbook, moved the car to the back door, and lifted Sally laboriously into the trunk. She went back into the house and gathered the bloody rags into a pile. She threw them into the trunk with Sally's body. She slammed the trunk lid closed and hurried to the driver's side of the car.

Had anyone heard? She must have made noise while hurrying about the yard. What about the neighbors' dogs? She cocked her head and listened. All was quiet. No one or nothing appeared to have heard her disturbance. Why should they? The nearest neighbors were a half a mile away.

She was sweating and out-of-breath when she climbed behind the wheel of the little car. She put the car into gear and pulled away from the garage. On an unconscious level she drove eastward. She disassociated herself with what she was doing by refusing to think about her actions. She drove several hundred yards before turning off the road onto a tractor path that ran alongside the property. She concentrated on avoiding the ruts in the tiny road, anything to keep her mind off her purpose. Finally she came to what she was looking for.

The original homestead had been back here at one time. The remains of a broken chimney stood against the gray sky. She stopped the car and set to work. She knew exactly where to look. She had played here countless times as a child with Aunt Paula's kids. She walked in circles several times in the same spot before she located the well. It was so over-grown, she almost missed it. The boards covering it were half-rotted and obscured from view with debris and vegetation. Strains of daylight were appearing through the trees as she finished what she came to do.

Back at the house, she filled buckets with hot, soapy water. She gathered sponges and rags and took a deep breath. With grim determination she entered the living room. She scrubbed the floors, the couch, and the boot scraper until it shone, without thinking about where the mess had come from. The sun was high in the sky before she sank into the bathtub and scrubbed away the evidence of the past few hours of her life. She dropped into the bed in the guest bedroom upstairs, totally exhausted. It wasn't until she awoke several hours later, that she realized what she had done.

Sally Blake was dead. She had killed her.

The first lie she told was to Mrs. Blake, Sally's mother.

"Noreen honey, have you seen Sally?" she asked tearfully.

The telephone had awakened Noreen from an exhausted sleep. It took a moment to realize what the worried mother was asking. "Uh, no ma'am" she answered. The lie came relatively easy. She was glad she wasn't in the same room with her. She doubted she would be able to sound so casual if they were face to face.

"I don't think she came home last night," Mrs. Blake said. "I don't know what could have happened to her. You haven't seen her today, have you?"

"No, ma'am. Not since last night." Not exactly a lie.

"I'm beside myself with worry. Mr. Blake and I called the police, but I can't wait for them to do their job. It could take forever. Could you do me a favor, honey, and call some of your friends who were at the party last night and ask if they've seen her? Could you do that for me, dear? I'm going to call as many as I can think of."

"Sure, Mrs. Blake. I'll do what I can."

And she did. The more telephone calls she made, the more concerned she sounded. By the time the police showed up on her doorstep an hour later, the lies had become the truth to her. The police were polite and friendly. They didn't notice the goose egg on her forehead with her bangs combed over it. They had no reason to suspect anything of her. They already had their sights set on James Steele. There was some concern on their part about him saying he had dropped Sally off at the house and left. Noreen simply said she hadn't seen James or Sally after they left the party. No more questions were asked.

She didn't realize her watch, a graduation gift from her parents, was missing for several days. When she noticed its absence, she searched her house, car, and everywhere else she had been. Horrified, she realized she had been wearing it during the struggle with Sally. What if Aunt Paula found it in the couch cushions or on the floor somewhere covered in Sally's blood? She would surely go to prison then. But the watch never turned up. She tried not to think of what could have become of it. Eventually she was able to tell herself it had never existed.

She had to go to the sheriff's department to write out a statement for the police saying that she was home all evening and never left the house. It was no big deal. Everyone at the party was there, filling out their statements too. That was the end of her involvement in the investigation.

Or so she thought. It turned out her statement about never leaving the house was her downfall. A deputy had taken a picture of her aunt and uncle's house the first time they came out to talk to her. The picture clearly showed her car parked by the back door. Many of the guests—including James Steele—wrote in their statements, her car had been parked in front of the barn during the party. A simple mistake on her part; a simple oversight on the part of investigators.

She told herself if James was formally charged, she would come forward and accept the blame. But why do that until absolutely necessary? It wouldn't bring Sally back. Without a body, James would be safe, and so would she.

She didn't see Tim until after she talked to the police. He was visibly upset. Like the rest of Jenna's Creek, he couldn't imagine what happened to Sally. He couldn't quite believe James Steele had done her harm, but what other explanation could there be? He talked to Noreen about the possibilities most of the afternoon.

All she wanted to know was if he and Sally had an affair. She couldn't come out and ask him. He would know she had talked to Sally after he left the party that night. So she contributed her theories about what could have happened to the conversation, and tried to act like nothing was between them.

She couldn't let go of the idea that maybe Sally had been telling the truth about her and Tim. Everything Tim said and did made Noreen more positive he had cheated on her. He barely talked to her anymore. She caught him staring into space with a pained expression on his face. She told herself she was only falling into Sally's trap, germinating the seeds of doubt she had planted about his infidelity. But try as she might, Noreen couldn't ignore them. She could almost see the wedge driven between them.

When Tim announced he was leaving his dad's farm to work for Mr. Blake, Noreen knew there was no repairing their relationship. She no longer trusted him.

Instead of healing her, the passage of time was debilitating. She continued her studies and went to work, but spent more and more time alone. She followed the case carefully as long as it lasted. With great relief, the police stopped actively pursuing James Steele. From the outside, it looked like the case had reached a stalemate. James left town and Sally's disappearance slowly moved to the back of the townspeople's minds and out of the newspaper headlines.

Tim's lifestyle improved significantly after he went to work for Mr. Blake. He began to make more money than he ever thought possible. Working with the public came easy to him. He was a natural salesman and people found it easy to trust him. He eventually married Joyce Davenport, a local girl whose father ran the feed and grain. Noreen was heart-broken when she found out, but powerless to change the way her life was turning out.

She continued to live with her parents until she saved enough money to make a down-payment on a house of her own. Her life became a dull routine. Noel Wyatt grew to depend on her. She was known and liked by everyone in town, even though they couldn't quite understand her. Her own family had a hard time comprehending what happened to their warm, personable daughter. She kept completely to herself outside of the drugstore, except for the three cats who shared her home. Their presence added to the growing consensus that Noreen Trimble was a bit strange.

As Noel pulled the Cadillac into the spot next to the one reserved for Vernon's cruiser, beside the jail, she realized in bittersweet irony that Sally Blake had gotten exactly what she wanted. Noreen had lost Tim because of her. Even if there had been no affair and no baby—which she prayed was the case—she still ended up alone. What truly hurt most was that Sally said she only spent time with Noreen to be near Tim. They had never truly been friends. Noreen could live with the betrayal that Sally had wanted Tim all along. But she hated to think their friendship had been a sham; that Sally had never cared for her. She—on the other hand—had loved Sally like a sister.

# Chapter Twenty-nine

After twenty-five years of suspicion and speculation, Jenna's Creek's citizenry finally knew what became of Sally Blake. The first few days following Noreen Trimble's arrest and confession found half the town hanging at their back fences, theorizing and debating with one another over what led her to do what she did. Now that it was all over, everyone claimed to have had their misgivings from the get-go. Some wagged their heads, clucked their tongues, and told anyone who would listen, "It's just as I figured all along. I always knew there was a cover-up and poor James Steele was framed." Others, more honest if only by a degree, proclaimed, "I always said Noreen Trimble was an odd bird. I knew she had to be hiding something—but this, my word!"

Noreen had been accused of being odd through the years, only because she lived alone, never married, and kept to herself, not because anyone thought for a second she was remotely involved in Sally Blake's disappearance. And until now, it never occurred to anyone that James may have been framed. Men like him found trouble easily enough without being some part of a conspiracy cooked up by law enforcement officials.

The most disturbing opinion that made its way to Jamie's ears, shared by a surprisingly large number of townspeople, was that Noreen shouldn't even be in jail at all. She was a good woman. She'd worked hard for the community her entire life. Hadn't she suffered enough? Wouldn't things be just as well if Jamie Steele had left well enough alone and let everybody go on thinking her dad had killed Sally Blake? What was the benefit of sending someone like Noreen to prison?

Judge Davis called Jamie to let her know that with Noreen's guilty plea, she would be eligible for parole in no less than a minimum of twenty years. At her age, it was almost the same as a life sentence. "You did it, Jamie," he said. "You wrapped up a case that had the rest of us stumped for over twenty-five years."

Jamie struggled to swallow the lump rising in her own throat. "Yeah, I guess I did."

"Don't be a stranger now," the judge admonished. "Bernice wants you to come over for dinner some night next week. Just let us know what night would be good for you. Bring your sister with you. We'd love to meet her."

"Okay, I will. Thanks."

She replaced the phone on the mount, but remained facing the wall. Why didn't she feel any better? Noreen Trimble was going to prison for the murder of Sally Blake. Her dad was innocent. She had proven it to everyone; especially herself. She could forgive him now and get on with her life like she promised Judge Davis she would.

She slowly turned away from the wall, lost in her own thoughts. Cassie was standing a few feet away. "Cassie!" She put her hand over her pounding heart. "You scared me. What are you doing sneaking up on me?"

Cassie's face remained impassive. "Who were you talking to?"

"Judge Davis." Jamie stepped to one side to get past her through the kitchen doorway.

Cassie stayed where she was. Jamie looked up, confused. "Excuse me."

"What did he want?"

"To tell me what's going to happen to Noreen Trimble. Now, will you please move so I can get through."

Cassie stepped aside, but followed Jamie into the living room. Jamie sat down on the couch and opened the TV guide. Cassie sat down beside her.

"Did you think Dad did it?" she asked suddenly.

Jamie froze. She hadn't talked to Cassie about the case since the night Henry was killed. Cassie hadn't mentioned that night again, except to wonder aloud where Henry had taken off to. She assumed he'd been scared off by all the racket and couldn't find his way home. Like Grandma Cory and Jamie figured she would, she went up and down the road, calling his name and asking neighbors if they'd seen him. Eventually she stopped looking. Jamie felt guilty for not telling her the truth, but at the time, she didn't want to get into the whole discussion of why it happened in the first place. Now Cassie was cutting straight to the chase.

How honest should she be? What did Cassie need to hear? She was only thirteen. If she thought her older sister had no faith in their dad, she might not be able to trust anyone again. Dad had looked guilty. There were moments when Jamie thought for sure he did it. She almost wished he had. At least then, she would know what she was supposed to be feeling right now. But she couldn't admit any of that to Cassie.

"I didn't know what I thought," she admitted truthfully. "I just knew I couldn't forget about it until I knew exactly what happened."

"You must have thought there was a chance he did it or else you wouldn't have tried so hard to find the truth."

"I suppose so."

Cassie looked down at her lap. "I thought he did it," she murmured. When she looked back up, there were tears in her eyes. "Isn't that awful? I'm a horrible daughter." By now she was sobbing. "How could I think my own Dad killed somebody?" she sputtered.

Jamie dropped the TV guide and pulled Cassie into her arms. She started crying too.

She thought, *"You're not a horrible daughter, he was just a horrible dad."* But she didn't say it aloud. It wouldn't do either of them any good. She had thought the same thing about herself. She had blamed herself for doubting him when it was actually his fault for giving her a reason to.

After a few minutes, the sisters cried themselves out. Jamie grabbed some Kleenex and they dried their eyes and blew their noses. Cassie sighed and put her head on Jamie's shoulder. Jamie stroked her long, thick hair. She remembered Mom doing the same thing to her when she was upset about something.

"I didn't want to think Dad did it," Cassie said after a few minutes of companionable silence. "But he could be so mean. Do you remember? He would get mad over the least little thing and fly off the handle. Sometimes, it was like he couldn't control himself." She paused and readjusted her head on Jamie's shoulder. "I thought maybe that's what happened between him and that girl. They got into a fight and he just lost it. You know, like he really didn't mean to hurt her, but then it was too late, and he didn't want anybody to find out. So he, like, hid her body or something. You know what I mean?"

Jamie nodded and kept stroking her hair.

"Do you remember how mean he was, Jamie?"

"Yes, I remember."

Cassie didn't speak for a few more minutes, but Jamie could almost see the gears turning in her head. "Do you think he loved us?" she finally asked.

Jamie stopped stroking Cassie's silky hair. She pondered the question carefully. She didn't want to blurt out the first thing that came to mind, nor did she want to tell Cassie what she thought she wanted to hear.

"Do you remember that one Christmas when Dad wasn't working and we didn't have any money?

"That was every Christmas."

Jamie chuckled. "Yeah, but this Christmas was really bad. You were about three or four. Dad hadn't worked since summer and Mom was waitressing almost every night. She hadn't even had the time to put up a tree. Money was really tight. I knew there probably wasn't going to be any presents, but you were still bugging Dad about what you wanted Santa to bring."

Cassie sat up and turned around on the couch to face Jamie. She wiped the last of the damp tears off her face and waited for the story to continue.

As Jamie talked, more and more details of that long-ago holiday came back to her. "On Christmas Eve, Mom was working and Dad was babysitting us like always. He brought us out to the farm and we went into the woods to pick out a tree. He kept saying we were going to surprise Mommy for Christmas. We found this scraggly little Cedar tree and took it back to the apartment. All afternoon, we cleaned until that dingy apartment sparkled. I guess Dad did learn something from Grandma Cory. Anyway, after that, we strung popcorn and cranberries to put on the tree. By that time, it was getting late and Mom was due home any minute. Dad had us turn out all the lights and we lit every candle we could find."

"I remember that!" Cassie interjected, slapping Jamie on the arm. "The candle Christmas! That was so cool. We hid behind the couch and jumped out at Mom when she came in. Dad was even hiding back there with us. I was so excited I couldn't shut up, and he kept telling me to be quiet or else Mom would know where we were hiding."

"Yeah, when she came in, she thought the electric company had shut us off again. We had to turn on the kitchen light to prove to her we still had electricity."

"And we stayed up all night." Cassie's eyes glistened with excitement as the faded memory came back to her little by little.

Jamie nodded. "Dad put all the blankets and pillows on the floor, and we stayed up as late as we could stand it; eating popcorn and telling stories and playing games. We slept right there on the floor in front of the Christmas tree. The next morning, it didn't even matter that we didn't have any presents. Mom and Dad weren't fighting. I think it was the best Christmas I ever had."

"Me too," Cassie agreed, even though she wouldn't have remembered it at all if Jamie hadn't reminded her.

They leaned back into the couch cushions. Finally Cassie spoke, "Thanks, Jamie. I'm glad you made me remember that." She leaned over and hugged her. "I love you. I'm sorry I don't say it more often."

"I love you too, Cassie."

They hugged again and then Cassie went upstairs to her room, leaving Jamie alone on the couch. She was glad too, that Cassie made her remember a happy occasion from their childhood. Now that she thought about it, she realized it wasn't the only happy memory she had. Living with James Steele hadn't always been one nightmare after another. He was a natural story-teller and loved to make people laugh, especially his girls.

If only he could've been funny and loving and thoughtful more often. If only he could have worked harder to control his temper, his daughters never would have thought he was capable of murder. If only he had been a more giving, understanding husband, his wife would have been better able to fight the cancer that took her life at such an early age. If he hadn't developed such a notorious reputation in the community, the townspeople wouldn't be blaming her right now for Noreen Trimble's arrest.

Jamie felt tears stinging her eyes again. *One decent Christmas didn't make up for the terrible things James Steele did in his life.* She clenched her fists and stared at the ceiling. *We wanted to love you, she cried silently. We wanted to trust you, but you wouldn't let us. It's all your fault. I'll never forget what you did. I'll never forget how you let Mom die.*

# Chapter Thirty

Jason Collier prided himself on his ability to remain comfortably detached from the personal problems of others. He seldom shared details of his own life. He had found when people often asked seemingly caring questions, it was to either appear sympathetic when they really didn't care about you one way or the other, or to get information to use against you later. Occasionally, he considered majoring in psychology at the community college he attended, so that he could better understand man's capability to harm another; and his own resulting cynicism. People were just plain nasty. He didn't need a degree to figure that out.

Today he was having a hard time maintaining his usual distance. Jamie was having a rough week. She was punishing herself for what happened to Noreen, although he couldn't imagine why she thought herself to blame. So what if a few small minded people in town seemed to think it was better to go on thinking James Steele had killed that girl than for the actual guilty party to be punished? She needed to develop a thicker skin if something like that could bother her. In a small town, people were always talking trash about somebody. He wished he could say something to help her see that; something that would make her feel better. He had always liked Jamie. She was an okay girl in his book. More than okay, actually, even if she did take herself too seriously at times and didn't laugh enough for what he considered to be healthy. He detected a dry sense of humor in there somewhere and a plucky personality she didn't seem to know she possessed.

He kept quiet for much of the morning, reminding himself that whatever was on her mind was none of his business. It was Friday; her last day at work before going back to school on Monday. If she could just hold up for today, she'd be away from all the local yokels who came into the store, pointing fingers and whispering behind her back. Then he realized the same thing would be going on at school, if not worse. He needed to say or do something. No sense in beating around the bush.

"Jamie." His voice was brusque and unsympathetic. "You're going to just have to forget about what everybody around here is saying about you."

Her face wrinkled. *Good going, Collier,* he berated himself, *'lotta help you are.* Jamie's chin quivered and her eyes pooled with tears. He felt like every other man who had found himself in the presence of a woman about to cry; as if he was standing on the deck of a ship, rolling and pitching on a storm-tossed sea, his feet unstable beneath him, knowing at any minute he would be thrown into the angry waves. He held his breath, planted his feet on the concrete floor to steady himself against the coming storm ... and waited.

Jamie turned her face away from him—her emotions dangerously close to the surface—to stare at the opposite wall. "Yeah, I know," she mumbled.

Hey, he'd tried. He offered his advice and made himself available if she wanted to talk to someone. He had tried to talk to her a few weeks ago when she asked him if he'd heard about the body they found in the well, but she made it clear she didn't want to discuss it. She didn't want to talk then, and she obviously didn't want to talk now. If he had any sense at all he'd go back to work and leave her alone. But no; for some reason, he wasn't thinking clearly today. He couldn't leave well enough alone. Maybe it was because of the fresh smell of apricot—or was it peach?—he detected in her hair. Maybe it was those huge brown eyes with the green and gold flecks, so sad and despairing this morning, they cried out to him for understanding. Ah, who was he kidding? It was because he wanted to come to her rescue, to comfort her, to be her knight in shining armor.

He reached out and put his hand on her chin to turn her face toward him.

"Don't let 'em get to you," he said much more softly, his eyes full of compassion. "They're all a bunch of hypocrites anyway."

Jamie jerked her head back, away from the soft touch of his hand on her chin. "Just leave me alone," she snapped. "You don't know what you're talking about."

Jason's compassion and concern drained out of him like icy water from a bucket; so much for a knight in shining armor. "Maybe I don't know what I'm talking about," he snapped back. "But I do know you've been moping around here ever since they found that girl's remains like the weight of the world was on your shoulders. You got what you wanted, didn't you? You proved your dad was innocent. Now you're feeling sorry for yourself for a whole new set of reasons." The injured look in her eyes only made him angrier. "Is that what it is? You like feeling sorry for yourself and this is as good a reason as any? 'Look at me. Poor Jamie'," his voice mocked cruelly. " 'My daddy didn't love me. Boohoo. Now that he's not around, I'll kick anyone else in the teeth who tries to get close to me.'"

Her eyes flashed angrily and he wondered if he'd said too much. "You don't know what you're talking about, Jason. I'm not feeling sorry for myself. It's not like that," her voice trailed off. If she uttered even one more syllable, she would burst into tears.

"Jamie." The compassion was back in his voice. "You're going to have to talk about it sooner or later."

"I—I—know. L—later I will." She gulped hard to stop the outburst from bubbling forth, but it was no use. The tears broke loose like a flood. She covered her face with her hands. Jason wrapped his arms around her and drew her against his hard chest. She sagged against him, her resistance gone, and let the sobs wrack her body. She cried for a long time. Her inhibitions of displaying such raw emotion in front of Jason, of all people, forgotten as the tears flowed freely down her cheeks—until the door suddenly opened.

"Oooh, sorry," Tate said sheepishly. "I didn't mean to interrupt anything." The look on his face let them know that was his very intent.

Jason felt her body stiffen and he tightened his arms around her. Jamie didn't look up but kept her face buried in his shirt. Tate was the kind of person to use something like this against her, and he wasn't going to let that happen. "Get out, Tate." He motioned toward the door with a wag of his head.

"I came in to get something," Tate explained lamely.

"Well, get it later." Jason's voice was subtly threatening.

"I need it now." He advanced farther into the room.

By now, Jamie's tears had subsided into muffled sniffs. She stepped out of Jason's embrace and dried her tears with the backs of her hands. Avoiding Tate's eyes, she scanned the stockroom for a box of tissues.

"I said, get it later," Jason said softly, but firmly.

"Well, actually," he admitted, "the reason I came in here was for Jamie. You wouldn't believe what I've heard people saying out there. I knew she'd be upset. It looks like I got here just in time." He advanced toward the two of them, his face a mask of concern.

Jamie located a box of tissues on the desk and blew her nose, loudly and without a hint of decorum. She deposited the used tissue in the wastebasket and reached for another. "Tate, I'm fine, really." She blew her nose again even louder.

To his credit, only the slightest hint of distaste showed on his face at the noises she was making. "You don't seem fine," he said, sounding almost concerned. "Listen, I know I can be a pain in the neck sometimes, but really, all I want to do is help."

Jason stepped forward and put a hand on Tate's chest, giving him a push toward the door. "Thanks for your concern, Tate, but everything's under control."

"If you need anything, Jamie," he called as Jason forced him backward out the door, "you know where I'll be."

Jason shut the door firmly behind him. This knight in shining armor business was kind of cool.

Jamie tossed the crumpled tissue into the wastepaper basket. With an appreciative smile in Jason's direction, she sank into the battered office chair beside the desk. "Thanks."

"Are you ready to talk?" he asked. "I really think you should."

"You don't want to hear me whining about my hard knock life." She dabbed her eyes with a clean tissue and gave him a shaky smile.

He smiled down at her, relieved she was teasing him about what he said earlier. That meant she wasn't mad anymore. "Oh, go ahead. I guess you've earned the right to whine; but only this once."

She sighed and leaned back in the chair, the tired springs squeaking in protest. "You're right about me feeling sorry for myself. I didn't think I was, but that's exactly what I was doing." She took another deep breath and stared past him at the wall. "When I found out about Sally Blake, I had to know if Dad had anything to do with her disappearance. I couldn't let it rest until I knew the whole story. I just couldn't." She turned her head to look at him. "But now ... I don't know. What good did all my nosing around do?"

He perched himself on the edge of the desk and looked down at her. "There was nothing wrong with you wanting to find the truth."

"It was better off hidden. Everybody tried to tell me that."

"Better off for whom? Noreen? Your dad? Sally Blake's folks? Can you imagine how relieved they must be to finally know what happened to their daughter? They don't have to wonder anymore if she's just going to come waltzing through the door. At least now they know the truth, no matter how terrible it is."

"I suppose," she mumbled.

"For a parent, that'd be the most important thing. I imagine they've probably suspected for years she was dead. I'm sure they even accepted it. But it'd be agony to not know what became of her. Now it's finally over and they can put it behind them."

"But Noreen is going to prison. I feel like I'm the one who sent her there."

"Jamie, she sent herself there." He reached out and took her hand. She looked earnestly into his face as she listened to his words. "I believe Noreen is repentant for what she's done," he continued, "but she still has to be accountable for her actions. It wouldn't be fair to Sally or her parents to forget the whole thing happened just because everybody in town thinks the world of Noreen Trimble. A young woman did die. Shouldn't some penance have to be paid for that?"

He cocked a questioning eyebrow as he looked down at her, hoping she was getting the point. "It could even be that Noreen is glad that it's over for her too. I'm not saying she's happy about facing jail time, but if she is repentant, it must be a relief to her that she doesn't have this hanging over her head anymore. Can you imagine the burden it's been for her to carry this around all these years?"

Always thoughtful. Always practical. Jason made it easy for her to see reason. "I suppose so," she admitted. "I never thought about it like that. I just feel terrible about what's happening to her."

"We all do," he said sincerely.

He straightened up and rose to his feet. Jamie stood up too; it was time to get back to work. Standing in front of him, she was surprised to notice he was a good six inches taller than she was. Why hadn't she noticed it before? She tipped her head back and looked into his deep blue eyes. She hadn't noticed those before either. Where had her mind been this summer to cause her to miss all these wonderful details right under her nose? He put his hands on her shoulders, his eyes suddenly lost in hers. The shared moment was no longer over mutual sympathy for Noreen Trimble. The instant before their lips met, she became aware he was going to kiss her.

Her first kiss. She hoped he wouldn't realize she was seventeen-years-old and had never truly been kissed.

When he drew back, the corners of his mouth pulled up into that quirky smile of his. She smiled back, her lips trembling and her cheeks a rosy pink. She studied his nose, his ears, his neck, anything but those deep, fathomless blue eyes that seemed to reach right down inside of her to her very soul. When she did make eye contact, she knew he wanted to kiss her again. She wanted it too, more than anything. She relaxed under his touch and forgot age and inexperience as his lips lingered on hers, longer and more ardent this time.

"I—I need to be getting back to work," she stammered as she stepped out of his embrace.

"Yeah, me too."

She gave him a quick smile and lowered her head, hoping he wouldn't see how shook up his kiss left her. She hurried to the other side of the room and busied herself in her work, her face hot and hands sweaty and trembling. As she unpacked cases and priced items to go on the shelf, she did not think about Noreen, prison, her dad, or what the good people of Jenna's Creek were saying about her. She thought about deep blue eyes, sandy blond hair, and lips she never dreamed could be so soft.

It was well after two o'clock before Jamie and Jason left the stock-room for their lunch break. Jason didn't say anything, but he knew it would be easier on Jamie to go out into the store after the usual lunch crowd was gone.

Noel spotted her and called to her from behind the pharmacy

counter. Jamie swallowed hard and left Jason sitting on a stool to go see what he wanted. She hadn't talked to Noel since Noreen's arrest and she wondered how he felt about the whole situation. Was he blaming her too? Noreen was a friend of his, and Judge Davis said he was there for moral support and even drove her to the sheriff's office when she was taken into custody. Now he was working around the clock behind the pharmacy counter in Noreen's absence. He sent out feelers to hire a new assistant, but everyone wondered if he would ever be able to bring himself to replace her.

Anxiously, Jamie approached the pharmacy counter. He finished explaining to a customer how to give a medication to her ailing father and then turned to Jamie with a smile in place. She allowed herself to relax just a little.

"Jamie, you've been doing an excellent job here this summer."

"Thank you, Noel," she breathed warily and felt a blush creep into her cheeks.

"Can I count on you to stay on after you go back to school?"

She exhaled, relieved. "Oh yes. I was hoping to."

"Good, good. I wanted to let you know this is Deidre's last week. It's too far for her to drive back and forth from Blanton and go to school during the day. So I'm going to need you to work the registers out here."

Jamie's first thought was she would miss working with Jason every day. Then she realized this was good news. She didn't want to be stuck in the stuffy stockroom her whole life. She would still see him whenever she came to work. Unless he quit work altogether when his fall semester started.

"If you can come to work right after school Monday," Noel was saying, "Paige can start training you."

Her face fell. Anyone but Paige. She thought about declining his offer. She'd rather keep sweating out the real work in the stockroom than look at Paige's sour face every day. No, that was silly. Maybe God had a purpose in all this. If she allowed Him, she could use the opportunity to glorify Him by witnessing to a woman obviously in need of His love.

"Thanks a lot Noel, but I'll have to check with my grandma about working right after school. I'll still have my chores to do on the farm."

"Sure. No problem. Just let me know." He turned his attention to a customer who had walked up behind Jamie. She stepped out of the way and hurried back to the lunch counter. She hopped onto the stool beside Jason who was already half-way through his tuna on rye.

"Well, that must have been good news," Barb mused at Jamie's pleased expression.

"Oh, it was. Noel is going to start working me at the cash registers Monday."

"Wonderful," Barb exclaimed. "You deserve it, honey. Now what'll you have for lunch?"

"A turkey club, I think."

"Boy, you must have worked up an appetite," Barb said over her shoulder as she moved away.

Jamie immediately thought of Jason's kiss and wondered if Barb could see it on her face. She stared at her hands until Barb was at the other end of the counter and out of earshot. "So, what do you think?" She leaned her elbows on the counter and turned to Jason.

"About what?" he asked between bites.

"Oh, no, not this again. You know what I'm talking about."

He gave her a playful nudge in the ribs. "Noel told me about your promotion last week. Now I've got to train another flunky." He wrinkled his nose distastefully.

"Hey!" she cried indignantly. Inside she was thrilled. If he would be training the person to take her place in the stockroom, that meant he wasn't going anywhere either.

He ignored her outburst. "We're losing Tate too." When she lifted her eyebrows questioningly, he added, "Football season."

"You're still not off the hook for that 'flunky' comment."

"What comment?" he asked with an innocent shrug.

Barb set a plate on the counter in front of Jamie. "Can you believe this guy?" Jamie jabbed her thumb in Jason's direction. "He'd drive a person crazy."

"Oh, you don't have to tell me that, honey." Barb patted her hand. "But he's a sweetheart underneath all that gruff and grumble."

"I'm beginning to figure that out."

Jason watched their exchange out of the corner of his eye, his mouth around his sandwich, and tried to look perturbed.

Barb went back to scrubbing the grease off the grill from the lunch crowd.

"Are you going to need a ride home at the end of your shift?" Jason asked.

She paused, not wanting to sound too eager. "Are you offering one?"

"Maybe," he said, rolling his eyes in mock sarcasm.

"Then I guess I could use a ride."

He wagged his head noncommittally and shoved the rest of his sandwich in his mouth. He didn't look nearly as excited as she felt, but she had learned from working with him all summer that he was a closed book. His true feelings seldom showed through his aloof exterior, unless of course, he was being kissed.

# Chapter Thirty-one

By late afternoon, a pleasant breeze made its way down the city streets, taking with it the last chalky residue of summer's relentless heat. A sudden gust of wind sent a shower of green leaves into the parking lot behind the drugstore as Jamie followed Jason to his car. Fall was definitely on its way. Her summer was over. Her first summer working. Her first summer without either of her parents. Her first summer of standing up for herself and going against what everyone else thought was best. It was over, and she had survived. The old Jamie Steele had been replaced by a more confident, stronger young woman, not easily frightened by things outside her realm of control. She was ready for Monday morning; ready to face her last year at South Auburn High School and whatever it might bring.

Jason revved the motor of his compact car and pointed it out of town toward the farm. Jamie leaned back into the upholstery and trailed her hand out the open window. The tension from the past week was gone. Jason was right. She had done nothing wrong in helping discover what really happened to Sally Blake. Whether it was her dad or someone else falsely implicated, the Blakes deserved to know the truth. She felt lighter and freer than she had in weeks.

Suddenly she sat up straight and pulled her hand back inside the window. The last time she rode in this car flashed through her mind. It was the day Jason drove her home from Mrs. Wyatt's house after they'd had lunch with Mrs. Wyatt and Noel. She remembered crying on the old woman's shoulder and telling her that she didn't know if her dad loved her. She told her she hated him; she blamed him for being dead, and worst of all, she suspected him of killing Sally Blake.

Mrs. Wyatt hadn't been shocked or disgusted by her revelation. She simply told Jamie to stop feeling sorry for herself. Sort of like Jason had done this morning at the drugstore, just in different terms. Jason said she liked feeling sorry for herself. Mrs. Wyatt hadn't been so blunt. She said she could waste the rest of her life hating him, or she could let go of the pain and forgive him.

Hadn't she planned to do that anyway. At the beginning of her search for what happened on the night Sally Blake disappeared, she vowed that she would forgive her dad if and when he was proven innocent. It sounded like a simple plan back then. So why hadn't it happened yet? He was innocent in Sally's murder. He did love his daughters, and maybe even his wife. She had convinced Cassie of that the other day, along with herself, with the retelling of the candle Christmas story. His part of the bargain was fulfilled. The only one keeping it from happening now was Jamie.

But how could she forgive someone who didn't want forgiveness? She knew her dad too well. If he were here right now, he would never admit he had anything to be forgiven for. She couldn't forgive someone like that. No one could. Nothing would erase the terrible things that he did to her, Cassie, and Mom. He was still guilty of that, regardless of how much everything else changed.

Mrs. Wyatt's words came back to her in crystal clarity. *"All you need to worry about now is if you love him or not. You're still here. You can change. He can't. You can waste the rest of your life hating him and torturing yourself, or you can let go of the pain and forgive him. It's up to you."*

"Jamie?" Jason's voice cut in. "Is everything okay?"

"Oh, I'm sorry. I was just thinking. What did you say?"

"I just asked if you wanted to see a movie or something tomorrow night? Anything you want to do is fine with me."

She smiled. Did he seem nervous? "That would be great."

The compact car turned off the highway onto Betterman Road. "I'll pick you up tomorrow night around seven then."

"Perfect."

Jason pulled the car into the driveway. Dusk had settled over the little farmhouse. Several lights were already burning inside. In the fading light, Jamie saw Grandpa Harlan rocking back and forth on the porch swing. It was odd to find him sitting outside by himself. Usually at this time of day, he was in front of the television set while Grandma Cory fixed supper. Jamie wondered if he was waiting for her. Not likely. He never waited for anyone or anything, his television programs notwithstanding.

"Thanks for the ride," she said, suddenly uncomfortable. Would Jason want to kiss her again? Even though she wasn't against the idea, she hoped he wouldn't try in front of Grandpa.

He reached out and squeezed her hand instead. "I'll see you tomorrow night."

"Bye," she said breathlessly, squeezing his hand in return. She stepped out of the car and climbed the porch steps. She lowered herself beside Grandpa Harlan on the porch swing. Together, they watched Jason's car back out of the driveway and pull onto Betterman Road. Only after the car disappeared around the bend, leaving a suspended cloud of dust in its wake, did she look over at Grandpa Harlan. He was still staring unseeingly at the cloud of dust as the breeze slowly broke it apart and scattered it into the cornfield across the road. She reached over and took his hand. "Grandpa? Is everything all right?"

He looked startled, as if he just realized she was there. Recognition registered on his face and he smiled. "Jamie."

She leaned into him, resting her shoulder against his. It was then she noticed the shoe box on the swing separating them. It was the box from Grandma Cory's closet; the one with the newspaper clipping and the letters James had written to Sally. She looked from the box to her grandpa's face, wondering what he was doing with it. Had he known of its existence all along?

Following her gaze, he looked down at the box. Then he slowly and methodically removed the lid. He reached in and took out a newspaper clipping, holding it up for her to see. It was from Jenna's Creek local paper; the one announcing James was being held for questioning.

Jamie took the newspaper clipping from him and scanned the now familiar article. She turned back to him, her eyes full of questions. Why was he showing it to her? Did he want her to know what had happened all those years ago? Was he still worried about what might have

happened to Sally? How could she put into words the discovery of
Sally's remains and Noreen's recent arrest so he would understand?

She searched his face helplessly, wishing she knew what to say.

He closed his large hand over hers, crumpling the scrap of paper
between her fingers. He brought his face in close to hers and stared
knowingly into her eyes.

"What is it, Grandpa?"

"That's my son," he said, wagging his head at the paper in her
closed fist.

"Yes..."

"Thank you, Jamie." He pulled her into a clumsy embrace, ignoring
the shoe box squashed between them. He rested his chin on the top
of her head and began to push the porch swing back and forth with
one foot. She felt warm dampness falling onto her cheek and forehead,
and realized he was crying.

He understood, she thought with a start. Grandpa Harlan knew
about Noreen and Sally and he understood what it all meant. Since
Noreen was guilty, it proved James was not.

Jamie's regrets for any pain she may have inadvertently caused
Noreen or the town or anyone else by exposing the truth about Sally's
murder, dissolved as the porch swing squeaked an accompaniment to
the evening sounds slowly breaking through the silence of the farm.
If she had believed when she and Judge Davis began their investigation, she could live without the truth of Sally's disappearance, she
saw now Grandpa Harlan could not. All those years he had suffered
alone, believing his son was innocent, yet unable to do anything to
prove it. Over time no one realized how much he understood, how
much he remembered, or how much he suffered the same doubts and
fears they did.

"Thank you, Jamie," he whispered again into her hair, his voice
cracking with emotion. "Thank you."

Tears welled up in her own eyes. Not only because of the intense
wave of love that suddenly engulfed her for Grandpa Harlan, but also
because of her father. Like Mrs. Wyatt had told her at the beginning
of the summer, Dad was gone. He couldn't change. But she could. She
could keep hating him and let it eat her up inside, or she could forgive
him. Did she want to spend the rest of her life hating her own father?

Maybe he didn't deserve forgiveness. Did anyone? She certainly didn't the first time she approached the throne of grace, seeking it. She wasn't perfect. She was stubborn, prideful, and slow to admit fault, just like Dad. Whether she deserved forgiveness or not, it was given freely; not because she was worthy, but because her Heavenly Father was merciful. A verse from the sixth chapter of Luke sprang to mind.

*"Therefore be merciful, just as your Father also is merciful."*

She squeezed her eyelids shut as tears of shame and remorse spilled down her cheeks. *"I'm sorry, Daddy. I don't want to be mad at you anymore. I love you."*

The unexpected admission brought fresh tears to her eyes. Yes, it was true. She did love him; regardless of the mistakes he made in his life. Even if her worst fears had been realized concerning Sally Blake's disappearance, he was still her father and she loved him. *"And I miss you, Daddy."* she thought silently.

The tears flowed free and cleansing down her cheeks.

After a moment, she sniffed and smiled to herself through her tears, breathing in the clean starched smell of Grandpa Harlan's shirt. A peace she hadn't experienced in a long time washed over her. It was clean, pure, like the freshly laundered smell of the shirt. It felt like... mercy. She had truly forgiven James with no strings, no conditions attached, just like forgiveness was meant to be. In return, her Heavenly Father could now forgive her. He would give her the strength to miss James without remembering only the bad things from the past. He would bring to her remembrance the Christmases, rides in the car, and plain ordinary days when Dad had made her laugh. She knew she couldn't snap her fingers and make the bitter memories of her childhood disappear, no matter how much she wished it could be that way. But someday soon, with God's help, she would be able to think of her dad, smile, and remember him with love and understanding in her heart. For now, she was free to mourn the father she had lost.

# The End

Coming Soon:

# *Beyond Redemption*

## The second book in the Jenna's Creek Series

As far as Jamie Steele can see, there's not a cloud on the horizon. She is finally at peace with the memories she has of her parents. She has a new car and enough scholarship money to pay for college. Her boyfriend, Jason Collier, is attending law school at the same university. Just when she has everything mapped out perfectly and life couldn't get any better, Jason makes an announcement that will change their lives forever; and she'll never forgive him.

Abigail Blackwood's entire adult life has been a sham, a masquerade. Only God knows of the hidden sin that could destroy everything she holds dear. When tragedy strikes, she realizes the secret she has safeguarded for the past twenty years isn't as well kept as she thinks. God can—and has—forgiven her for the selfish, cruel act she committed. But even God's grace cannot shield her husband and family from heartbreak and shame, should her secret be revealed. One person takes her secret to his grave. She will stop at nothing to protect what she has left, even if it means destroying the life of another.

Two women who share nothing more than love for one man—when their lives are shaken and faith tested beyond what either can imagine—will they trust the God of purpose who promises to remain closer than a brother, or will foolish pride drive them to take matters into their own hands?

If you enjoyed this book and would like to pass one on to someone else or if you're interested in another Tsaba House title, please check with your local bookstore, online bookseller, or use this form:

Name_____

Address _____

City _____ State_____ Zip_____

Please send me:

_____ copies of *Streams of Mercy* at $15.99          $ _____

_____ copies of *The Payload* at $15.99          $ _____

_____ copies of *Your Rights to Riches* at $14.99          $ _____

_____ copies of *The Parenting Business* at $15.99          $ _____

California residents please add sales tax          $ _____

Shipping*: $4.00 for the first copy and $2.00
for each additional copy          $ _____

Total enclosed          $ _____

Send order to:

Tsaba House
2252 12th Street
Reedley, CA 93654


or visit our website at www.TsabaHouse.com
or call (toll free) 1-866-TSABA-HS (1-866-872-2247)


For more than 5 copies, please contact the publisher for multiple copy rates.

*International shipping costs extra. If shipping to a destination outside the United States, please contact the publisher for rates to your location.